Almost Like Being in Love

Christina Dodd

Almost Like Being in Love

POCKET BOOKS
New York   London   Toronto   Sydney

This book is a work of fiction. Names, characters, places, and incidents are products of the author's imagination or are used fictitiously. Any resemblance to actual events or locales or persons, living or dead, is entirely coincidental.

An Original Publication of POCKET BOOKS

 POCKET BOOKS, a division of Simon & Schuster, Inc.
1230 Avenue of the Americas, New York, NY 10020

Cover design by Lisa Litwack
Cover photograph by George Kerrigan
Author type by Dave Gatti

Manufactured in the United States of America

For Bobbie,

an extraordinary woman who can do everything,

yet you're such a good friend, I like you anyway.

A huge thank-you to TJ Oatman for coming to my
assistance when I asked for help with ranching.
I had never thought of cattle as a herd
of puppies before.

Prologue

Eight-year-old Pepper Prescott woke to find the light shining down the hall from the kitchen. She blinked and, yawning, looked at the clock. The lighted numbers said two thirty-six, and she experienced a surge of triumph, because she knew she wasn't supposed to be awake in the middle of the night.

But that light meant Daddy and Mama were here at last. They hadn't been when Pepper got home from school. The house had been empty, something that had happened only a few times that Pepper could remember, and always involved a parishioner who had had an accident and was dying and a family who needed help coming to grips with mortality. Usually Mama left a note on the table, but this time there was nothing. Pepper even checked on the floor to see if the air conditioner had blown away the paper.

Then she did what Mama would want her to do, and rummaged around and found a snack. Well, not quite what Mama would want her to do, because she had cookies instead of an apple and she ate them in front of the television and watched the shows she wasn't supposed to watch. She enjoyed herself thoroughly until Hope came home.

Then Hope snapped the TV off and made Pepper do her homework at the kitchen table. Sixteen-year-old Hope always did the right thing. At school, Pepper's teachers always said, "I had your sister Hope, and she never talked all the time." Or, "I taught your sister, Hope, and she got straight A's." Pepper got sick of hearing about wonderful, perfect Hope, and she kicked the table leg the whole time Hope was gone getting the baby from the church day care.

She came home with a pucker between her brows, but she wouldn't tell Pepper anything. When Gabriel came home from soccer, she pulled him into a corner and they whispered in a worried tone.

Daddy and Mama didn't come home all evening, and they didn't call.

Pepper had gone to bed feeling like it was her fault because she'd eaten those cookies, but now she could hear voices in the kitchen, and that meant they were home. Flinging back the covers, she padded down the hallway toward the light.

She recognized Hope's voice, and Gabriel's, and they whispered as if someone were choking them. Pepper heard a man speak, but he wasn't Daddy, and she stopped short of the doorway. She had on only her nightgown. Mama said a girl of eight didn't come out in her nightgown in front of strangers.

Pepper peeked around the door and saw that there

were two strangers in the kitchen, a Texas man sheriff and a Texas lady sheriff.

Hope was sitting at the table. Gabriel stood behind her with his hands on her shoulders.

And Daddy and Mama weren't here.

The lady was saying, ". . . Car rolled five times about three o'clock this afternoon on an empty stretch near the Mexican border—"

Who was she talking about? Why was she here?

She continued, "—and not discovered until almost eight o'clock this evening by a passing officer. Both bodies were battered in a way that—"

The man sheriff dug his elbow into her ribs.

She finished, "They were killed instantly."

Killed, who was killed? Who were they talking about?

"I'm so sorry to bring you news like this." The lady looked like she meant it.

But Pepper still didn't understand. Who had been killed instantly?

The man asked, "Do you kids have anyone you can call to stay with you? Aunts? Uncles?"

"No. My parents didn't have family. They met . . . they were both orphans . . ." Hope dropped her head onto her hands and gave a sob.

Why did she do that?

Who were they talking about? In the depths of her heart, Pepper knew, but she couldn't believe it.

Gabriel, big old fourteen-year-old Gabriel, made a noise like Pepper had never heard, sort of between a whimper and a groan.

And Pepper . . . Pepper was making a noise too. She

didn't realize it until everyone turned and looked at her. Then she backed up out of the doorway, but the sound coming out of her throat was thin and high and kept getting louder.

Hope came to her feet and dashed toward Pepper.

Gabriel followed her and stood back, staring, the way he used to before Mama made him join the family.

Gathering Pepper into her arms, Hope said, "*Sh.* You'll wake the baby. *Sh*, Pepper, you'll make yourself sick. *Sh* . . ." She rocked Pepper.

But Pepper stood rigid, one foot on top of the other, her thin nightgown sticking to her suddenly clammy skin, and wailed because she couldn't help it. Her mama . . . they said her mama was dead. Her daddy . . . no! She'd seen him that morning. He'd looked tired, but he kissed her and told her to do right today. He said that every day when she left for school, and she never did, and now he was . . . he was dead? Her mama? Battered? Gone? Dead?

Hope scooped her up and carried Pepper into her bedroom, saying all the time, "*Sh, sh*, quiet, honey, you'll wake the baby, you'll make yourself sick, don't cry, don't cry."

Pepper didn't think she was crying. She had cried before, but it had never felt like this. This wrenching pain in the gut, the pounding in her head, the emptiness . . . everywhere.

The two girls sat on Pepper's bed.

Gabriel stood in the doorway. "Can I help?" he asked, but he was awkward and somehow out of place.

Of course. He'd only lived here a few years. Daddy

and Mama weren't his real parents. He didn't know what to do.

Pepper sobbed harder. Gabriel was her brother, the one who understood her when no one else did, and now everything was changing, disintegrating . . . destroyed.

Their lives were destroyed.

Taking Pepper's shoulders, Hope held her. She dipped down until she was on Pepper's level. She looked into her eyes. "Listen to me, Pepper. Listen. *Listen.*"

Pepper calmed a little. Just a little. Agony still ripped at her belly. She understood this was only a calm in the storm. But she caught her breath and listened.

"I will take care of you," Hope vowed. "Trust me. We're a family. I'll make sure we're together. I'll take care of you. Trust me."

Georgetown, Washington, D.C.
Early June
Seventeen years later

One

ackie Porter hoped she didn't embarrass herself by falling to her knees before her idol and kissing her hem. It was a distinct possibility, one she faced with a mixture of dread and amusement, but what was she to do? General Jennifer Napier was what Jackie wanted to be in twenty years—a woman successful in her own right.

For Jackie would succeed in her own right also. As she inched forward in the line that wound through the trendy Georgetown bookstore, she clutched her well-read copy of the general's autobiography and a copy of the new release, a book that clearly delineated and explained the principles by which General Napier had become a success. All the while, Jackie cherished the bright spark of hope General Jennifer Napier had created in her.

General Napier had lost her parents in horrible circumstances—just like Jackie. She had been raised in a series of foster homes—just like Jackie. She had made mistakes in her youth, mistakes so dreadful she hadn't believed she could ever recover from the disgrace and the shame—just like Jackie. Yet she had turned her life around, gone to West Point, joined the military, and was now the highest ranking female general in the U.S. Army.

Jackie looked up at the huge photo hanging over the table where General Napier was signing books.

General Jennifer Napier was fifty-five, an attractive woman with piercing blue eyes and dark, graying hair swept up and under her military hat. She exercised every morning, sternly regimenting her body to the peak of health. She was an acknowledged sharpshooter. She lived by the tenets of discipline that she outlined in her book.

Now Jackie lived by them too. She exercised every day. She practiced shooting and self-defense. She kept her eyes fixed on her goal and let nothing—not friendship, fun, or romance—get in her way.

General Napier had never married, dedicating her life to her career, and although Jackie had chosen a different career—horticulture—she dedicated *her* life to building a successful landscaping business in the Washington, D.C., area. She was doing well for a poor, orphan girl from Texas. And if sometimes at night she ached with loneliness, and remembered her one, dreadful mistake with a little too much fondness . . . well, in the daylight she had the life she had made for herself, and that was enough.

Now Jackie waited in line to thank General Napier for her guidance. Craning her neck to see past the other women in line, she caught her first live glimpse of her hero.

The general looked older and more worn than she did in her photo, and Jackie thought, *Airbrush.*

Then she chided herself for being cynical. After all, the general had been on an extensive book tour. She'd been interviewed on television and on radio. She was probably exhausted. And she was, in every other way, absolutely as Jackie had imagined her. The line inched forward and Jackie's heart thumped as she came closer.

Jackie had carefully dressed for this moment, wearing a dark blue skirt and white blouse neatly belted at her waist and designed to make the most of her five-foot-seven-inch height and to minimize her lavish bosom. Her sandals were dark blue and white, flat, and conservative. As the general advised, Jackie's jewelry was traditional, yet expensive: gold earrings, a gold chain, and a plain watch with a black leather band.

Each woman as she stood before General Napier babbled about how much she admired the general, saying almost the same words that Jackie had planned, but when Jackie stepped up to the table, all of her prepared speech flew right out of her head. Her fingers trembled as she handed the general the books.

General Napier fixed her gaze on her. "What's your name?"

"Pep—" She caught herself. "Jackie. Jackie Porter." She must be really rattled—she'd almost given the general her real name.

"How do you spell that, Jackie?"

"J-a-c-k-i-e P-o-r-t-e-r."

"Do you want me to say anything special? Happy birthday? Or . . . ?"

"No. No, I just wanted to say—" Oh, dear, she *was* going to fall on her knees and kiss the general's hem.

General Napier opened the new book and started signing. "Yes?"

"I just . . . just . . ."—*come on, Jackie, spit it out*—"I wanted to tell you how much you inspired me. I'm . . . I was from . . . I'm from Texas, and I was raised in foster homes just like you. I just . . . I messed up a lot, and when I read your autobiography, I felt as if we were soul sisters."

The general was nodding, listening as she signed her name with a flourish, then went on to the autobiography and signed her name again. "I'm glad I could help. That's why I wrote the books. I felt I had something to say." Once again she looked directly at Jackie, and she folded her hands on the table before her. "It's important that no matter what the obstacles before you, you never give up."

"I know!" Speech was becoming easier. "When you said in your book, 'I've disappointed people who believed in me, and I've disappointed myself, and I owe it to them and most of all to myself to become a success,' that struck a chord in me."

"Really!" General Napier's gaze warmed. "I'm so flattered that you've memorized my words."

"I've memorized all of your tenets for living. You see, my father was a minister, and I was eight when the police came and said he and my mother had been killed after embezzling funds from their church. The authorities separated me from my sisters and my foster brother, and my sister helped them. I was so angry I wanted to make the rest of the world pay for my grief." The people in the line behind Jackie were getting restive, and the lady who was handing the general the books looked as if she were about to interrupt, so Jackie talked faster. "I threw tantrums, I got tattoos, I ran away from the foster homes, I shoplifted—"

"I never got a tattoo," the general said reflectively, "but otherwise it does sound familiar."

"I had one foster mother who tried to straighten me out, but I was too far gone."

The general nodded. "You had to straighten yourself out."

"Exactly! And I did, and I have, but one day when I got lonely and discouraged, I found your book and it was as if you were speaking to me."

General Napier's aide stood on her left—Jackie recognized him from his picture in the book; he'd been with the general for five years, his name was Otto Bjerke— and he looked grim, as if he'd heard too many tales like hers and believed none of them.

Jackie didn't care. The general was interested, her eyes sparkling as she listened. "I have to thank you for more than simple support and inspiration. You said you couldn't have done it without the help of God, and I . . . since my parents died and I lost my family, I refused to go to church. Because of you, I got my faith back, and for that I can't thank you enough."

General Napier offered her hand, and when Jackie took it, the general pressed it between both of hers. Tears sparkled on her lashes as she said, "It's stories like yours that make all the difficulty of writing worthwhile. Thank you for telling me. I really appreciate it."

Tears sparkled in Jackie's eyes too. "No, thank *you*."

General Napier released her hand. Jackie picked up her books.

And her moment was over.

As she moved away from the table, she tingled with excitement. The meeting had been everything she'd hoped for. She'd made the general happy and made herself happy in the process. That was one of the general's tenets. *Give generously of compliments where they're due, and the pleasure you'll see on their receipt will return to you doubled.* Once again the general had been right.

As Jackie moved through the bookstore, she eyed the stack of General Napier's new release—and realized she should have bought a copy for Mrs. Dreiss. It would be Mrs. Dreiss's birthday in less than two weeks, and those two women—Mrs. Dreiss, who had taken in a rebellious foster child, and General Napier—reminded her of each other in their strict moral code and their commonsense sayings.

More important, she *needed* to send Mrs. Dreiss occasional indications of her affection. She hadn't gone back to see her. She just . . . hadn't gone yet. She couldn't face the memories, or the chance she might meet *him* there, so she told herself that next year she would go and visit, and in the meantime she sent presents.

Guilt drove Pepper.

Grabbing a copy of the general's book, she whirled and started back toward the table—and stopped. General Napier was speaking to someone else, signing for someone else. The line wound around the entire bookstore, and there was no way Jackie could start at the back and make it through before her appointment with Mrs. Maile to discuss her landscaping.

Catching one of the clerks as he hurried past, Jackie asked, "How long will General Napier be here?"

"Until everyone's had their books autographed." He indicated the line with a grin. "That'll be a while. Isn't she great? Usually the authors only stay for an hour or two, but she says if people come and stand in line for her, they're going to get their books signed."

"She is great," Jackie agreed fervently. "How long do you figure it's going to be?"

He studied the line. "Two hours at least."

She glanced at her watch. Mrs. Maile wasn't more than a mile away, her Georgetown yard was tiny and exclusive, and if Jackie bought the new book now and hurried through her consultation, she could probably make it back to the bookstore in time to get another autograph. She thrust the unsigned book at him. "Ring this up. I'll come back for her autograph as soon as I can."

Mrs. Maile insisted on looking at every garden in every yard design magazine she owned, and she owned quite a few. The hour Jackie had imagined turned into two. By the time she ran back through the Georgetown thoroughfares, streetlights were popping on one by one in the late spring twilight. She arrived in time to see the clerk flip the CLOSED sign on the door. She held the three books with one arm, the stitch in her side with the other, and stared in a kind of frozen despair. She had thought of several more things she wanted to say to General Napier, important things, things she could say in the time it took the general to autograph Mrs. Dreiss's book.

But she couldn't now.

General Napier was off to the last stop on her book tour. Off to New York City, where she would be feted by her publisher like the goddess she was.

Jackie breathed hard, fighting the disappointment. Then she remembered: *Obstacles were there to be overcome.* General Napier said so. This wasn't a disaster, it was an obstacle, and Jackie could overcome it with a little intelligence. God knew she'd had to do some quick thinking at other times. Times when quick thinking had probably saved her life. Compared to those moments, this was easy.

Turning, she strode toward the parking garage under the building. General Napier's car might still be parked there. Jackie would hand her a pen and Mrs. Dreiss's book, the general could sign it while Jackie *wouldn't* say anything else because that would be tarnishing a blessing—that was what General Napier called it when one tried to take advantage of a kind act—and Jackie would be on her way with autographed books and a happy heart.

The garage was gray concrete and reinforced steel, half full of cars and SUVs, including one long black car with government plates. The general hadn't left yet.

Jackie put her hand to her chest and breathed a sigh of relief.

The fluorescent bulbs overhead threw light and shadows across floor and ceiling. Heat and air-conditioning ducts hung close to the ceiling by metal straps, and the place smelled of tires and dust.

Jackie's footsteps echoed up and around. Feeling suddenly foolish, she stopped behind a pillar and considered whether she had the nerve to approach General Napier while her attaché looked on. It wasn't that she didn't like Otto Bjerke; in her book, General Napier had spoken highly of him. Yet Jackie's confessions had seemed to neither interest nor convince him.

Perhaps he'd been instructed to stop troublesome fans.

Embarrassment crawled along her nerves. Was she being too pushy?

The elevator doors opened. She heard footsteps, Otto Bjerke's heavy ones and the general's lighter ones. She heard General Napier's voice saying, "That went well, and we still have time for dinner."

Jackie knew if she didn't at least try to get that signature, she'd never forgive herself. She had to *try*. She started to step out from behind the pillar, when Otto's footsteps stopped, and in a low, serious voice he said, "Look, General, I've been trying to get up the nerve to say this for a week."

General Napier's footsteps stopped also. "What's wrong?" She seemed alert, concerned.

His deep voice rumbled in the stillness. "I know what you're doing."

Jackie froze into absolute immobility. He sounded serious, accusatory. She had inadvertently stepped into a tense moment.

"What are you talking about?" General Napier's voice became clipped too. "What do you mean, you know what I've been doing?"

"I was working late. I heard you talking on your private line."

General Napier snapped, "Major, what are you trying to say?"

Most of Jackie's early years had been spent with the scent of danger in her nostrils. She smelled its acrid odor now.

"You're selling information to the terrorists." Otto Bjerke sounded calm and businesslike as he made the dreadful accusation. "General Napier, I'm going to have to turn you in."

A heavy silence followed. Jackie held her breath as she waited to hear General Napier deny it, explain . . .

"I don't suppose it would be any use telling you I'm part of counterintelligence," she said softly.

He sounded sad. "No, General, it wouldn't."

"Or to offer you a cut of the profits. It is a very tidy sum."

Jackie's heart stopped. Her idol had just admitted her guilt.

Now Otto Bjerke's voice grew heavy. "General, I've admired you every day I've worked for you. That's the only reason I'm giving you warning. I owe you so much."

She sounded ice-cold when she said, "And I owe you."

"General! Ma'am!" Panic sounded in his voice. "Don't—"

The gunshot crashed against Jackie's eardrums.

When the sound had cleared, she heard General Napier murmur, "You never should have given me warning."

Numb and stupid with terror, Jackie dropped the books.

Two

The books landed flat on the concrete, their thud as loud as the gunshot.

"Who's there?" General Napier's voice whipped across the rows of cars.

With the well-honed instinct of a wild cat, Jackie ran. Crouching low, she weaved in and out of the cars. She knew where she was headed—if she could get there.

Another shot smashed through the air. A windshield cracked, showering Jackie with glass.

"Stop!" General Napier commanded.

Every instinct told Jackie to run, and she trusted that instinct as she never had before. She dodged behind a pillar. Another shot sounded. Another windshield broke—but further away.

When General Napier again shouted, "Stop!" her voice was going in the opposite direction.

She'd lost track of Jackie.

And Jackie had gained her goal—a thin, yellow, plastic

rope that hung close to a pillar from one of the high, broad heating vents. She'd glimpsed it on the way in. Back in Texas, her dad had made a swing out of this kind of rope. All of them—her older sister, her foster brother, and her baby sister—could swing on it at the same time. Carefully, she tugged on the rough yellow plastic, half fearing it would fall in her face and bring General Napier running.

The rope held.

Using her arms and legs, she slithered up the rope. With adrenaline coursing through her veins, she scarcely felt the pull on her muscles, but my God, did she have to breathe so loudly?

When she was even with the heat vent, which spiraled away into the darkness, she eyed it with trepidation. In her girlhood, during the long progression of foster homes, she had run, many times. She'd even hidden once in a parking garage much like this one, so she knew that when she slid onto the thin metal box, her weight would compress it and the tin might make the sound of thunder—and alert General Napier.

But there was no choice. General Napier was scanning the whole garage. She'd stopped calling, but her footsteps moved with a surety that chilled Jackie.

Gently, Jackie lowered herself onto the vent.

As the tin bent and crackled, a car screeched into the garage.

"Son of a bitch!" General Napier said viciously.

Palms slippery with sweat, Jackie pulled the rope up and onto the vent.

"Police!" A man's voice echoed through the garage. "Put down your weapon!"

Now Jackie wanted to curse.

Police. If she were a normal woman, she would consider the police her saviors. But with her record, they wouldn't believe her when she said the distinguished general had shot her own aide. And even if they did, by the time they performed the tests on the gun and confirmed that Jackie was innocent, the general would be long gone—after having had Jackie eliminated.

For Jackie knew that the same principles that had guided General Napier's actions in her climb up the ladder of the American military guided her actions now. The general would be ruthless in her pursuit of a scapegoat.

That scapegoat was Jackie.

Keeping her head down, Jackie crawled swiftly toward the garage entrance, depending on the shouting of the police and General Napier's furious replies to block the noise of her escape. She had only a few moments before General Napier convinced them of her own innocence.

Jackie made that time count. The vent burrowed up against the concrete wall beside the wide opening. The fresh air enticed her, drawing her onward.

But no convenient rope dangled here. There was no way down, and it was ten feet to the concrete floor.

She had no choice. After a swift intake of breath, she slid off the vent, dangled by her hands for a single second, then dropped to the ground.

The shock reverberated through her ankles. She couldn't move. She fell.

A yell confirmed that she had been seen.

She rolled and came to her feet running. Running toward freedom.

The chain gate began rattling down. The shouts became more emphatic. Footsteps pounded toward her.

She didn't think they were close.

She didn't dare look back.

A shot blasted a hole in the concrete wall just ahead of her.

She was almost there.

The gate was almost down.

In the moment before the gate rattled closed, she dropped and rolled beneath it.

At once she was on her feet again, running as hard as she could up the ramp. Another shot exploded behind her, striking the gate, ricocheting close by her head.

Behind her, men and women bellowed.

She could hear the gate clattering up again, but she turned the corner onto the street. A few people stood about, staring into the garage, but they backed away as she raced past, down the block, and around the corner.

Here no one had heard the ruckus from below. The band playing at the sidewalk café masked any noise. The tourists and locals enjoyed the warmth of the June night. Ignorant of the drama taking place so close by, they sipped their drinks. They chatted.

Although Jackie's breath hurried in her throat, she ambled past the sidewalk café. Snagging a woman's red jacket that hung on an unattended chair, she slipped it on. She reached into her purse, pulled out a clip, twisted her hair up off her neck, and fastened it into place.

Her fingers shook. She heard a shout behind her, and her body jolted as if she'd been shot.

But she hadn't been. Not yet.

A quick glance behind her proved the policemen hadn't spotted her. They fanned out, moving quickly.

She marched on like someone who knew where she was going. She turned the corner again, leaving the brightest lights and the largest crowds behind. Spotting an alley, she crossed the street. At the far end, she could see an exit. An escape.

She entered the shadows and took a breath. Here she could smell her past—garbage, darkness, panic, and betrayal.

Staying low and close against the fences, she skirted the Dumpsters, trotting over the broken asphalt. She couldn't twist her ankle now. Not with death following so closely on her heels.

The sounds from the street were muted. She was moving away from respectability, back toward the underbelly of life. She heard the scurry of rats in the refuse, the mumbling despair of a street person huddled in a cardboard box.

She slid her hand into her purse. Inside one zippered compartment she kept the remnants of her past, for a woman like her never trusted that bitch Fate. A woman like her never got entirely comfortable. A woman like her always looked over her shoulder.

She would go to Dulles International Airport to her locker. Inside was a backpack loaded with ten thousand dollars in cash, two IDs, a small bag with toiletries, and a change of clothing. She would buy a ticket on the first plane out and she would be gone, hopefully before the police could assemble a composite drawing of her and get it out on the wires.

Did the bookstore have a security camera that would show her face? Probably. If her crummy luck held, they had her photo.

Stopping before the end of the alley, she pulled out a small Swiss Army knife. She located the scissors.

Five minutes later, when she sauntered out of the alley, her hair was cropped close to her scalp, her shirt tails were tied under her breasts so the tattoo at the base of her spine would show, and she had wiped her face clear of makeup.

Jackie Porter was dead.

Pepper Prescott had taken her place.

Three

Lieutenant Dan Graham didn't sleep on the floor every night. Most nights he slept in a bed like a normal person. But sometimes, when the moon was full and the ghosts came to visit, he found himself stretched out against the wall in the living room, wrapped in blankets, sleeping as lightly as he had on those missions when every sound brought peril, and death was only a breath away.

He didn't worry about his tendency to wander the house at night. Restlessness was the price he paid for his years in the army.

Besides, the last time he had slept on the floor, the temptation of an empty ranch house had proved too much for some of the kids from town, and they had tried to break in. When they discovered the house was not empty, which they did in a terrifying manner, they ran so hard they left scorch marks across old Mrs. Dreiss's lawn.

Dan had laughed quietly and then gone back to bed.

Now the soft chime of his perimeter alarm woke him up. He opened his eyes to a total lack of light; on a moonless night, the Idaho mountains *defined* dark. A quick check of the intruder panel confirmed that something large had broken the laser beam that cut across the gravel road as it wound past the barn. Typically a deer did the damage, though sometimes a bear blundered down from the mountains into range.

But it was after midnight, and only during a full moon did those animals wander at night to feed.

Rising from his makeshift bed, he donned his jeans, tucked his small Beretta 9mm pistol into the back of his waistband, and wondered, was this it? Was this the moment he'd been waiting for? Perhaps *they* had found him at last.

Light, firm footsteps climbed the stairs to the wide wooden porch. A woman's footsteps.

Women were usually less dangerous than men. Usually. But he didn't make the mistake of assuming they all were.

The front doorknob rattled, but when it didn't open, she walked on the porch around the corner of the house.

Adrenaline flowed in his veins, but he controlled it, let it burn around the wounds on his face and belly. He took a deep breath, scented with the need for revenge. For justice.

He followed the footsteps toward the kitchen at the back. He saw no glint of light through the lacy curtains, so she didn't carry a flashlight. He waited for her to trip on the porch swing.

Without hesitation she moved around it. Either she wore night goggles, or she knew the layout of the Dreiss house.

Distantly he noted that, by the sound, she was wearing boots of some kind and stepped as if she had no fear of discovery. Did she think the house was abandoned? Or had she come looking for him, anticipating a showdown?

No. Unlikely. The people who hunted him never played fair. They never showed their faces, never let their true selves be revealed.

So who was this intruder?

She stopped by the storage crate Mrs. Dreiss always kept on the porch. He heard the *snick* of the rusty latch as she lifted the lid. She wouldn't find anything in there to steal—and sure enough, she put the lid back down and walked on.

In the old-fashioned kitchen, the clock gave off a phosphorescent glow, giving him enough light to see the dim outline of the wooden table, the wood-burning stove, the high countertop . . . the window where the woman stopped. It was locked, of course, a simple slide lock, but she jiggled it as if she knew what she was doing, and before long the slide squirmed free of its clasp and the window glided upward, the warped frame creaking all the way.

Fascinating. She knew the secrets of Mrs. Dreiss's home.

With a flick of the hand, she raised the window shade.

He let her get her leg through the opening, then her arms, her head and shoulders. As she straightened up, he tackled her, taking her down, rolling with her flailing body and coming out on top.

And immediately he knew her. Recognized her by her shape, her scent, by the memories that assaulted him.

"Pepper," he said. "Pepper Prescott. I've been waiting for you."

The tackle left Pepper winded. She couldn't see a thing.

Yet even before he spoke, she knew who lay on top of her. She recognized the weight of him, the scent of him, the glorious impression of his body stretched across hers.

Dan Graham. Her lover. Her heartache.

How could she ever forget him?

She knew there were things she should say. Questions she should ask. But all she could think was *Dan.*

His heat warmed her chilled body. His voice lowered to a croon. His hands slid into her hair. "Where have you been these last nine years?"

But he didn't seem to care about the answer, for he blocked her mouth with his.

For one stunned and helpless moment, a fragment of memory held her brain, the remembrance of an excited teenage girl's voice confiding to her . . . *Dan is the best kisser ever.*

That had been a challenge to Pepper. To find out if it was true.

And it was. Damn. It was.

His lips opened over hers, and she forgot the past, forgot the present. All that existed was his lips on hers, the hard floor beneath her body, and a long-banished warmth welling up from the depths of her soul.

His tongue thrust slowly, thoroughly, into her mouth.

He didn't wait for permission.

He never had.

He drew her into the kiss with an inviting curl of his tongue, teasing with a dark probe that imitated the first, tentative thrust of intercourse. He took pleasure from her as if it were his right. But he gave pleasure in equal measure, ladling on her a richness of passion that bestowed enjoyment and promised fulfillment. It was as if each part of her filled him with a delight that over-flowed into dark and smoky passion.

She could almost smell the sizzle between them.

He tasted of mint toothpaste and of Dan, a spiciness she had never forgotten, and he fed her the flavor as if he knew she had ached to taste him again.

Yet she didn't answer him. How could she? She was still off balance, reeling from the fall, reeling from almost being murdered, from being on the run for the last five days . . .

As she stiffened, he gave an impatient exclamation, and the tentative, loving kiss became a claim. He thrust, and thrust again.

Her reluctance skittered away as she remembered. Remembered the way he had felt inside her. The strength and the need and the heat.

She had never forgotten. No matter how hard she had tried, she had never forgotten.

His fingers massaged her scalp, spreading shock waves of delight through the nerves of her skin to her breasts, her belly, and it was as good as it had been before.

Better, because she had missed him so.

He slanted his lips to seal them with hers, not allow-ing her a moment to think, and possessed her so thoroughly that each thrust of his tongue brought her body arching up, trying to get closer to him. They were already mated from shoulder to knee. He was between her legs, and the fly of his jeans was stretched across the bulge of his erection. It was an enticement she hadn't felt in reality for nine long years, although she'd dreamed about it.

No matter how disciplined she was in the daylight, her dreams had been wild and sensual, filled with Dan and that night, the pain of losing her virginity and the ecstasy of being with him.

And the guilt afterward, the overwhelming sense of having gone too far in her defiance and her rage. Of finally going much, much too far.

Now, under his handling, heat roared through her. She stroked his arms and his T-shirt-clad shoulders, finding the long-lost contours and reveling in them. She remembered him, inside and out. She wanted him, inside and out.

She'd never stopped wanting him.

As if he'd heard her acknowledgment, his kiss lightened, grew softer, more tender . . .

He lifted his head.

He said, "Pepper." And that was all.

Damn him. She had betrayed herself before she'd even seen him.

She reacted as she always did when all her plans had gone awry—with hostility. She shoved at his shoulders. "Get off me."

"No." That was all. Just *no* spoken in a calm, flat voice that betrayed nothing of the man he'd become.

Except he didn't feel much different. He was tall, six foot three, and heavy-boned, with large shoulders that made her feel dainty. He'd always been well muscled. Every summer he had worked as a ranch hand for his father, and by the time he was seventeen, he'd been a hardbody, sexy and swaggering, the hottest guy in the town of Diamond. The coolest guy in Adams County. The guy who tangled himself in her mind and meshed with her soul.

But she didn't want to remember that.

She shoved again. "You almost broke my leg tackling me like that."

"No, I didn't." He sounded absolutely certain, darkly menacing, and dangerous. He didn't sound like the Dan she had known. The Dan she had loved.

That Dan had been fiery and wild, an unbroken colt bred to kick down fences and race into the sunset. This Dan was . . . frightening and still.

The old, curling edges of Mrs. Dreiss's linoleum bit into the center of her back, and she noted the familiar scents of her home—clove sachets and starch and Lemon Pledge. Now, in addition to the old smells, the added odor of dust twirled faintly through the air.

Alarm stirred in her. Mrs. Dreiss would never allow a speck of dust to settle in her house.

"How did you get here?" he asked.

Her awareness shifted from him. She listened to the silence of the house and said absently, "What do you mean?"

"You didn't come by car."

Oh, no. He had noticed. Her hands jumped away from

him as if he had become superheated. Her fingernails scraped along the floor. "Why do you care? What are you doing here? Where's Mrs. Dreiss?"

He peeled himself off her body. He stood. He extended his hand. He didn't wait for her to grab it but caught her arm and lifted her to her feet.

"Where is she?" Pepper didn't like the slightly breathless, anxious tone in her voice. Didn't like the thoughts that whirled in her head.

Dan switched on the light.

Pepper blinked at the sudden illumination from the plain light fixture at the center of the nine-foot-high ceiling. The large, old-fashioned kitchen with its small table in one corner and chipped white sink looked much the same as it had when she had lived here.

Dan did not. He'd always been dark-eyed and dark-skinned; his great-grandmother had been Shoshone Indian, her genes had dominated his mother's family ever since, and clearly, American Indian blood coursed through his veins. But Dan had somehow confounded the genetic gamble, and at seventeen his hair had been a gorgeous burnished gold. At seventeen as well he'd had a purity of countenance and a clarity of features that made the girls babble and giggle when he turned his gaze on them.

Now he was . . . harsh. The charm of a young hunk was gone. Now cynical lines bit into the skin around his mouth. His black eyes watched her as if he would have his answers from her by any means. Not a muscle in his face stirred, yet danger shimmered in the air around him.

This was a ruthless man. This was a man with night in his soul.

She saw it all in an instant: the similarities, the changes. The changes . . . She took a step toward him. His straight hair hung almost to his collar. The sun had tanned him a uniform bronze. Across his cheek and over his nose a scar zigzagged—a wound that had been skillfully repaired. The place beneath the scar looked slightly indented, as if the cheekbone had been smashed. The thin white line was drawn like war paint across his skin, making him look, ironically, more like an Indian than ever before.

He'd been hurt. Badly.

And now he was here, in Mrs. Dreiss's house, when he should have been at home at the Graham ranch down the road.

She rubbed her hands up and down her arms, trying to warm them through the slick material of her jacket. "Is she ill?"

All the answer she got was the sight of his back as he walked toward the front of the house, clicking on lights as he went.

She followed, her cheap boots making a muffled thump as she walked and rubbing new blisters on top of those that had already burst.

The house had been constructed in the twenties, with the living room, the dining room, and the kitchen laid out in a row from front to back. Off each room was a bedroom. The dining room hadn't changed, with a built-in buffet that ran the length of one wall and a table large enough to feed a threshing crew of eighteen. Only the computer added an odd, out-of-place touch of the contemporary. The plants scattered throughout the rooms looked neglected: dusty, dry, suffering as Pepper now suffered. In the living room, starched tatting still decorated the arms of the chairs, lace curtains still covered the windows. Pepper saw that the door to Mrs. Dreiss's bedroom was still open.

Stepping aside, Dan let Pepper walk through first.

The dresser was made of solid oak, which had darkened with age. Mrs. Dreiss's nylon brushes, her silver barrette, her collection of glass perfume bottles were laid neatly on a dusty mirror. As always, the bed was made with a wedding ring quilt done on a dark blue background.

The room was empty.

Dan didn't have to say a word. Mrs. Dreiss was gone.

"When did she . . . pass on?" Pepper whispered. She couldn't say the word *die*. Not now. Not in reference to Mrs. Dreiss.

"Ten months ago."

"Did she suffer?"

He didn't move. Didn't show any emotion. "Heart attack. I found her myself. She died in the garden."

Relief, minor but real, eased the tension in Pepper's muscles. "So she died happy."

"She looked peaceful and pleased with herself."

"Thank God." Pepper felt odd, disconnected from him, from this place. Her head buzzed heavily, and she swallowed. "She wasn't that old."

"Seventy-one."

"No, not that old." Pepper was grateful that he didn't reproach her for the misery she had caused Mrs. Dreiss, both in the months she had lived here and later, when she had left and never looked back.

Although she *had* looked back. She'd sent tokens, occasionally, small gifts and brief bulletins so Mrs. Dreiss wouldn't worry. She had bought her a book and tried to have it autographed . . .

But she hadn't wanted anyone to trace her, and she'd always thought she had time. Time to come back. Time to make things up to Mrs. Dreiss.

She, of all people, should have known better.

Going to the closet, she opened the door. Mrs. Dreiss's clothes hung there, and the scent of a lavender sachet rushed out to envelop Pepper. "I never thought she would pass away."

Stupid. Everyone dies.

But he agreed. "Neither did I."

Pepper touched the dress Mrs. Dreiss wore to church every Sunday in the summer. A wash-and-wear cotton— Mrs. Dreiss didn't have time to fool with ironing—its simplicity symbolized Mrs. Dreiss for Pepper. A no-nonsense, straight-talking woman, tanned from a life spent outdoors among her plants, with blue eyes that could see a sixteen-year-old's lies for what they were and the fearlessness to call her on it. Pepper faced Dan. "No one thought she should take in an orphan."

He lifted one brow as if the sentiment surprised him. "She didn't care what anyone thought."

"No." Pepper stared at herself in the yellowing, wavy mirror over the dresser. Her face was distorted, too broad across the forehead, too narrow around the chin, her hazel eyes overly large and filled with disbelief. For the first time since she'd heard the gunshot that killed Otto Bjerke, the terror faded, replaced by bitter grief.

"You really didn't know." It was a statement, yet he seemed to be asking.

The world was distorted, off-kilter, knocked off its axis by General Napier's betrayal, by Mrs. Dreiss's death, and by the man standing behind her, so familiar yet so different. Her gaze met his in the mirror. "No."

He had an expression on his face, a slight curl to his lips, as if he didn't know whether to believe her. "I'll be in the kitchen if you need me."

He left her alone, to cry if she wanted, she supposed, but the hurt was too new. Too shocking. She couldn't cry. She couldn't even feel. For the last nine years, she had thought she had a place to come to when she was a success, and a person to brag to who would be wholly happy for her. She had planned it in her mind a thousand times.

She would drive up to the ranch in a great car—a Mercedes, a Beemer, no, wait, she'd come in a helicopter—she'd bring presents, and Mrs. Dreiss's eyes would gleam with pride. Mrs. Dreiss wouldn't scold her for running away either. Mrs. Dreiss was a great believer in water over the dam. Many a time during the year Pepper had lived here, Mrs. Dreiss had told her to stop looking back, told her she had the future ahead of her. Long before Pepper had discovered General Jennifer Napier and her axioms, she had had Mrs. Dreiss and her common sense.

And Mrs. Dreiss had lived as she believed. Mrs. Dreiss would never have betrayed anyone. Not like that bitch, that murderer, General Napier.

Going to the bed, Pepper traced the pattern of the quilt.

Instead of coming back in triumph, she'd come back in need of a haven, sure that she had a home she could run to when life got too difficult.

The haven was gone. Mrs. Dreiss was gone, and all that was left was the bitter knowledge that Pepper had received what she deserved. No pride, no help, no love.

Mrs. Dreiss was gone.

With a painful grimace, Pepper removed her boots. Crawling awkwardly onto the bed, she curled up on the quilt, put her head on the pillows and grieved for the woman who had taken in a rebellious teenager and made her straighten up, made her take a look at herself and decide she had to change—or die.

Four

Walking out onto the porch, Dan closed the door behind him, careful to be silent. He shivered in his T-shirt; it was cold out here, as always at night so high in the mountains. Opening his wallet, he pulled out a tiny, flat earpiece and microphone. He walked to the corner of the porch. A billion stars shone down brightly, obscured by neither clouds nor smog. Up here, a man could look up and see eternity—and know that hell existed right here on earth.

He knew. He'd lived there. He lived there still.

Somewhere in the heavens was the satellite that would pick up his call and beam it to one place, one office, one phone. Punching the call button, Dan listened to the series of burrs and whistles.

"Lieutenant Graham." Colonel Donald Jaffe's voice spoke clearly in his ear, and despite the fact that it was two hours later in Washington, D.C., he sounded alert. "Is there a problem?"

"I caught an intruder." As his eyes adjusted to the darkness, Dan descended the steps, walked to the drive, and looked toward the garage, then down the hill toward the barn. "A woman I knew when I was a teenager."

"Get rid of her."

"I would." Squatting down on the graded gravel, Dan looked for tire tracks. Standing, he dusted his fingers. "But it seems odd she would show up now, in the middle of the night, by herself . . . without a car."

Colonel Jaffe's voice grew crisp. "Sounds like a career criminal."

"Given her past, it's a good possibility." Although even with the hair, she looked more middle class than criminal class. But Dan knew enough not to be taken in by appearances or to think Pepper Prescott had eschewed crime. She'd been well on her way to trouble when she'd lived in Diamond.

Of course, so had he.

"Yes, let's check her out. Better to be safe." Now Dan heard the weariness in Colonel Jaffe's voice. "What's her name? What do you know about her?"

"Name, Pepper Prescott. Age twenty-five. Born in Texas—or so she told me once. Raised in foster homes. She lived in Diamond, actually here on the ranch, for eleven months when she was sixteen." Dan tried to think what else he knew about her, but a description of the heat inside her and out would scarcely help with the search. "That's about it."

Colonel Jaffe asked incredulously, "That's all the information I get?"

"It's the best I can do. After Mrs. Dreiss's death, I

briefly tried to trace her myself but couldn't. I believe she's been living under assumed names."

"Why were you trying to trace her yourself?" *Trust Colonel Jaffe to see what was important.*

If Dan told the colonel that Pepper was the new owner of the ranch, he'd blow a gasket. He'd want to close down the operation, and Dan couldn't allow that, so he said only, "Personal matters, sir."

"Personal matters. Personal involvement?"

"Long ago."

"Hm."

Dan knew what the colonel was thinking, because the idea had occurred to him too. "Yes, sir. Our friends might have discovered the old connection and planted her."

"But that's a far stretch." Dan could almost hear Colonel Jaffe weighing the possibilities. "All right. I'll get your information as quickly as possible. We don't want her there if she's an innocent civilian."

"Don't worry about that. All I have to do is scare her." With a cynicism honed by time, Dan said, "She'll run away. That's what she does best."

"We want to interrogate her if she's not a civilian."

"Yeah." Dan planned to anyway. Hell, he looked forward to it, for he hadn't told Colonel Jaffe the whole truth. Dan's need to investigate Pepper was more than business. It *was* personal. It was curiosity about an old lover and his own reactions to her. Tonight Pepper had broken into more than the house. She had broken through to the man he had been before. When he had given in to an irresistible compulsion and kissed her, he had felt something vivid, overwhelming, old and yet glittering new, and he recognized it.

Lust, clean, pure, and primitive—and not surprising at all, for he had been thinking about Pepper, on and off, for nine years. Been seriously looking for her since Mrs. Dreiss died. And she'd walked right into his world. She wouldn't find it as easy to escape this time. He'd find out where she'd gone, what she'd done. He'd find out the truth of why she was here. And God help her if she was one of *them*.

As if he couldn't bear not to ask, Colonel Jaffe asked, "Any sign of the boys?"

"Nothing. Do you still have tabs on all of them?"

"Of course." The colonel sounded irritated that Dan would even ask. "They landed in Vegas two weeks ago. They gambled for a couple of days, lived it up like men who might die tomorrow, then one by one they slipped away. All except two, and they're still gambling. The rest of them are scattered over the Northwest. They can get to you within twelve hours."

With satisfaction, Dan said, "They're waiting for Schuster."

"You're obviously weak from your wounds and conspicuously unprotected. We planted the information about your activity and your location. What's keeping him? Why haven't they tried to kill you yet?"

Dan grinned at Colonel Jaffe's freely expressed desire to see Dan get shot. "They've got a bad sense of direction? They've realized the error of their ways and decided to become decadent Americans?" He sobered. "They decided to save themselves a lot of trouble by sending in an old girlfriend to take me out?" He heard movement from inside the house. "She's coming. Let me know what you find out about her."

Without fanfare the two men shut off transmission.

Dan slipped back inside while Pepper was shut in the bathroom, and although it was past midnight, he poked up the fire in the stove to chase the chill out of the kitchen and started the coffeemaker. Pepper loved her caffeine, and long ago the two of them had spent many an evening over a cup of powdered espresso, pretending they were in Seattle—or Paris. He needed to know more about her, what she was doing here, and the smell of the coffee would lure her to his side.

This wasn't some casual visit. She was on a mission. His task was to find out what kind before it was too late for her, or for him.

As she walked back into the kitchen, he analyzed her movements, her facial expression, the way she held her hands. She'd discarded her boots, and her cheap white socks looked as if they were going to fall off. She still wore her jacket, hugging it to her as if she were cold—and she had been when she crawled through that window. Her eyes looked stunned, as if she'd had a blow she'd not anticipated.

Had she? Or did she know the truth about Mrs. Dreiss and the ranch?

He leaned against the counter, poured a mug, and pushed it toward Pepper.

"Thank you." She didn't look at him, didn't come any nearer than necessary to wrap her hands around it. Then she stood there, staring at the steaming brown brew as if fascinated by the color, and that allowed him the leisure to look her over.

The years had wrought changes. A lot of changes.

Nine years ago she'd worn her hair wavy and long down her back, braided around her face, and the color had constantly changed. Red, blond, brown, with outrageous highlights of pink or blue or purple. Now the color was black, and the cut was short, uneven, and wildly curly.

But the cut was the only sign of the old, rebellious Pepper. The new Pepper's features had matured from the roundness of adolescence to a slender grace, and the constant animation, the open hostility had been replaced with a thoughtful intelligence that fascinated him against his will. The new Pepper's hazel eyes didn't spark with green but tonight appeared to be a misty gray, and they were tired, sad—and wary.

Where had she been? What had caused such changes? *Who* had caused such changes?

Maybe it was a man. She was one of those women that men fought for. No matter how old she got, her face would launch a thousand ships—or with that haircut, at least a dozen.

To his surprise he didn't like that image any better than the idea that she had come to find him and kill him.

He pushed the sugar bowl toward her, a harsh scraping across the green Formica counter.

She started at the sound. She looked at the sugar bowl. Looked at him. Her gaze sidled away. "Thank you." She sounded subdued, as if she'd had a shock.

Maybe she truly had. Maybe none of the letters had

caught up with her. Maybe she'd shown up here *now* by accident.

Yeah, and maybe James Bond really preferred pink squirrels shaken, not stirred.

In a voice that sounded almost routine and very civilized, Pepper asked, "So . . . what have you been doing since I saw you last?"

With cynical appreciation he realized she was making conversation, as if it was a normal occurrence for her to arrive at midnight after an absence of nine years.

Too bad. He used to play this game with skill and charm. He didn't have the patience anymore. He didn't care anymore. "I joined the service."

She put down the mug. As if they'd suddenly grown sweaty, she wiped her palms along her pants. "The . . . service. Like the army?"

His sharp gaze noted every movement. "Exactly like the army."

"Any . . . particular thing you did?"

Special Forces, Terrorist Unit. But he didn't tell anyone the whole truth, and certainly not this woman. "Nothing in particular."

He saw her bosom lift and fall as if she were fighting to get breath, and her voice sounded constricted. She touched her face where the scar sliced across his face, and her finger trembled. "Is that where you got . . . ?"

"American soldiers aren't welcome in many parts of the world," he said in considerable understatement.

"No. No, of course not."

Did she know about the scar that sliced his belly? Had

they told her that was his weak point? Had they convinced her she could take him out?

But if she had come to kill him, this was not her first job, for she leaned against the counter in a parody of relaxation. "How long have you been home?"

"Less than a year."

She picked up the mug. "You must have missed Diamond. I'm surprised you ever left."

His gaze moved to her mouth. Her wide lips were slightly swollen, the only sign that their kiss hadn't been an erotic dream. She had tasted the same. Hungry, horny, wistful . . . his.

But that was an illusion. She wasn't his. She was . . . God only knew what she was, or why she was here, but abruptly, he was done with being civilized. "I couldn't stay here. Not after we screwed each other."

She flinched. The coffee slopped over the edge of the cup. But her voice was studiedly casual. "We were a couple of stupid kids. What existed between us was nothing more than a youthful infatuation. I'm over it. I'm sure you are too." She paused as if waiting for him to agree, and when he didn't, she shrugged. "Anyway, I never look back on the past. I don't even remember what happened."

Emotion swept him along with the fury of a roaring mountain stream, and that emotion was rage. The memory of that one night had driven him away from Diamond. The dreams of that one night possessed him in the jungle, in the desert, in Germany, and in the Philippines, bringing him out of deep sleep to face sticky sheets and a night of pacing the floor.

And she didn't remember?

Taking a paper towel off the roll, he squatted down and wiped up the coffee, then looked up at her. A non-threatening position, one that yielded a position of superiority to the weaker of the duo. Here he could pretend he felt nothing but mild interest in her and her replies. "What did you think? Did you think I could stay here after *you* ran away?"

She stammered, "I . . . I don't understand why not."

He bludgeoned her with the truth. "Everyone knew what we'd done."

She turned pale enough for the sunburn on her nose to glow like a beacon. "How could everyone know? It was dark. There was no one around. No one saw us."

"What else were they to think? One night you and Mrs. Dreiss have a knock-down-drag-out because you skipped school—"

Pepper looked as truculent as she had on the winter day she had gone to McCall and returned with a tiny dragon tattoo at the base of her spine.

"—You go off with me like a bat out of hell, stay out all night, we steal beer from a convenience store in McCall, we drink, we drive, then you leave town so fast you leave skid marks on the highway and me hanging in the wind." He wadded the paper towel into a ball and tossed it, hard, into the garbage can. "The gossip was I'd raped you."

Her head snapped around at him. "Rape!"

"Mrs. Dreiss thought so. She called me down here and ripped a strip of hide off of me—"

"I acquit you. You didn't rape me." Pepper looked

everywhere but at him. "Could we talk about something else?"

Not damned likely. He'd been waiting for this chance for too many years. *Why the hell had she run?* "I know it wasn't good."

"Please be quiet."

"The funny thing was, even back then I had better technique than I showed you. But I had wanted you for so long, I lost control. Somewhere in the back of my mind, I was embarrassed, because I was such a clod, but I was drowning in pleasure."

"*Sh!*" She looked around as if there were someone who could hear.

He relentlessly continued, "You were a virgin. I was horny and clumsy—"

"No, you weren't!" Her voice was low and intense. "It wasn't like that!"

Still he knelt before her. "Then why did you take off?"

"It was what you said afterward!"

He strained, trying to remember. He'd been half-drunk and totally blown away by her. He couldn't remember mumbling anything except a feeble attempt to comfort her. But he tried to bluff, to pretend he recalled what he'd said. "Why did that offend you?"

She tried to speak. Closed her eyes. Tried again to speak. Sputtered, "You . . . arrogant idiot. You haven't changed a bit! Never mind. Just forget it."

She wasn't going to give him a clue, at least not right now, so he stood up. Let her remember how tall he was. Let her feel nervous around him. "You left me to face my dad, Mrs. Dreiss, and everyone in the town." And even now, that pissed him off.

"No one knew," she repeated.

"By the time I'd got done drinking and brawling, they did."

Her eyes narrowed. "Your fault, then."

She had grown thinner. She wore not a drop of makeup. Her forehead and nose were sunburned, a blotchy red on the fair, freckled skin. She wore a beige, long-sleeved camp shirt and matching slacks, cheap clothes, as if she'd bought them at a discount store. Boring colors, as if she had been interested in anonymity. The slacks were a little too long for her. The hem was ragged, as if she'd walked a long way, stepping on them all the way. And she was nervy, like a cat on the Fourth of July.

More important, she was tired—always a great time to interrogate a suspect. Stepping back, he gave her some space and changed the subject to something less personal but important on a different level. "What have *you* been doing?"

Too quickly she asked, "What do you mean?"

Interesting reaction. "For a living."

He saw her relax. "I'm a landscaper." She spooned sugar into her mug and stirred the coffee.

"Not doing too well, I guess, or you wouldn't be here."

Fury flashed through her, lighting up her face, illuminating the old Pepper from the inside out. "Maybe I came to brag."

"Maybe." Had she been successful? If she had been, why wasn't she dressed to impress? What was she doing here? And more to the point—"How *did* you get here?"

She took a breath. "Get here?"

She understood him, but she was stalling. He waited without comment, knowing from experience that silence would work where words would not.

He was right. The silence made her uncomfortable, and in a rush, she said, "I had an accident a few miles down the road. I had to walk in."

"You all right?" She was. He knew she was. She moved without pain.

"I'm fine."

But she didn't want to talk about what had happened. Curiouser and curiouser. When people had survived an accident, they always wanted to talk about it, even when they were at fault. "You had an accident. You weren't hurt. You . . . walked here?"

"Yes. Walked."

"Nobody came along and picked you up?"

"I got a little lost." She tried to take a swallow of coffee, but her hands were shaking. "I drove off a gravel road."

He tensed. A little lost? The highway wound through the mountains, but it was paved all the way to Diamond. She had to have come in the back way to have driven on a gravel road, and for no one to have come by, it had to have been so far back the birds couldn't find it. "You'll need to call the rental car company. Tell them what happened."

"No. No, the car was mine." Her voice got higher, more breathless. "I bought it. From a man. I have the papers. Or rather, had them. They were in the glove compartment."

A lot of information to prove she owned that car. "The insurance company then."

She looked as if the thought had never occurred to her. "Yes, I'll call them tomorrow."

He'd made assumptions about her trip here. Which parts were true? "So you didn't fly into Boise. You drove all the way here."

"Yes."

"From where?"

She shrugged as if she couldn't see any reason not to tell him, and her words grew clipped and decisive. "I drove in from Denver."

"So you've been living in Denver." He surveyed her thoughtfully.

She stirred so hard the coffee formed a whirlpool in the cup. "No."

One of the postmarks on one of the letters she'd sent Mrs. Dreiss was Denver, and when Mrs. Dreiss had died, he'd looked for Pepper there. He hadn't found a trace of her, and he had pretty good connections. "Where have you been living?"

"I move around a lot."

Still the same old Pepper. No commitments and no confessions. "Roads must have been slick driving. There's still a lot of snow out there."

Putting down her coffee, she went to the sink, reached into the window shelf where Mrs. Dreiss kept her collection of African violets. Pepper touched the wilting leaves. "Going across the Rockies was scary."

"That's probably why you slid off the road. You hit a patch of ice."

With a reproachful glance at him, she poured water into the bases of the pots. "You could water these plants occasionally."

"I'll take you back to the site of the wreck tomorrow. Pick up your stuff. Bring the car in." He recognized that expression on her face: the outthrust lower lip, the direct, steely-eyed gaze. She was about to tell him to go to hell, and he wasn't ready to go there yet. Not alone, anyway.

"I'm starving. Is there anything to eat?"

Every time she evaded him, he became more suspicious of her. "Cookies."

Her face lit up. Her eyes glowed, her wide mouth smiled. Then her smile wavered, her brow knit, and she looked lost. Uncertain. "Who . . . ?"

He went to the freezer and pulled out the Tupperware container. "Mrs. Dreiss made them before she died." Prying the cold, stiff lid off, he offered Pepper the container. "I saved them for you."

She took a long sniff of Mrs. Dreiss's chocolate chip cookies. "How did you know I would be here?"

Ah. The moment at last. He punched her with the important information. "I knew you'd show up when you heard Mrs. Dreiss left you the ranch."

Pepper's face went slack. The Tupperware fell from her nerveless hand.

He caught the cookies before they hit the floor.

So she hadn't known.

"She left me . . . the ranch? All of it? I mean . . . the *ranch*?" Pepper started shaking, a low-level tremor caused by, he diagnosed, sleeplessness, hunger, and stress.

Taking three cookies, he put them on a paper towel and heated them in the microwave. It took exactly sixty-six seconds to get them to the right consistency. He knew that; he'd done it often enough for himself. "Here." He broke off a chunk and held it to Pepper's lips. "This will make everything better." It wouldn't, but it would sure help.

As she chewed, the color came back into her face. She was not quite so wild-eyed, not quite so drawn. She let him put another piece in her mouth.

He enjoyed the texture of her lips against his fingers. Toyed with the idea of kissing her and tasting the dark warmth of the chocolate, the rich flavor of the black walnuts.

But she wasn't thinking about that. About him. All her attention was on the situation she faced. "Is that why you're here? Are you taking care of the place?"

That wasn't the reason. Not at all, but he couldn't tell her the truth. So he lied with the adroitness that came from much practice. "Dad and I have been tending the ranch since old Mr. Dreiss died anyway. Mrs. Dreiss was only interested in her garden. You know that."

"I remember," Pepper said faintly.

"Staying here made it easier for me to keep an eye on things." Staying here was part of a reckless plan to get justice for too many deaths.

Dan tried to feed Pepper again, but she had recovered enough to recognize the intimacy of the gesture. Taking the cookies out of his hand, she ate the rest of the first one and all of the second one. Putting down the paper towel, she looked him right in the eyes. "When she died . . . when the will was read . . . did you look for me?"

"We've been searching for you, following the trail of postmarks from the packages you sent Mrs. Dreiss." He took the step he'd been wanting to take, the one that put him so close Pepper had to look straight up at him, and she looked up with alarm. "If one of the letters didn't find you, if you didn't come to claim the ranch as your own, why are you here?"

Her pupils dilated as she stared up at him. She swallowed. "I did come to claim the ranch. That is why I came."

"Liar."

Her chin jutted out. She took a breath. "Believe what you like. Call me what you please. I've been called worse. Now, I'm pooped. I'm going to bed."

"Your bedroom's made up." Deliberately, he poked a stick at her. He needed to see the evidence of her pain. "Mrs. Dreiss wanted it ready for you when you came home."

That jutting chin trembled, but Pepper knew him well. Knew he was being cruel. She smiled with all her teeth. "I'll wash up before hitting the sack." Gathering the last cookie, she turned away—and staggered a little.

He didn't know what she'd been doing, but she was exhausted, harried, and lying through her pearly white teeth, and he intended to find out why. He watched her disappear around the corner, his gaze on her skinny rump.

Then she stuck her head back in, and for one

moment, he saw a flash of the old, mischievous Pepper. "By the way," she pointed at the jumble of blankets on the dining room floor, "who's having the slumber party?" She smiled.

As it always had, her smile caught him by the throat. He wanted to smile back. He wanted to believe her lies. He wanted everything to be all right, for no one smiled like Pepper. No one shared joy so genuinely, so generously. The first time she'd smiled at him, he'd been lost, and he hadn't found his way back.

Pepper Prescott had a lot to answer for.

Five

Sergeant Sonny Midler pushed his cowboy hat back on his forehead, leaned his arm against the pommel of his saddle, and drawled, "Hey, Dan, next time you want to brand calves, maybe you ought to ride a horse who doesn't scrape you off on a tree."

Dan picked himself up off the ground, dusted himself off, flicked Sonny off, and walked over to Samson, who stood eying him with a grin on his stupid horse face. "You're an asshole," Dan said. He didn't know whether he meant Samson or Sonny, and it didn't much matter. Sonny had a score to settle with Dan; the sergeant really was pissed about having to work on a ranch again. And Samson had never been anything but ornery. Both had given Dan what he wanted this morning—a chance to burn off some of the frustration Pepper's advent had caused him.

"Better be nice, Sonny." Hunter Wainwright had been on the ranch for as long as Dan could remember, and he teased with a heavy hand. "Dan's the boss's son."

For good measure, Dan flicked him off too, and smoothly mounted Samson, the damned palomino who had been his horse for over twelve years. He didn't know why he bothered riding him; Samson really did scrape off his riders every chance he got. Maybe Dan kept him around because he was the biggest gelding anyone around Diamond had ever seen. Maybe it was because Samson always knew his way home.

Dan was ready to go home now. He'd spent three hours, from six in the morning until nine, over on his dad's property, branding calves. It was hard work, stinking and dusty, rough and filled with the bawling of calves and the cursing of cowboys.

The truth was, the surgery to repair his intestines had convinced Dan that he didn't want to bleed internally ever again. So he had listened to his body, rested a lot last fall and this winter, and figured he would work himself back into condition by the end of summer.

Some of the cowboys had made fun of him the first few times he'd bowed out of a workday. Then he'd looked at them, long and hard, and they'd shut up. He knew rumors flew about what he'd done in the service, dire rumors of death and desperation, but nothing they said could compare to the truth. What he had done—what he was doing—they couldn't begin to imagine.

That was why he was doing it. So the men who worked so hard on the ranch would never know desolation and hopelessness.

With a lift of the hand, Dan left the noisy scene behind, riding through the meadows toward Mrs. Dreiss's place.

The long valley stretched and twisted between the still-snowcapped peaks and the greening foothills. The valley followed the river that eventually made its way into the Snake. Two properties divided the valley: the Dreiss ranch and his dad's ranch. They took in a lot of surrounding mountains, where the cattle wandered in the winter when they wanted to get good and lost.

The mountains defined this land. It was the mountains that brought winter storms so sudden and vicious even an experienced cowboy could get caught and freeze to death. It was the mountains that provided summers so brief sometimes the piles of snow didn't melt until after Independence Day. People up here in the high country laughed about the weather, said there were only two seasons, winter and August, and they were right.

But the mountains had formed Dan's character, made him tough, made him solitary, made him a leader of men . . . and brought him home. All that agonizing time in the hospital, two things had kept him going: knowing that when he came home, the craggy peaks would be there, as they had been for all eternity . . . and knowing that it was time to find Pepper.

But he hadn't found her. She had found him. That meant something. He just had to find out what.

The hay barn looked fine when Dan rode in. He put Samson in his stall and groomed him. Then he picked up the phone, dialed his dad, and said, "She's back."

Russell was a rancher and no one's fool; it took him only a moment to deduce who *she* was. "Is she? Pepper Prescott rushed in to claim that legacy, did she?"

"Dunno."

Businessman that he was, Russell went right to the subject of paramount importance. "Does she want to sell the ranch?"

"Dunno."

"Because if she does, we're the first on the list. She ought to know that, she lived with—" Russell's voice snagged as he realized what Dan had said. "What do you mean, you don't know if she rushed in to claim her inheritance? That is what she's here for, isn't it?"

"She didn't know Mrs. Dreiss had passed away until she got here."

"Is that what she told you?" Russell's condemnation was flat and disdainful. "She's lying."

"I've gotten pretty good at telling a lie from the truth."

During the thoughtful silence on the other end of the phone, Dan could almost see his dad stroking the early morning stubble on his chin. Russell didn't know about the things his son had done in the service, but Dan's ability to discern a lie had something to do with them. His dad didn't know the truth of what Dan was doing at Mrs. Dreiss's ranch either, but the changes in Dan obviously made him uneasy. Dan knew it and was sorry, but the events he'd witnessed, the deeds he'd done, had blasted away every emotion except the need for revenge—until last night, when Pepper had brought him to a white-hot rage with her indifference, and blue-hot lust with her kiss.

"If she didn't come to get her inheritance, what did she come back for?" Russell asked.

The chickens clucked and pecked out in the yard,

scratching for grubs and complaining softly. "Dunno." But Dan was going to find out.

"Knowing that girl, it's trouble."

"Yeah." Yeah, Dan would say she brought trouble. It was trouble when the first thing he did was tackle her and kiss her, and more trouble when she kissed him back. Trouble when he'd listened as she washed up before going to sleep, and imagined how she looked naked. Trouble when he wanted to go climb in bed with her and show her what he'd learned from the women he'd used to forget her. Yeah, that was trouble, all right.

Russell's voice turned cautious. "Are you okay with her being there?"

"Sure."

"It's her ranch," Russell said. "You could leave her to it."

"It might be her ranch," Dan reminded his father, "but she can't run it by herself."

"I didn't say that, but she can take care of the house. You could live here, ride over and do the chores." Russell's voice turned eager. "Son, come on home."

It was good to know his dad wanted him back in the house but typical of Russell to forget that they hadn't gotten along when Dan was a teenager, and they still got along best when they lived in separate houses.

That was because his dad always knew everything. He'd given Dan advice on how to heal those wounds on his face and belly. He'd told him how to invest the money he'd made in the service and which truck to buy. He'd even picked out the best girl for Dan to marry. So Dan had moved in with Mrs. Dreiss, ostensibly to help her out. In reality, if he hadn't got away from his dad, the two strong-willed men would have come to blows.

Still, they loved each other, so Dan said, "I can't come home yet, Dad. Maybe later. We'll see how it goes."

Samson poked his head back over the side of his stall, snuffled at the phone, then blew into the receiver.

"What the hell was that?" Russell shouted.

"Samson." Dan scratched the horse's nose.

A disgruntled tone entered Russell's voice. "I don't know why you ride that big, mean gelding. He's nothing but trouble."

"He reminds me of you." Dan looked into Samson's brown eyes.

The horse stared back, then shoved his nose harder into Dan's hand.

"Very funny. I heard you were branding calves this morning."

That news got back to Russell in a hurry. "I try to earn my keep."

"No worry about that." It was a measure of Russell's worry that he brought the conversation right back to Pepper. "Son, don't let her get her claws in you again."

"Don't worry, Dad. I can handle her."

"She hasn't already got her claws in you, has she?" Maybe Russell knew him better than Dan realized.

"Dad, she never got them out of me." While Russell was sputtering, Dan hung up the phone.

He gave Samson a last scratch, then donned his down vest to disguise the bulge made by the pistol and holster beneath his shirt, and strode out into the cool morning. As he stretched the kinks out of his muscles, he gazed around in bone-deep appreciation of this valley. Of his home.

From here, Dan couldn't see his dad's house. The houses sat on opposing ends of the valley, miles away and out of sight from each other, which was the way the two families had liked it. His family had always been ambitious, making a good living out of ranching, working three sections, with the federal rights to another three. The Dreiss men had never been worth much, according to Russell, ranching one section and doing a poor job on rich land. Russell had rubbed his hands when old man Dreiss had died, leaving no heirs except his wife. Russell had thought Mrs. Dreiss would sell him the land.

Dan remembered the kickup when the old lady had refused, and briskly too. She said, with the forthrightness that characterized her, that she wasn't going to give up her garden and go live in town with a bunch of store-keepers, loggers, and ne'er-do-wells, and that was that. She had kept her home, and she and Russell had come to a reluctant understanding. His family ran her ranch for a healthy cut of the profits, and she got to live in her house and tend her garden, which she had done with vigor and enthusiasm.

Now he thought maybe she'd known that she had heart problems, because before she passed on, she'd let the house and the barn get run-down and concentrated all her attention on her beloved garden. Only once, when they were sitting on the porch watching the sun set, had she talked about Pepper and how she hungered to see her again. She'd reminisced about what Pepper had done while she lived there, what she might be doing now. She had speculated concerning Pepper's early life and how it had contributed to her wildness. She hadn't said anything he didn't know, but he hated to hear the old lady talk with such fondness about a girl who had left.

Pepper should have come back. She had to have known Mrs. Dreiss wanted to see her.

Since early spring Dan had spent a lot of time scraping and painting, fixing fences, and pulling a few weeds in the flower beds. Sometimes, when he glanced at the garden, he thought he saw Mrs. Dreiss straightening up, her hand on her back, her big hat flopping in the breeze.

He'd seen a lot of death in the military. He'd come to accept it as part of life, but he still couldn't believe she was gone. After he came back, she was the only one who understood his need for solitude.

She didn't realize he had a raging thirst for revenge too.

When Mrs. Dreiss had died, Dan had invited Colonel Jaffe out to the ranch. Colonel Jaffe was short, plump, fair, a desk jockey with a genius for organization and an uncanny way of predicting the enemies' movements. He had been as out of place on the ranch as he would have been on a battlefield, but Dan had an objective in mind. He had shown him around the two ranches, impressed him with the isolation and difficult terrain, then that night, in Mrs. Dreiss's kitchen, Dan had mixed them both a scotch and water and proposed his scheme.

Dan handed Colonel Jaffe his drink. "Colonel, would you say I was one of the best terrorist fighters in the unit?"

Colonel Jaffe looked surprised, then cautious. "The

best. I'd see you were given the Purple Heart and Medal of Honor, but you know that's not possible."

"I don't care about that. The army taught me a lot. Taught me how to think on my feet. Taught me honor. Taught me what's worth fighting for. What's worth dying for." Leading the way into the living room, Dan said, "I've been thinking: I'm not so sure that I'm content being dead."

Colonel Jaffe followed on his heels. "Lieutenant, you don't have a choice. You killed Schuster's only son in hand-to-hand combat. We had to disseminate the information that you were dead and make it look convincing, or Schuster would never rest until he killed you."

Dan gestured Colonel Jaffe into the rocking chair. "I know. I know." Sinking onto the couch, he sipped his drink and waited.

Colonel Jaffe pulled an afghan over his chubby knees and fussed with it until it was just right, then looked Dan in the eye. "Are you saying you want Schuster to know you're alive?"

"He's evaded our forces for six years. He's masterminded more bombings than I can remember. There's only one thing that would bring him out of hiding. One thing that could lure him onto our ground . . ." Dan allowed his voice to trail off enticingly.

"You. And you owe him." Colonel Jaffe rubbed the rim of his glass, then as if recalled to his senses, he shook his head. "Too dangerous. We could set a trap with you as bait, but for it to work, you'd have to be here alone, or pretty damned close."

"I already live alone in the house," Dan pointed out.

"And since I've returned, I've kept to myself. Cowboys come by every once in a while, but I don't visit in town. I wouldn't have to change a thing about my habits or the way I live."

Dan could see Colonel Jaffe was tempted, but he was bound to make objections. "You said you didn't own this place. Won't the new owner come and make a claim soon?"

"No, I tried to inform her of her inheritance and can't find her." And Dan wanted to find her. He suffered intense curiosity about what had happened to Pepper Prescott. But she—and his curiosity—could wait. "I made the attempt. She can't sue me for that, and when we're done, I'll find her somehow and turn the place over to her."

"You mean what's left of it after Schuster gets done!" Colonel Jaffe struck the arm of his chair. "Dan, be reasonable, it won't work. It's too dangerous. You would really be killed."

Dan leaned forward. "There's a cabin up in the hills, built into the rock, the old homestead. We could put our equipment up there."

"That might work," Colonel Jaffe conceded, "but we're not going to do it."

"We're not any closer to finding Schuster, are we?" Dan heard the answer in Colonel Jaffe's silence. "How many more Americans does he have to kill before we're desperate enough to do anything to get him? How many more children have to be murdered? How much more fear and anguish does he have to cause?"

Colonel Jaffe took a drink of his scotch.

"What if he heard a rumor that I was alive, retired and

unprotected, living like a king in splendid isolation in the Idaho mountains . . ."

A slow smile spread across the colonel's lips. "He'd have to come in to take care of you."

"He'd have to come in personally." Tall, brown-haired, blue-eyed, with an open smile and a hearty manner, Annar Schuster was the one man in the world Dan longed to see. To capture. To kill.

For all the innocents he had destroyed.

For one dear little girl.

"Schuster can't afford to have it known that I bested his son—"

Colonel Jaffe snorted. "Killed his son."

"Exactly. And even if that information never leaked out, it would eat at his insides to know I was alive and that kid of his was dead."

"We could get him," Colonel Jaffe conceded. "I just don't know if we can save you at the same time."

"I know the odds." No better than fifty-fifty if everything went well. "Have some faith. I'm a damned fine soldier. I've survived more than one fight when I shouldn't have."

"You've got a reputation for luck, Graham, but luck runs out. It almost ran out for you last time."

Dan concealed his sense of triumph and talked logistics. "You'd have to get the information that I'm alive to him. Have one of his men steal it or something."

"I can do that."

Lifting his glass, Dan said, "I figured you could."

Colonel Jaffe stared at the blank television. In crisp syllables he said, "Schuster's terrorists know where we are, what we're going to do before we do it. They've been picking off my men one by one and in whole groups."

Dan hadn't known that, but he interpreted the information correctly. "They've tapped into a source in the military."

"Yes."

"You have to use me."

"Yes." Dan could see Colonel Jaffe doing calculations in his head. "In about a month. It'll take us that long to discreetly bring in the firepower and fix up a perimeter guard. You'll need backup in town and on the ranch."

"We get drifters through town occasionally. Artists and folks who like fresh mountain air. Send a couple of soldiers to live in the hotel."

Colonel Jaffe named a couple of men from Dan's old unit. "Wagner and Yarnell— and won't they be surprised to hear about your resurrection."

"As for the ranch, before he joined up, Sonny Midler was a cowhand down in Colorado. He's mouthy, but he's good with a gun and I'd rather have him guarding my back than anyone else. I'll hire him to work the cattle. He'll blend right in." Dan grinned. "Poor guy. He joined up to get the hell off the ranch."

Colonel Jaffe's tired brown eyes narrowed. "You've been thinking about this for a while."

"Since I got out of the hospital, recovery has been both boring and painful. I could have spent the time either feeling sorry for myself or making plans." Dan smiled unpleasantly and let the scotch burn its way down to his stomach. "I made plans."

Six

Dan strode up the path. The white clapboard house sat on a knoll with a view of the valley and the mountains. Tall blue spruce surrounded the lawn, providing a windbreak in the winter and shade in the summer.

Inside the house Pepper slept in the same bedroom she'd used before.

Frustration sizzled in his veins. Frustration, passion, and a clawing need to enforce his domination over her. It had been like this nine years ago. When he was a teenager, he'd been the biggest stud in three valleys, driving the hottest car, winning every rodeo prize, screwing the most popular girls. And he'd been good at everything, the driving, the riding, the screwing. Everyone had thought he was irresistible.

Then Pepper had come to town.

Dan paused on the porch. He hung up his hat on the hat rack. He peeled off his boots. Mrs. Dreiss forbade him to stomp mud on her clean kitchen floor. Now that he was the one doing the mopping, he had a grim appreciation for her sense. Standing barefooted in the kitchen, he listened to the silence. Had Pepper slipped out while he wasn't looking?

No. That was impossible. Even if she hadn't come to kill him, she had an inheritance. No matter how successful she'd been or not been with her landscaping, she would be a fool to walk away from a ranch if she had an anxious buyer—and she did.

Going into the bathroom, he washed his hands and face, then lifted his head, expecting to turn and see her standing in the doorway. Instead the silence was deafening.

Placing his palm flat against the wall between the bathroom and Pepper's room, he could almost feel her. She was in there, and her presence made everything about the day distinctive. Pepper was back, and he wanted revenge, satisfaction, justification, closure. . . . Hell, he didn't know what he wanted, but he knew Pepper would provide it. She owed him. She owed him big-time.

He strolled into her bedroom and stood looking down at her in her pristine single bed.

She was still asleep, deeply asleep, on her back with one open hand flung against the wall, the other tucked under her cheek. She wore a long-sleeved white nightgown left behind on her previous stopover, and she'd pushed the covers down to her waist. Her lips were plump and open, and she breathed deeply. Her faint snore disarmed him, and his hand hovered over her ear.

She looked better today. She had color in her face, as well as a few creases caused by the pillow. Her black hair stood up in peaks and down in valleys. She looked charming. Disarming.

Innocent.

Pepper came out of the first sound sleep she'd had in five days to find a tall man hovering over her. She didn't know where she was. She didn't recognize him. She remembered only that someone wanted to kill her.

Instinctively she reacted by defending herself. She punched at his groin.

He moved in time. Barely in time. As her fist hit his thigh, the man swore soundly. Now she knew who it was.

It was Dan. This was Mrs. Dreiss's house.

She was safe.

She looked up at Dan. He looked like a warrior. A savage.

At least she hoped she was safe. From him, and from herself.

Her heartbeat, which had accelerated to Mach speed, throttled back a notch.

"What the hell do you think you're doing?" He spoke in a low, vibrant tone, almost in a whisper, but she didn't make the mistake of thinking he was indifferent. "You could have destroyed the future generations of Grahams."

Hackles rising, she came up on one elbow. "What the hell do *you* think *you're* doing, coming into my room while I'm sleeping?"

"Honey, the alternative is to come into your room when you're awake, and that'll lead to a whole different set of results." He wore a blue denim shirt and a faded camouflage green vest. A pair of work jeans hugged his narrow hips. He looked even better than he had last night, and that was saying a lot.

Last night, he had been almost kind. Today, he was a jerk. A tall, broad, handsome jerk.

With a snap, she said, "Believe me, it won't." No matter what he said, no matter that his kiss had been as welcome and sweet-tasting as hot chocolate on a cold day, no matter that her belly clutched at the sight of him . . . He wasn't getting into her bed. She'd screwed him once. She couldn't stand to suffer the consequences again. "You scared me to death." To cover the admission she asked, "What are you doing in here?" *Here* being her bedroom bright with sunshine and decorated with posters of movies made ten years ago.

He surveyed her in her old flannel nightgown, designed to be worn in a country where winter was a horrible trial, in a house where central heat had never been installed. And although nothing changed in his still face, she thought he was amused.

Fine. He could be as amused as he liked. Up here on the ranch, as soon as the last snow around the house had melted, she used to sleep with the window open, celebrating her freedom from the fear that was rife in the cities. She wasn't changing her ways now just because he had seen her in her nightie.

The hint of humor in his expression faltered. "I thought maybe you had slipped away."

"How could I?" She bit her lip. She hadn't meant to remind him she had walked here.

"That's right, you don't have a car," he said mildly. "We'd better tow it back today."

She had removed every bit of identification from the cheap wreck she'd bought in Colorado. She'd pulled her backpack out of the back seat and slung it over her shoulder. She had pushed the car off the highest mountain on the most remote road she could find. She definitely didn't want to go after it. "We can't. It went off a cliff."

He went still. "You said you drove off a road."

"I did. It was a really high road."

"A cliff. How the hell did you get out?"

If he only knew . . . "I jumped."

Obviously, trying to hold on to his patience, he asked, "How did you drive off the road? Did you go to sleep?"

She had to tell him something. "I must have."

"Why didn't you stop and rest? You know how dangerous mountain roads can be." His eyes were so dark a brown as to be black, and he scolded her as if he were concerned.

She wished he were indifferent. "I was in a hurry to get here. I got confused."

"Which road did you say you were on?"

"I didn't. I don't know which one it was." She gestured vaguely. "It was gravel. It was windy."

"But you managed to find your way here with no problem." He leaned toward her menacingly and grilled her as if he had experience in interrogation. "You must have had some idea where you were."

She wished he would shut up. "I started walking downhill and this is where I eneded up."

It took him a long time to reply. "Fortunate."

"Very." She bit her lip and did her best impression of a poor, feebleminded female. "It was all so horrible, it's a blur."

Leaning down, he planted his fists on the mattress beside her, looked her in the eye. He appeared sternly unimpressed. "Why do I think you're lying to me?"

Because she was. What kind of man saw through the helpless woman act and responded sensibly?

Only Dan, who knew her so well.

She thrust her face close to his, ignoring the warmth he exuded, ignoring the familiar scent of him, pretending to be unaffected by his nearness. "Do you have to be here?"

He straightened up easily enough and walked over to the dresser. "Here? Like in your bedroom? Or here? Like on the ranch?"

"You know what I mean. On the ranch." He irritated her like a burr in her sock. "You said Mrs. Dreiss left me this place."

"You said you came here to claim it."

She was still dull with sleep, but she realized that, last night, he'd told her of Mrs. Dreiss's death. He realized she hadn't known about the inheritance when she arrived. She had told a stupid lie brought on by exhaustion and defiance, and she had to sweep away the falsehood and start anew now. "I didn't really know about the inheritance before I got here. I said that because—"

"Because you always strike out when you're being attacked. You always challenge people to believe the worst of you."

She straightened her shoulders and tried to tell him he was no longer dealing with the defiant, angry girl he'd known before. "No! Not anymore."

"You did last night."

"Last night was . . . last night I was off balance. When you told me she was gone . . . my God, I still can't believe she's gone." That much was true, anyway, and the tears that had eluded her suddenly arrived, closing her throat, trickling down her cheeks.

As calmly as a man who faced a crying woman every day, he handed her a tissue off the dresser.

She cried for more minutes than she cared to realize, bound by her sorrow and regret. Yet she struggled against the sentiment: Why did grief overwhelm her now, in front of Dan? She needed to be the woman she had created out of the fragments of her former life—ambitious, cold, and logical. When she could get hold of herself, she blotted her cheeks and blew her nose. "Sorry. I didn't mean to change the subject." She tried to look him in the eye, but she couldn't get any higher than his chin. "I don't encourage people to believe the worst of me anymore. I've changed."

"People don't change."

His cool comment banished her diffidence and brought her gaze to his.

He'd been in the army, he said. He'd been a soldier. Where? Who was his commander?

Did he know General Jennifer Napier?

Pepper felt ill.

Had Dan worked under General Napier's command? Did he mindlessly admire her as Pepper had? How would he look at Pepper if she was accused of murder? Would he hand her over to the law on General Napier's order?

Those were the questions Pepper didn't dare to ask. She didn't want to be involved in Dan's life. More important, she didn't want Dan involved in hers.

The general's favorite axiom came to her. *Don't defend. Attack!* Good advice. "*You've* changed."

He inclined his head. "So they tell me."

He *had* changed. Before he had been an insolent boy, walking in a sensual saunter that had caught every female eye in all of Adams County. He had moved as if he commanded the sun and the moon and the north wind, and old and young, all the women had noticed Dan Graham.

Now he moved differently. Now each movement was catlike, alert, as if any moment he expected a blow from behind. He walked like a man who could defend himself. Who *had* defended himself. And behind that face with its bronze skin and its still expression, she sensed a darkness, a vortex so deep and black it sucked all the light from his soul.

He displayed a deep, masculine awareness of everything around him, even her. Especially her. He seemed satisfied to have her close to him, and that made her wonder . . ." After Mrs. Dreiss's death, how hard did you try and find me?"

"We wrote to your last known address."

"I moved."

"Quite a lot."

Pepper's actions in Georgetown had haunted her every step of her way to the ranch. The night of the autographing she had told General Napier everything about herself. That she was from Texas. That she was an orphan. That her parents had committed a crime. With that information and Pepper's alias—Jackie Porter— written in the autographed books she'd dropped, the general would eventually be able to trace the footsteps of Pepper's life.

What was the general's axiom? *Be thorough in every endeavor.*

Sooner or later the trail would lead her here. To Diamond. To the ranch.

And it would be sooner, if Dan stirred up the sediment with which Pepper had covered her tracks. "Did you write everywhere I'd lived? Did you talk to the police? Did you search the Internet?"

"I couldn't find a trace of you, not even on the Internet, and the police were profoundly uninterested. They don't care about locating a missing person who doesn't wish to be found."

"When did you last look?"

"It's been a few months."

She relaxed a little. In the past, she'd assumed more than one name. If Dan couldn't trace her from Diamond to Washington, it would take time for General Napier to trace her from Washington to Diamond. Pepper needed to watch the news and see if there were any reports about that bitch. That traitor to her country. Traitor to every person who stood in that line in that bookstore and admired her as fervently as Jackie Porter had.

Pepper needed to look around the countryside, see where she could go to hide, see what she could do to defend herself if that e-mail she'd sent from the cyber-café in Denver didn't reach the proper authorities in time.

She swallowed. She didn't know if she'd sent that e-mail to the right person, or if Senator Vargas would recognize her name. Pepper had landscaped his townhouse over a year ago, and he'd been pleasant and sincerely enthusiastic about her work, but senators met a lot of people in the course of twelve months.

And if the senator did see the e-mail, would he believe her? She'd pointed out to him that she was not only concerned about her own safety but about the safety of the country: There had been a high-level breach of national security. Was he the right person to inform? She didn't know how these things worked; she was a landscaper who had spent most of her life avoiding anything to do with the government, its agencies, and the law.

Until the general was caught, Pepper could never rest easy—and every time there was a bombing anywhere in the world, Pepper would wonder if General Jennifer Napier was involved.

She needed Dan off this property. She might not like him anymore, but she didn't want his death on her conscience.

She adjusted her nightgown until she knew it decently covered her rear and climbed out of the bed.

Her bones creaked as she moved. She'd walked for six hours last night, through freezing cold and down gravel roads, carrying the heavy backpack she had then stashed in the old trunk on the porch, and she ached from the exertion. She felt as if she could have slept another twelve hours. But she had to get going. She had to make plans to protect herself and the ranch—and Dan.

Dan observed her clinically, as if he were a doctor, but he made no comment on her stiffness. "My dad said you were dead."

"I'll bet." Mr. Graham hadn't liked her dating his son, and he had let her know it in no uncertain terms. Opening the closet, she looked at the clothes hanging there. The clothes she had abandoned nine years ago. Clothes to work in: flannel shirts and heavy jeans. Clothes to wear to school: sequined tops and tight jeans. And clothes guaranteed to tease Dan: tight T-shirts, low-cut jeans, and a sexy light-blue camisole.

"I knew you had gone underground. I was waiting until you popped your head up again," he said.

She turned and glared at him. "I'm not the groundhog predicting the spring."

He looked her up and down. He didn't leer.

Yet she found herself shifting one foot atop of the other. Her nightgown was *not* see-through, the flannel was too thick for that, but she wore nothing underneath.

He behaved as if he knew it too, as if it didn't matter whether she wore clothes or not, whether she hid beneath the covers or stood on her own two feet. He appreciated the way she looked. He had always liked the way she looked, and he had a way of gazing at her that made her feel he could protect her from any threat, from any challenge. For a woman who stood teetering on the brink of disaster, that illusion was almost irresistible.

"No," he said. "No, I've never compared you to a groundhog."

She needed to do something about this man before she forgot all the lessons she'd learned in all the years since the day her family had left her.

No one felt loyalty to her. No one would protect her. No one could be trusted.

Those weren't General Napier's axioms, but her own. She'd forgotten them for a little while, and look at the jam she'd landed in.

Yet even though General Napier was a traitor, her advice was still good. *Be decisive,* she had said. So Pepper turned on Dan and gestured toward the door. "Leave! You don't need to stay here. Why don't you just leave?"

"I cared for the place while Mrs. Dreiss was alive," he said, "and I've cared for it ever since her death. I've got a responsibility to make sure nothing happens to the ranch before it passes into your hands."

Impatience and desperation drove Pepper. She wanted him *out.* If he left, she could make plans to defend this place and herself. "I can handle everything. I lived here before."

An expression of innocence and surprise crossed his face. "Really? I would have said no one person could ever handle everything on a ranch."

She didn't trust him. It seemed as if he were donning masks, one after another, and none of them represented his true feelings.

"What with the cattle and the chickens and the gardening," he continued, "*I've* barely managed to keep up, and the cowboys help with the heavy work."

Oh, yes. She'd forgotten how much outright back-breaking labor ranching involved. Dawn to dusk, all summer long, mending fences, chasing cattle, trying to snatch a moment for the garden. She pulled a pair of jeans from the closet. "You can live at your dad's house and drive over."

"On gravel roads?" Folding his arms across his chest, he looked as stern and immovable as a stone face on Mt. Rushmore. "It takes an hour. I don't have two hours a day to waste."

The year that she'd spent living with Mrs. Dreiss had been full of work for her, for Mrs. Dreiss, for everyone. In the distance she could always see the cowboys working the cattle. And Dan had been there a lot, working usually. Trying to get in her pants the rest of the time.

She shifted uncomfortably. She stared at the dark blue jeans in her hands, then put them behind her back as if he could read her mind.

"But if you want to go into town," he said, "see the lawyer and sign the papers, I'll be out of here."

He had unerringly ferreted out her weakness. "God, no."

He raised an eyebrow. "No?"

No. She didn't want anyone in town to know she had arrived. She certainly didn't want to sign papers, not with her real name, not with her pseudonym. She had been lucky so far. She had watched CNN in the airports, and while there had been a brief mention of Otto Bjerke's death, the reporter had said no one knew the identity of the murderer. She had thought very hard about what that meant, and she had decided that the general didn't want Pepper brought in by the police. No doubt General Napier feared Pepper's testimony. So the general must be hunting Pepper by herself, or perhaps with some of her terrorist cronies. That meant more danger. Dan had no idea of how much trouble was stalking her.

With bleak despair Pepper wondered if she would be in hiding for the rest of her life—her short, easily terminated life. To Dan she said, "I don't know how long it will take me to settle in and figure out what I want to do with the place. I can wait a while to lay claim to the ranch, can't I?"

"I don't see why not."

"If you . . . if you want to stay, that's okay."

His other eyebrow came up. Obviously, such a shabby appeal wouldn't satisfy him.

The words almost choked her. "I would appreciate it if you would stay until I get on my feet."

"Until we get the cattle moved up to the high country," he conceded. "That'll be two weeks."

Two weeks. As long as General Napier and her soldiers and her bounty hunters stayed away for two weeks, he would be safe. "That'll work." It had to.

He rubbed his jaw with his fingers and considered her thoughtfully. "Pepper, is there anything you want to tell me?"

She stared at him. At the long, tall temptation he represented.

If she turned the matter over to him, he would somehow make it right . . . wouldn't he? He would trust she was telling the truth. Surely he would. He wouldn't recall her wild youth and the time they'd shoplifted beers out of a convenience store in McCall. He wouldn't wonder why she'd moved so often after she left Diamond or suspect her of perpetrating more crimes, and even a murder . . .

She thought of poor Otto Bjerke, the general's aide. He had been an honorable man, and he was dead because of his principles. Killed by a woman so ruthless she didn't hesitate to murder the man who had served her for years.

Now General Napier pursued Pepper. Pepper looked at Dan. If General Napier found her, Dan stood a chance of being murdered for being in the wrong place at the wrong time. What had she been thinking? She couldn't let him stay here.

"Pepper, what's going on?" Dan asked, watching her intently.

A soft chime sounded from the dining room. She jumped. "What's that?"

Dan looked down at the beeper hooked to his belt, read the message there, and as if the beeper could hear him, said, "Took you long enough."

She started to ask what he meant. Then a sound on the drive brought her head around. A vehicle, bumping over the gravel washboard. In her mind she envisioned a car. A long, black, government-issue car.

Tense and on alert, she demanded more forcefully, "Who's that?"

"Why? Are you expecting someone?"

"No!"

"You look"—his gaze lingered on her face—"uneasy."

"I'm not. But who *is* it?"

With uncanny certainty, he said, "It's only my father."

Outside, the car's wheels spat gravel as it stopped. A door slammed, and a man's voice bellowed, "Danny! Where are you?"

Dan uncoiled his length from the edge of the dresser. "No doubt about it, that's my dad."

"What is *he* doing here?"

"I told him you'd arrived." Dan headed for the door. "He's always had rotten timing."

How did things go wrong so fast? Pepper asked herself. Dan suspected she had a secret and Mr. Graham knew she had arrived. She might as well take out a billboard to advertise her presence. "I wish you wouldn't spread the word yet."

Dan turned to look back at her. "It's just my dad," he said gently.

The screen door slammed in the kitchen. Mr. Graham shouted, "Dan? Are you in here?"

Hustling over, she caught Dan's arm. "Has he told anybody?"

Taking her hand, Dan held it in his own. "We can tell him you want privacy."

For a moment, she let the warmth of him soothe her. Yet no safety could be found there. "That would be good." She jerked her hand away.

"But he's fretting about you and me getting back together. No use giving him more to worry about. As appealing as you are in your nightgown, why don't you get dressed and save me a lot of trouble?"

"No man alive can accuse me of wearing a long flannel nightgown to be appealing."

"It just happens that way." With one more long, hot, all-encompassing look, Dan went out to meet his father, shutting the door behind him.

Seven

As she dug through a drawer of her old clothes, she could hear Mr. Graham's voice boom through the door. "What were you doing in her bedroom?"

"Waking her up," she heard Dan say laconically.

She pulled out underwear, a bra, and an Idaho T-shirt that proclaimed "Darth Tater" and showed a potato clad in black armor.

"How?" The panicky edge to Mr. Graham's tone was hardly flattering.

"With my lips."

Glaring at the door, she whipped off her nightgown. Dan knew she could hear them.

"You're kissing on her already?" Mr. Graham sounded aghast.

The bra and panties were a little too big around and the elastic was feeble, but Pepper got them on in record time.

"Dad, I *told* her to get up," Dan said.

She paused with her T-shirt half over her head and waited to hear him add that he had kissed her the night before.

He didn't.

Good thing.

She ran a comb through her shorn hair—that didn't take long—and zipped the jeans. She put Band-Aids on her blistered heels and donned socks and shoes.

"She was still asleep?" Mr. Graham had a lifelong rancher's disbelief that anyone could sleep past sunrise. "It's after noon!"

She burst through the door and into the kitchen, talking as she went. "I didn't get here until after midnight. Tomorrow I'll be up with the birds."

The two faces that turned toward her were as different as father and son could be. They were the same height, but where Dan was big-boned and raw, Mr. Graham was muscled and sinewy, with no butt except for a wallet and a folded handkerchief. His thinning hair was a reddish blond, his skin was fair and freckled, and his blue eyes displayed every emotion. Right now they surveyed her with a snap and derision that made her want to snap right back.

But she got herself in hand. No longer was she little Pepper Prescott, the rebellious orphan who had lured Russell Graham's son down the path to perdition. She had transformed herself into a successful, responsible landscaper with a nose for business, and because of a recent inheritance, she had become Mr. Graham's neighbor. Plus, she had to depend on his goodwill to keep this ranch going until she could decide what to do with it—or until General Napier had killed them all.

Then Mr. Graham's gaze landed on her hair. He chortled. "What did you do? Back into a lawn mower?"

She answered before she could think better of it. "I find that's easier than tweezing it off like you do."

Mr. Graham ran his hand over his overly high forehead to the receding edge of his hair. "It's not nice to make fun of your elders."

Old instincts kicked in, and she stepped up to Mr. Graham and stood toe-to-toe with him. "It's not nice to make fun of a bad haircut either."

"That's one of the reasons Mom divorced you," Dan said. "You never could keep your mouth shut about her hair. Isn't that right, Dad?"

Mr. Graham glared at his son. In a lofty tone, he said, "There's more to marriage than a haircut. Your mother had so many reasons for dumping me, I can't remember them all."

Pepper found her lips twitching with amusement. According to local legend, before their separation when Dan was six, the Grahams had been famous throughout the county for their shouting matches. Now they lived amicably apart, she running a bed-and-breakfast in McCall, he on the family ranch. If Dan had suffered any trauma from the divorce, he was long over it, given a sense of security by two parents who loved him deeply.

Pepper's expression soured. It must be nice to be so certain of affection. She wished she didn't envy Dan, but she did. She wasn't proud of her resentment, but it remained, solid and immovable.

Mr. Graham looked at his son. "Speaking of haircuts, when are you going to get one, Danny?"

Pepper grinned again, not a bit surprised that Mr. Graham nagged his son about the length of his hair. He'd been doing it for as long as she'd known him. "I know a barber," she offered. Then her gaze collided with Dan's, and her breath stopped.

He stood by the sink, watching her like a predatory shark, as if her smile fed some starved part of his soul. Without a word or a move he told her he wanted her, and her body responded. Unwillingly, resentfully, but it responded, remembering, softening, and reaching for him.

His voice was still and deep. "If it's the same barber who cut your hair, I'll have to decline."

Mr. Graham looked at her, then looked at Dan, then looked back at her, and his gaze cooled perceptibly. "Pepper, how long are you going to stay?"

Widening her eyes, she said, "As long as it takes." Let him make of that what he would! Then Dan cleared his throat, and she remembered she had to appease his father. "Sir, I'd appreciate it if you didn't tell anyone I've moved back."

"No one in town's interested in you," Mr. Graham said.

Pepper snorted. Over the foothills and about thirty hard miles down the road sat the town of Diamond. It had a population of eight hundred and thirty-five, one main street, a single stoplight, and a school where all the farm kids from the surrounding ranches got their education. Everyone did their grocery shopping at Diamond's one store and divided their drinking time between the two bars. There was a Congregational church, an LDS church, and a traveling Catholic priest who came once a month to hear confessions and give communion in Mrs. Buckley's front room.

Occasionally someone new moved in. Free spirits usually, people from the cities who imagined a bucolic existence in the country and moved up to get in touch with nature. Once nature touched them in the way of freezing temperatures and howling blizzards, most of the free spirits were pretty much finished with roughing it. They couldn't wait to sell and move back to civilization, so for the most part the same families always lived in the vicinity of Diamond.

The Graham family had lived here since the nineteenth century. They had ranched and they had logged. They knew everyone and everyone liked them. They married into other ranch families, and no one as wild as Pepper had ever threatened the decency of the Graham family.

Now she'd inherited the Dreiss ranch.

No one in town was interested in her? *Everyone* in town was interested in her.

Even Dan hooted. "Dad, what a lie! I haven't been into Diamond for more than an hour a month since I arrived home. Everyone knows everyone else's business, and I don't like them prying into mine."

"Wouldn't hurt you to go in a little more often, Danny," Mr. Graham grumbled. "Everyone asks about you every time I go in, and that nice Johnson girl would love to keep company with you."

"Rita?" Pepper asked incredulously. "Oh, please. When we were in high school, Dan scared her, and he's a lot more—" Pepper stopped. She had been going to say *dangerous now,* but she didn't want him to know that she'd noticed. "Besides, isn't she married yet?"

"Once." Dan pulled a ham out of the refrigerator and started slicing it. "It didn't work out."

"Poor Rita! She said she would never divorce." Pepper stared at that ham, all pink and sweet-smelling, and her stomach growled.

"Life has a way of changing your mind. You going to call her?" Dan asked.

No. "After I settle in," she said aloud.

"She'd love to hear from you." In a reminiscent tone, Dan asked, "Remember Mark Jeffers?"

"The kid with the open-door ears? Sure." She was more than hungry. She was starving.

"He's an artist. A pretty good one. He lives in a cabin up in the hills on his family ranch and sends his stuff to New York for showings."

"Wow." Opening the loaf of bread, she put pieces on three plates. "I'll bet Mrs. James is pleased."

"She always said he had the makings of a great artist, although how she knew, I've never understood." He handed her the mustard, got out the tomatoes, washed them, and sliced them.

As they chatted and worked together, Mr. Graham watched with sour displeasure. They were excluding him. He knew it, and he didn't like it. "So, Pepper, why don't you want anyone to know you're here?"

"I don't want to deal with any gossip or any welcome receptions or"—she tried a self-deprecating smile—"more likely, any condemnation. Not yet. Not until I get settled in. Please."

Mr. Graham got that grin on his face, the one that meant trouble. "If you two are going to live here together, who's going to cook dinner?"

Pepper wanted to protest that she hadn't said they would live together. Not in the way Mr. Graham meant.

But Dan gave a response guaranteed to drive both her and Mr. Graham berserk. "I'll be busy with the cattle and the farming all day, so I figured Pepper would."

Pepper opened her mouth to furiously object.

Dan put the sliced tomatoes on the plates. "At least for the summer. Then this winter I'll do it."

After one glance at Mr. Graham's appalled expression, Pepper subsided.

"Dan, you're not going to stay here that long!" Mr. Graham rounded on Pepper. "You're not planning on staying, for sure. You're going to sell this place!"

"I hadn't thought about it." That was the truth. She'd arrived only last night. She hadn't had time to think about what she would do. "Mrs. Dreiss left it to me. To sell it seems cold."

"I'm not going to maintain it for you, I can tell you that!" Mr. Graham said.

Dan moved behind his father. He pulled a long, disbelieving face.

Dan was, she realized, coaching her. She managed not to laugh. "I suppose if I got a good-enough offer, I might sell."

"Don't expect to get more than two hundred thousand for this place." Mr. Graham tucked his thumbs into his belt and rocked back and forth on his heels. "It's rundown. There's no federal land grants connected to it. It's not really worth that much, but some poor sucker will probably give you two hundred."

Dan held up five fingers, pointed to his father, and gave her the thumbs-up.

Her eyes widened. *Really? Five hundred thousand?*

Mr. Graham continued, "I imagine two hundred grand is a lot of money to a girl like you."

Dan covered his eyes with his hand.

An upswell of rage caught her. Through hard work, scrimping, and saving, she had fifty thousand dollars in a bank in Georgetown, and she not only couldn't get to it, she was standing here being patronized by an Idaho rancher who needed to have his butt kicked. Smiling with saccharine sweetness, she said, "But thinking it over, I really couldn't let the ranch go for less than a million. Sentimental value and all that."

"A million dollars?" Mr. Graham roared. "That's a helluva lot of sentiment!"

"I've got a helluva lot of sentiment!" And she found herself blinking back an unexpected rush of embarrassing tears.

Mr. Graham looked as horrified as any man would who spent most of his time with cowboys and cattle. "Now see here, missy! None of that. We all miss Mrs. Dreiss, but you don't see Danny and me breaking down and sobbing like girls."

"Dad, she *is* a girl." Dan pressed her into a chair. "Pepper, when was the last time you ate?"

She remembered far too well, but those cookies had hardly been a meal. "Yesterday at lunch." She had to stop this! All this unbridled emotion. It wasn't like her. But oh

God, she was so scared. She missed Mrs. Dreiss. She wanted . . . she looked at Dan. She didn't know what she wanted, she only knew she couldn't have it.

She didn't know which of the Graham men put the sandwich in front of her, but as she sank her teeth into the nutty brown bread, she clearly heard Mr. Graham say, "Damn, son, haven't I taught you that a hungry woman is a dangerous woman?"

She didn't stop eating

Dan didn't answer.

Mr. Graham seemed to read that as a reproach, for he said, "You can stop glaring at me. I haven't said anything to her she hasn't heard before. I'll never forget how she looked the first time I saw her."

With an odd, pained tone in his voice, Dan said, "I remember the first time she walked into school too."

Eight

She was tattooed, she was pierced, she wore makeup like a weapon, and Pepper Prescott walked in the door of the auditorium on the first day of school like she owned the place. The entire high school, all one hundred and fifty-three of them, stopped talking and stared. Her hair was bleached blond with highlights of red—and not a red God had created. Red like a pie cherry or the side of a barn. She had a series of rings stuck through both ears. Her shirt was tied up under her lavish boobs, displaying her pierced belly button and a narrow waist. She wore a scornful smile and jeans that cupped her tight ass. No one moved while she posed in the doorway, well aware of her impact on the conservative country school.

The expressions on the girls' faces were priceless as they realized how boring they were compared to Pepper. The guys' expressions as they soaked in her wild sexuality were equally hilarious.

Dan, sitting slouched in his seat, knew he wore the same

expression. It went with his hard-on; the same reaction had every straight guy in the school squirming, trying to get comfortable. But Dan knew he had the advantage in pursuing Pepper; he was a Graham, he was a senior, he could fight, and no one else drove a vintage '66 El Camino. He was the most dangerous guy in school.

Then Pepper's gaze slid over him without an ounce of interest, and he found himself straightening up in indignation. She didn't realize how important the Grahams were. She didn't notice him at all.

Mrs. Sweet, the principal, had obviously anticipated Pepper's arrival, for she gestured and said, "Sit down, Miss Prescott. We're about to have our opening assembly. After we're done, you can come to my office and we'll discuss the appropriate dress code."

Everyone waited, tense and excited, to hear the new girl smart off to Mrs. Sweet.

Instead Pepper nodded her head and subsided into a seat beside the head cheerleader, Rita Johnson, a girl so clean and conventional she got embarrassed gazing at the cover of Cosmopolitan. Now Rita looked as if she were about to faint in horror, and she actually turned and sniffed at Pepper as if trying to catch the scent of illicit drugs or, worse, body odor.

Pepper grinned at her. For the first time he saw that sudden sweet burst of high spirits, and he smiled too, as if her merriment were contagious. More important, after a startled moment, Rita smiled back at the wild, pierced, exotic student. Before long they were whispering, and halfway through Mrs. Sweet's welcoming speech, the principal had to stop and chide them. It was the first time Rita had ever gotten in trouble in her life, and to Dan's surprise, she didn't burst into tears. She looked rather defiantly pleased, as if she'd achieved a goal she'd set for herself but didn't know how to accomplish.

Of course, when Mrs. Sweet finished with Pepper, she had her shirt tucked into her jeans and one ring per ear, and she carried an outraged note to Mrs. Dreiss on the unsuitability of sending children to school dressed in a way that was sure to be a bad influence on the other students.

Mrs. Sweet was right. Because from that day on, Pepper wore T-shirts and jeans, but the damage had been done. Everyone in high school scrambled to be terminally cool too—even Rita Johnson. Especially Rita Johnson, who sewed her own clothes and managed to do a pretty credible job of changing her wardrobe from modest to eye-popping in less than a week.

The funny thing was, Pepper didn't sneer at Rita's efforts or anyone else's, for that matter. She didn't talk about the other places she'd lived. She didn't compare Diamond to the big city, or tell them that such a tiny burg was tedious beyond belief. She didn't talk about herself at all. And everyone, even the cheerleaders, even Mrs. Sweet, liked her. No matter what Pepper did, no matter how much she goofed off, no matter how often she skipped school, everyone liked her.

He liked her.

He liked the way she talked, slow and thoughtfully, as if she weighed every word. It was almost southern in its cadence, but she didn't have that twang, and when someone asked her if she were from Texas, she shrugged and said, "I'm not from anywhere."

The drama of her statement impressed him.

He liked the way she stopped every afternoon as soon as she stepped foot off the school grounds and replaced every single earring while in sight of Mrs. Sweet's office. He liked the way she walked, with a languid roll of her hips that bewitched every guy in Diamond High School. He really, really liked when that idiot Peck Maltkin, whose family thought they were better than the Grahams, tried to grab her tit in front of the girl's bathroom. She seized his wrist and twisted, bringing him to his knees and holding him there until he begged forgiveness for everything, including being born.

Yes, Dan liked her, but the trouble was, she didn't like him. No matter what he did, no matter how much he showed off in front of her, she paid him no heed. He didn't understand it. Every girl in town wanted to be with him.

What was wrong with her?

For the first time in his life, he had to chase a girl. Carefully, he planned his assault. He started by visiting Mrs. Dreiss. She'd been their neighbor ever since he could remember, and she made the best cookies in town, so it was no nuisance to wander over, sit in the kitchen, and watch Pepper learn how to bake.

Only Mrs. Dreiss didn't put up with slackers, so Dan found himself wrapped in an apron, squashing rounds of peanut butter cookie dough with a fork and sliding them into the oven.

Still Pepper didn't say much to him, except for "Pass the baking powder" and "Will you stop hogging the beaters?"

Mrs. Dreiss watched them with a sage expression and pretended she had no idea why he was there.

He went to school the day after his first kitchen experience, expecting that Pepper would have told the whole town that Big Dan Graham had been baking cookies. He would have never lived it down.

Instead, she didn't tell anyone in school what he'd been doing, almost as if she were embarrassed to have spent time with him.

What was wrong with him?

So he instructed Karen D'Amato, his first girlfriend and the one who taught him how to steam up the windows of a car, to give Pepper the full rundown on his sexual prowess.

That backfired. Pepper ignored him even more faithfully, dedicating her time to helping Rita pierce the cartilage in her ear and Meghan Dawson learn how to give henna tattoos. He would have guessed Pepper wasn't interested in guys, except for the way she looked at him when she thought he wasn't looking—warily and with an irrepressible curiosity.

So as winter deepened, he dated a few of the other girls—hey, he couldn't help it if they all wanted him—but he kept dropping by Mrs. Dreiss's. He helped with the daily chores and learned way more about plants than he ever wanted to know, because Mrs. Dreiss loved them and Pepper loved them more. They kept a greenhouse under the window of the back bedroom, where it could catch the most sunlight, and they experimented with growing perennials that would survive the stunning cold of the mountains and vegetables that would ripen in half the time and thus double the crop yield. He asked Pepper about her background, but all he got for his pains was Pepper's treating him like a brother who wasn't quite right in the head.

Finally, after she'd been there for six months and Christmas had come and gone, the day arrived when the high school braved the cold for the annual "These Kids Are Driving Us Crazy" field trip to Warm Springs Pool to swim. The air temperature hovered at twenty degrees, ice formed on the sides of the pool, and the chaperones sat above the kids in an enclosed, heated booth and only came out for necessary admonitions. But the pool itself stayed a toasty eighty-five degrees. The only thing that was as good as climbing up on the diving board, posturing, then diving into the warm water was watching the girls do it. While they stood up there in their one-piece bathing suits (Mrs. Sweet didn't allow bikinis), they laughed and shivered and showed off, and every guy took notice. Like Dave Geary said as he stared up at Laura Berners, "Her nipples are so hard they could cut glass."

When Pepper climbed up on the diving board, she confirmed what every guy in the high school already knew. She had a figure that would stop traffic. If anything, her bathing suit was more conservative than the others, but it didn't hide those long legs. Her hips were slender and her waist tiny, but her bosom swelled over the top of her suit in lush abundance, and he wanted to drown the other guys for slobbering in the pool. She dove in, executing a perfect jackknife, and swam as if she were born to the water. Her swimming ability created another mystery about Pepper, a mystery that made him all the more determined to make her like him.

He didn't realize that his luck was about to turn, and he was about to spend all spring dating the wildest girl around.

Mrs. Sweet and Mrs. Dreiss came down to yell at the guys for throwing each other across the pool, and they stayed for a while to talk to the kids. Everyone liked them: Mrs. Sweet was stern but fair; Mrs. Dreiss was stern but fun.

Right before they went back up to sit with the other chaperones, Mrs. Sweet said to Mrs. Dreiss, "Pepper Prescott is settling in well. It would be good for everyone if she remains in Diamond. She'll forget all this wildness and be a good, steady member of society. I predict she'll find herself a husband before long—one of the Yeagers perhaps, or maybe the Michaels boy."

Mrs. Dreiss answered sharply, "She's too good for them, and she's fine on her own."

But the damage had been done.

He heard Mrs. Sweet. So did half a dozen other kids. All of them went right to Pepper and told her, word for word, what had been said.

Pepper looked stunned. Then she looked sick. The Yeagers were poor and stupider than a bottle of Jack Daniels on Tuesday night. The Michaelses' son was a mama's boy, cautious, tight-lipped, and judgmental. Mrs. Sweet liked Pepper, yes, but she couldn't have been more plain: She thought Pepper should settle for what she could get, and be grateful.

Pepper was not grateful.

She swam over to Dan, whispered, "Meet me in the girl's locker room," and lifted herself out of the pool.

The way she walked was completely different from the way he'd ever seen her walk before. Her strides were long and slow. Her hips swung back and forth hypnotically. She was looking for trouble.

He would help her find it. He waited a few moments, long enough that no one connected the two of them. Then he followed her.

She met him at the door, covered with goose bumps. She flung herself into his arms and kissed him.

He could still remember the way she tasted that day. Like chlorine, chewing gum, and defiance. Their two bodies clung together, heating quickly under the pressure of his hormones and her rebelliousness. When at last he let her go long enough to breathe, she said against his mouth, "Let's get dressed. Let's go."

"Sure. Where?"

"Anywhere you want, baby." She touched his lips with her fingers. "Anywhere you want."

Nine

"So, Pepper, where have you been? What have you been doing?" Mr. Graham asked, returning to the attack.

Now that she'd finished eating her sandwich, she felt refreshed enough to spar with him and take him down. "I'm a landscaper. I decorate rich people's yards."

Dan listened, his gaze shifting from his father to Pepper as he absorbed every bit of information.

"Did you go to college?" Mr. Graham asked.

"No. No college. I didn't need it." She would have enjoyed the classes, the learning, the chance to earn a degree and be a respected professional, but that wasn't in the cards. "Mrs. Dreiss taught me about plants, and I got a job with a nursery. I learned everything I could there, then moved on until I could design plants for any yard, any size, anywhere."

"Where are you working now?" Mr. Graham peered at

her. "At another nursery? That's not much of a job for a woman."

She stared incredulously at him. "It's hard to believe they still make misogynists like you."

"It is, isn't it?" Dan interceded easily. "I'm constantly amazed myself."

Mr. Graham's eyebrows bristled as he glared from one to the other. "I'm not a misogynist. I just know what goes where."

Before Pepper could spew forth more indignation, Dan said, "But yeah, Pepper, I'm curious, too. Where are you working now?"

In feigned innocence, she lifted her eyebrows at him. "Here, apparently."

He nodded, apparently content to wait for another time—and she knew there would be another time.

"After you left, I barely finished high school," Dan said.

"I didn't graduate." She wanted to be out of the system, be judged not for her family, not for her past, but for herself. In every city, she'd been able to buy a driver's license, use that to open a bank account and rent an apartment. She had always made a life for herself out of nothing. Neither of these men had an inkling of how much she had accomplished.

"What kind of employer's going to hire you if you don't have a high school diploma?" Mr. Graham asked.

She spoke with pride. "I work for myself."

"You're *here,* and Danny claims you didn't know about your inheritance, so you must not have done well."

She crumpled her napkin in her hand. Her business

had been thriving, and now having to bite her tongue rather than make an insolent retort to Mr. Graham took all her strength. "Maybe I came on vacation."

"Funny sort of vacation where you don't call ahead," Mr. Graham said.

Dan shoved a plate of cookies toward them.

Taking one, Pepper shot him a sideways glance. He was like a zookeeper shoving meat between the bars of the cage toward two combative lions.

It worked too, for as long as it took Mr. Graham to chew and swallow. Then he turned to his son. "I invited some people over for dinner a week from Saturday. You'll come. I need you to make the numbers right."

Unfortunately for him, Dan looked none too thrilled to be included. "I don't like parties."

Pepper pushed the plate of cookies toward Dan. "Better have one."

Dan took a cookie and bit into it.

As Pepper stared at him, the conversation faded to an annoying background buzz. They were still talking, but she couldn't comprehend the words, for at last the shock of seeing Dan in the flesh was sinking in. She had dreamed about him for so many years. Wondered what he was doing. Tried to justify her own actions in her mind. Now Dan sat opposite her, warm and alive. He had kissed her, held her in his arms, aroused her. He had relentlessly questioned her. He had given her the news about Mrs. Dreiss. But until Pepper had slept and eaten, until she had recovered from her flight, the shock of her situation had robbed the events of reality.

Yet he was here in truth, and with his blond hair and

brown eyes he captured her senses. He fed her. He pursued her. He made her aware of her body as she hadn't been since the day she left Diamond. She wanted him as much as ever. She wanted to put her trust in him and didn't dare, for she would get him killed.

My God. How had such a simple plan to survive become so complicated?

Dan glanced at Pepper. Saw her staring intently at him, absorbing the essence of him, and he raised his eyebrows inquiringly.

With a thump, she landed back in the present. Shaking her head, she tore her gaze away from his. She had to get a grip on herself.

In disgust, Mr. Graham pushed back his chair. "Gotta go back to work." He looked hard at his son. "Sure you don't want to come home to live?"

Grabbing his father by the arm, Dan walked him to the front door. "Dad, let me be blunt. In a choice between living with a crusty old man like you and a pretty woman like Pepper, you're going to lose every time."

"That's my boy." Mr. Graham slapped Dan on the back, took his hat off the rack, and set it carefully over his balding head. As Pepper joined them, he grinned at her. "Always had an eye for the ladies, and they always had an eye for him. Right, Pepper?"

She had to give Mr. Graham credit. He might not be subtle, but he got his point across. A lot of girls had crossed Dan's path. She was one of many who had fallen for him. Still, she didn't want him now, and it wouldn't hurt her to reassure Mr. Graham about her intentions. "Yes, sir. None of us ever could resist him. Still, I'm going to try."

"That's a girl." Mr. Graham went out the door.

Dan flashed her a look that weighed her determination and found it lacking. Taking his hat, he set it low over his eyes and plucked the remaining hat off the rack.

Reluctantly, she took the hat from his hand.

Had it hung there all these years? Or had he located it this morning while she slept?

The buff-colored hat made her recall the shining memory of an old-fashioned Christmas such as little Pepper Prescott had never imagined.

Pepper couldn't remember being part of a group before. Not like this, with thirty high school kids crowded into Mrs. Dreiss's kitchen, pulling taffy until it lost its pristine whiteness and turned a kind of gray.

Mrs. Dreiss laughed at the teenagers and warned, "No matter what it looks like, you have to eat it."

Pepper jostled Rita on the shoulder. "You have to try it. It's good!" It was. In honor of the holidays, they had made peppermint taffy, and each sweet bite held the tang of joy and goodwill. "Come on, you coward. I dare you."

Cautiously Rita put a blob in her mouth and chewed. Her all-American blue eyes widened. "It is good!"

"Did you think I was going to poison you?" Mrs. Dreiss asked from behind them.

Rita looked horrified. "No, ma'am, of course not. I never thought that."

Pepper exchanged a grin with Mrs. Dreiss. Pepper liked Rita, even though the cheerleader had no sense of humor. Blond hair, petite and curvy figure, bubbly personality—Rita looked and acted like a teenager from a fifties beach blanket movie. Although Pepper didn't know why, Rita liked her. She laughed at Pepper's jokes and timidly imitated Pepper's rough language, which made Pepper crack up because Rita swore so badly. At the same time, Pepper found herself reining in her ribaldry. Rita had a belief in the goodness of mankind that had been destroyed for Pepper when her parents abandoned her, and with bleak honesty, she knew she could never be like Rita.

Feeling the weight of eyes on her, she looked around and found that damned Dan Graham staring at her. He used his dark eyes like a mower, knocking girls off their feet and into the back seat of his car. If half of what she heard was true, he'd slept with every girl in town—except for Rita, of course—and most of the divorcées. Certainly he thought he was God's gift to women, and he irritated Pepper with his swagger and his half-cocked smile. She told Rita he probably practiced it in the mirror, and he was using it on her now, summoning her with a jerk of his head.

She heard the buzz of whispers start up, and she noticed Christopher Bardey offering a bet to Charlie James.

They could all go to hell.

Dan could go to hell. She might be the wildest girl in town—not that that was saying much, not in this little burg—but she was not going to sleep with Dan Graham, and not just because she'd never made it with any guy. She knew, better than anyone, that Dan wanted her to fall on her back so he could brag that he'd nailed her. She wasn't going to be anyone's trophy. She would tell him where to go, but . . . Her gaze shifted to Mrs. Dreiss. Mrs. Dreiss, who had two towering boys by the ears and was dragging them outside.

By coincidence, the boys were Christopher Bardey and Charlie James.

Mrs. Dreiss liked Dan. She welcomed him into her home, she kicked him in the rear when he was lazy, and he obeyed her. Jumped like a puppy dog when she snapped.

Well, so did Pepper. She'd never had a foster parent like Mrs. Dreiss. Mrs. Dreiss was old, about sixty, but spry and lively, with a sharp tongue and a no-nonsense way about her. She was thin, tall, and she dyed her hair black. She did chores in the barn every day, even when she was sick or they were snowed in. She told bawdy jokes and recited naughty poetry, and she taught Pepper about plants and people in equal measure. So when Mrs. Dreiss said Pepper should show courtesy to Dan and his rude, awful father, Pepper was polite.

But she didn't have to go when Dan beckoned, and she didn't. Instead she enjoyed the rest of the party.

When the kids were piling in their cars to go home, she stood on the porch and shivered and waved and exclaimed as if she were a normal girl with a normal life. It was a lovely illusion, and she had tears in her eyes as she thanked Mrs. Dreiss.

"You are a normal girl," Mrs. Dreiss said. "A normal girl who's had a tough time. Don't let it tear you apart. You're as good as you say you are."

"Right." Pepper almost believed her.

"Dan's still here. He has something for you." Pepper wanted to groan, but Mrs. Dreiss hugged her shoulders and whispered, "He's not as tough as he'd like to believe. And neither are you." She went inside and shut the door, leaving them on the frozen porch.

The lights from the house shone in squares on the wooden floor. Dan stood in the shadows, wrapped in his sheepskin jacket and wearing his black cowboy hat. He held a large, beautifully wrapped round box in his hands, and when Pepper came toward him, he thrust it at her. It was the first time she'd ever seen him behave awkwardly. "Here. For you."

She looked down at the box and felt foolish. "I don't have anything for you."

"I know, but I wanted to . . . and my mom helped me pick it out . . . She wrapped it . . . Aren't you going to open it?"

Pepper sat on the porch swing while Dan stood before her and rocked on his heels as if her reaction mattered to him. As she pulled off the ribbon, he snatched it away. Carefully she untaped the gift wrap, and he groaned, "You're not one of those people, are you? The ones who save the paper?"

She could have told him she didn't care about saving the paper, she only cared about prolonging the rare excitement of receiving a gift. Instead she said, "Yeah, I care about the environment. Too bad you don't."

"I do. I do! Have you got it open?"

She did, and when she lifted the lid, she found herself looking at a lady's buff-colored cowboy hat. Reverently she lifted it out and smoothed the felt brim.

How had Dan known she wanted one? She'd been careful to be scornful as the ranch kids talked about the spring rodeo and what events they were going to enter and what they would wear to make themselves look like the real thing. Like real cowboys. She had known she would be the *odd man out. But she always was; Mrs. Dreiss wasn't rich, and a good cowboy hat cost a lot of money. "I can't . . ." she whispered.*

"Yes, you can. I asked Mrs. Dreiss before I bought it, and she said it was okay." He added defiantly, "You can ask her."

"Really?" She was still whispering in that awed tone, and she cleared her throat. "If she says it's okay, then I guess . . . it's beautiful."

A smile broke across his face, a smile so broad she realized he had been nervous. He wasn't cool Dan Graham now; he was just a guy who wanted to know he'd done the right thing. "Do you like it?"

"So much."

"Try it on." He couldn't wait. Lifting it out of her hands, he placed it on her head. "It fits."

Like Cinderella's slipper. *But she couldn't say that. So she stood up. She said, "Thank you." And taking his lapels in her hands, she stood on tiptoe and kissed him, a chaste kiss, then hurried into the house and left him standing on the porch, staring after her.*

Now Dan took the hat and placed it on her head. "It still fits."

It did. It fit perfectly . . . like Cinderella's slipper.

Ten

As Pepper stepped out on the porch holding her cowboy hat, Russell didn't like the way she stared at his son, like Dan was the champion bull rider at the rodeo. There was no call for that. No call at all, and he knew how to fix her. He'd seen her look around the ranch half-prideful, half-fearful, and with the bulldog bluntness that he took pride in, he said, "There's a lot of things out here a woman like you can't handle."

Dan made a move toward him. Then he stilled.

Casually, she looked at Russell. "What do you mean, a woman like me?"

"A city woman." Was she offended? Tough. "Steers get mean, and bulls get out of the fence and they've got an attitude that never stops."

"Imagine that." Her gaze lingered on Russell. "Testosterone poisoning at its purest."

Dan watched her with eyes so dark and intent Russell turned his head away so as not to intrude on a private moment. It looked like all Dan wanted to do was pick her up and run off with her to the first available bed.

Russell remembered feeling like that about Dan's mother, and look where it got them. Years of good sex and bad fighting. A divorce that tore his guts out and a love that made him unfit for any other woman. There had to be a way to clear Pepper out before Dan got tangled in her web.

Russell was determined to scare her away. "Bears come blundering down the mountain, and wildcats sneak around during calving, looking for an easy meal. What are you going to do if you accidentally get between a mama bear and her cubs?"

"Just what you would do, Russell," she said. "I'd wet myself."

He wanted to laugh but forced himself to remain stern. "Don't be insolent, missy."

"I was being honest, mister."

Some things never changed. She still had a smart mouth on her.

"Worse, if you stay on this ranch, word will get around to the scum who live in the mountains that you're a woman alone. What are you going to do if some rustler comes around for your cattle?"

She smiled so pleasantly, Russell got worried.

Opening the screen, she stood on tiptoes and reached for the rifle that Mrs. Dreiss—that every rancher—kept on hooks above the door.

Dan kind of jumped, as if he didn't want her to have it.

Russell concurred. "Damn, woman, be careful with that thing!"

Then, looking calm and amused, Dan helped her get it down. He stood close by her shoulder, watching as she examined the rifle. "What's the matter, Dad?" Dan asked. "You nervous?"

On finding the rifle loaded, she released the safety. Lifting it to her shoulder, she asked, "Mr. Graham, what do you want me to shoot?"

"Nothing!" Russell said. "There's no reason for a demonstration. If you say you're good with firearms, I'll believe you."

"So you say, until you drive away. Then you'll mutter about how I ought to play poker because I'm so good at bluffing."

"It's scary how well she knows you, Dad," Dan said.

It was scary the way Dan was so proud of Pepper. When he thought no one noticed, he looked at her as if she were Christmas and his birthday all rolled into one. Ever since he'd returned from overseas, Dan had been solemn, responsible, and so cynical it made Russell's teeth ache. Russell found himself praying that something would bring the old laughing, hell-raising Dan back. But not Pepper. Dan couldn't survive another heartbreak like the last one.

Pepper waved the barrel at his truck. "I could shoot out your tire."

Russell lifted his hands as if she'd pointed the rifle at him. "I told you I believe you." With his luck, she'd miss the tire, hit the gas tank, and blow up his F350.

"But I might miss the tire, hit your gas tank, and blow up your truck."

At the look on his dad's face, Dan laughed out loud.

"She knows everything you're thinking, doesn't she, Dad?"

Pepper shot Dan a glance, and for one moment they shared a connection, the memories of Pepper's long-ago defiance of Russell. She'd been more shrill then, less skillful at baiting him, but even then she'd been able to get Russell's goat. Now she had such a polish and a sure knack for teasing Dan's old man that Russell didn't know which way was up.

"The truck looks pretty new," Pepper said in a conversational tone, "so instead I'll shoot off that dead branch. See it on that Douglas fir down there? Dan, how far away is that?"

Dan barely had to glance to know. "Two hundred yards." Dan doubted his dad could make that shot. In fact, Dan would be damned impressed if Pepper succeeded. Impressed . . . and wary. He made sure he was standing close enough to take that gun if she seized the chance to off him or his dad right now.

Russell squinted to see the branch; he clearly expected Pepper to fail. "Well, now, if you manage to shoot that off, I'll eat my hat with sawdust for break—"

The blast cut through his words.

The branch exploded right where it connected to the trunk and fell to the ground.

Russell's mouth dropped open.

Dan hid his own amazement with a mildly inquisitive tone. "What were you saying, Dad?"

Russell looked at Pepper, and his eyes were wide and round.

She lowered the rifle, gazed at the place where the branch had been, and nodded as if unsurprised.

"You were talking about eating your hat, Dad? For breakfast?" Dan's opinion of her had just been confirmed. She was—always had been—one hell of a woman. She wasn't afraid of anybody. Not of his dad, not of him. Wasn't afraid to say what she thought. When he looked at her, he saw the kind of open honesty he thought he had left behind forever.

But Dan didn't know if she was honest. She could very well be a traitor awaiting her chance to off him. In fact, where had she learned to shoot like that?

Dan took the rifle away from her.

Russell demanded, "Dan, did you know she could shoot like that?"

"No. She never did it before." Dan placed the gun on the table. "Pretty amazing, huh?"

"Yeah, well"—Russell's lip stuck out like a sulky boy's—"not as good as you."

Good point, and Dan was glad his dad had made it, for if Pepper had aspirations to outshoot him, she'd have to catch him asleep. "Yes, but I've been shooting since I was a kid. You taught me. The army taught me more."

Dan knew it would grate on Russell to see a woman shoot so well, and it did, for he said, "I bet it took ten men to teach you, huh, Pepper?"

"Mrs. Dreiss could shoot just as well." Pepper made her point. "She taught me a lot, and after that I practiced for months and months and months at the shooting range."

"All right, you can shoot," Russell said, "but what if some guy breaks in and you can't get to a gun?"

As if she'd anticipated the question, she grabbed his

wrist and the front of his shirt, said, "This," and flipped him over her hip.

He landed with a thud that shook the wooden floor, flat on his back looking up at the ceiling of Mrs. Dreiss's porch. "Needs paint," he remarked.

Watching Pepper best his dad was the most fun Dan had had for . . . he didn't know how long. As an added bonus, Pepper was showing him her skills—and that spoke well for her innocence. He didn't know why she could shoot, he didn't know why she could do judo, but a terrorist plant would hide her skills behind a screen of incompetence. Pepper showed her every skill seemingly without guile.

Pepper looked down at Russell. "Did I hurt you?"

"You know you didn't," Russell said grumpily. "You laid me out as cleanly as one of those judo champions in the movies."

Dan touched Pepper's cheek. Just a single long caress down to her jaw. "Smooth. Nice moves. Who taught you?"

She moved her head aside as if she didn't like his touching her, but she wet her lips. During his stay in the hospital, Dan had seen his fair share of Oprah, and Oprah would say Pepper was a woman conflicted.

"Master Han. He was a Vietnamese champion. He moved to George"—she corrected herself easily—"to the U.S. and opened his own school.

"Where was that?" Dan asked.

As if he hadn't interrupted, she continued, "I've been studying for three years."

Dan let her ignore his question—for now.

"Got your black belt?" he asked.

"Yes." Pepper didn't brag on herself, she simply extended a hand to Russell.

Russell let her help him to his feet. He dusted off the seat of his pants. And of course Dan knew his father *couldn't* let her get the last word. "All right, Miss Smarty, what are you going to do if there's more than one man and they come at you with firearms?"

Color washed from her cheeks, and she looked no longer like the teenager she'd been but more her age. And tired. She looked tired. "Then I'll die."

She spoke so plainly, so hopelessly, Dan wondered if she'd learned to shoot and to do judo to protect herself from someone. From a stalker. From a husband. From a lover.

Russell wasn't a cruel man, and he looked horrified by Pepper's flat pronouncement. "It's not likely to happen," he reassured her.

Dan added, "Especially since I'm not leaving yet."

Pepper looked at him as if she were afraid for him, and that added weight to his theory of a stalker. "You should," she said. "Your dad needs you."

Russell opened his mouth to agree.

Dan answered before he got the chance. "My dad got along dandy without me for years."

"People will talk about us staying here together," she pointed out.

Russell nodded and tried to put in his two cents.

"Not if they don't know you're here," Dan replied before Russell could speak. "That is what you want, isn't it? That no one knows you're back?"

She sagged as if Dan's arguments had defeated her. "Yes. That's what I want."

"Then we'll be fine. Frankly, if everyone in Diamond knew I was living with you, it wouldn't make a bit of difference to me."

Russell pranced with the need to say his piece. "The problem comes when she sleeps with you."

"I'm not sleeping with him," Pepper said with absolute conviction. "I am not going to sleep with him."

Dan fixed Russell in his gaze. "Since when did sex become a problem, Dad? You've been herding me toward every woman in town like I'm some sort of stud bull. Why not sex with Pepper?"

Pepper hated having them talk about her like this. "Why not sex with Pepper? Pepper is standing right here, and Pepper isn't here for sex with anyone, most especially not Dan Graham. Pepper has learned her lesson."

"What lesson is that?" Dan looked wickedly dangerous.

She enunciated the words very carefully. "Sex isn't worth the trouble or the mess."

Dan took a step forward to stand right in front of her. He looked down at her, as he had last night, and even though she had had enough sleep and enough to eat, he still intimidated her with his height and his closeness. But he spoke so quietly she had to strain to hear him. "We'll see."

He was threatening her with sex so good she wouldn't care about the trouble and the mess. As long as she stayed here, as long as he was here, the danger would stalk her . . . because she still wasn't over Dan Graham.

Dimly she heard Mr. Graham say, "Son, I brought over that compressor you wanted. It's in the back of the pickup and damned near a hundred pounds. Could you go get it out?"

Dan stepped away from her.

She took a breath, light-headed with relief.

Dan gave his father a hard look, then left the two of them on the porch. "Be good, Dad."

She watched Dan walk away, her gaze glued to the promise in his long stride. Just watching him walk made a woman think he would be a lover she would never forget.

Last time had been a triumph of defiance against authority. This time what she felt wasn't a young girl's rebelliousness but a woman's response to Dan's raw, undiluted masculinity. It frightened her, this tug of the senses. A totally out-of-control, heart-stopping need, a blatant essential. When she looked at Dan, when she heard his voice, when she smelled his scent, she was torn between the instinctual impression that he could keep her safe and the more wanton desire to give him whatever he wanted.

"I hope to hell you're not planning on staying," Mr. Graham said roughly. "The last time you slept with my son, it took him eight years, fourteen countries, and two life-threatening injuries to get over you. He doesn't need to suffer like that again."

She wanted to protest, to say she'd suffered too. But she faced the truth she had learned the hard way—nobody's parents cared for her the way they cared for their own kids. Mr. Graham didn't care about her pain. "Dan can take care of himself."

"You'd think so, wouldn't you? But he hasn't been interested in women, or cars, or company since he's been back. Even his mother's gotten no more than two words out of him, and that woman can nag a man to death." The truth was written on Russell's face. He might be a fussy, interfering old busybody, but he loved his son and suffered for him. "Worst of all is the way his eyes look, so old, as if he's witnessed terrible things."

Yes, that was it. She'd seen that look on Dan's face, as if he were viewing another time, another place, and the only way he could survive was to step away, into a place where emotion and color did not exist.

"When you came here from wherever you'd been, we gave you every chance to be one of us." Mr. Graham's gaze was fixed on his son as Dan wrestled the bulky compressor out of the back of his truck. "But you had to stick out like a sore thumb."

"You mean I didn't want to be like everyone else in Diamond? I'm *not* like anybody else in Diamond."

"That's for sure. Who the hell ever named a girl *Pepper*?"

His scorn stung. "My parents."

"Parents. We don't know who your family is." Mr. Graham talked fast, for Dan was on his way back. "Even *you* don't know who your family is. Who your parents are."

Dan must have the hearing of a cougar, for he answered from across the yard. "Yes, she does."

Her breath caught in her throat. She could count on two fingers the people she'd told about her past—General Jennifer Napier and Dan. And now Dan was going to tell his father. In a voice that vibrated with emotion, she said, "Please, Dan. Don't."

Dan paid her no heed. "She's the daughter of a Texas minister and his wife. When she was eight, they were killed in a car wreck. She was separated from her two sisters and her foster brother and sent to live in foster homes. That's why she was so rebellious when she was here before, and that's why she's so determined to make a go of this ranch now."

His father swiveled on his heels. He stared at her. "Is this true?"

She crossed her arms and refused to answer. Mr. Graham didn't need to know about her. For a lot of reasons, she was sorry she had told Dan, but right now she was sorry because he was using it to whitewash her reputation. She didn't care one damn bit what his father thought of her. She didn't need him. She didn't need anyone . . .

And she heard the echoes of the rebellious, teenage Pepper in her mind.

The truth was, she *did* care what Mr. Graham thought of her. She *did* need him. She needed him to help her care for the ranch. Taking a fortifying breath, she admitted, "It's true."

He considered her incredulously. "Why the hell didn't you tell me before?"

"Because you were having so much fun thinking I was a mongrel who would lead your little Danny boy astray."

Dan took his stance beside her. "You did do that."

"I didn't lead you anywhere you hadn't already been."

"The way I heard it, he led you a few places *you* hadn't

ever been." Mr. Graham observed her while the hot color rose in her cheeks. *"Humph."* He shot a glare at Dan; for a moment, his voice reminded her of her own dad's. "Damned teenage boys. Keep all their brains in their underwear." Turning so he stood beside her, Mr. Graham pointed at the south meadow. "Dan says the alfalfa's ready for the first cutting. What do you think?"

He was, she realized, acknowledging her ownership of Mrs. Dreiss's land. Because of one little piece of information, he gave her respect.

"I don't know, Mr. Graham. You'll have to advise me."

"Call me Russell."

As Russell launched into a detailed explanation of when to cut and why, Pepper reflected that she'd not only given him the one thing he loved more than anything in the world—a chance to expound on something he knew well—but also an excuse to like her. He was the kind of man who was happier being a friend than an enemy.

She . . . she was happier too.

And Dan looked smug, as if he'd fixed a problem. She didn't want him fixing her. She didn't want to be indebted to him in any way, ever. She couldn't afford the repayment plan.

When he was done talking, Russell said, "All right. We'll cut your section next week. If you have any questions before then, ask Dan."

"Please don't tell anyone I'm here," she said.

He walked toward his truck and lifted his hand in acknowledgment, obviously not taking her too seriously.

"Really," she said for emphasis, as she and Dan followed. The afternoon sun slid along her shoulders, taking the chill out of the air, warming her skin, her muscles, heating her all the way to her bones. "I came to see Mrs. Dreiss. This"—she waved an arm around her—"was the last thing I expected to find. I want some time to cope with Mrs. Dreiss's death, and I need peace and quiet to do it." More important, she had to figure out if Senator Vargas had read her e-mail and if not, what other action she could take to protect herself from General Napier and get her life back. Somehow, from her own land in this place out of time, the task seemed doable. "In a couple of weeks. I'll be ready for company then." *Or dead.*

"Pepper, what about your landscaping company?" Dan asked. "Don't you have to go back to . . . where was it you said your company was located?"

"I didn't."

The silence stretched as he considered her set expression and then continued, "Don't you have to sell it or get a manager for it or something?"

She thought about the inevitable consequences to the reputation she had worked so hard to build. Her exclusive customers were going to be furious to be deserted by their landscaper, but resolve stiffened her spine. Pepper Prescott had always run away from her problems, but this time there was no way to run far enough and fast enough, and this time she had lost something precious to her. Yes, Pepper Prescott would stand and fight General Napier. "I've got a manager, of course. She's competent. She'll take care of things while I'm gone."

"Really?" Dan said in disbelief.

Russell shrugged. "Okay. Sounds like you have it in

hand, Pepper. Dan, I think you'll want to leave as soon as she settles in and starts acting like she owns the place."

"I do own the place," Pepper said.

"See? It's started already." Russell donned his hat. "Dan, when do you go to the doctor?"

Dan cast a dark glance at his father. "Day after tomorrow."

"Would you let me know what she says? Please?" Russell sounded humble for the first time Pepper could remember.

She considered the two men. What was going on here? How seriously had Dan been hurt?

Russell's humility must have pulled some weight with Dan, for he conceded, "Sure, Dad. I'll give you a call."

"Great." Russell started the truck. "I've got to admit, this is the prettiest spot for fifty miles."

As he drove away, Pepper shouted after him, "In Idaho!" Turning, she looked back at the house. Hydrangeas rimmed the wide porch, their white clusters flourishing. Beneath them, anemones bloomed in clumps of blue and purple, their golden stamens striking to the eye. In a sunny spot behind the house, the rich black earth was turned in the extensive garden. From her experience all those years ago, Pepper knew that the barn was close enough so she could do the chores in the winter, but far enough away so the smell of cow and horse never wafted up on the breeze.

"It *is* the prettiest place in Idaho," Dan agreed.

Pride swelled in Pepper. Here civilization had not won the battle against nature. Could never win the battle, for wildness hovered in the mountains that rose in mighty peaks around the valley, threatening and protecting, sending murderous winters and blessed summers. Always the scent of pines spiced the air. Brooks murmured across their rocky beds. The rich soil sprang to life every spring and rested, dormant, every winter. Wildlife thrived: That one spring, Mrs. Dreiss had called Pepper to the window countless times to see a deer picking its way across the lawn, or chipmunks dashing along a branch, or a bear bumbling down from its hibernation.

And Pepper owned this place.

Pepper had never allowed herself to dream about owning anything. First she hadn't had the money. Then when she did, she'd been afraid to put her phony name on such a permanent legal document. And at last she'd had to face the truth—settling in one place terrified her. If she lived somewhere for long, she'd have to get to know her neighbors, learn the names of the people in church, become part of a community . . . It had begun to happen in Georgetown anyway. She'd had her business and lived in the area long enough that she'd made friends, friends who liked her for herself, who showed interest in her opinions. Friends who asked personal questions.

Mrs. Dreiss's legacy had taken the choice from her. This—she turned to look over the valley—this was hers.

She experienced the familiar clutch of fear at the thought of being trapped in one place.

Taking a breath of the fresh spring air, she eased the constriction in her chest. If she found she couldn't stand to be stuck in one place, she could sell Mrs. Dreiss's place. Pepper Prescott's place.

And to her surprise, dismay seized her. She looked around again. Sell this? How could she?

What did she want? General Napier said a successful person had to have goals. Pepper had had her goals—to make money, to flourish so completely that where she came from and who she really was did not matter. But now she had land. If she sold it, she would be rich enough to be her own person for the rest of her life.

On the other hand, *if* she could manage to stay alive, and *if* she could figure out a way to get General Napier behind bars, all of this was hers. She could live here if she wanted. If she stayed here, she would live the life of a rancher: difficult, worrisome . . . and free.

With a jolt she realized she wanted to stay here. She wanted this ranch. In a dazed voice she said, "This is mine. It's really mine."

But there was a fly in the ointment.

Dan stood beside her, straight and tall, the kind of man a woman could lean on.

The kind of man Pepper Prescott dared not have.

Boston, Massachusetts

Eleven

"What do you mean, you know where to start our search for Pepper?" Hope Givens stared at Griswald, ignoring all of the guests, all of the family gathered at the Givens mansion to celebrate her graduate degree from Harvard and the imminent birth of her and Zack's first child. Through the sheer power of her gaze, she compelled their elderly butler to answer her *at once*.

Zack Givens, CEO of Givens Enterprises, knew well the power his wife wielded when she fixed her large blue eyes on a man and demanded an accounting. He'd had plenty of training with the experience. They had been married for seven years, and Hope was the sweetest, most easygoing of women. *Was*—until she saw an injustice that needed righting or perceived a need among the hundreds of people she called her friends or found an obstacle in tracing her long-lost family.

Now, as Griswald stood on the patio at the sumptuous Givens mansion, his forehead broke out in a sweat. He ran his hand over his bald head, turned his basset hound eyes on Zack, and in his crisp British accent, said, "Sir, with Madam's graduation party going on and Madam in an advanced stage of pregnancy, I submit that it's not good for her to get excited in this manner. Might we not take this into your study where I can give you a complete report . . ."

The sound Hope made could only be described as a growl.

Griswald's voice trailed off, and he had the good sense to look terrified.

Zack's parents and his aunt Cecily shook their heads as if bewildered by his folly.

Zack moved between his butler and his wife, hoping to protect Griswald from bodily harm.

At eight and three-quarters months, Hope had enough hormones coursing through her veins that she cried at reruns of *I Love Lucy*, laughed at the Three Stooges, and threw tantrums a three-year-old would be proud to perform. All this from a woman everyone valued as calm and reasonable.

Of course, Zack had experience with her temper; before their marriage, she had ripped into his character and shredded his self-esteem. He'd deserved it, but he had never again made the mistake of assuming that Hope was a pushover.

For Hope had lost her two sisters and her foster brother when her parents were accused of embezzling church funds. Their death in a car wreck immediately afterward had left Hope alone and bewildered. When Zack met her, she had been searching for the other children, and the only way he had been able to convince her to marry him was to bribe her with the discovery of her foster brother, Gabriel. Since that time seven years ago, the entire family had been hunting for the two girls, and Hope just would not wait another second to hear whatever news Internet guru Griswald had unearthed with his search.

Gabriel stood beside Zack now. Gabriel's hair was black and smooth, his eyes as green as emeralds, and although the family didn't know his background, his Latino ancestry showed in his stark cheekbones and wide forehead. He showed his presence of mind when he suggested, "The family should adjourn to Zack's study and hear what Griswald has discovered."

"Excellent idea." Zack put his arm around Hope and helped her out of her chair. To the hovering guests, he said, "Please go ahead with the celebration. I promise that soon we'll have more to celebrate."

The guests, close friends and relatives, nodded and murmured their agreement. They all knew the story of Hope's lost family; they all helped with the search when they could.

As Hope walked before Zack, he noted that she moved slowly. She looked tired, and he thought that before long their daughter would be born. He prayed it would be soon, for he couldn't wait to hold the baby in his arms. And he hoped they would find Pepper too, because he wanted Hope to celebrate the birth wholeheartedly.

She stopped at the doorway of the study. "I'm sorry. Before I hear the news, I must pay a visit to the restroom."

The three men nodded. All of them were familiar with her recent habits, and the news surprised none of them.

"But don't you *dare* discuss Pepper until I'm there," she commanded.

Gabriel waited until she was in the bathroom with the door shut before muttering, "No, ma'am. Whatever you say, ma'am."

Zack stared at the closed door and shook his head. "It's a sad day when three grown men are afraid of one very pregnant woman."

"I'm not afraid of her, sir, I simply respect her condition too much to upset her. Now if you will excuse me, sir, I'll go in and pour libations." Griswald paced into the study.

Out of the side of his mouth, Gabriel said, "He's in denial," and followed him in.

Zack stayed in the hallway, waiting to see if Hope needed him.

She came out and smiled as if the sight of him pleased her. "Have I told you recently what a handsome guy you are?"

"No." He sighed theatrically. "And you know how tough that is on my ego."

She sputtered with laughter, and when he opened his arms, she went to him at once. "Your ego needs no strokes, my boy. It's quite large enough."

"Only because I have you." He felt an upswell of love. "And the baby." He couldn't quite reach around her enlarged girth, and at the pressure on Hope's belly the baby kicked vigorously.

Hope snuggled her head into his chest. "She's a miracle."

"She really is."

Their start together had been rocky, but the last seven years had been the sweetest he'd ever experienced, and he wanted nothing more than to make her happy.

"Do you think we'll find Pepper this time?" she asked.

He stroked her brown hair, but he couldn't raise false optimism. "I don't know. I hope so." His wife had braved years of poverty and privation while trying to discover any information about her family. She had been thwarted at every turn, as he had been, and now, at last, he confessed his deepest thoughts. "I find it suspicious that no attempt was made to keep you children together, and the fact that *you* were sent so far away from home is odd."

"I know," she whispered. "I've always thought that too."

"It's even more suspicious that with my money and my family's influence, we've still been unable to find any trace of the other girls." Some great force seemed to block their every inquiry.

"I know this is probably paranoia caused by being too uncomfortable to sleep, but lately I've been wondering"—Hope raised her head from his chest and looked up at him—"do you think the fire at the Hobart Courthouse was deliberately set to destroy our records?" Quickly she added, "That's ridiculous, isn't it?"

"To think that someone would burn down the county courthouse in Hobart, Texas, to get rid of your adoption records? It *is* ridiculous—but I've wondered too." Although he knew that Gabriel was convinced that was the case, Zack didn't want to tell her that just yet.

She held her breath, then sighed. "It's almost a relief to think that's what happened. It's better than thinking you and I and all of us are so incompetent we can't trace my family."

"And worse thinking that someone's trying to hide the truth." Gently he added, "A truth that must be terrible."

"I told you my parents were good people." Her mouth was set in a grim line. "They didn't steal that money."

"Then someone killed them."

Tears shimmered in Hope's blue eyes. "I can't bear to think about it."

He cursed himself for bringing it up now. Now when she was so emotional. "Then don't. Let's go in and hear what Griswald has to report."

In his study Zack helped Hope into his most comfortable leather chair and sat on the arm, where he could hold her hand.

Gabriel pushed the ottoman beneath her feet.

Griswald handed her a glass of water, then took his position before the fireplace and recited the facts that Zack and Gabriel knew but Hope did not. "Miss Pepper was residing in the Washington, D.C., area. She is a successful landscape gardener."

"Landscaping?" Hope hung on his every word. "She was always such a rambunctious child. I would have never expected her to go into such a quiet profession."

"Yes. Well." Griswald took a breath. "Because of my difficulty in tracking your sister in the foster care system, and because Pepper is an unusual name, I have long suspected that she changed it, or that it had been changed. At first I thought she had been adopted. Since she was eight when she . . . left Texas, that seemed logical, but my search through the adoption records yielded nothing."

"The adoption agencies allowed you access?" Gabriel asked with interest.

"Er . . . no. *Allowed* would be a generous term," Griswald answered.

"You hacked into the records?" Gabriel managed to sound stern and not at all amused, which Zack knew very well he was.

"Gabriel, you know he did, so be quiet," Hope said crossly. Hope had searched for her sister on her own, and she knew well how little information adoption agencies willingly gave out. "I want to hear what Griswald has discovered."

"Thank you, madam." Griswald sneered at Gabriel with the superiority only a British butler could muster. Then he rumbled on, his voice reflecting the excitement of his investigation. "I caught up with the woman I thought might be your sister Pepper in Albuquerque, New Mexico. She lived there four years ago for a short while and called herself Pepper Porter. I spoke to people who knew her, and the description matched Pepper as we believe she would look today."

Zack had had experts scan in the photo of the eight-year-old Pepper and with a complicated software program, create the face she would have developed as she matured. It was eerie, to see those hazel eyes staring at them so calmly. Hope had cried when she'd seen it, for it looked like the death mask of a loved one—and that, Zack knew, was Hope's fear. That they couldn't find Pepper because she was dead. He could only imagine the anticipation and desperation Hope felt now, to know they had located Pepper's trail at last.

"She *had* changed her name. Several times." Griswald gave a huff of indignation, as if Pepper had thwarted him on purpose.

Hope sat up straighter. "Why?" she demanded. "Was she in trouble?"

"Not that I could tell, madam."

Hope exchanged a telling glance with Gabriel. Zack knew why. He'd heard the tales about Pepper. How she was the typical minister's daughter, rebellious, impertinent, and daring. He knew Hope and Gabriel thought Pepper *must* have been in trouble.

Zack unerringly led them back to the topic at hand. "What did she do for ID?"

"She bought false identifications through the Internet," Griswald informed him.

Hope raked her fingers through her hair. "Isn't that illegal?"

"Yes, madam. Very. So although I couldn't trace her back to her origins, I put pressure on the gentleman who sold her the identities." Griswald smirked with justifiable pride. "I was thus able to follow her trail from Albuquerque to Minneapolis, then to Tampa, and at last to Washington, D.C. In her most recent incarnation, she called herself Jackie Porter. I didn't locate her home immediately, for although she worked as Jackie Porter, she rented her condominium as Jacqueline P. Peters, an identity she bought from an entirely different source."

Unable to remain still, Gabriel paced across the study. "We were so close to finding her. We barely missed her in Washington. She disappeared. Zack and I traced her to

Denver, where she bought a car, drove into the mountains and . . . we can't find a trace of her now."

"Why? Why did she abandon a thriving career as a gardener and disappear?" Hope demanded.

"Because . . ." Griswald hesitated. "I fear I found an article in *The Washington Post* that gave the name of Jackie Porter and listed her as . . ." With a worried glance at Hope, Griswald pronounced, ". . . wanted for murder."

Zack came to his feet. "Good God."

Gabriel stopped pacing and turned ashen. "Of whom?"

Only Hope spoke with unassailable certainty. "That's impossible. She's innocent."

"I found someone who agrees with you. With us. Once I located Miss Pepper's home in Washington, I hacked into her computer and found an e-mail professing belief in Miss Pepper's innocence and offering to help her. With this woman's assistance, we can surely locate Miss Pepper and clear her reputation. For the lady who believes in Miss Pepper's innocence is"—with triumph, Griswald produced the name of the renowned celebrity— "General Jennifer Napier."

Twelve

"Come on," Dan said. "I'll show you around the ranch."

Without looking to see if Pepper followed him, he walked toward his truck.

This truck was a working man's vehicle, tall, tough, pale green, and cared for as a valuable piece of ranch machinery. Its four-wheel drive and big tires had kept him out of snowbanks, and its powerful motor climbed the steep roads without a whimper. Its long bed hauled bales of hay and the occasional recalcitrant calf, and he kept his tools in a locking toolbox flush against the cab. Dust from the gravel roads covered the vehicle from top to bottom, and mud splattered the inside of the wheel wells. His truck looked like every other ranch truck in the county.

But it contained something extra. He kept a monitor behind the seat, one connected to the monitor in the house. His pager alerted him whenever something—or someone—broke the laser beams that surrounded the house. He could read the size and direction of the intruder. He kept weapons back there too. Not the usual rifle every rancher kept on a rack behind him, but weapons that most civilians didn't own, didn't even know how to use.

Pepper *had* followed him, and aggressively she said, "Okay, you can show me around. You can teach me everything I need to know. In two weeks, you said. Right? Two weeks until you drive the cattle to the high country, and no more."

"If I didn't know better, I would think you didn't want me around." He opened the door for her and watched her thighs stretch as she pulled herself up on the step. With the skill of an experienced observer, he examined the curve of her slender bottom as she seated herself on the bench seat in the cab. *He wanted to kiss her.*

"It would be better if you go."

"Better for who? Not for me." Dan flexed his hands. The kind of kiss he planned to give her had to be exchanged reclining and without clothes. There would be others, preliminary kisses that softened Pepper's ire and eased her into lovemaking, and he plotted those with equal care. Yet the kiss that sprang fully imagined into his mind was desperate, open-mouthed, and intimate.

He found it interesting that he, who had put all his substantial concentration on catching the elusive terrorist who had killed so many men, women, and children, now found equal fascination in planning Pepper's seduction. "I'm enjoying myself, being here with you. It's like old times—fun and rebellious, but without the sex."

He heard her hard intake of breath. Saw her eyes widen in shock. "You're a smart-ass." Leaning out, she grabbed the door and slammed it in his face.

He came around and jumped in, and considered how very much he enjoyed prodding her to see her temper flash. He did it to check her honesty, of course, not out of some remnant of boyish mischief that unexpectedly surfaced when she was around.

As he set the truck in motion, he watched her out of the corner of his eye. The bad haircut had sent her wavy hair totally berserk. It curled around her face in wild black ringlets, framing her naturally pale complexion; patches of lingering sunburn flaked on her nose and forehead. Yet her eyes were large and thoughtful, her lashes thick and dark, and her Barbie-doll figure looked good in those jeans and that T-shirt.

No wonder his dad worried about the two of them staying together. Most men wouldn't be able to keep their hands to themselves. Wouldn't want to. Dan sure didn't, and he had reasons, good reasons, for being wary of her. But being wary meant he had to watch her closely, and that duty was more enticing than it should have been.

Stopping at the barn, he said, "Stay here. I'll only be a minute."

"Take your time," she replied acidly.

Inside the barn he pulled his transmitter out of his wallet and plugged it into his ear. With a push of the button, he reached Colonel Jaffe. "Any information on the woman?"

In a tone of great forbearance, the colonel said, "I've

been looking less than twenty-four hours. I take it she didn't try to murder you in your sleep?"

"No."

"Did she try and seduce you?"

"No, damn it."

Colonel Jaffe chortled. "So there's one woman in this world with some sense."

"She was exhausted," Dan explained loftily. "I'm sure she'll sneak into my bedroom tonight. That is, if the boys are still lolling around the countryside waiting for Schuster."

The colonel's tone turned businesslike. "No movement yet. Has she done anything suspicious?"

"She doesn't want anyone to know she's here. Doesn't want to visit old friends. Won't tell me where she's been living or where her business is located. Insists I keep quiet about her."

"Because she doesn't want to be identified after she offs you."

"Anything's possible," Dan acknowledged.

"She can stay a little longer," Colonel Jaffe decided. "If she's innocent, and if anybody's watching you, she adds a nice touch of negligence to your setup."

They had discussed it before, but—"*Is* someone watching me?"

"Not unless it's one of your faithful cowhands, and Sergeant Midler thinks they're all in the clear."

"All right. Then Pepper and I are off on a tour of the ranch, where I'll wow her with my ranching knowledge and my"—Dan lowered his voice to a manly voice—"big hat."

"I understand there are women who are impressed with that sort of thing," Colonel Jaffe said in a tone of complete boredom.

"All of them, Colonel. All of them." With a grin, Dan hung up. Donning his work gloves, he hefted a forty-pound block of salt and carried it out to the truck.

He found Sergeant Sonny Midler, Hunter Wainwright, and a young cowhand, TJ Loving, standing beside the truck, hats in their hands, talking to Pepper.

Sonny was a handsome man, if women were to be believed, with his curling auburn hair and his easy smile, and he had the gift of gab. Too much of a gift, so Dan told him on the frequent occasions when Sonny said too much.

Wainwright's mature good looks always drew the women. Women had a thing about those silver streaks in his hair.

And TJ was young, really young, and if a woman was attracted to boyish good looks, he was her man.

They were all muscular and handsome, and Dan hadn't been kidding when he told Colonel Jaffe that women loved a cowboy. Dan hoped Pepper had too much sense to be influenced by a big hat and a load of bullshit, but he suffered stabs of jealousy anyway.

That surprised him. He wasn't an unreasonable man. He would never expect any woman to be celibate for nine years. Certainly he hadn't been.

Yet his feelings for Pepper were different. With her, lust mixed with possessiveness to form a fervent brew of need. He *needed* to sleep with her more than he had needed to sleep with any woman for the past . . . well, the past nine years. The greedy craving had to be because he had taken her virginity. For some reason his heart insisted she was his for the taking.

Actually, the insistent organ was lower and ached fiercely.

She didn't want to be seen, for whatever reason, and now these guys would gossip that Dan had a girlfriend. When he approached the truck, he imagined he looked grim.

Pepper had her hat pulled far down on her forehead, a feeble disguise, and she nodded as the cowboys spoke, but she kept remarkably quiet. When the guys saw the expression on Dan's face, silence fell. He stopped and looked them over.

They straightened.

"Looking for work?" Dan asked.

Sonny turned the brim of his hat in his hands as he spoke. "Yes, sir, we wanted to know if you want us to mend fences." His voice sounded respectful, but he grinned irrepressibly. In the battalion he was second only to Dan for female conquests, and he loved nothing better than trying to steal one of Dan's women. He had never succeeded, but that didn't stop him from giving it a shot. As Dan raised the salt to load it in the back of the truck, Sonny rushed to his side. "Here, sir, that's pretty heavy. Let me help you."

As if Dan were an old man! "Sure." Dan let him take the forty-pound block, and while Sonny lifted it, Dan smacked him hard in the belly with the edge of his hand.

Sonny dropped the salt onto the truck bed. It hit with a smack. The truck rocked under the impact. As the air rushed out of his lungs, Sonny doubled over.

The other cowboys burst into laughter.

Pepper kept her gaze straight ahead.

In a fatherly tone, Dan said, "Is your hernia bothering you, son?"

"Yeah," Sonny gasped. "My hernia."

More quietly, Dan said, "All's fair in love and war, *son*." Raising his voice, he said, "Get to work, guys. I'm taking the lady for a tour of the ranch, and then she's leaving town."

"That's what Miss Watson said." TJ sounded disappointed.

Who? Dan thought.

"I was hoping she could come to the Gem Lounge tonight," TJ continued, "but she says she has to catch a plane."

Sonny had recovered his breath. "No use spending the night with Grandpa Graham here. He's no good to any woman anyway."

"You could be washing dishes," Dan said.

Sonny skittered away. "No, sir, no KP for me. I'm off to work."

As the cowboys rode away, Dan got in the truck and slammed the door. "Damned idiots. What did you tell them?"

"Nothing except my name, which is Glenda Watson." Irritation vibrated in Pepper's voice. "Men never grow up, do they?"

He reversed the truck and headed in the opposite direction from his dad's place, going past the house again, around the end of the valley and toward the salt lick by the river. "What do you mean?"

"That business with the salt. Then Sonny calling you Grandpa and assuming all I'm here for is sex. You're all smirking little smart-asses."

"Yes, ma'am."

His laconic reply made her eyes spark brighter. "You were a smart-ass the first time I met you, and you're still one."

"As were you." An understatement if ever there was one.

"*I* had a difficult upbringing. What was your excuse for being such a rude, cocky little delinquent?"

"I didn't need an excuse. I was seventeen, and I was the only Graham son. Hell-raising's an old family tradition." His truck rattled along the gravel road, pitching as he drove through ruts and over frost heaves. "Plus, I was a boy. Boys are supposed to be wild."

He heard her take a hard breath. Saw her head swing toward him as she assessed his sincerity. He kept his expression carefully impassive and added, "Girls are supposed to be quiet and well behaved."

"I'm going to throw up on the floor of your truck," she declared flatly.

"Don't do that. It's the only vehicle we have between the two of us."

Her jaw tightened.

She was worried he would ask about her car again. He might as well oblige her. "Later today, we'll go after your car and tow it back."

She bit off the words. "It's at the bottom of a cliff. It's unsalvageable. I'll call the insurance company when we get back to the house."

"Good idea, but we still should get it. The insurance adjuster will want to look it over before he declares it totaled."

Pepper drew a long breath, turned toward him, and in an attack so sudden it took him by surprise, she snapped, "You always have to take over, don't you? It's your way or no way."

He braked the truck to a stop. He waited until the cloud of dust had settled, then he turned off the motor and rolled down the windows. He turned to study her, his arm across the back of the seat.

Her full mouth was compressed; her jaw jutted out. She met his gaze steadfastly, and she radiated resentment. She no longer looked like the sophisticated Miss Prescott. Once again she was the sixteen-year-old Pepper, and he welcomed her arrival. This girl he knew. This girl he understood.

"You don't have any idea what I'm talking about, do you?" she asked truculently.

"Not a clue." That was the problem. She wanted him to know what she wanted without being told. He didn't have—had never had—the foggiest idea. But now he was smart enough not to pretend. He simply invited, "Tell me."

"You had to tell your dad about my parents, but you didn't tell the whole truth. You had to fix it up pretty, so he would like me. You didn't ask me what I wanted. You just decided on your own."

"What did I fix up?"

"You didn't say my parents stole money from their church and abandoned their children." If anything,

Pepper's bitterness had grown greater through the years. "And were killed trying to get away. Killed leaving us behind to be . . . torn from each other and sent . . . to be alone . . ." Her chest heaved. Her eyes burned. But she wasn't crying. She was incandescent with anger.

Did she want to assassinate him? Maybe, but the more irritated she was, the more he relaxed. Guilty women always tried to screw their way out of trouble, and if this was seduction, she was very bad at it . . . and yet surprisingly good, for he wanted her. "Did you fear I would think less of you because of your parents' crimes?"

"No. No, that's not it!" She took a breath. "When I told you about my parents all those years ago, and explained that they had abandoned me, what did you do?"

"I tried to find them."

"You tried to find them," she repeated. "You tried to find my family. You sent a letter to Hobart, Texas, asking about my family."

He had. In the misery that followed her disappearance, he had forgotten about that—and about her stunned reaction to his revelation.

Dan pulled up his pants, tucked in his shirt, tried to pretend nothing extraordinary had happened when in fact the sex had been mind-shattering, unlike any experience he'd ever had. In the darkness of the El Camino, he could hear Pepper frantically straightening her clothes, and the occasional sniffle as if she were crying.

Damn. He'd been wild for her. He'd hurt her, he knew it. And now he didn't know what to say. He'd feel better about sleeping with her if she was going home to her own family. Not that Mrs. Dreiss wasn't great, she was, but she was kind of old and set in her ways, and most important, she wasn't Pepper's mother.

So he waited until the sounds on Pepper's side of the car had quieted. Reaching over, he pulled her against him and hugged her.

She was stiff, rejecting him.

But he kept hugging her until she relaxed a little. Just a little. Then he offered the best comfort he could imagine, the one thing he'd done that was so good she'd forgive him anything. "You know that stuff you told me in confidence? About your family?"

She stiffened again. "Yeah?"

"I did something really great."

Trembling, she asked, "What did you do?"

"Nothing bad! I didn't tell anybody. It's not like that." He was a little hurt that she thought he'd do that. "I did something to help you find them. I wrote to Hobart to the courthouse and asked for records about your sisters and your brother."

He hadn't thought Pepper could tear herself out of his arms, but she did. Her breath sounded harsh and rasping, and she erupted with resentment. "You . . . you . . . how could you? How could you do that to me?"

"What do you mean?" He couldn't believe it. She wasn't thanking him. She was attacking him. "I didn't do anything to you. I just did what I thought was best."

"Well, thank you very much, George Washington. I don't know where I'd be without your guidance."

She pissed him off so much. "Hey! No one talks to me that way."

"Of course not. Not to the great Dan Graham." Sarcasm

*bubbled out of her. Then, "Did you ever think I might have
tried to get their attention myself and nobody bothered
to—" She stopped talking. Just stopped. In a small, tight
voice, she said, "Take me back to the Dreiss ranch. I gotta
get out of here."*

He had thought she meant out of the car.

She had meant get out of town.

He'd never heard a word back, nothing acknowledging his query, and that seemed *odd*. Dan didn't like odd.
He had learned since then to be wary of *odd*.

But Pepper raged on. "You want to know why I left
Diamond? I left because you acted like a Graham. High-
handed and without a single thought as to what I
wanted."

He had her trapped in the cab of a truck. She had
nowhere to flee. So he leaned toward her and pressed
harder for answers. "Why wouldn't I try to find out about
your family? It was the right thing to do."

"In your judgment! Are you always so sure you're
right?"

Memories rose in him. Memories of last summer: the
heat, the scents of a foreign country, the sunbaked
house, the child who lived within . . . the explosion that
had shattered his life. "Not always."

"But you felt qualified to make decisions for me. You,
an eighteen-year-old boy."

"So you ran away from me."

"I didn't run away from you."

Logically, he said, "You just admitted you did."

"It wasn't about you. It was about me. All right? Not
everything in the whole world is about you."

He damned well wasn't supposed to have to explain this stuff to a woman. Women were supposed to *know*. "That night wasn't about you or me alone. We were tangled together in every way. We were angry together, we made love together. It wasn't me or you, it was us."

When he was in a fury, most people stepped back from him. Pepper met him head on, her eyes sparking. "*Us* is over now. Forget it."

"Forget it?" With an effort, he controlled his temper. "There are moments in a man's life that are turning points. Moments that define who he is for the rest of his life. That night, my darling, was one of those moments for me." His other moments . . . weren't good. But that one was, and he cherished the memory. "Are you saying that night wasn't one of those moments for you?"

Thirteen

That night had changed everything for Pepper.

The shame of stealing, of drinking, of deliberately hurting Mrs. Dreiss, the one person she could depend on. The heat of passion and pain between her and Dan. The fear of knowing that with Dan's help, her family might be able to find her . . . but might not care to.

But Pepper couldn't discuss her emotions. Not about that night. Not about any night . . . or day. She'd spent nine years banishing emotions. Her rampant, childish reactions to every situation in her life had led her to hell and back, and she was afraid to allow them to struggle to the surface again. Especially now. Especially when death stalked her and she needed every bit of logic and sense she could dredge up in order to survive.

Pepper's gaze raked Dan. His eyes blazed with fire. One hand gripped the steering wheel, the other the back of the seat.

If she stayed here, he would always be around. She didn't know what he ultimately wanted from her, but in the short term she knew very well. He'd been pretty plain about that. He wanted to be in her bed.

Would she be strong enough to tell him no?

Was she strong enough to convince herself she didn't want him?

She didn't know from what depths of her soul the question arose, but she blurted, "Why do you have to go to the doctor?"

"That's all the answer I get? I asked if that night defined you, and you ask me why I have to go to the doctor?" Dan asked incredulously.

"I just . . . I remembered what your dad said about your doctor's appointment, and I . . ." Inching back, she pressed herself against the door.

Fiercely, he asked, "Does your answer depend on mine?"

"No." She straightened her shoulders. "I don't intend to answer you."

The expression on his face turned hard. She knew he was trying to intimidate her, but she refused to crumple.

Instead she settled back and buckled her seatbelt. "Apparently you don't intend to answer me either, so I guess we're even."

Dan started the truck and drove toward the salt lick. "So we're back to high school," he said tightly. The road needed to be graded after the spring runoff; the truck bumped over it.

Dan finally broke the silence that had stretched between them. "I've got a belly wound."

She gazed at his face, then down his shirt as if she could assess the seriousness through his clothing. "How'd you get that?"

"I was in a fight."

"A fight. You mean like between two guys who are mad at each other? Or a fight like a battle?"

"Both. I had a couple of men with me, so you could call it a battle. But I was definitely pissed at the other guy."

"How bad is your wound?" she asked, feeling somewhat subdued.

"I got shot. I lost a piece of my intestines." The truck splashed through a creek icy from snow and rich with silt. "I got peritonitis."

Her hand made a fist against the window. "Are you going to be all right?"

"I am all right." He stopped the truck on the slope overlooking the salt lick, a flat stretch along the river where the trees crept down the mountain and wilderness and pasture mingled.

"If you're all right, why do you have to go to the doctor?"

"You know the army. They've got rules. This is my last six-month visit. After this, it'll be once a year. More of a checkup than anything."

Finally she asked, "What did you *do* in the army?"

"Soldier stuff."

She flinched at the harsh sound as he put on the parking brake.

Soldier stuff? What did that entail? She knew he had been overseas. Russell had said so. But General Napier had worked overseas too. Had they met? Had he served under her? Regardless of Pepper's account, would he feel a soldier's loyalty to a commanding officer? Would he hand her over?

The old Dan would have died for her. The new Dan watched her, judged her, found her wanting. She couldn't put her finger on it, but during their years apart, he had lost something: kindness, hope, a belief in mankind or God or goodness.

He was changed, and she couldn't depend on him. Pepper shook her head.

Everything out here was so vast. Long and narrow, the valley stretched away from them, cattle dotting the landscape. The mountains towered above and around, craggy and covered with pines. Reigning over it all, a blue sky blazed so bright and clean Pepper felt naked beneath it.

Where could she hide? Not in the pastures or even the mountains. The tracking equipment General Napier could call in would find her.

"See anything unusual?" Dan asked, pointing at the two dozen head of cattle that grazed on the new grass.

She tensed. Something unusual? That was precisely what she feared.

But he sounded relaxed, interested.

Then she saw them, picking their way among the lumbering steers—two slender does with their dappled fawns. The deer made their way to the slim blocks of salt and delicately licked their fill, lifting their heads occasionally, sniffing for danger. The fawns gamboled together, their coats glistening in the sunshine. Their joy was infectious, their gait amusing and graceless.

Caught unaware, Pepper laughed aloud. Opening the door of the truck, she eased out, careful not to startle them.

On his side Dan did the same and came around to join her. "They come down here for the salt. And to the house for the roses." He made a face.

"They're beautiful," she whispered. The faint mist of green grass glowed beside dirty mounds of snow left in the shadows where the sun never reached. Here and there, gray boulders rose where they had been placed by the spring runoff. The wind skipped through the tree-tops, making them creak and groan like old men dancing after a long winter. Beyond the sun slanted across the river, turning the water to a bracelet of molten gold.

In her time away she had forgotten how the space, the loneliness, and the immensity here spoke to her soul. This place, a light-washed composition of colors and textures, echoed with the beat of eternity, and she had been so worried, she hadn't heard. Now she did see, and hear, and her heart lifted.

The storm missed us; don't look to the sky for clouds.

Who had said that? General Napier or Mrs. Dreiss? Right now, Pepper couldn't remember.

Smiling, she turned her head and caught Dan's gaze on her.

He watched her without expression, his dark, grave eyes considering.

There are moments in a man's life that are turning points. That night, my darling, was one of those moments for me.

She heard the echo of his words in her head.

Was it true? God knows, when they were young, she

had loved him. He had been an icon to her, the someone everyone wanted to be: accepted for his family name, his handsome face, and his great car. In the intervening years, she had told herself that that was all her grand and glorious passion had been—a superficial teenage urge to date the coolest guy around.

Faintly she heard Dan talking as he gestured. "From here, you can see the alfalfa field. The cattle try to get in, so the cowboys watch that fence."

Yet she had come to Dan's arms, not with a grandiose need for acceptance but with a fiery desire to reject everyone and everything. In him she had found another wild spirit. They had been so different, and so alike.

"If the cattle get in there, they're dumb enough to eat until they die," he said.

Their backgrounds had been different, yet they had both cherished a love for books, and they had talked about the places they would go when they finished school and could heed the call of adventure.

He warned, "Remember, cattle are like people. Some are smarter than others, some are meaner than others. Don't ever turn your back on a steer."

They had talked for hours . . . and they had kissed for hours. She had crawled into his lap and driven him wild, and he had returned the favor. They had been crazy for each other. "I know. I remember the cattle."

"I know you know, but I'm reminding you anyway. They weigh ten times what you do. Don't take chances."

She nodded. "Really. I know."

"I'll deliver this salt to the lick," he said. "Then we'll go."

Time and distance had proved one thing—whatever desire she and Dan had had between them was intrinsic to them, like lava and ice, meeting and blowing everything to bits with the violence of the explosion. She saw him heft the salt block and walk down the slope toward the lick, his strides long and gloriously smooth. The does leaped away, their fawns after them, escaping into the woods. The cattle stood unimpressed as he placed the salt, then headed back.

The sun kissed his face. Of course. Even the sun worshipped Dan.

That kiss last night . . . At the touch of his lips to hers, her body had readied itself. Her breasts had grown heavy, her legs had trembled.

Her mind had emptied—dear heavens! Her mind had vanquished every sensible thought, every practical fear, while her body surged with need. Even now she wanted to rush to meet him, let him pull her to the damp ground, where they would mate as nature intended.

The instinct to mate with Daniel James Graham overwhelmed even her drive to survive, and as nothing else could, that frightened her back into good sense. Scrambling for her side of the truck, she opened the door, climbed in, slammed it after herself. She didn't want him acting like a gentleman. Didn't want to feel his gaze on her and know that his hands could so easily touch her. Didn't want to wonder whether she would reject him or not.

She huddled close to the door as he started the truck. She had better get used to thinking like a rancher. She'd better start learning how to do what needed to be done—now.

"Tonight I'll help with the chores," she said.

"Tomorrow," he said comfortably as he reversed and drove back up the road. "You're still tired. Tonight if you'll fix dinner, that'll be plenty for me. I'm sick of my own cooking."

A yawn caught her by surprise. She *was* still tired. "What do you have for me to fix?"

He gestured vaguely. "There's some cans of stuff you can fling together."

The pure, male absurdity of his words relaxed her as nothing else could. "Sounds great. I love cans of stuff flung together."

"You used to be a pretty good cook."

"I still am. With real food. You know, fresh vegetables, fresh meat, herbs . . ."

"We don't have any real food."

"I'll make you a list. When you go to the doctor, you can stop at the grocery store. In the meantime, let me see what I can do." She yawned again. "What time in the morning?"

"For chores? Five."

"Of course. Five." She sighed heavily, then made sure. "O'clock?"

"Five o'clock. In the morning." He sounded amused. "We've got to feed Samson, muck out his stable, and turn him out to pasture."

"It's the same Samson?"

"The very same. He's older, but just as strong. With the good weather, I've been cleaning out the barn, getting the old straw out and getting ready for the new. I've been working the compost pile for the garden." As he shot her a sideways glance, he added solemnly, "We have to gather eggs."

A wave of remembrance hit her. "Ooh." She thumped her head back on the seat. "I hate to gather eggs. The hens always sneak off and hide them under the barn in all these horrible, spider-ridden—"

"Snake-ridden?" he suggested helpfully.

"—snake-ridden, dark places"—she shuddered—"and I'm sticking my hand around trying to find the eggs."

"Use a flashlight."

But he didn't sound callous. Rather, he seemed comfortable, settling into the kind of dialogue they had once shared. Yet beneath their camaraderie, a sensual awareness shimmered. They could, and did, talk about everyday things, and all the time a heat grew in Pepper's belly.

Dan kept his attention on driving the rutted road, yet the sense of being wanted filled the distance between them.

She lifted weights and was proud of her muscle tone, but now her arms seemed more naked than bare, a deliberately feminine enticement to a man already seething with passion. When she got back to the house, she would find one of her long-sleeved shirts and cover herself more completely, and she didn't think she would bother to dig out her shorts until she had mastered the running of the ranch and he was gone.

She glanced around. If General Napier allowed her the chance.

The house came into sight, surrounded by tall trees and looking cozy and mellow. With no forethought,

Pepper said, "I think a helicopter would have a rough time landing anywhere close to the house."

"You own a helicopter?" Dan asked mildly.

She shouldn't have brought it up. "No."

"Your boyfriend owns a helicopter?"

Her boyfriend? "Forget I said anything."

Dan pulled in under the shade of the trees.

She put her hand on the door. He leaned across her and held the door shut. "Do you have a boyfriend?"

"No. No boyfriend." She considered smacking his hand, but it was big and broad, placed far too close to her. "No husband, no entanglements. I live alone. I work alone. I like it that way." She had, she hoped, made her point.

He was very close. Close enough for her to feel claustrophobic. Close enough for her to realize he didn't believe her.

Her temper flared, and this time she did smack him on the knuckles. For her trouble, she hurt her own hand, but he let her go. She slammed out of the truck and stormed toward the house.

He caught up with her in a few long strides. "The house is set up on a rise," he explained. "The mountains go up behind it. There are tall trees for one hundred yards to the front and the sides. No helicopter could land without losing its blades."

"As if you would know," she snapped.

"I would. In my time I've made a few risky helicopter landings."

As she climbed the steps, curiosity slowed her down. "You were a pilot?"

"No." He held the door. "I've answered your question, now you can answer mine. Why do you care about whether a helicopter can land here?"

For the first time, she was grateful to Russell Graham for handing her a sorely needed excuse. "I imagine your father knows what he's talking about, occasionally, and I'd heard that rustlers use helicopters these days."

"They do. But they'd be out where the cattle are, not up by the house."

"Oh. Yeah. I didn't think about that." She hadn't worried about the cattle at all. She had been thinking of herself, trapped in the house with nowhere to run. "Your dad spooked me this morning. He made me want to increase security before you move out, in case someone *did* try to break in."

"Besides shooting them or using judo on them?" Dan's gaze expressed very nicely his admiration for her skill.

So nicely she shifted and once again resolved to dress more conservatively. "It would be nice to have warning. That's why I was thinking about security."

"So you could call the sheriff?"

"And run." She went to the large camellia that hung in a basket in the window. The poor thing drooped; only one creamy white blossom was open. With the hem of her T-shirt she wiped the dust off the shiny leaves and tested the soil with her finger. "I find," she said, "that plants, like people, need water to flourish."

"I forget that stuff."

She swept him a scathing glance.

He watched as she fetched the watering can, but

he didn't seem to see her. He was thinking, frowning, deciding. At last he said, "You don't need to worry about anyone getting in here. I've installed a security system."

"You mean around the house?" She gave the camellia a good drink.

"Yes, around the house, but in a wide perimeter—down by the barn, up along the hills, across the road."

That caught her attention. He wasn't talking about a normal security system. He was talking about something more.

"No one comes close without my knowing it." He gestured toward the cabinets in the dining room. "You'll hear an alarm go off whenever anybody, or anything, comes close."

"Why would you do that? Are there so many intruders here?" Did she truly need to be worried about rustlers as well as the general?

"Everyone knows Mrs. Dreiss died and that you haven't been found. Vandals are always keen for a little fun. They did some damage before I moved in, and I've chased off a few since." Putting his hands on her shoulders, he looked into her eyes and said reassuringly, "Trust me, you're safe here from any threat, no matter how big or how small."

His palms warmed her through her shirt. His scent both reassured her and stirred her, and she realized he was lying—because he posed the biggest threat, and she had no resistance to him. No resistance at all.

No. No, that was impossible. Cautiously, she said, "Thank you. I feel safer."

"That's what I wanted." He released her.

Yet this preparedness made the question of his past press harder on her consciousness. "Dan, what did you *do* in the military?"

"Security." He grinned easily. "Nothing more than security."

Fourteen

Five o'clock came way too early the next morning.

At Dan's knock, Pepper stumbled to her feet and tried to remember where she was and why she was up.

Chores. She had to do chores. For the rest of her life, short though it might be, she would have to rise at five, get dressed, and go feed the chickens, muck out the stable, feed Samson . . .

Yet Dan's assurance that his security system would keep her safe had allowed her to sleep. For that fragile sense of safety she was profoundly grateful.

Although . . . was there another reason why he had surrounded the place with lasers and beepers and alarms?

But no. That was ridiculous. She was borrowing trouble, as Mrs. Dreiss would say, and it was time to stop.

As she threw on her clothes—jeans, light turtleneck sweater, long-sleeved shirt, and boots—she glanced at her dresser. Last night, while Dan was down at the barn, she had brought in her backpack. She had stashed it in the trunk on the porch the first night, before she broke in, and now she had her ID and her cash hidden. She hoped to God she didn't have to run again.

Straightening her shoulders, she pretended to be awake and aware as she strode into the kitchen.

She needn't have bothered. Dan didn't care whether she was awake or how carefully she covered every inch of her body. His sexy dark eyes took note of her conservative garb and mocked her for imagining she could so easily distract him from his desire. "Nice," he said.

He meant it. She could wear burlap and he'd still be interested. Still make her break out into a fine sheen of sweat. "I thought it would be cold this morning," she mumbled.

"Not bad. About forty degrees." He shoved a cup of coffee in her hand and waited while she took a few slurps. He placed her buff-colored Cinderella cowboy hat on her head, then walked out with her on his heels.

It *was* nippy. She could see her breath as she hurried down the winding path toward the barn. A light frost touched the grass blades with silver. The sun's rays spread golden across the horizon, then the orange rim peeked over, setting the few lingering patches of snow on fire. The sky turned a pale wash of blue and the few clouds brightened to a miraculous combination of gold and pink. It was pretty, she supposed, but it would be prettier if it happened later in the morning. Around ten would be good.

The hay barn was warm and redolent with the smell of horse and leather. It was a familiar smell, one she hadn't realized she missed. A row of stalls stood open, waiting for the cows that no longer resided there. In the wide-open space beneath the hayloft, a workbench stood loaded with tools: a cordless drill, a can of paint smeared with white, and a paint brush. Nearby stood two old wooden chairs, one fixed and painted, the other with a broken rung and a listing leg. A thoroughly male place, more like a workshop than a barn.

Dan handed her a pair of women's work gloves and pointed her toward the hen house. She had to shoo the little bantam rooster away before she could crawl in; he stalked away in masculine indignation. Only six hens were in residence, sleeping on their nests, and they squawked when she stuck her hand beneath them to look for eggs. "I know," she mumbled, "it's an obscene hour of the morning." She looked the oldest hen firmly in the eye. "You didn't go off and lay eggs anywhere else, did you?"

The old hen returned her stare without flinching.

"Figures." By the time she finished searching for more eggs and scattering grain, Dan had mucked out Samson's stall. He led the big gelding out to a pasture and she followed, keeping a sharp eye on the horse's restless hooves. "He never liked me," she announced.

"He likes you. He doesn't want anyone to take him for granted, so he kicks occasionally." Dan never changed tone. "Like my dad."

She surveyed the big horse's hindquarters. "I see the resemblance."

"I'll make sure I tell Dad." Dan shooed her toward the house.

She was awake now—resentful, but awake—and she

noticed the giant canoe birches that lined the path and the fresh green leaves misting the branches. The peonies put forth clumps of new growth. She stopped to smell one white blossom, finding the scent sweet and heady. Spring came later to the mountains, but it bounded from the earth in a hurry, anxious to make the most of the warmth and sunshine.

She decided to ask once again the question that had worried her last night, and again this morning. "Dan, what did you *do* in the military?"

"Security." He grinned easily. "Let's go get some breakfast. Cold cereal all right with you?"

"Cold cereal is great." She started to press him for details about his military past.

But he said, "Then I'll fix breakfast."

"Ooh, thanks." The first smile of the morning broke across her unwilling face.

He pulled her to a halt. He adjusted her hat, settling it so it sat on her head just so. Then he stood looking down at her.

He was going to kiss her. She knew he was going to kiss her. Her lips trembled. She wanted to sway toward him.

But she had to put up resistance. She couldn't fall into his arms whenever he made a move toward her.

Instead he stroked his thumb down her cheek. "I love your smile."

The simple compliment took her breath away. *He* took her breath away. The crisp breeze stirred his blond hair. The sharp, early sunlight turned his tanned face to bronze. The white scar slashed his skin, a sign of ugly violence. He was so much a man, strong, silent, uncomplaining, that her heart clenched and she ached with the desire to hold him, to seek comfort from him and offer succor to him.

And that proved that worry had made her lose her mind, for what could she offer him except a berth in the family cemetery, courtesy of General Napier?

Pepper looked down at his chest and grappled with her rapidly dwindling good sense. She needed to remember the lessons that life had taught her.

Never trust anyone. Never love anyone.

"Pepper?" His deep voice called her out of her contemplation of the past.

Looking up with a smile that denied his right to be concerned, she moved casually away. "We'd better get that cereal. I'm starving!"

"Pepper," he repeated, and her name was a command.

Unwillingly, she turned back.

He watched her with an intensity that stripped her pretense away and made an exhibition of her cowardice. "This isn't the end. We will talk, and when we do, you'll tell me the truth."

With an irony she thought lost on him, she said, "I hope we both live that long."

"Mrs. Dreiss got the plants I sent her!"

Dan watched as Pepper clasped her hands and gazed at the large garden behind the house. He had known she would be excited; he hadn't realized she would flush pink with delight.

She pointed. "Look at the greenhouse. It's twice the size it was before!"

Like some sort of construction peacock, he strutted his manly skills. "Mrs. Dreiss wanted someplace to try out the seeds you sent her, so I added on."

"Did they grow? Do you know? She and I used to cultivate new flower colors all the time, and we tried to create some winter-hardy varieties of the more tender perennials. After I left, I kept trying and I sent seeds and shoots back every chance I got . . . look!" Pepper bounded across the garden. "This is a new variety of primrose!"

What he knew about plants he'd learned from being around Mrs. Dreiss and listening to her. Now Pepper chattered in the same way, with affection and exhilaration, and he experienced an expanding gratification. Flowers didn't feed the cattle or paint the barn, but they had been important to Mrs. Dreiss, and they were important to Pepper, and he had kept up the garden for them.

Pepper knelt beside a row of large green leaves sprouting from the ground and brushed the mulch away. "Look at the size of these hostas! They're so big. She must have cross-cultivated them with an elephant!"

He should be more wary of Pepper. She had torn his life apart once. She could do it again with a smile—or with a gun.

He didn't like to remember the day he'd received his belly wound—the day he killed Schuster's son. His previous encounter with the bastard had left Dan's face stitched together like Frankenstein's monster. Dan had had the scent of revenge rich in his nostrils, and he hadn't cared if he died achieving it. *He hadn't cared if he died.*

He still hadn't regained the instinct that had carried him through so much action—the compulsion to survive at all costs. He found it odd that he went through the motions of keeping this place safe, yet faced life bolstered only with the determination to bring that bastard Schuster down.

Yet ever since that night Pepper arrived, he'd felt stirrings. Lust, need, anger . . . What an interesting thing, to face a woman and wonder if she was his deliverance, and to know that it didn't matter if she was, because he had to have her—even if she was his damnation.

He'd told her about the security system, downplaying its sophistication, and waited to see if she would try to sabotage it.

She hadn't. She had slept without moving all night.

He knew. He had gone to her bedroom several times to check, and had remained to stare at her, wishing she would wake so he could join her on the mattress.

"Look at that raspberry patch. She was trying to develop a seedless blackberry when I was here. Dan, do you know where she kept her records?" Pepper called. "I need to look them over as soon as possible."

"I put them away for you. Remind me this evening and I'll find them." If Pepper was a terrorist, she played the part of an innocent to perfection, for with each passing moment, he grew more certain of her innocence.

He should have her removed from the ranch.

But he didn't want to. He wanted her here where he could try to unravel the mystery that was Pepper Prescott. Schuster hadn't arrived in America yet.

Schuster's boys were still scattered across the Northwest. It was safe to keep her here a while longer.

"Look at how much she's done in nine years." Pepper's arms embraced the garden area. "This is beyond belief!"

When Dan was an adolescent, he had found a kindred spirit in Pepper. Like her, he hadn't wanted to be in Diamond. He considered Diamond a quiet backwater, set apart from America by the mountains and made different by the hearty souls who lived here. As he watched TV and read books, he longed for the adventure he knew lurked down the road.

Now he knew what kind of adventure lurked out in the world. He wished he didn't, but he could never go back to being the innocent he had been before. He would never again step into a room without assessing every person in it; he would never again ignore a footstep behind him.

"This must be the rosemary I sent her." Pepper pinched off a branch, sniffed it, and laughed. "I did it. I created a winter-hardy rosemary! I tell you, we can start a seed company and make a tidy living."

Now Pepper's animation and her enthusiasm washed over him. She wore the cowboy hat he had given her. It protected her from the sun, which burned so intensely at this altitude, and he experienced the satisfaction of a barbarian who sheltered his woman.

"That's what I thought Mrs. Dreiss and I would do when I came back . . ." She faltered. Her head dropped, and her fingers trembled as she touched the rosemary lovingly. "Rosemary for remembrance."

She was mourning again.

Making his way through the rows waiting to be planted, he knelt beside her. Sliding his arm around her back, he removed her hat and pulled her into his chest.

She came willingly, burrowing into him, accepting his solace. He loved the weight of her leaning against him, and the scent of her, a combination of woman, earth, and rosemary.

Would it have been like this if she had stayed in Diamond, conversations and closeness, or would Russell and the burden of the town's disapproval have separated them?

Drawing away, Pepper said, "Thank you. It's still a shock to realize she isn't here. I keep expecting her to call me from the house to come in and do my homework." Smiling feebly, she dabbed at her nose with her sleeve.

Because she was vulnerable, he pressed his advantage. "If she were here, what would you tell her you'd been doing while you were gone?"

Pepper's gaze flashed up to meet his, then sidled away. Coolly she stood and brushed the dirt off her knees. "I would tell her I'd been doing landscaping. What else?"

There it was again. The sure knowledge that she was lying, hiding from something or someone. He needed to remember that when his lust threatened to overwhelm him and caution slipped away.

Pepper Prescott hadn't come back to seek him. She had come back to seek safety, or to set him up.

He had to determine which.

Fifteen

On Pepper's third day on the ranch, a knock sounded on her bedroom door. Cool air nipped at her nose. Dan's voice called, "Rise and shine."

Without opening her eyes, she snapped, "I am not a star."

He chuckled. The sound of his boots moved into the kitchen.

Five o'clock. In the morning. Again.

This morning it was colder, and Pepper tried futilely to keep both of her feet off the chilly floor as she hopped into her clothes. She raced for the kitchen, wanting the warmth of the stove and the heat of the coffee.

"Morning, sunshine," a man's voice said. A man who was not Dan.

She blinked at the two masculine figures. It was that red-haired cowboy, the obnoxious one who had leered at her, who had made fun of Dan for being old . . . who had dropped the salt block into the truck. Desperately, she tried to recall his name. "Sonny."

Sonny was almost as tall as Dan, a buff guy with rangy long legs. On the basis of a few minutes' conversation, she knew he was impressed with himself and his abilities with women. Putting his hand over his heart, he said, "What a honey. You remembered my name!" He smacked his fist into Dan's shoulder. "I told you she liked me best."

Enigmatically, Dan said, "Sonny, when you're handed rope, you don't always have to make yourself a noose."

But she'd told Sonny she was leaving that afternoon and now he knew she had stayed over. She knew this kind of guy; he would put the worst possible interpretation on her presence, and he probably thought it was okay to make a pass because she was easy.

Some things never changed.

She stammered, "I . . . I didn't leave because . . ."

"I know, Dan told me." Sonny winked at her.

She took a long breath, preparing to berate Dan for what he'd said. What he must have said to put that smirk on Sonny's face.

But Sonny continued, "It was a good thing you had him to call when your car conked out, but you could have called me."

Gradually she let out her breath. The two men looked nothing alike, yet still they resembled each other. Something about the way they stood, the way their eyes moved around the room, as if they were always aware of what was hidden from lesser mortals. "Better the devil you know," she retorted.

Sonny laughed out loud. "No wonder the lieutenant is keeping you here. He likes 'em witty." He flinched as if he'd said too much. "Not that he's a lieutenant anymore."

Coolly she answered, "Nor is he keeping me here."

Sonny blundered on. "No, of course not. This ranch is your place, so technically, you're keeping . . . him . . . here." He withered under Dan's narrowed eyes. "Sorry, sir. I'll just . . . um . . . wait out here on the porch."

"Go on down and do the chores," Dan ordered.

"Yes, sir. Ma'am." With a nod in Pepper's direction, Sonny slipped out the door.

Dan poured her a cup of coffee and handed it to her. "Sonny may act like a blithering idiot, but he's good in a tight spot."

Hostility radiated from her. "So?"

"So I've got a doctor's appointment today. Remember?"

"I remember." The aroma of fresh-ground beans lured her into taking a sip and then another. Glaring at Dan over the rim of her cup, she said, "Which doesn't explain why Sonny knows more than he should."

"He brought over Dad's car for me to drive so you could use my truck. I don't want to leave you here without wheels in case anything . . . in case you need to go somewhere."

"But that doesn't explain why—"

"He's going to do the chores this morning and tonight."

"I can do them." In irritation, she walked away from him. "In fact, I don't want Sonny doing them."

Dan thoughtfully considered her.

She flushed. She sounded like a petulant child. As caffeine spread warmth through her veins, she used a more reasonable tone. "I want to do the chores myself. After you leave, I'll have to, won't I?"

"So you will." His deep voice conveyed meanings the mere words did not.

His blond hair shone with golden highlights. He wore a black, starched, long-sleeved shirt that made his broad shoulders look even broader, and a pair of tan wool slacks that hugged his long legs and his tight ass. Dressed like a ranch hand, he was handsome. Dressed like this, he was mouthwatering, and her hands itched to stroke the contours beneath the clothes.

Sinking down on a chair, she wrapped her hands around the cup, soaking in the heat.

Thank heavens he was leaving. If he stood around, she'd be hard pressed not to bring him down like a . . . well, like a gazelle bringing down a lion in some surreal National Geographic special.

Dan said, "When I drive by the barn, I'll tell Sonny to leave the evening chores for you. But if you need him, give him a call at the bunkhouse. The number's by the phone."

"Sure." She realized he was watching her watch him.

As usual, he seemed to know exactly what she was thinking.

Snapping out of her daze, she asked, "Why did you tell Sonny I owned the ranch? Now he knows my name!"

"A slip of the tongue. You don't have to worry. I'd trust Sonny with my life—and yours."

Was Dan trying to tell her something?

When she tried to speak again, Dan said, "I apologize. It won't happen again. I'm usually very discreet."

She wanted to rail at him, but how could she? She didn't believe him. Dan Graham's tongue didn't slip. So what was he trying to do? She watched him uneasily, and realized that for all that sexual tension stretched between them like a taut line, she didn't trust him. "Well . . . okay. As long as you don't tell anyone else. No one else, Dan!"

"I promise."

She looked down at the pale curl of steam coming off the coffee and wished she could free herself from the tangle her life had become. This was what happened when she got involved with other people. This was what happened when she got involved . . . with Dan.

"Pepper, tell me what's wrong. I can help you." His warm voice caressed her, inviting her to give over her inhibitions.

But she knew no one could help her. "Don't worry about me. I'll be fine while you're gone. I can keep busy in the garden. I'll uncover the rest of the plants."

He walked to the table, stood over her until she looked up into his face. "Don't uncover the plants. We're getting a cold front and possibly snow."

"But it's June."

"It's the mountains. The mountains weed out the weak and leave the strong behind."

Was he talking about her? Was he trying to tell her something? It was too early in the morning for enigmatic messages.

"If I'm going to get to Boise in time for my appointment, I'd better scoot." He shrugged into his coat. "I've got the grocery list, but if it snows, I'll spend the night down in the lowlands."

"That would be great!"

His face lost all expression. "Will it?"

"I mean . . ." She meant that it would be a relief to have a day alone without the strain of pretending she felt nothing for him when what she really wanted to do was rip off his clothes and her clothes and . . . "I mean I can get a lot done around here without you underfoot."

"It'll be late tonight, if at all." Dan removed the cup from Pepper's grasp, slid his arm around her waist, and brought her to her feet. "Try to miss me."

Fool that she was, she hadn't foreseen this. Yesterday he could have kissed her and didn't. Today he touched her as if he could not stop himself, as if he were leaving for battle and might never return. The slow sensuality with which he drew her to him frightened her with its power. She couldn't look away from him and his deep brown eyes and his sculpted face, and when their bodies met, she lost her breath at the burning sweetness of their joining. Bending her back, he pressed a single, close-lipped kiss on her—a kiss no less intense for its restraint.

He released her, handed her her cup back, and walked out the door.

The brisk wind swept through the kitchen, but she stood staring, her coffee forgotten.

If she defeated General Napier and gained control of Mrs. Dreiss's land, what was she going to do?

Dan might move out, but still he and his lush sexuality and his unspoken promises of pleasure would reside right across the valley. She would see him often, he would make sure of that. She'd spend her time with her breasts and loins aching while her heart longed for something she dared not take.

Pepper blinked in dismay. Rushing toward the window, she watched him as he fit his long body into a low-slung, bright red Corvette. Although he couldn't see her, she lifted her hand to wave as he drove away, then snatched it back and cradled her fist to her chest.

When had she become a living, breathing country-western song?

Dan pulled the car into the barn, where Sonny stood waiting.

All Sonny's swagger had vanished, and he was grim and businesslike as he helped Dan fit the Corvette with a tracking device and a screen that tapped Dan into a satellite view of his surroundings.

Wiping his greasy hands, Sonny said, "Okay, Lieutenant, there you go. You'll know it if someone follows you. But if they do, what are you going to do about it?"

"I've got my pistol and a few other surprises. Plus, this car does move out." Dan patted the Corvette's hood. "Thank God for Dad's midlife crisis."

Sonny didn't grin back. "I still say I should go with you."

"I need you here."

Sonny tossed the rag aside. "I haven't spotted any sign of trouble around the ranch. It's as quiet as a grave, and just as boring."

"Colonel Jaffe worries about a possible terrorist plant among the cowboys."

"Other than me, there's no one new except for that

kid. TJ. Wagner and Yarnell are staying in Diamond, and they say nothing suspicious is going on. Unless the terrorists bought the loyalty of one of your old hands, this place is clean as a whistle."

"And just as boring," Dan finished for him. "Anything's possible, and you know it. That's why you're needed here."

"To keep an eye on *her*?" Sonny pointed toward the house. "That's babysitting, sir. Glenda, or Pepper, or whatever her name is, is no terrorist."

Dan's amusement faded. "Do you have a reason for trusting her—besides the fact she's one good-looking woman?"

"Yes, sir. You seem to have confidence in her, and you're better at reading character than any man I've ever met."

A dull pain ripped through Dan's gut where young Schuster's knife had sliced him, and his mouth curled with a bitterness he could taste. "Thanks, Sonny, but if you'll recall, I'm not infallible, and this is too important a mission to mess up now."

"Exactly," Sonny argued. "You're too important to this mission. You shouldn't go to Boise. It's a three-hour drive through open country. Far too risky, sir."

"If someone is watching me, I want to give the impression of being carefree and unprepared for attack. I don't want to change my schedule."

"Who's going to know?" Sonny argued.

Dan cast him an eloquent glance.

"All right, it's true," Sonny admitted grudgingly. "Everyone in Diamond is familiar with your schedule."

"I don't want to scare off Schuster's boys. I want to lure them in, and right now, every one of them is still accounted for and far away. I'm as safe as can be. You know it." Dan squeezed himself into the low, tight seat. "You just want to get out of chasing cows in this weather."

Sonny gave up. "Can you blame me?"

"Not at all." Dan gave the equipment one final check. "So you stay here in the barn and keep an eye on the road. Don't let anyone come in. Don't let her go." He revved the engine. "Keep her safe."

Sixteen

"*Brr.*" Dr. Melling shivered as she walked Dan out of the Veterans Hospital in Boise. "I planted my tomatoes yesterday, and today it feels like snow."

He cast a knowledgeable eye at the gray sky. "Not down here, but in the high country for sure. I won't get home before it starts."

"Should you stay in Boise overnight?" She huddled into her light, surgical scrubs and made her offer. "I can put you up."

Dr. Melling was a combat-toughened soldier. She was attractive, articulate, and intelligent. She'd read the reports; she understood what he'd been through in a way no one else could. If there had never been a Pepper, Dr. Melling would have had a boarder tonight.

She never stood a chance.

With innate courtesy, he said, "Thank you, but if it's going to snow, I have to get the cattle in."

She nodded as if her offer had meant as little as his

rejection. "Sounds like rough work. I gave you a clean bill of health, but you should take it easy if you want to get back into combat soon."

She didn't realize that right now he was on active duty.

She misunderstood his silence, for sternly she said, "I outrank you, Lieutenant, and I'm ordering you, take it easy."

"Yes, ma'am."

With a wave, she strode back into the hospital.

It wasn't yet noon when he headed up Highway 95. As he drove into the mountains toward Diamond, it grew wintry. The cold front was moving in.

He checked the satellite screen. No one was behind him. No ambush lurked ahead. He was right, the trip to Boise had been uneventful—damn it.

Now, more than ever, he wanted the waiting to be over. He wanted to know where Pepper's loyalty lay and what she was hiding from him. He wanted to know whether the interest she showed in the ranch was real, whether that interest could be nurtured into a desire to remain. For if she decided to stay, that would relieve the sense of urgency that drove him to stake his claim on her.

He smiled in biting amusement. He was lying to himself. Nothing would relieve his sense of urgency except the act of claiming her itself.

And he hoped, with a fervency that rocked his world, that he was right about her. That Sonny was right about her. That she was innocent, that he could claim her—and not arrest her.

Before he reached Diamond, he held a brief, cheerless conversation with Colonel Jaffe during which he reported an uneventful trip. Colonel Jaffe told him the terrorists had not moved yet and reiterated his desire to see Dan attacked. Dan agreed.

Then he drove into Diamond, down the single main street, parked by the stoplight, pulled out his grocery list, and strode inside Hardwick's General Store. When he saw the crowd, he wanted to groan. Half the ranchers in the area were there with their wives, and a chorus of, "Hey, stranger!" went up as soon as Dan set foot in the door.

He raised his hand in greeting. He knew them all. Had gone to school with them or their kids. He needed to get in and out without trouble, and that included keeping Pepper's secret as well as avoiding a terrorist attack.

His gaze slid to Wagner and Yarnell, seated right in the midst of the ranchers and looking like a couple of goobers. That was their disguise, to pretend to be low-landers who came looking for the clean life, and as silly as they looked in their overalls and their fishing hats, they might have been born to the part. Dan hoped to hell they remembered how to shoot an AK-47.

To the owner, he said, "Cold snap must be good for business."

"It sure is." Mrs. Hardwick was old enough to be his mother, and she always checked out his ass as well as his groceries. "It got you in here, didn't it?"

Everyone laughed.

"Come on out to dinner sometime," Rebecca Hunter called. Mrs. Hunter cherished hopes that he would be stricken with admiration for her oldest, Gloria. As Gloria had once told him, she didn't need a husband to run the ranch when she inherited it, but if she did, he would be the one. He had been flattered, because Gloria was a hell of a woman.

"I'll do that, Mrs. Hunter," he said, not meaning a word of it.

"When are you coming in for a haircut?" called Rita's father. "A *man's* haircut." Mr. Johnson had been the barber in Diamond for more years than Dan could remember, and he only knew one kind of haircut, one that involved a pair of electric clippers and a bare scalp. Dan hadn't been to him since he was old enough to drive himself elsewhere.

Dan kept his hat firmly on his head and lied, "Just got one."

He consulted his grocery list. He didn't know where half this stuff was, and when he told Mrs. Hardwick what he wanted, her bushy gray eyebrows went up. "Are you learning to cook?"

Her loud voice put everyone on alert.

She headed for the meats. "I would have never guessed you even knew what to do with a pork tenderloin."

"Cooking's not so hard," Charlie James said. "Except for my wife."

His wife landed a smack on his arm hard enough to break it.

"You know what it means when a man starts cooking," Chris Bardey said. He and Charlie put their heads together and yodeled, "He's getting a little."

Those two guys had been assholes in high school, and they hadn't grown up one bit. Dan felt sorry for their wives, red-faced and embarrassed.

Grabbing a basket, he walked off toward the canned goods, hoping to find artichoke hearts and wishing that he'd stopped in Boise for the groceries. Terrorists posed less of a threat than running the gauntlet in here, facing the people he'd known all his life and realizing he had nothing in common with them. It was spooky to come back to a town and see that nothing was different. Nothing had changed . . . except him.

As he made his way back up to the checkout, Rita Johnson stepped into the store.

Dan almost groaned aloud.

Poor Rita, head of the cheerleaders, all-American girl, honor student. She'd done only one wild thing in her life—befriending Pepper Prescott. The adults had thought she did it out of charity instead of a desire to be crazy just once before she settled down. Now she was the worst thing a woman could be in Diamond—divorced with two kids.

But the brave young woman looked around at the two dozen inquisitive, pitying eyes, lifted her chin, and walked right in.

When she spied Dan, she almost walked right out again.

Her father came off the bench, grabbed her, and dragged her toward Dan. "Rita, look who's here! Only the other night, you were wondering how Dan was doing, living all alone by himself." For emphasis, he added, "Lonely."

She probably had wondered, poor girl. Not because she wanted to bear his children, as her father—and his— so obviously hoped, but because she was a nice woman who had known him since kindergarten. "Good to see you, Rita," he said. "Heard any gossip lately?"

She blinked at him in bewilderment, then caught his drift and bit her lip to stop her smile. "Doug Weber's going with Vicki White."

"I thought she was married."

"Not anymore." With relish she added, "There's been a rash of divorces around town."

The avid gazes throughout the room started falling.

"Your dad's seeing someone in McCall."

Startled, he said, "But that's where my mom lives. Couldn't he do his catting somewhere else?"

"He's a man, and like most men, a creature of bad habit." She condemned the gender with relish. "And Cheryl Kenner made a pass at me."

"Wow." Dan was startled. "I guess she came out of the closet."

"She did. Myself, I'm thinking about becoming bisexual."

Mr. Johnson coughed so hard someone smacked him on the back.

"Why's that?" Dan asked.

Rita delivered the line with style and panache. "It'll double my chances of getting a date on Saturday night."

Rita had just confirmed Dan's suspicions. She had developed a sense of humor sharpened to a razor's edge by marriage, divorce, and disappointment. With a grin, he asked, "Is that all?"

"That's it," Rita assured him, and nodded reassuringly.

"Great! My grocery order is made up. I have to go." He paid Mrs. Hardwick and ducked out with his bags.

Rita had not told him that Pepper Prescott was back in town, but what did that reassuring nod mean? Either Russell had kept Pepper's secret—or he'd warned Rita to keep quiet. Rita would be discreet, Dan was sure, but he would speak sternly to his dad.

At last he was ready to do what he'd wished to do since the moment Pepper had walked back into his life. He set out to find the place where her car went hurtling down a cliff. He hoped the snow held off long enough for him to find the spot, for while the Corvette handled beautifully under dry conditions, it wasn't worth a damn on ice, and Dan didn't look forward to driving down a snowy road at ten miles an hour.

But he would. He had deliberately misled Pepper about his intentions for tonight. Nothing could keep him away from the house where she slept. Sure as hell not a little spring snowstorm.

Luckily, he didn't have many places to look. Not a lot of areas around here had a gravel road and a steep drop-off and were located close enough to Mrs. Dreiss's house that Pepper could have walked in after an accident. First he headed up toward Kauffman Creek, but a slow drive up the incline produced nothing. No skid marks, no slide where a car would have gone over the edge.

Next he drove toward Reformation Butte. Again nothing. But the road had obviously been graded not twenty-four hours before; any marks she'd made would have been obliterated by the blade.

It was three o'clock, and the clouds piled in as he cut across to Gray Peak. The winds were picking up, making the pines creak and groan, and he drove slowly, his head out the window, watching the side of the road for signs that something had gone down the steep grade toward the creek far below.

He found marks at the top of the last rise, on the downward slope toward the valley. He stopped, got out, and examined the road. There were no skid marks, no signs that she'd been driving too fast or hit a loose patch of gravel and lost control. But the mound of dirt on the side of the road clearly showed where the tires had passed over it.

As he suspected, she hadn't had an accident. She'd sent that car off the cliff on purpose.

Standing there at the top of the steep, tree-laden slope, he could see the glint of metal far below. More important, he could smell the faint scent of melted plastic, scorched paint, and heated metal. The car had burned, or she had set it on fire.

This confirmed one thing—she hadn't been sent by the terrorists. The terrorists who wanted to kill him were professionals, and they would never manage this job so badly. She would have appeared, carefree and beautiful, dressed to kill—armed to kill.

His mind clicked off questions and possible answers.

Why had she pushed her car off a cliff? Why did she look at him with such wariness, such fear?

She was running away.

From the police?

Maybe.

Was she running from an obssessed lover? A husband?

No, not a husband. She didn't wear the mark of a ring on her finger.

Dan himself was on his way to feeling obsessive about her. Obsessive and, as he looked at the twisted ruin of Pepper's car, angry. She had lied to him. Why? Why risk her life to perform such a dangerous act? If she was in so much trouble, why didn't she tell him?

He needed information, and he needed it now.

He was going back to the ranch. To Pepper. There he would find all the answers he could possibly desire.

Pepper turned off the television. Still no mention of an investigation involving General Jennifer Napier. In fact, CNN said the general had returned to Washington, D.C., after a successful book tour.

In Washington the general would use her considerable power to search the Texas records to determine how many married couples had committed crimes approximately fourteen years ago, to discover Jackie Porter's real name and to trace her through the foster care system.

Yet . . . the one time Pepper had tried to trace her siblings, the records from Hobart, Texas, had been unavailable because of a fire at the courthouse. If Pepper were lucky, and she was praying she was, that would slow General Napier down.

Looking out the window, Pepper laughed aloud in a brief explosion of heady relief. White flakes drifted on the wind, and the afternoon faded into premature night.

Sonny Midler had been told to stay home. General Jennifer Napier couldn't arrive, either alone or with her terrorist friends.

Best of all, no Dan Graham roamed the house to fill the atmosphere with the erotic scent of his sexuality and his intentions. He said he wouldn't be here until late tonight. He promised he'd stay in Boise if it snowed. For the first time since she had seen General Napier shoot her aide, Pepper was alone and wholly safe. She intended to enjoy herself, to be herself, away from the brooding gaze of Dan's dark eyes.

She shrugged uncomfortably. What was this emotion that possessed her when he was around? It couldn't be love. Lust, yes—she recognized that. But the love she'd felt for him all those years ago hadn't been this madness of pleasure and devastating want. When he was with her, guilt roiled in her, for she hadn't removed him from harm's way. Satisfaction plagued her, for against all logic, she believed he could keep her safe. Gratification bedeviled her, for he observed her with such obvious desire.

But she'd lost him before when she'd run away and she had survived. She could survive not having him now. For this evening, he was gone, and she could put the past—her past, his past—behind her. Tonight she would do as she wished. As soon as she got done with chores, she could do girly things—a manicure and a facial perhaps. Or she could get the scissors and improve the hack job she'd done on her hair in that alley.

Slipping into her coat, her boots, and her winter hat, she hurried along the path to the barn, the swirling flakes dancing in the beam of her flashlight.

Dan never seemed to care what her hair looked like. His seductive gaze lingered on her curls as if the sight gave him pleasure. She shivered at the memory and told herself it was the cold.

At the barn Samson stood impatiently by the door, waiting for her to let him in. He glared at her, the whites of his eyes showing, and as she fumbled for the lock, she said, "I do see the resemblance between you and Russell."

Giving a snort, Samson shoved her with his nose.

Slipping in the mud, the manure, and the snow, she landed on her hands and knees. Half-liquid, half-solid, all stinking, the muck splashed up her arms and all over her jeans.

Samson tossed his head and nickered as if laughing.

"You miserable beast." She climbed to her feet, wiped off the worst of the slime, and glared at him. "If you weren't already a gelding, I'd make you one."

She opened the door and Samson trotted right in, more pleased with himself than any one horse had the right to be.

The interior was still and quiet, rich with the smells of leather, hay, and horse. The hens huddled in the warmth of their house. Satisfied that he had triumphed over the lowly creature who cared for him, Samson went right to his stall. As she fed him, she asked him, "You and Russell are brothers, aren't you? You have different mothers, but you both think you know what's right for Dan and you both think you can push me around. You can't."

Samson chewed his grain and examined her wet, stinking clothes with a jaundiced eye.

"Sure, you can knock me in the muck, but I'll rise again." With a flourish, she shut the stall. "And you'd better be nice to me, or there'll be no breakfast!"

From his impatient shake of the head, it was obvious Samson didn't take her threat seriously.

She finished the chores and hustled back to the house, freezing as the cold cut through the sopping material at her knees and cuffs.

On the porch she prepared to strip out of her clothes. But first she glanced around to see if anyone was watching. *Foolishness.* In the darkness and the cold, with the snow blowing sideways, there was no one to see her. Yet Dan had left his imprint on her, making her aware of her body as she hadn't been since those long-ago teenage days in Diamond.

God, she wanted him. She *wanted* him. She feared him. She feared the desire he elicited from her. She feared the control he had over her mind, the way he visited her dreams at night, and not only her dreams, but her waking fantasies.

She tossed her outerwear on the swing, then struggled out of her jeans. The wind whistled at her bare skin, turning her blue in an instant, and she scampered inside. Dropping the jeans and her shirt in the washer, she turned it on and headed for the bathroom, leaving an aromatic trail behind her.

That shower was the longest she had ever taken. Removing all trace of the barnyard, she scrubbed herself until her skin turned pink and she glowed all over.

With the water running, she didn't hear the alarm buzz in the dining room.

She ran barefoot back to her room and rubbed her hands together. It was chilly in here, but if she went into the kitchen and turned on the oven . . . she grinned.

There was never really a doubt what she would do tonight.

She would bake.

Swiftly she donned a red cotton sweater and a matching red wraparound skirt. She was warm, she was comfortable, and she was ready to make cookies.

She found the recipes in the small, flowered tin box set on the shelf over the stove. She spread them out on the counter and examined the yellowed cards, written in Mrs. Dreiss's elegant penmanship.

Peanut butter. Oatmeal butterscotch. No . . .

Snickerdoodles first. She hadn't had snickerdoodles since she'd left Diamond. Old-fashioned, homey, cinnamony cookies with the elegant crunch of whole wheat, snickerdoodles were her favorite. She set the oven to three fifty, gathered the ingredients on the counter, and assembled the dough.

The wind blew around the eaves. She hummed as she worked. She didn't hear the car door shut or the boots on the porch.

But the sound of the door shutting made her drop the spoon. She jumped.

General Napier.

Pepper whirled to face . . . Dan.

He was here, a dark shadow against the white painted wood, a menacing figure who dominated the room with his size and his impatience.

He looked angry. He looked edgy. He looked dangerous, more dangerous than the men Russell had warned her about. More dangerous than any attack General Napier could launch.

First Pepper sagged with the release of tension.

It wasn't the general. Pepper was safe.

Then her heart leaped with the joy of seeing Dan so unexpectedly.

Finally, she stiffened with shock, exhilaration . . . and a different kind of fear entirely.

This man wanted her. He made it clear every moment he was with her. Now without moving or saying a word, he clarified his need . . . and his impatience.

She backed up until the edge of the table dug into her thighs. She clutched the painted surface so tightly with her hands that the blood left her fingers. "I didn't expect you back today."

"I can see that." His voice caressed her nerves like velvet made audible, and he lingered in the shadows. He was created to linger in the shadows, and the shadows loved him.

"You're interrupting me. I was"—nervously she gestured at the laden countertop—"baking. How was the doctor's visit?"

"I got a clean bill of health." He stepped away from the door.

Toward her. "Good. Good." She sidled toward the dining room. "If you'll give me a minute, I'll change into my jeans and we can talk."

"Don't bother." His voice was rough, as if he'd been ill. But he hadn't been; she knew that as clearly as she felt the blaze of lust emanating from him. His difficulty in speaking rose from too much desire, restrained too long. "I warn you, that scheme of yours is worthless."

Alarm skittered along her nerves. What did he mean?

Running from General Napier? Hiding here? Proving her innocence? "Wh . . . what are you talking about?"

"The way you dress." He indicated her bare legs, her bare feet. "You might as well wear a skirt every day. You wear those jeans all the time, and you imagine they'll keep me at bay, under control."

She couldn't see his eyes; they were dark, shadowed pools, yet she knew how he looked at her. With a passion that fed on the sight of her legs—and the knowledge of what was beneath her skirt.

He continued, "Yet those worn jeans cling to your thighs, caressing every muscle, and I watch you walk and work and imagine how it will feel when your thighs are beside mine, I'm inside you, and you're riding me, up and down, taking me so close to the sun we're both going to burn alive."

Her knees gave out. She sat against the table and raised a shaking hand to her throat. She wasn't afraid of confrontation. She made her way intrepidly in the world. But his bold speaking roused passions in her, and she feared those, and what would happen when they were unleashed.

His eyes glittered with dark fire as he removed his hat and dusted the snow from the brim. His blond hair was wild and tousled. He moved into the light, and she caught her breath at the stark ruthlessness of his face.

"What happened?" Her own voice rasped in her throat, tight with the tension of fear and desire. "Why are you like this?" What had lifted his restraint and vanquished his patience?

"What happened?" he repeated. "That's my question.

What happened to you? Where have you been? What have you been doing?"

"When? Today?" Then she realized: He was asking more than that. He wanted her story since the day she'd left him, and he wanted it now.

But she wouldn't tell him. The man who stood before her was not some kindly confessor who would soothe her fears and help her get justice. He wanted everything from her, and he would give nothing. She straightened her shoulders and lifted her chin. "I'll tell you where I've been when you tell me what you've been doing."

"You're a changeling. I think I know you, then you surprise me." He stepped close against her, his broad shoulders throwing his shadow on her. He didn't touch her, yet he stood so close she could feel the heat radiating off him. "I think you're all that's genuine and wholesome, and you push your car down an embankment and set it on fire."

She blanched. "How did you . . . ?" Oh, no. She had just admitted everything.

"Are you a criminal, my darling?" He stroked the ends of her short hair with his fingertips. "Did you steal the car? Are you running away from the police? Tell me." The scent of him enveloped her, soap and shaving cream and a warm, masculine aroma redolent of unhurried, wet kisses and sex that lingered far into the night.

She wanted to tell him. But an innate caution held her back. She had sent that e-mail to Senator Vargas accusing General Napier of murder. Surely by now someone had read it, had assessed it as from Pepper and genuine, and was taking action. Surely soon she would hear something on the news that indicated an investigation was in progress.

If not, she would contact Homeland Security. She feared that then they—the general, the police, the government—would trace her here, but she had to act for her own safety, for Dan's, and the country's.

She drew a shuddering breath. "I can't, but I'm not . . . I'm not . . ."

"Honest?"

Abruptly, she realized he was more than aroused. He was furious.

He had his reasons.

But she had her reasons too, and she didn't take that kind of insult from anyone. Clenching her fists, she said, "Let me be honest now. The truth is, I don't trust you. I don't know you. You're not the boy I loved. You're not the man he should have become. You're someone else, and you won't tell me who. So why should I tell you anything? Tell me that, Dan. Why should I be *honest* with you?"

He stared into her eyes, and she saw right into the tumultuous depths of his soul. Fury, desire, old love, and new betrayal shivered and moved in his soul like boulders before the force of a creeping glacier. Tonight he had left civilization far, far behind.

Right now he didn't care that she didn't trust him. He wanted her, and he was going to take her. The patience she'd imagined in him had never been there; he had only been waiting. Waiting until he couldn't bear to wait any longer.

Now he couldn't bear it anymore.

"But I am the boy you loved, because I remember

every last moment of our time together." Leaning down, he inhaled above her hair. "Do you know what you did to me when you left? You left me the memory of how you smelled, the little sounds you made, the way we fit together so perfectly. You branded me with yourself, and I could never lose myself in another woman." For a second, just a second, he rested his cheek on the top of her head. "Did you think I would forgive you for that?"

Her legs quaked as his words ruffled her hair. "I never asked for your forgiveness."

"All too true. I never wanted you to." His hand slid around her neck. "You're going to beg for it."

Beg? For forgiveness? Or sex?

She wanted to demand the answer, but she couldn't.

Because he tilted her head up and kissed her.

Seventeen

Dan possessed her with his mouth, scraping his teeth along Pepper's lower lip, rasping the sensitive nerves. He slid his tongue around her mouth, then entered slowly, dragging out the anticipation and bringing her to her toes.

She wouldn't fight; she wasn't stupid enough for that. She was alone with a man barely brushed by civilized behavior. With very little encouragement, he would bop her on the head and drag her to his cave.

But she could refuse to reply to his enticement, and she did. She clutched the table with her fists, rejecting the urge to embrace him. She wasn't afraid of confronting him, but she was afraid of him sexually. He wouldn't hurt her, not physically, but he could wound her in the secret places of her soul, and she would be a fool to give in to him.

He drew back from her. "That's right, darling. Resist. That makes your surrender all the sweeter." Lifting her onto the table, he slid his hands up her thighs, opening the edges of her wraparound skirt. His callused palms chafed her smooth skin, and the intimacy made her breath rasp in her throat. He stroked her as if the sensation of her skin against his gave him pleasure.

She didn't know what kind of satisfaction the contact gave him, she only knew he sapped her strength with his touch. Or . . . not her strength. Her good sense, because she wanted to plead that he go higher.

Dear Lord, she *was* a fool. For him.

His fingers slid up and down the seam of her panties at her crotch. "This is in my way."

"Heaven forbid anything should ever be in your way." Her attempt at sarcasm fell flat when he pulled out his pocket knife. With a flip of his thumb, the blade slid out, long and sharply gleaming. Before she had an inkling of his intention, the cool metal slid along her thigh, under her panties, and sliced them away. The spandex material curled up around her waist, then the knife slid up her belly and even the shreds fell to the table.

The shock of his action gave her an illicit thrill. A stupid thrill. "Are you crazy?" she demanded.

"Absolutely. We can definitely say I'm crazy." The blade slid smoothly back into the handle and he pocketed the knife. A long breath lifted his chest as he stared at her.

Fear scuttled along her nerves. He was too big. Too fast. Too much of a bully. Too demanding.

And looking at him made her damp between the legs. Ever since she'd arrived, she had ached inside, suffering from a need strong and sharp in her womb, in the center of her being. Every minute of the day, he made her aware she was a woman who craved her man. Her denials availed her nothing in this game of desperate desire. Denials only made her want him more.

Now his finger slid along the crease between her thigh and the hair that protected her womanhood.

A damned ineffectual protection it proved, for she shuddered as the sensitive nerves tingled in reaction.

"Tell me. Tell me what you're running away from." He thrust his finger inside her. All the way inside her.

"Bastard," she breathed. "You bastard." He tormented her, using her body against her to gain information. She was wholly involved—wanting him, overwhelmed with passion. And he wasn't. He retained enough sense and distance to interrogate her. "You dirty son of a bitch!" She kicked at him.

He caught her foot, lifting it to rest on his shoulder. "Bastard? Son of a bitch? Why? Because I'm giving you what you want?"

She struggled to stay upright, not to tumble onto her back. "I don't want this!" She leaned back on her hands, tried to jerk her foot free.

"Really?" He drew his finger partly out of her very slowly, using the moisture of her body to smooth the way. She was slick inside, and with his assistance she was slick outside too. "Honey, you can lie all you want. Your body tells the truth."

She jerked her foot again. She was wide open, but this time when she kicked with her other foot, she connected with his thigh.

He didn't flinch, but he did let her foot go. Yet his finger was still inside her, moving restlessly. "What are you running away from?"

She couldn't tell him. Not about General Napier. Not when he was a soldier. Not when he remembered her larcenous past.

She scooted away.

He never lost contact, and he was demanding. He would know the truth, or at least part of the truth, so she said, "I got involved with the wrong person."

"Ah," he breathed. "That's what I thought."

"What do you mean, 'That's what I thought?'"

He twisted his finger, driving her to the edge of excitement. "I always wondered why you left, and finally I decided you ran away from me, from what we had, because you wanted to taste the world. So tell me, how many others were there?"

"How many what?"

"Tell me"—his breath brushed her ear—"how many men were there?"

She wanted to hit him. She wanted to hurt him. He was manipulating her, and all for information he had no right to know. So she lied. "Dozens."

"Really?" He withdrew his finger, then slowly he worked two fingers inside her. As she stretched, discomfort threatened to become pain. "Were they all needledicks? Because you're damned near as tight as the night I took your virginity."

The man knew too much about women. He knew too much about her.

"How many men?" He coaxed her now, his voice a glorious, beautiful rumble. "The truth. How many?"

What difference did it make? Sooner or later, she would give in. Taking his collar in her hand, she lifted her head and spoke into his neck, knowing *her* breath caressed *his* skin. "If I tell you, will you shut up about it?"

"If you tell me the truth." Dan's thumb rubbed in circles around her clit.

The truth? She could barely speak. "Ah, God, Dan, you're killing me."

"I'm not even close to killing you. I've been waiting nine years to do this to you. I've barely started." His thumb rasped over her, his fingers caressed her internally, and she convulsed, the tiny, preliminary tremor of an orgasm.

At once he stopped. "Not yet, darling. You can't come yet."

Gathering handfuls of his shirt, she glared up at him. "I'll come when I come."

He laughed, a deep, throaty chuckle. "I can talk you into coming. I can touch you into coming. I can unzip my jeans and lay you across the table, spread your legs wide and work myself inside you, in and out, in and out—"

Unanticipated climax took her, sweeping her along. Blood rushed through her veins. Her inner muscles clenched at his fingers. She arched against him, her body seeking to extend the sensation, and she gasped for air. When she had finished, she sagged against him.

He supported her and laughed. Laughed low and deep in her ear. "Don't tell me," he said, "that you're in control of your body and your climaxes. I'm in control, and if you're very, very, very good, I'll give you what you need."

That was what she was afraid of. That he would give

her what she needed. Then she would need more. It was an endless cycle of needing and satisfaction that he offered, and she had already suffered the agony of forgetting him—and forgetting his passion.

She didn't know if she could forget again.

"How many men?" Dan interrogated her like a professional, tormenting her, keeping her off balance, and never forgetting his objective.

She hated him for that. She hated him for making her talk. Through a throat tight with anticipation, she said, "None. There were no men for me."

He wouldn't believe her. She was sure of that. Then what would she do?

Lie, of course. That she did very well.

But Dan didn't snort or laugh or protest. Instead, in that cool tone she hated, he asked, "Why not?"

So rather than lie, she told him the truth. "I couldn't. No one else was you."

He slid his hand into her hair. He lifted her face to his and looked into her eyes. Just looked until he plumbed the very depths of her soul. "Damn you," he whispered. "You tear me apart."

His breath touched her face. His gaze stripped her of all her masks. "Does that mean you believe me?"

"I believe you." Moving as swiftly as lightning strikes, he let her go, stepped away. He pulled his starched shirt open. He flung it aside. He wore a wide-sleeved T-shirt underneath, and the muscles in his arms bunched and flexed as he pulled it over his head. His belly was flat, and his joy arrow pointed right at the fly of his slacks.

And he had a scar, white, jagged, right across his ribs and down to his hipbone.

But at her silent expression of concern he shook his head. "It's fine," he assured her. "I'm fine."

He tugged off his boots. He eased himself free of his slacks.

She watched, mesmerized by the ripple of his belly, the power of his thighs, the bulge in his shorts. The bulge that promised so much.

Her mouth dried. Her first time had been in the back seat of his car, at night, filled with teenage fumblings and the bitter realization she couldn't stay and be his lover.

This was wholly different. The overhead light illuminated the kitchen. Like exotic perfumes, the scents of vanilla and cinnamon filled the house. She was no longer a stupid child bound by anger and resentment to bring destruction down on herself, but an adult with needs she hadn't previously recognized.

It was those needs that he knowingly fed. He didn't flex and pose, but he moved in slow motion, giving her time to run, to scream, to change her mind . . . or to appreciate his assets.

Dragging one of the hard kitchen chairs into the middle of the kitchen, he seated himself. At last, he painstakingly peeled back his underwear. He lifted his hips and slid them down the length of his legs. His thick erection jutted up.

Her heart thudded in her chest, filled her throat with a mixture of cowardice and expectation. She was exposed, sitting up here on the table, the shreds of her panties beneath her. She felt awkward, inspecting him so blatantly, yet she couldn't tear her gaze away. She didn't know what to do, what he expected her to do.

He slid down on his tailbone, stretched out his legs, and gestured. "The first time, I screwed you. This time, you screw me."

She couldn't believe he had the gall to make such a demand, to pose so unashamedly, to entice her without remorse.

She shouldn't go to him. She would be mad to go to him. But the compulsion ignited in her. He had cut her panties away, opened her. He had readied her with his touch. Now she stared at him until her eyes burned.

He silently demanded she do as he wished.

As she wished.

Finally, when her lungs ached as if she'd been holding her breath—ah, she had been—she made her decision.

It was absurd to deny herself for fear of the visceral reaction she'd experienced the first time. She was mature now, an adult who no longer believed that the act was the union of two souls. She understood sex was merely the clashing of two bodies.

She could handle this.

Sliding off the table, she walked, barefoot and silent, across the floor. Taking the two edges of her wraparound skirt, she parted them and, oh so carefully, she straddled the chair.

She straddled him.

Foolish woman, to do as he demanded. It would have been better if he had taken her.

But she knew him. He wasn't the impetuous eighteen-year-old who had rolled with her in the back seat of his car. He was a man, and if he had decided she would take him, then she would. Sooner or later, she would take him, or she would face another stalking, another trial, more nights filled with the knowledge that he slept in the next room and that he wanted her.

And she was too far gone to face another night of aching arousal with equanimity. She had to have him, and she had to have him *now*.

He steadied her with his hand on her rear and like a magician doing a trick, he produced a condom. The foil was wrinkled as if he'd held it in his palm, and she accepted it knowing full well what he expected.

He held himself at ready as she discarded the packet and placed the condom over the head of his penis. Slowly she rolled it down the length of him, and as she did a warning bell rang in her head. The skin was smooth, the head was broad. She had had him once and run afterward. Did she really know what she was doing?

Then he groaned. She looked into his face and she saw how he strained against the bliss her touch gave him.

And although the warning bell still rang in her head, she no longer heard it.

With her feet braced flat on the floor, she lowered herself onto him. As he grazed her sensitive flesh, she thought she would finish even before they'd begun.

Then, with a shiver, she controlled herself and moved her hips until he was placed at the entrance to her body.

It felt right. It felt good. To look into his face, to see the beloved eyes, the harsh brown face, the scar, the sharply cut, golden hair.

As she pressed her hips down, as he began to enter

her, that felt right too. He filled her, hard and hot. Yet it was true, what he'd said about her. She was tight. He was too big for her. The pressure of his entry made her grit her teeth against a moan.

But if she were in pain, he was in agony. He threw his head back, his face contorted, the cords of his neck strained. She could feel the small jerks of his hips as he fought his impulse to thrust inside her. Sweat beaded his forehead as his thighs tensed beneath her, as she sheathed him with herself.

As long as he struggled too, she was satisfied. A small smile stretched her lips as she sank lower, then lifted herself, then sank again, going ever deeper.

Her fingers began to curl on his chest, trying to find a grip in a world spinning out of control. She panted, she could hear herself, and trembled from a combination of a deep ache and a greater need. "Dan. Please, Dan."

She didn't know what she asked for.

It didn't matter. He would give her what he wanted. His hand tugged at the knot at her waist. He tossed her skirt aside, and his fingers came back to her, between her wide-open thighs. He touched her lightly, a circling caress that galvanized her, that opened her to him without reservation.

With a harsh breath, she lost control. She slid all the way down, felt his legs and belly beneath her. Swiftly she lifted herself, exulting in the glide of his penis inside her. She heard him groan and laughed. Laughed to be caught in this whirlwind of unruly passion with him.

Perhaps the sound of her laughter destroyed the last of his discipline. Perhaps he had never intended to remain passive. But with a thrust, he met her. His rich texture filled her, and she thrust back at him, determined to dominate.

The slow beginning became a frenzy of action, of sound, of feeling. The chair scraped on the floor, small, harsh sounds that echoed in the large, bright kitchen.

His fingers pressed into the flesh of her bottom.

The floor beneath her feet was cool.

He groaned, a deep, shattered sound.

Her fingernails dug into his shoulders, and her thighs quivered from the strain of lifting herself above him, over and over.

Each thrust of his hips, each of her downward efforts brought them closer together. Brought them closer to paradise.

Her eyes closed as need rushed toward her. There was no lingering moment of bliss, no holding off her climax. Orgasm struck like lightning, searing her flesh with his, fusing them together. Deep within her, fever burned, obliterating every sensation but the pleasure and the agony of being one with this man.

He didn't slow. He lifted her, guided her, but he didn't join her. He forced more and more pleasure on her until the blood thundered in her veins, her body arched over him in a great and marvelous spasm, and she screamed out loud, an incoherent cry of inexpressible fulfillment.

At last he allowed the pace to slow enough for her to regain her breath and a faint semblance of consciousness.

She heard him say, "Pepper."

She opened her eyes.

She became aware of her surroundings. What had seemed like necessity a few moments ago now seemed like madness. She faltered at the realization of what she had done. What she was doing.

His dark gaze challenged her. Taking her hands, he again placed them on his chest.

The heat of his skin rose to meet her palms. She could feel his heart thudding with need.

His black eyes burned with a possessive fervor. "Who am I?" he demanded. "Tell me who I am."

She didn't understand what he was asking. "Dan," she whispered. "You're Dan."

"Who's holding you? Who's inside you?" He thrust, and thrust again. "Who's making you come?"

Now she comprehended. He was maddening her and at the same time holding back his own climax—all to enforce his possession. He wanted control over her. He demanded that she acknowledge her master.

She hated him for that. Hated him. Needed him. Had never, ever forgotten him.

"Pepper. Tell me." He moved her on him, faster and faster.

She rode him. Climax rode her. Again the breathless spasms swept her. She moved on him because she had to have him. Because her body demanded, and she had no choice except to surrender.

"Who are you screwing?" He looked into her eyes. "Who's inside you?"

She couldn't look away. She could scarcely speak. "You are. Dan. Dan, please . . ."

He gave in at last. Feverishly, he moved her on him.

His hips gave a final surge, then he clamped her down on top of him. Inside her, his penis jerked as he came, filling her with his passion.

She struggled against him, her body demanding more satisfaction, and more, until it seemed she would die from the merciless rapture.

Finally, when the pleasure had gone beyond all bearing, it gradually retreated, taking with it strength, thought . . . everything except sensation.

She drooped. He was still inside her, still too large, still too hot, yet she couldn't hold herself above him anymore. Although this slow slithering down atop him felt like a surrender—more of a surrender than this frenzied joining—she at last let her muscles loosen and came to rest on his lap.

As if that were the signal he was waiting for, his arms came around her, pulling her close, urging her head down on his shoulder.

She relaxed against him, trusting him with her whole weight. She knew as soon as coherent thought returned, she would have a whole slew of problems to face—like what to do with the large, sexually demanding, angry man beneath her.

But right now this felt right. More right than anything had been since she'd run away from him the first time . . . and with that thought, doubts began to bubble in her mind.

Eighteen

As passion retreated, Dan felt Pepper stiffen—in rejection, in fear, he didn't know. He only knew he wouldn't allow her to recoil from him this time. With an exclamation of disgust, he gathered her tightly against him and stood. Without withdrawing, he strode toward his bedroom. She clung to his shoulders, and that gave him some small satisfaction. At least she was too weak to try to get away from him. At least he'd managed to accomplish that.

Pulling back the quilt and blankets, he laid her across the sheets.

She looked fragile. She kept her eyes closed, as if she feared to meet his gaze.

He wanted to get her a cold, wet cloth and stroke it across her feverish face. He wanted to comfort her, to murmur mindless words of reassurance. But he knew Pepper. If he relented for even a single moment, she would arise like a phoenix and try to establish her independence once more.

So instead he opened her legs as wide as possible and thrust himself deeply inside her.

Her eyes flew open. She stared at him wildly. "Didn't you . . . haven't you . . . ?"

"Yeah, I did." He pulled back, a long, slow stroke, then filled her again. "But with you, it doesn't take much time to recover." He pressed hard with his hips, pushing her into the mattress, putting pressure where it would bring her the most pleasure. "I've got no common sense when it comes to you." That was the truth. He had exploded inside her, a glorious release, and now he experienced a slow build of heaviness in his groin, like a dam refilling after a flood.

She stared at him, her lips slightly open, her breath rapid.

"What did you expect? I've waited nine years for this." He groaned as he eased his way out of her again. His brain urged patience, and strategy, and a coolly plotted manipulation that would keep her in his bed, so he could continue to make love to her. His body had other plans.

She was gloriously hot inside, and wet with her excitement. "My cock's got this crazy idea that if it's inside you enough, you'll get the message."

She groaned as he stroked inside her again, but she didn't ask the question he wanted her to ask. She didn't say *What message?*

He damned her, and he damned himself for letting it matter.

Light pressed on Pepper's eyelids, a clear indication that, as always, morning had come way too early. And with that knowledge came another—last night had been magnificent, glorious . . . and meaningless.

Turning her head into Dan's pillow, she took a deep breath of his essence. Without opening her eyes, she knew he was gone, leaving her on the field of battle after bringing her to orgasm so many times all her muscles ached and a special ache had formed between her legs— an ache that told her she had been well and truly possessed.

She flung her arm over her eyes and groaned.

Possessed by a man who looked at her as a conquest that had escaped him and now presented itself once more. Last night she had melted on him like an ice cream cone in the summer sun. She had done every sexual act he had demanded . . . suggested . . . cajoled. She had come again and again, until she thought she would never stand again, much less walk a straight line.

Her fingernails dug into her palms.

Dan had imprinted himself on her. What a fool she had been! And what further surrender would he expect from her today?

She sat up to escape her roiling thoughts and looked around his bedroom. In their lust they'd tangled the sheets and made the old-fashioned bedsprings squeak. She would never again recline on a bed in this house without thinking about Dan and last night, and—

"Shit!" Reality hit her in a tidal wave. It was ten o'clock. She had missed chores. Tossing the covers back, leaping out of bed, she dressed as quickly as she could. She brushed her teeth. She washed her face. She brushed her hair and, after squinting into the mirror at her own reflection, she dashed into the kitchen and slapped on her hat. There was no time for breakfast. No time to do anything but to get down to the barn and busy herself with . . . whatever she could find to do. Racing out the door, she skidded to a halt as Dan rode up to the porch on Samson.

The horse was so tall, and the man was so lofty, she had to look up, up, up . . .

Dan controlled Samson with his knees and a casual hand on the reins, his muscles rippling with each movement. The stern lines of Dan's face had relaxed; he almost smiled, and he gazed at her flustered expression and her heavy eyes as if he enjoyed the sight and relished the memories. The morning sun caressed his hair, penetrating each strand and lending it a gloss that might have looked like a halo—except after last night, she knew better. This man was no angel but a determined devil who urged her, lured her, carried her away with ardor.

And as prosaically as if the night had never occurred, he said, "Let's go on a picnic."

"What?" She glanced around. "Today?"

"The snow's melting fast."

And it was. Overnight, the late season cold front had retreated. The wind had shifted to the west. Snow covered the ground in uneven patches, melted off the roof, and ran in rivulets down the hill.

"Come on." He extended his hand. "Samson can carry us both."

She breathed in the fresh air and considered. Last night she had spared nary a thought for today, but if she had, she would have expected Dan to be confrontational and overbearing. Instead he came riding up on his over-sized horse, a picnic basket strapped to the horse's rump, and expected her to ride off with him as if they were two children playing truant from school. As if they were young and carefree and didn't need to face the consequences of their misdeeds. As if . . . as if they were living the last days of their lives.

And maybe they were.

Walking down the steps, she took his hand and let him hoist her into the saddle behind him.

"Hold on tight." He sent Samson away at a gallop, and asked, "Do you know where we're going?"

"Oh, yes." She hadn't been on a horse since she had left Diamond, yet she recognized the sensation of Samson's rolling gallop and the scent of his warm body as if it had been yesterday. The motion pulled at her weary muscles, yet the air rushing at her face recalled that spring nine years ago when Dan had come to get her every Saturday morning and taken her around the two ranches and into the mountains. She had always brought sandwiches. He had always brought sodas and chips. The two of them had gamboled like lambs in the spring, and always, always the days had ended with them stretched out on a blanket, petting until they were both flushed with desire and frustration.

Now that sense of freedom and youth buoyed her. Samson, with his big hooves and his broad back, carried them up the steep, narrow path into the mountains. As Dan guided his ornery horse, his body moved in her arms. His heat mixed memories of long ago and last night into a potent brew that carried her along toward . . . probably toward disaster.

More disaster.

As they climbed, the pines pressed in. Pepper sensed the primeval spirit around her, took long breaths of air so fresh it hurt her lungs, and experienced a prickle of warning along her skin. The wildness was contagious. If she was not careful, the old recklessness would claim her and she would succumb to Dan before anything between them had been settled.

After last night they needed to talk. They really, truly needed to talk.

They broke out into a flat, and there stood the first Dreiss ranch house, originally a single room dugout built into the corner of the hill for protection from winter winds and snow. At some point in the nineteenth century, a Dreiss woman had insisted the cabin be enlarged, so a portion now extended beyond the slope, a wooden cabin with a porch and glass windows facing out into the forest. The trees had originally been cut back to create a yard, but when Pepper had lived here before, seedlings had sprouted close to the cabin.

Now the seedlings were gone. The brush had been removed. The yard had once again been cleared back to the lines of trees about thirty feet away. The summer sun shone on the uneven patches of grass, melting the snow, and all around, Pepper heard the trickle of water as drops became creeks and creeks raced downhill toward the river.

Dan brought Samson to a halt, then swung out of the saddle and stood looking up at her as if she were some sort of prize he had captured in battle, making her only too aware of their primitive surroundings and his smoky hot sensuality. She blinked as he reached up to her and commanded, "Come down to me."

And she, silly woman, did as he wished. She slipped out of the saddle into his arms. He caught her around the waist, brought her close and allowed her to glide down his body so gradually, her breath stopped in anticipation.

When her face was level with his, he stopped her. The expression in his eyes as he gazed at her heated her from within, while his muscled body warmed her from without. She was foolish, so foolish, for she wrapped her legs around his waist and clasped him close. Her face descended to his, and their lips touched. In one long, savory moment, they would be moving toward the porch and another session of grand and glorious sex. She was willing. Dear God, more than willing.

Without warning, Dan jerked his head back from hers, and he scowled. "Damn it, Samson!" Dropping her feet to the ground, Dan sprang away.

Her sexual flush faded to amusement as she watched Dan chase after his recalcitrant horse, making for the barn.

Dan caught the reins and brought Samson to a halt, then led the big gelding back up the path. She hugged herself as she watched Dan stride toward her. The long, slow caress had proved one thing—last night had not satisfied him. Their affair had extended beyond a one-night stand and become . . . become what?

As Dan tied Samson to one of the posts that supported the porch, she eyed it with alarm. "Are you sure he won't pull down the whole structure?"

With an odd crook to his smile, Dan shook his head. "It's surprisingly sturdy. The pioneers built for the future. Come on." He lifted the hamper off Samson's back. "Check it out."

She walked through the damp grass toward the porch. "The cabin looks as if it will crumple in the breeze." Cautiously, she mounted the steps, expecting the boards to turn to dust under her weight.

Nothing creaked. Nothing moved. The wood was deceptively strong.

"This place is safe. It withstood the earthquake twenty-some years ago. If anything ever threatens the house in the valley, this is the place to come." He spoke without emphasis, so calmly his comment might have been nothing more than casual conversation.

But it didn't feel casual. Not when General Napier hunted her with such deadly intent. Pepper examined him cautiously. Had she talked in her sleep? Had he somehow discovered what she feared?

He paid her trepidation no heed but strode up onto the porch and opened the door. "It's a bit of a cave."

It was dark in there. "Or a grave."

"It's easy to see why the Dreisses built here." He gestured inside. "No one could attack the house without warning, and whoever is inside has the advantages of an impenetrable defense to the back and the high ground in front."

She stepped forward, then halted when the scent of earth issued forth from the door. Stalling, she said, "I love it when you talk like a soldier. It makes me hot."

"What are you afraid of?" Dan asked. "You've been in here before."

But she had never liked it. Still, Dan stood there as if he would not be satisfied until she stepped inside, so she did. The room contained an assortment of tumbledown furniture casting shadows across the wooden floor. A long table, a few stools, a bench, and a deep trunk were all pushed toward the center of the room. A tall, wide fireplace made of rounded gray river rock dominated the shadows inside, and a squeaking issued from the opening.

She jumped back. "What's that?"

"Bats. There are a few mice too, but the place is perfectly safe."

She shivered and hastily exited. "I don't like mice and bats, and I really don't like caves."

As he shut the door, he smiled at her. "Do you know how beautiful you are?"

She looked down at herself. She had done no more than wash her face and brush her hair and teeth, and he thought she was beautiful? "I'm wearing work clothes," she pointed out.

"Yes." His possessive gaze lingered on her figure, then rose to her face. "Very attractive."

How could she have imagined that wearing unappealing clothes would repel him? He wanted the body beneath the flannel shirt and blue jeans, *her* body, and maybe . . . maybe the woman inside too. For Pepper, who had been unwanted for so long, that was a heady combination of desires.

"Come on." He strode to one sunny corner of the

porch. Delving into the basket, he pulled out an old quilt, blue and red on a white background, and spread it across the aging boards. With a flourish, he laid a napkin across his arm and produced a bottle of Frappucino.

She caught her breath. She hadn't had breakfast. She hadn't had coffee. Her mouth watered as her caffeine-starved system lurched to life. In a tone of awe, she asked, "Where did you get that?"

"It's from my private stash. No one knows about it except me . . . and now you." He placed it on the blanket and brought forth another one. "I only have one on special occasions. This morning definitely qualifies as a special occasion."

Taking the bottle, she shook it up and opened it. The sweet, creamy coffee flavor spread across her tongue, and she closed her eyes as she savored every drop. When she opened them, she saw Dan on his knees on the blanket, spreading out a feast of . . . *hm*, it looked like salami sandwiches, pickles, and gummy bears. Ah-ha, an artful combination of seduction and bad cooking. And some unfortunate character defect in her found his incompetence absolutely charming.

He gestured hugely. "Shall we?"

The darkness in him seemed far away today, still there, but smaller.

She settled herself on one corner of the blanket. She accepted a plate and sank her teeth into the sandwich. The rich flavor of garlic and the pungent bite of horse-radish complemented the nutty bread, and she thought idly that this might be the most perfect breakfast food she'd ever tasted. The bread-and-butter pickles crunched between her teeth with their sweet, vinegary flavor. The sun had warmed the boards and the blanket beneath her. The warm breeze brought the birds back to life, and they chirped in the trees, in a frenzy to welcome the spring once more.

Time shifted, altered, and déjà vu carried her into the past. She had been here before, on a day like this, nine years ago. They had ridden up on Samson. She had brought the picnic basket. They had drunk sodas, not bottled coffees. But like now, the breeze sighed through the trees. Just like now, the forest had been exuberant with life. And like now, Dan had watched her with a hungry intensity that sent blood rushing through her veins and desire sliding down her spine.

After last night, how could she want him?

How could she not? Last night he'd bullied her, and treated her with a passion reserved for only the most treasured of lovers. Today he waited on her and cared for her. Who knew what tomorrow would bring?

Who knew if General Napier would kill them both?

Pepper burst out, "This is the busy time in ranching, and I worry that you should be caring for your ranch now."

Dan put down his sandwich and pushed it aside. As if he'd been waiting for this opportunity, he said, "Tell me the truth. Why do you want me to leave so badly?"

"I feel badly because you're not working your own place." But her gaze fell before his. She couldn't look at him and lie.

"Why did you burn your car?" Reaching across the blanket, he caught her hands and pulled her close. "Why are you here now?"

What could she tell him that he'd believe? The truth. Yes. Yes, she could tell him. She opened her mouth. A gust of panic caught her, squeezed her lungs, made her skin prickle. All the old fears gripped her around the throat, and she couldn't speak. She didn't dare.

So she distracted him the only way she knew how. Leaning forward, she kissed him.

It wasn't a sacrifice. She had wanted to kiss him since she'd laid eyes on him this morning. No, since the first time she'd seen him. The heat he radiated, the scents of leather and working man, the way he'd stood up for her with his father, introduced her to his cowboy friends, acted as if he was proud of her—all combined to arouse her senses. Now she needed to shut him up, and she got to fulfill her desire at the same time.

What a bargain.

His lids fluttered shut, shuttering those piercing dark eyes. He sat stock-still as she pressed her mouth to his, outlining the form, loving the softness and the texture. Goose bumps skittered up her spine as his lips parted and his warm breath slid across her skin. She answered by opening to him, pressing her tongue into his mouth. A surge of tenderness washed over her, a tenderness such as she'd never experienced before. It was almost as if she could taste the years and all his pain. She wanted to absorb him into herself, give comfort where only bleak sorrow had existed.

Perhaps he tasted the same anguish in her, the loneliness that living on the run had produced, for he slipped his arms around her waist and brought her close. Her fingers wavered between them before coming to rest on his shoulders. He heated her from breast to thigh. His lips moved against hers, reminding her of the untutored kisses they had exchanged, the youthful passion they had roused in each other. Now there was more; the empathy of two adults who had shared so completely—and lost so much.

Lost each other.

Her hands slid up to his neck. Her arms pulled him close, and she loved him with her mouth, giving in to her gradually escalating passions. Their tongues touched, retreated, danced in ever-upward spirals of desire. She stroked her fingers into his golden hair, gasping with satisfaction as the brightness seared her palms.

He cupped her bottom, then worked his arm beneath her thighs and lifted them onto his lap. Slowly, he dipped her until she lay flat against the blanket. He leaned over her, pressing his chest to hers, wrapping her in his arms, easily dominating her with his powerful body. Control slipped away from her, taken by the need that brought her shortened breath and a heightened awareness—of him. Only of him.

His hand skimmed beneath the hem of her T-shirt, up her ribs, and beneath the loose underwire of her bra. As his tongue probed her mouth, his fingers stroked the skin of her breast, making every nerve quiver. The pleasure and the anguish almost broke her heart.

His thumb circled her nipple, and she wanted him to press his mouth there. She wanted to open her legs to him. She wanted him to take the choice away from her. She wanted him to relieve the demands of years of lack and longing. She wanted to face the consequences later.

No, never.

But as she sensed his pain, so he sensed her uncertainty. With a growl of impatience he grasped her wrists and pulled her arms from around his neck. "That answered some questions. Not all of them, but at least the most important ones."

Her lungs hurt from the breathlessness of kissing him, and she could scarcely get enough air to ask, "What do you mean?"

"You're scared to death." He looked deeply into her eyes. "Are you being stalked?"

His inquiry struck her so hard, again she lost her breath. "What? Stalked? You know about . . ." About General Napier.

But what he said astonished her. "I suspected a former lover, but last night you proved that wasn't possible. Is it some guy you refused to date? To sleep with?"

She stared at him and slowly, slowly her brain comprehended. Dan didn't know about General Napier. He had thought of an explanation that had never crossed her mind. An explanation that made total sense.

Dan continued, "Is some guy obsessed with having you? Because if that's the case, I can take care of him. Trust me. I can take care of anything."

On a long exhalation of breath, she told the truth, and let him believe a lie. "Yes, I am being stalked, and I'm scared half to death."

Nineteen

It wasn't that Pepper was an inexperienced liar. From the time she was eight, she had told falsehoods to foster parents and to social workers. From the time she was sixteen, she had told falsehoods to everyone about who she was and where she was going, and it was only in the last few years that she'd tentatively begun telling a few truths.

But she hadn't done a good job lying to Dan. Maybe she was out of practice. Maybe the way he looked at her, his sharp eyes an X-ray to read her soul. It didn't matter. As she fabricated the tale of her stalker, she made mistakes. She had to backtrack. She contradicted herself. And all the while Dan listened without comment and nodded as if he believed her.

Her story had put a pall on the afternoon, especially when he said he would talk to the police and asked where the stalkings had occurred.

She'd begged him not to, assuring him the police had

never done more than issue a restraining order and ignored the question of where she had been.

He had nodded again, told her she was safe, and suggested they return to the ranch. They mounted Samson, and the ride down the path was silent, not with the easy silence of friends or the smoky silence of sexual tension. This silence was painful, the kind that clogged her ears and weighed on her mind until she could think of nothing else.

She should have told him the truth. She would tell him the truth. She tried to speak, but every time she rehearsed her opening phrase, she cringed.

Dan, you know that stuff I told you about the stalker? I was lying.

Dan, I did a silly thing. I witnessed a murder and ran from the police because I've been living under an alias for so many years, I knew they wouldn't believe me.

Dan, I'm being hunted by a bestselling author and the highest-ranking female general in the army because she's really a terrorist accomplice.

Pepper couldn't bring herself to say any of that. Those words violated every code she'd lived by for seventeen years. If she said them, she'd be putting her trust in another human being.

But she had to speak. She had to trust him. At the house, she promised herself, face to face.

Yet when the house came into sight, someone stood on the porch. A woman, but not the kind of woman Pepper could ever mistake for General Napier. This woman was petite and blond, wore a blue blouse with a paisley scarf, and waved when she saw them and jumped up and down like a kid.

Pepper squinted, trying to see, trying to tamp down her feelings of relief that she couldn't talk to Dan, at least not now. She had another half hour, or hour, or maybe she could avoid making her confession for another day, and what difference would that make? There had been no sign of danger yet.

"Who is that?" she asked. Then she recognized the visitor, and slapped him on the shoulder. "Rita. Dan, it's Rita!"

"I'd say you were right. My dad didn't keep his mouth shut."

Pepper would be furious at Russell later. Right now joy overwhelmed her, and she waved and bounced too. "Rita!" she called. "Hey, Rita!" Before Samson had even stopped at the door, Pepper slid down.

Rita rushed at her. Pepper saw a brief flash of teary, cornflower blue eyes before Rita flung her arms around Pepper's neck and hugged her as if they were best friends long separated.

Pepper found she hugged Rita back with equal fervor. She had missed Rita's mysterious knowledge of makeup application, her ability to match her nail polish with her shirt, and the way she giggled guiltily when she told a dirty joke. Other than Mrs. Dreiss, Pepper had missed Rita more than anyone, except for Dan. And during those years of exile, she had tried never to think about Dan.

Rita was still Rita; the first words out of her mouth were "Pepper, what did you do to your hair? You look like Heidi in an alpine windstorm."

Pepper laughed. She couldn't help it. "You look good too."

Rita did. Of course she did. She was cute and perky with a ready smile and a peaches-and-cream complexion. She wore her long blond hair tucked into a clip, and strands of it curled artfully around her face. Even her jeans looked tailored, and probably had been, for in high school she'd won awards for her sewing at the Adams County Fair.

Yet on closer inspection, she looked tired, and Pepper wanted to ask her what was wrong. But a real friend would have known, and Pepper fought the urge to apologize for leaving all those years ago. She'd only lived in Diamond for eleven months; it wasn't as if she'd abandoned her best friend when she left.

She only felt as if she had.

Without a sign of awkwardness, Rita said, "Hi, Dan. Listen, I know you hate guests, but your dad told me Pepper was home and I couldn't stay away. I made a fresh cherry pie to ease the sting of having me here."

Dan spoke in a slow, gentle voice. "You're always welcome, Rita, you know that."

To Pepper, Rita confided, "Sometimes when I have to get away from my parents and kids, I sneak out here. But I can't let anyone know where I go or the gossip machine will rev up." She rolled her eyes. "You can imagine."

"Wow, can I." Pepper risked a glance at Dan. He watched them, hat in hand, smiling. Something about Rita always called forth that male response, a kind of indulgent amusement that made her the most popular girl in Diamond High School. No wonder Russell wanted her to marry his son. She was everything Pepper was not—domesticated and homegrown.

Oblivious to Pepper's thoughts, Rita patted her shoulder. "When Russell told me Pepper didn't want anyone to know she came home, I grabbed him by his scrawny neck and informed him if he told another soul, he'd never see another pan of cinnamon rolls from me. It's killing him, but he's kept his mouth shut."

Dan chuckled. "Never underestimate the power of a domestic goddess."

Rita chattered on. "Dan, before you take Samson to the barn, would you be a dear and get me the scissors and a comb? And a towel to put around Pepper's shoulders. I need to fix this mess someone made of her hair."

"Sure, Rita." Coming up on the porch, he kissed her cheek, accepted a hug around the waist, and entered the house.

As the door slammed behind him, Pepper experienced a twinge of jealousy and a surge of possessiveness. Dan was *hers*. Clearly nothing but friendship existed between Dan and Rita, but logic made no dent in the surge of rivalry that seized her. Pepper wanted sex with Dan to be casual, carefree, the kind of sex other women had on Saturday night and forgot by Monday morning. Instead, a superheated awareness warned her that Dan was close . . .

And silent as a wraith, he returned.

Rita jumped and gasped.

Pepper did not. She didn't need some supernatural connection with this man—but she had it.

With a wave of her hand, Rita dismissed Dan. "Go on, now. You'll distract me if you stay, and fixing this haircut requires concentration."

"I kind of like Pepper's hair." He swung himself into the saddle. "It makes her look like a demented pixie."

"A compliment any woman would cherish!" Rita called after him as he rode toward the barn. In a normal tone she said, "I don't understand how a man wearing cowboy boots can walk so quietly. He makes me jump out of my skin every time." She sat Pepper down, ran the comb through her hair and made distressed clucking noises. Tossing the towel around Pepper's shoulders, she made the first cut. "What's the word on his physical?"

Startled out of her morose contemplations, Pepper asked, "What?"

"His physical. Everyone in Diamond knows he went to the doctor yesterday." In a sly tone Rita said, "I'll bet he was too modest to tell you he almost got killed in defense of our country—twice."

"I knew he was wounded, but I don't know the particulars." A relentless curiosity drove Pepper, when she would rather be indifferent. "What happened?"

"Nobody knows, but his mom and dad spent about a month in Washington at the hospital, waiting to see if Dan was going to live or die." Rita clipped and talked, clipped and talked. "When Russell came back, he said Dan's commander told him he had seldom had the privilege of dealing with a man of such upright honor and integrity. He said Dan had an uncanny ability to sniff out a crime and the utter ruthlessness to carry out the punishment."

At those words a shiver ran up Pepper's spine.

"I'm sorry." Rita stopped cutting. "Did I hit a nerve?"

"Yeah. Yeah, I guess you did." A big, tender one. Dan

was suspicious of Pepper. Why wouldn't he be? She acted suspiciously, and he had performed some job in the army that had taught him to watch the world through narrowed eyes, to look for trouble everywhere. He had grown from a teenage boy who laughed at the law into a man who dispensed swift and brutal justice. Now she'd compounded the matter by lying to him—and he knew that too.

She was in such trouble. Last night she had taken all the experiences she'd gathered in her years away and held them before her as if they were a shield to protect her from the deepest intimacies with Dan. He had smashed through the shield, and she couldn't even explain to herself her own inexplicable submissiveness.

What kind of instinctive female nonsense had made her straddle him? Was it simply a desire to please him? She had clung to him like the weakest female in the world, and she knew the interpretation he would put on her surrender—and she feared what would happen next.

First he'd think he had won. Then he'd wonder if he really wanted her. Then he would start easing away, making excuses to avoid her. Or maybe he wouldn't bother with tact. Maybe he'd shrug and walk away.

Or maybe he wouldn't, and that frightened her more than anything.

She wanted to tell him not to worry about her stalker, that her life was her business, but she couldn't imagine Dan Graham abandoning her in her need. If they never had sex again, he would still help her.

She was in a mess of her own making, and it grew deeper and more complicated with every passing moment.

The scissors started again, and Rita said, "Anyway, he won't ever talk about his physicals, but I figured he'd told *you*."

He hadn't told her. Pepper hadn't even thought to ask him. "Don't know," she mumbled.

Rita giggled. "I know why. I'll bet you've hardly had a chance to say a word since you got home." Leaning down, Rita whispered in Pepper's ear. "Is he as good in bed as they say he is?"

Shocked to the core, Pepper said, "Rita!"

"Come on. I'm the only woman for a hundred miles he never slept with. Satisfy my curiosity."

"Rita! You never used to say stuff like that." Belatedly Pepper added, "Besides, we have not spent every moment in bed."

"That's too bad." A wistful note entered Rita's voice. "I'd like to think somebody's having fun. *I* married Brian Domokos. Remember him?"

"I remember him." Brian had been a pale imitation of Dan, handsome, witty, a stud, but only in his own mind—and in Rita's.

"You never liked him, did you?" Rita asked.

Pepper shrugged uncomfortably.

"You were right. I used to think he was a Greek god. Now I think he's just a goddamn Greek. He dumped me and went off to pursue his singing career." Brian had worn his hair like an underage Elvis; he played the guitar and sang like Clint Black with a bellyache.

Freed of the necessity to be polite, Pepper asked sarcastically, "How's that going?"

"He doesn't check in with me. If he did, I'd sic the

sheriff on him for nonpayment of child support." Rita had quite an attitude going. "One time I asked Mrs. Dreiss why she never married again. She said, 'You know how it is with men. You can't live with 'em, can't hold a pillow over their heads long enough to make 'em quit whining.'"

Pepper laughed. She'd heard Mrs. Dreiss say the same thing.

"I was so shocked." Rita mocked herself and her innocence. "Now I know what she meant. My kids and I are living with my folks. I've got no education. No way out of Diamond and no way to support myself."

Pepper was livid at Rita's husband and even more livid at Fate, who had played them both so callously. Pepper had been chased here by murder and deception, and she carried danger on her heels. Rita lived stuck in a little town where there were no good men who could rescue her, and she had no way to rescue herself. Pepper didn't know which of them she should pity more.

As Rita cut Pepper's bangs, she caught sight of Pepper's expression. "Don't look like that. It's not so bad. The kids barely miss Brian, and if there was one thing I learned while I was married, it's that there's nothing worse than being with the wrong guy."

"There could be." Like being with a guy who felt so right, in a place that felt like home.

Rita hugged Pepper's shoulders. "Everything's going to work out. We're strong women. In the end, no matter what happens, we're going to prevail."

What was the saying? *If you keep your head while everyone around you is panicking, you obviously don't comprehend the problem.* That was Rita.

Yet Pepper offered a tentative smile. It wasn't Rita's fault she always looked on the bright side. It was a personality flaw.

Rita went back to cutting, until Pepper worried she would have no hair left. In a coaxing tone Rita said, "Tell me everything that's happened while you were gone."

Pepper's mind jumped to poor Otto Bjerke's murder. "That would take a long time."

"And you never like to talk about where you've been." Rita sounded hurt, as if she had confessed her deepest secrets and Pepper had failed to reciprocate.

Which was true. "Rita . . ." Pepper faltered.

"No, it's okay. I understand. With your background, it must be tough to trust anyone. After you've been here for a while, maybe you can tell me some stuff. I've never been out of the state, and it's getting stuffy here." The note of mischief came back into Rita's voice. "But I guess you came back for *your* fantasy. At last you're living with Dan!"

"We're living together from *necessity*. I need him to help me until I can handle the ranch and . . . things. We can't help but know each other well." Pepper was proud of her prosaic tone. "I know he eats too fast. He knows I won't wash the dishes until the last second. I know he belches every time he drinks a Coke—"

"I know you belch louder," Dan declared from the corner of the porch.

This time Pepper jumped too. So he *could* sneak up on her.

Rita giggled. "You always were the best belcher, Pepper." She removed the towel from Pepper's shoulders and shook out the strands of hair. "What do you think of the cut, Dan?"

As if he needed an invitation to express his opinion!

He strode across the porch, and this time his boots made a steady thumping on the boards.

Pepper rose as he approached and tried very hard to feel indifferent. She looked him in the face, but as his dark gaze met hers, her lids fluttered, lowering a veil over her eyes. Over her soul. He was scrutinizing her, she knew he was, for her heart beat too quickly, her skin heated, and she wanted . . . wanted him.

"Very pretty," he said, and his voice was deep and slow, reminding Pepper of the night before and all the things they'd done together as darkness wrapped them in secrecy and the only promises made were passionate and physical.

Rita must have recognized the tone, for she said, "Whew." She fanned her cheeks.

Pepper knew she could never be indifferent to him, but too clearly, she remembered Rita's words—*Dan had an uncanny ability to sniff out a crime and the utter ruthlessness to carry out the punishment.* Pepper had planned to tell him the truth about General Napier. Now . . . she was afraid. Again.

She was sick of being afraid. Resolve stiffened her spine. When Rita was gone, Pepper was going to drive down to Boise, go to the FBI, and make a report. Perhaps they wouldn't believe her. Perhaps she would face a cruel justice at their hands. She could face their disbelief. But not Dan's disbelief, and never Dan's justice.

Linking arms with Pepper, Rita said, "Let's show you your hair."

Dan followed them through the door and into the house, observing the two women with deepening satisfaction. In one way, he was glad his dad had tattled on Pepper, for Rita's friendship would be another tie to keep Pepper here. And keeping Pepper on the ranch had somehow become a goal of his.

He watched from the bathroom doorway as Pepper looked in the mirror and gaped. The cut accentuated her large, hazel eyes and the fine bones of her face. Pepper whispered, "I look like Audrey Hepburn."

With palpable satisfaction, Rita said, "I've always thought so."

Pepper faced her. "I always thought you were the fairy-tale princess who would live happily ever after."

"It could still happen. I'm not dead yet." That was Rita, smiling with plucky courage in the face of disaster. "I keep telling Dad all I need is the capital to open an Internet outlet to sell my quilts, and I could make a tidy sum. But he won't help me."

Dan stepped back to let the women exit. "Why not?"

Rita pulled a long face. "He thinks the Internet will never last."

Pepper laughed.

"I'll front you the money," Dan offered.

With a surprising haughtiness, Rita said, "I wasn't hinting."

"I didn't think you were." At Rita's sniff, Dan explained, "Look, we've known each other since we were kids. You're organized and motivated, and I'll keep my nose out of your business. More important, I don't know about you, but I'm sick of having our parents throw us together. Once you have enough in the bank, you could move away. But if you don't want my capital—"

Rita almost jumped at him. "I'll take it."

"If everything goes well," Pepper said, "I'm going to sell some unique seeds and plants. Rita, you could put together a Web site selling quilts and flowers. Maybe some of the other women in town have things they could sell. You could charge a commission."

Interest lit Rita's face. "The Web site would be like a general country store for women."

Fascinated, Dan asked, "Would that work?"

"Sure. Let me show you." In the living room, Rita turned on the television. "If I can find the infomercial where they sell stuff like that . . ."

As she flipped through the channels, Oprah's face filled the screen, and in her warmest, most interested tone, she asked her guest, "With this most recent heartbreak, do you worry that tragedy stalks you?"

Dan never took his gaze off Pepper, so he saw it. She jolted so hard she looked as if she'd grabbed an electric fence. Her face turned white. Her gaze was riveted on the screen, and Dan looked too. He recognized the woman.

General Napier, with her piercing blue eyes and her neat upsweep of hair. She gazed out of the television and answered, "Not at all, because I always turn misfortune into a positive for myself and for someone else."

While Pepper stared so hard her dark pupils swallowed all the color in her eyes, General Jennifer Napier blathered about the death of her aide and how she would hunt his killer until the perpetrator was found.

"You and O. J.," Rita said in a disgusted tone. "I don't like this woman."

"Wait!" Dan stopped her when she would have changed channels.

"I'm sorry, Dan," Rita said. "Do you know her from the service?"

Watching Pepper, he answered absently, "I met her once, but I served in the field. I didn't have much to do with generals." He had as much respect for generals as any soldier did: They were a necessary evil, pompous windbags, or great politicians, and usually a combination of all three.

But it was obvious Pepper knew this general, and not in a good way. Pepper hung on her every word, and when General Napier said the police sketch artist had drawn the perp following General Napier's description, Pepper gasped so loudly, even Rita noticed.

Rita hurried to her side. "Pepper? What's wrong?"

On the television flashed a sketch of a white woman in her forties with dark hair, dark eyes, a large nose and a receding chin. Dan didn't recognize her.

But Pepper did. Or did she? Rita pressed her into the chair, and Pepper obeyed without taking her gaze from the screen, without seeming to be aware of Rita or him or anything beyond the drawing. She stared, listening intently as General Napier gave the woman's name— Jackie Porter—and urged the public to report any sightings. A tremor shook her when General Napier announced that, because of the great demand, she had agreed to do extra autographings in the western states.

Only when a dancing bleach bottle filled the screen did Pepper relax.

He saw the moment she remembered that two other people were in the room. Her gaze flicked around, tangled in his gaze, and he clearly saw fear in her eyes—fear of him.

Pepper asked, "Rita, did I hear you say you don't like General Napier?"

"She's cold," Rita stated. "Every time I see her, I think she's the coldest woman in the world. Why?"

"I used to admire her. A lot." Pepper rose as if nothing had occurred. "When do your kids come home from school?"

Looking faintly bewildered, Rita said, "Shelley gets home in about an hour."

"I know you. The perfect mother. You probably want to be there for her." Pepper urged Rita toward the door. "But thank you for coming. I've enjoyed this so much. And I missed you." Her voice wobbled. "I really did. I hope we can visit again soon."

Twenty

Dan walked Rita to her aging Sentra and held the door while she got in.

"Are you glad to have Pepper back?" Rita answered before he could. "Silly question, I can see you are. But are you going to keep her this time?"

"I didn't try to chase her away last time." And he didn't know if he would have the chance to keep her this time. Her behavior in front of the television proved one thing to him: She might be the victim of a stalker, but she was also guilty of . . . something.

Rita shut the door and rolled down the window. "This time you need to give her what she wants."

"What's that?"

"A reason not to run." She waved as she drove off, leaving him to stare after her and wonder if any woman knew how to say what she meant.

Then, with a glance at the house, he walked around a black walnut tree and leaned against the broad trunk, hidden from view. Pulling out his transmitter, he made a call, and as soon as the connection clicked open, Dan asked, "Sir, what do you know about General Jennifer Napier?"

An astonished silence followed, then Colonel Jaffe said, "She writes books?"

"It appears Pepper Prescott knows her or something about her. Whatever it is, it's not pleasant."

"Really?" Interest quivered in Colonel Jaffe's voice. "I've not heard any rumors about . . . no, wait. General Napier's aide was killed about two weeks ago."

"I know. In Washington. I just saw her on *Oprah*."

"Of course. You saw it on *Oprah*." Colonel Jaffe's voice was as dry as a good chardonnay. "You think Pepper Prescott has something to do with it?"

"I think she must have at least witnessed it."

"Good. At least now we know why she suddenly showed up at the ranch." The colonel spoke with the satisfaction of a man who liked his riddles solved. "Let me poke around and see what I can find out about the crime and her part in it. I'll get back to you as soon as possible."

"And Colonel?"

Colonel Jaffe knew what Dan was going to say. "No sign of Schuster. Over and out."

"Damn it!" Being a decoy had been a great idea, but Dan wanted it over with. He wanted to be able to decisively handle the situation with Pepper, and he couldn't do that until the operation was complete.

He was beginning to realize that finding out what Pepper needed in order to stay with him might take the rest of his life.

He was military. But he didn't have to be. With his wounds, he could be discharged at Colonel Jaffe's request. He had never considered the matter before because he'd had nowhere else he had wanted to be. Now . . . his gaze scoured the valley and the surrounding mountains. He knew these lands, he loved these lands, and he wanted to keep them safe. They were the best of America, the grandest, highest, wildest part of the country, a symbol of the past and a hope for the future. If Pepper lived here, Dan would never want to be anywhere else.

But he had to bring Schuster to justice first.

He headed back to the house, determined to settle a matter or two such as why Pepper had lied to him about her reasons for coming to Diamond, and failed to tell about the murder of General Napier's aide. He didn't believe for a minute she had pulled the trigger, so what was she hiding?

Why didn't she trust him? So many problems existed between him and Pepper, he scarcely knew where to start.

Pepper was nowhere inside.

For one moment, his gut tightened. Had she run away?

But no. He'd been outside; he would know. Looking around, he saw that her hat was gone, and her gardening gloves.

Like a bird seeking sustenance, she had gone out to the garden.

Outside he saw that with the return of the spring warmth and the heat of the afternoon sun, the late snow had melted into puddles between the garden rows. Pepper was not here, but he saw her blurred outline in the steamy windows of the greenhouse.

She said she had a stalker, and Dan believed her. He recognized the bitter embarrassment of a woman who halfway blamed herself for her predicament. Women had a tendency to believe they were at fault when some crazy crossed their path. But the other stuff she'd told him—that it was a man, a powerful man, whom she'd met through her work—was all lies. Under his interrogation, she'd contradicted herself, and when he'd offered to contact the authorities, she'd forbidden him. And he'd seen the crescent marks in her skin where she'd dug her nails into her palms.

Then she'd kissed him again.

Did she think Dan was stupid? She had kissed him to distract him, and it had worked. What man wouldn't be distracted when the woman of his dreams pressed her lips to his and produced his fantasy in living color?

More than that, she had wanted him. Her eyes had met his, then fluttered away. Her lips had softened against his. Her nipples had pressed into his chest, poking at him, demanding attention, and he had heeded the siren's call. He had touched her breasts, cradling them in his palm. Her skin was glossy and smooth, and the roundness brought his passions roaring to life.

Was she protecting someone?

Had she killed someone?

Had she witnessed a crime and feared an accusation?

Picking his way along the muddy path, he pulled opened the door, and stepped into the moist, perfumed air of the greenhouse. "Let me help you."

She swung around.

He caught a glimpse of wide, panicked eyes as she threw the trowel she held at his head. Dirt sailed in all directions.

He ducked, said, "What the hell . . . ?"

The trowel crashed through a pane of glass. Shards blasted him like shrapnel.

Pepper's hand flew to her mouth in a gesture of dismay. She stared, trembling.

Touching his fingers to his forehead, he brought them away covered with blood.

She started toward him at once. "I'm sorry, I'm sorry. You frightened me. How badly are you hurt?"

"I'm fine." With his handkerchief, he dabbed at the blood that trickled down his brow.

She flung off her gloves. She put her hand on his arm. "Is the glass still in your skin?"

"I'm fine," he said again, irritated as hell. He'd come in here to play the grand rescuer and been wounded by a garden trowel. "I've had worse."

"Of course you have." She tugged at his collar until he bent toward her. "But I didn't do it to you." Gently she pressed the handkerchief to the wound. "Does that hurt? Is there any glass inside?"

"It's *fine*." He took advantage of being at eye level to look her in the face. "You're sure jumpy."

She let him go. She drew back. Her eyes filled with tears and defiance. "I didn't see you coming. I'm sorry."

"Remind me not to sneak up on you when you're holding a gun. With your aim, it would be deadly."

"Come on. I'll put a bandage on you."

He let her take his hand as she guided him across the carpet of shattered glass and into the house, into the bathroom. Putting the lid down on the toilet, she made him sit. She peeled back the handkerchief and examined the wound, and she gave a sigh of relief. "It's going to be fine."

"I believe I said that." He stared at her in her old, loose, grubby gardening clothes, with a smudge of dirt across her cheek, and thought she never looked as beautiful as when she suffered concern for him. This woman tangled him up in emotions he could scarcely acknowledge. Emotions beyond lust, beyond need. And what was beyond that? He didn't know. He only knew he wanted her . . . and she wanted him. She could hide nothing from him. Her wide hazel eyes showed her worry for him, and her desire, and he experienced a surge of triumph that started in his gut and rose to his heart . . . No, not his heart.

His mind.

He believed in gut instinct. He believed in logic and thought.

But when he contemplated feelings, everything in him shied away. After what he'd experienced in the last couple of years, he didn't relish the idea of reviving feelings—at least not deep feelings. At least not the kind that could leave him scarred and anguished.

She bit her tremulous lip until he wanted nothing so much as to kiss it better.

He reached up for her.

She swayed toward him.

Then, as if she'd been stuck with a pin, she leaped

back. With that expression of fear he couldn't understand, she thrust the bandage at him, and fled into the dining room.

He followed her. "We've got to talk."

Looking like the young, almost-savage Pepper, she turned on him. "About what? About my burned-out car? About my stalker? About my family? Can't you trust me to handle anything? Can't you trust me to know what I need?"

"Did you hear what I said to you in the greenhouse?" At her blank stare, he repeated, "I can help you. Let me help you."

"I don't want help. I want—" Walking away from him, she flung the words over her shoulder. "I want the freedom to find my own way in the world."

God, she was stubborn. He followed her into the kitchen and caught her hand, half turning her toward him. "From what I can tell, your freedom is going to get you killed."

Her gaze slid away from him.

"All you have is me."

Snatching her hand out of his, she declared, "No, I don't have you. You're not mine!"

She was right. He wasn't hers. When he was with her, he reveled in the sweet grandeur of their lovemaking—and remembered the pain of their parting. "Then who will you lean on? You haven't got a family to help you."

She paced away from him.

And because he didn't know if he trusted her, this woman with the guilty face and the lonely eyes, he shied away from the intimate issues and took up the cudgel for her family. "You could find your brother and your sisters if you searched the Internet."

Going to the sink, she sluiced water over her face. "Why would I?"

"Curiosity, if nothing else. Don't you want to know if your sisters and your brother are out there somewhere looking for you?"

"They are not," Pepper said belligerently.

"If I had siblings, I would want to keep them close." He moved in, trapping her against the counter. "Yours weren't very old when you were separated."

"Not the baby. Of course, I've never expected Caitlin to find me. She was only nine months old when they took her." Pepper's voice contained a wealth of pain. "But the other two were older than me. They could have looked."

Dan persisted, "How do you know they didn't?"

Taking a paper towel, she scrubbed the smear of dirt off her cheek. "If they'd been looking for me, they would have found me by now."

"That doesn't make sense. *I* couldn't find you."

"Because after I left Diamond, I didn't want to be found." Pepper looked around as if seeking escape and found it in a seat at the table. She twisted the paper towel in her hands, shredding it in her distress. "But before I came here the first time, I was scared and lonely. I lived in crappy foster homes and I did wild things, thinking something would attract their notice." She shrugged as if she didn't care, when clearly she did. "They didn't notice. They weren't looking. They don't want me to find them."

"But if you're not actively looking, you definitely won't find any messages they leave you on the Internet."

Taking the towel away from her, he tossed it in the garbage. When he was young, he had barely comprehended why she would be reluctant to find her family. Even separated, his dad and mom had done everything they could to enfold him in a loving family. Yet now he'd been out in the world. He'd seen the worst of human beings, and he knew that the very establishments that were supposed to make you strong sometimes grievously failed. "Was your family not a happy family?"

"It seemed happy at the time. I guess I was wrong, and I'll tell you one thing—I'm not going to long for them and sigh for them when they don't care if I live or die." When Pepper stood, her chair shot backward, scraping the linoleum. "Now I'm done talking about it."

"I'm not."

She ridiculed him with a half grin and tightly clenched teeth. "Of course not. You haven't changed a bit. When you were eighteen, you were positive you were *always* right, positive you *always* knew the thing to do. Sure, you went with me to steal beer, but *you* were a Graham. Your cousin was the sheriff. You knew nothing bad was going to happen to you." She lifted one shoulder. Her pose echoed Pepper's old defiance, and at the same time, her hands shook.

In anger? Dan didn't think so, for she still watched him as if she feared him.

She talked faster and faster. "You tell me that I *have* to find my family, because you're so sure you're right and I'm wrong. Let me tell you, mister, I like not having the burden of a family. I don't want to know if they're alive somewhere in the world."

With perfect logic Dan said, "You were a kid when you lost them. Have you considered that what you remember isn't the way it happened?"

Pepper stood with her arms straight at her sides and her fists clenched. "I remember that night my parents were killed. Hope comforted me. She said, 'I will take care of you. Trust me. We're a family. I'll make sure we're together. I'll take care of you. Trust me.' Then when they took me away, she told me to be a good girl and she'd find me soon. She promised. I believed her. Believed her until I was thirteen and one of my foster mothers told me the truth. No one wants a kid who cries at night and throws tantrums all day long. Hope was glad to get rid of me."

Incredulous, he asked, "You believed a bitch of a foster mother?"

"She wasn't too bad. She never beat me, and she fed me three good meals a day." Pepper squeezed out a smile. "She simply had five kids of her own and she wanted me to stop whining. I did."

"But—"

"Let it alone." She walked away, into the dining room. "Just let it alone."

He couldn't. He followed her. "What if all your angst is for nothing? What if your family is dead?"

"Don't be stupid," she lashed out, spoiling for a fight. "They're healthy."

"Things happen. Accidents happen." He walked toward her, using all of his persuasive abilities to convince her. "There are thieves and thugs all over the world. Don't you realize—"

The blood drained from her face. "What if *I* die?" She appeared to consider her death a very real threat.

And like that, they were back to the danger that stalked her. "You won't," he assured her.

She turned stark eyes toward him, but she didn't seem to see him. "You can't know that."

When he took her hand, her ice-cold fingers rested limply in his palm. "I'll keep you safe. I swear I'll keep you safe."

"I have to think." She took quick, shallow breaths. She strode into the dining room, toward the computer sitting on the table. "I need to write a letter. A couple of letters. One to Hope. I need to tell her it's okay, that all those things I screamed at her when they took me . . . weren't true. One to Gabriel, he was always nice to me." Tapping her fingers on the keyboard, she stared at the blank monitor. "I wonder if I could find them . . ."

"I'll help you look. We'll get on some of the search sites—"

She grabbed his arm. Her eyes flashed at him. "No! Don't get on the computer. Don't go looking for my family. *Not now.*"

He pried her fingers off his arm.

"Please. Not now. I don't need the addresses right away. I have to think of what to say anyway. And I don't want—"

"—anyone to know you're here," he finished for her. "So you've said. You were going to tell me why you came here now."

"There's no mysterious reason. I came here for a sabbatical, to visit Mrs. Dreiss and to see the ranch. I'll leave here a wealthy woman. In the meantime, I might as well—"

"Lie to me?" That unexpected fury rose in him. She always stirred it with her distrust, and now . . . now it was worse. More powerful. More personal. "You're nervous as a cat on a porch full of rocking chairs."

"I am not!"

"You pushed your car off the road. You threw your trowel at me. You told me you had a stalker, remember?"

She dropped the casual façade. "You don't trust me and I don't trust you, *remember*?"

Her fierce rebuff astounded him. True, he was waiting for the report from Colonel Jaffe before *he* could have confidence in *her*, but women should be softer, sweeter, more trusting. "So we solved nothing last night?"

"We scratched an itch we'd both been suffering for a long time."

The little witch. How dare she put such a disagreeable interpretation on what had been the best night of his life? "We didn't scratch it very well, because I'm still suffering." Swooping down on her, he enfolded her in his arms.

She tore herself out of his arms as frantically as if she feared him. "No!"

It took all of his discipline not to snatch her back. "I don't understand you at all."

"I don't understand you either." She waved her arms like a windmill gone mad. "First you're irate with me about my family and about . . . about everything. Then you want to have sex with me."

"I want to make love with you all the time. The other

emotions exist separately from that." It made perfect sense to him. How hard could that be to comprehend?

"Look, I know you could seduce me."

Damned right.

"But you said that wasn't what you wanted."

"I did?" Had he lost his mind?

"Last night you wanted me to seduce you."

"That was last night." And *seduce* wasn't the word he had used.

"We need to step away from our obsession with each other until we can each honestly say that we trust each other. We can't keep having sex—"

His simmering temper boiled. Stepping close, he deliberately towered over her. "We made love. We didn't have sex. We made love." Before he could grab her and show her exactly what he meant, he walked rapidly away. But he stopped at the door, looked at her mortified face, and said, "Repeatedly."

He strode out the door and off the porch. In his pocket, he felt the vibration that signaled an incoming message from Colonel Jaffe, a vibration that quickly turned into a beeping.

Relief rolled over Dan. At last. At last. This had to be it. The end of the operation—or information on Pepper. The situation had grown intolerable. Something had to break. He placed the receiver in his ear.

And without preliminaries, Colonel Jaffe said, "Schuster's in the country."

This *was* it. Dan started back for the house. "Where is he?"

"In Utah."

"I'll get rid of Pepper at once."

"No!" Colonel Jaffe's frustration bit at Dan's ear. "No one's moving."

Dan stopped. "What do you mean? Schuster's men were waiting for him."

"Apparently not." Colonel Jaffe repeated, "No one's moving."

Dan wanted to throw something. "What are they waiting for?"

"I don't know, but the logical explanation is that they suspect a trap, and if someone is watching your movements, you can't get rid of the woman now. That would tip them off that we know."

Dan wanted this revenge so badly he could taste it, and it was delayed—again. Now Pepper was in the way. "It doesn't matter. She can't stay. I can't lose another civilian."

"You want to scrap the plan? I don't think so, Lieutenant! We've got too much invested in this, and we're on the cusp of success. Schuster's going down. Pepper stays." In Colonel Jaffe's voice, Dan heard the echo of his own determination.

But things had changed. Schuster, the most ruthless, bloodthirsty slimebucket in the entire world, waited a few hours from the ranch. He wanted to kill Dan, and he wouldn't care who got in his way. "It's a trick," Dan said.

"That's possible, but we'll take our chances." Colonel Jaffe's voice changed to a kindlier tone. "Look, I know you're afraid for her because of what happened to you last time, but Pepper Prescott is no child. Maybe she's not an accomplice to the terrorists, but she's probably guilty of something."

Dan remembered her behavior, and he couldn't argue that point. "What did you find out about Pepper and General Napier?"

"Nothing yet. My query's all tangled up in some kind of stupid bureaucratic bullshit with Napier's commanding officer. But what are we going to find out that changes my mind? Pepper stays," Colonel Jaffe said with finality.

Dan wasn't going to win, but he could bargain. "All right, but if she's going to stay here, Sonny's got to watch her."

"He needs to watch your back."

"What if she's innocent? What if she is simply a civilian?" Deliberately, Dan released the information that would protect Pepper—and get his own ass in trouble. "What if I told you she's the missing owner of this property and she came home to make her claim?'

"Damn it, Lieutenant! Is that the truth?"

"Yes, sir, it is. If she's killed in action, you know all hell will break loose."

Colonel Jaffe swore viciously.

Dan knew he had won.

Biting off his words, Colonel Jaffe said, "Tell Sonny he's her bodyguard. I'll tell Wagner and Yarnell to patrol the road to the ranch. But you will watch your own back, Lieutenant, or by God, I'll know the reason why."

"I'm not going to be killed." *Not now.* "You'll let me know as soon as something happens? Anything happens?"

"Right away." The line went dead.

Dan replaced the microphone and earpiece. He was beginning to think it didn't matter why Pepper was here, only that she was and he had a second chance. A chance to save her. A chance to prove he *did* know best. A chance to win her, to keep her . . . to give her a reason not to run.

He continued on his trek back up to the house. He walked heavily across the porch. He didn't want to give Pepper another reason to throw something at him.

When he stepped back into the kitchen, she still stood there, her arms wrapped around her own waist, her chin raised defiantly against the world. But when she saw him, the defiance wavered, misted over, and she walked into his arms. She hugged him as hard as she could. "You came back."

"I'm not going to leave you."

"I know, and I—"

Love you for it?

But she didn't say that. "I want some answers. I wish Mrs. Dreiss was here. She used to see things so clearly. She always gave me good advice, and even if I didn't follow it, I always remembered what she said." With an earnestness that ripped at his heart, Pepper said, "I'm confused. I don't know who to trust."

Trust me. But her trust was worth nothing if she hadn't given it on her own.

Time was ticking away. Schuster was waiting for something they didn't comprehend. Dan was stuck on the ranch with a woman he wanted, *needed* to keep safe. But she appealed not to him but to Mrs. Dreiss, the woman who had taken her in so many years ago.

He supposed that was fair. "Come with me." Going to

the wall of cabinets in the dining room, he reached up to the top shelf and pulled out a cardboard storage box, long and narrow, decorated with flowers. He put it on the long dining room table. "Here."

She approached the box with caution. She lifted the lid, and he knew what she saw.

A file of letters, with dividers periodically placed between them. The first divider was marked with Mrs. Dreiss's handwriting and addressed to Pepper, nine years ago. She flipped through the dividers. She saw the contents.

Letters inscribed in Mrs. Dreiss's spidery penmanship, all addressed to her. Some had been returned to sender. Most had never been mailed. But they were written, they were sealed, they were stamped, they were ready to go to her whenever Mrs. Dreiss discovered where Pepper lived. Mrs. Dreiss had written at least one letter a month. There were over a hundred letters here, and they were all for Pepper.

As if strength had abandoned her, Pepper sat heavily in a chair. Helplessly she looked up at Dan.

"You said you wanted answers." He gestured at the box. "See if you can find them in there."

Twenty-one

"Hope used to be so sweet." Gabriel strode with Zack out of the corporate jet, through Logan Airport, and toward the parking lot where the stretch limousine waited. "I never knew pregnancy turned women into predatory wolves who would as soon rip your heart out as look at you."

"You're exaggerating." Zack wished he could speak with conviction. As her pregnancy progressed, Hope became more and more feral. He, Gabriel, and the legal counsel of the Givens Corporation, Jason Urbano, had traveled to Washington, D.C. They had been away eleven hours, looking for Pepper. By now Zack imagined Hope would be positively homicidal with anticipation.

Gabriel grimaced. "I love my sister, but I hope she has this baby before she ties us up and starts hunting for Pepper herself."

That was exactly what Zack himself feared. More than once he had come awake at night and checked to make sure that his wife had not taken the corporate jet and gone off without him to find her sister.

Gabriel clapped Zack on the shoulder. "Did I mention I'm really glad *you* have to deal with her?"

"You're riding home with me, and you're going to help give the report," Zack replied.

"I'll take a cab."

"Like hell you will."

Zack's tone was low and menacing, but he was only half joking.

Cautiously the two men approached the black limousine parked at the curb. Coldfell, Zack's female chauffeur, stood at attention beside the open back door, and at Zack's questioning glance, she waggled her fingers in the universal not-too-bad-not-too-good gesture.

Gabriel sighed.

But Zack experienced a joyful leap of his heart. He hated being away from Hope, especially now as her body blossomed with his baby. No matter how difficult she might be, for him the sight of her always affirmed his love.

He stepped into the limo, cool after the unseasonable heat of a Boston summer day. The windows were tinted, the upholstery was black, the interior reeked of money; he was happy his fortune could make Hope comfortable.

She sat waiting, her fingers tapping her distended belly, and the look she bent on him was demanding to say the least.

He slid along the leather seat. Wrapping his arm around his wife, he put his finger over her lips. "Before I say a word about the meeting with General Napier, first I want to know, how are you?"

"Pregnant." Her eyes blazed with impatience. "What did the general say? Can she help us?"

Gabriel slid in and sat on the seat facing them.

"More information," Zack prompted. "You're pregnant and not yet having contractions? You're pregnant and the doctor said . . ."

"That I'm dilated to two centimeters and it could be two more weeks. All right? Is that enough information? Can I hear about my sister now?"

Putting the car in motion, Coldfell pulled away from the airport curb, but the window between the driver's seat and the back seat remained open. She was frankly listening. All of the Givens servants knew how desperately the family was searching for Pepper, and in their own ways they were all involved.

That was what Hope had done for Zack. She had taken a man set apart from society and brought him into the human family.

So he would do everything to help her reunite with *her* family. He gave the report precisely. "We met General Napier at Pepper's. The general was waiting in an official limousine, and when we went to Pepper's apartment, the door was unlocked. The apartment had been ransacked."

Hope sucked in a shaken breath.

"We were pretty shocked." Zack had never expected to see such wholesale destruction in Pepper's apartment. It was almost as if whoever had searched it harbored a personal malice toward Pepper. "Whoever did it was thorough and looking for something quite specific."

"Like Pepper's identity or location?" Hope guessed. "Do you think they found anything?"

"I don't know." Zack exchanged a glance with Gabriel. "We didn't find anything, and we looked."

"Did General Napier help you?" Hope asked.

"No, she said she didn't want to interfere in a crime scene." Gabriel's lip curled at such squeamishness. "But she promised she would use her considerable resources to find Pepper before the real murderer did."

Hope's shrewd gaze narrowed. "Pepper is wanted for questioning in the murder of General Napier's aide, right?"

"Not really." As the car sped through Boston traffic, Gabriel leaned forward, his elbows on his knees. "We talked to the police. They're referring to Pepper as a 'person of interest.' They want to question Pepper—or Jackie Porter, as they call her—but there seems to be doubt that she actually pulled the trigger. They know she was there, and General Napier seems convinced that if they bring her in, she'll be charged."

Hope shivered. "Why?"

"She said the police had made no headway in the case, that they probably wouldn't find the real killer, but that Pepper—or rather, Jackie Porter—had been seen fleeing the scene. She had dropped the general's book, the one that General Napier had autographed to her, and that made her the prime suspect in the murder." Gabriel leaned back. "General Napier said the police like to make arrests and convictions, and she was sure they would arrest Pepper because she had done the wrong thing and run as if she were guilty."

Zack watched Hope as she absorbed the information. Her intelligence had impressed him almost from their first conversation. Actually, it had been her voice that impressed him first, calling to him like a siren. Next had been her capacity to care for everyone she met. But as he had watched her work toward her college degree in the toughest circumstances, he had grown to admire her as he had never admired any woman before.

Now she knew what they were saying but didn't yet want to believe it.

With staccato impatience she asked, "Who does General Napier think killed her aide?"

"She said she didn't know," Zack told her. "She said she was at an autographing. She and her aide went down to the parking garage. She realized she had dropped some papers and went back up the elevator while he went to get the car. When she went back down, he was dead and a woman was running away. She told the police that she thought her aide had interrupted a robbery and was shot."

Hope looked from one to the other. "What do you guys think?"

"If she wasn't there, why is she so sure Pepper isn't guilty?" Gabriel asked.

Zack replied, "She said that at the autographing she talked to Pepper for a long time, and Pepper impressed her as being reformed."

"Reformed from what?" Hope spoke sharply.

"According to the general, Pepper has quite a criminal record." Gabriel watched Hope with an affection rooted in their mutual background.

Hope was getting more and more irritated. "If Pepper had quite a criminal record, why didn't the police lift her fingerprints off the book and match them with other law enforcement offices?"

Gabriel nodded. "That is a problem, isn't it?"

"Generals send their aides to do everything," Zack told her. "Why did General Napier come to Pepper's apartment herself? If she was so squeamish about looking around Pepper's apartment, why didn't she call the police and report the crime?"

Shrewdly Hope asked, "When she dropped those papers, why didn't she send her aide back for them?"

Zack and Gabriel exchanged glances and nodded. They hadn't thought of that.

Hope looked from one to the other. "You two don't trust General Napier. You think she's guilty of something. You think . . . you think she killed her aide." Hope took a deep breath as the full measure of the calamity swept over her. "What did you tell her about Pepper?"

Zack and Gabriel exchanged glum glances.

Zack said, "At first we were so grateful that a renowned general was helping us, we didn't realize there were inconsistencies in General Napier's story."

Gabriel admitted, "We told her Pepper's real name."

"Dear heavens." Hope groped for a bottle of water. "With that and her government influence, she can force every state to open their foster child rosters and find where Pepper has been."

Coldfell floorboarded the limousine.

Zack nodded grimly. "We left Jason in Washington talking to the police. I called Griswald from Dulles Airport and told him that we've got to find Pepper at once, or we won't find her alive."

Twenty-two

The Dreiss cemetery occupied a sunny slope where the grass turned green early in the spring and stayed that way through the heat of the summer. Crab apple trees shaded the crumbling headstones.

This headstone was new and sharply etched. *Patricia Lois Dreiss.*

Last night Pepper had read all of Mrs. Dreiss's letters, save one. Now she rolled up her sleeves, ignored the chilly dampness that seeped through the knees of her jeans, and cultivated the ground around the grave, planting flowers that would bloom all summer long. Pepper knew that somehow Mrs. Dreiss would enjoy the fragrance of the hearty old-fashioned pinks and the blazing orange and yellow of the marigolds.

Regrettably Pepper's mind wasn't only on the sunshine or the way the dirt felt between her fingers. A ripening sense of pleasure filled her body, and a warring sense of panic filled her mind. She had said, to both Dan and herself, that they had had sex. It was a good term, not euphemistic like *sleeping together*, but a solid, modern term that expressed what had really happened between them.

But Dan used a different term entirely.

Made love. We made love.

Pepper shivered. She stared down at the plants as she shifted a few at a time into the soil. How could he say that to her? He insinuated that during their union, they had *exchanged* love.

Did he love her?

No. No, he didn't. He was like all the rest of the people in her life, the ones she loved, the ones who said they loved her, the ones she trusted. The last lesson was all too clear in her mind. She had trusted an author, a general, someone all of America looked up to, and now Pepper was being hunted because of her own weak need to depend on one person's integrity.

While she was with Dan, she had almost forgotten the danger that stalked her. Almost. But always on the periphery of her mind, she listened for a step behind her and the crack of a gunshot.

She spoke to the headstone, knowing that somewhere Mrs. Dreiss was listening. "Thank you for the letters. I loved them. Thank you for having faith I would return. I wish I'd been here for you, but you're right. There's no turning back the clock, and I won't give in to regrets. Last night Dan kept coming into the dining room, he said to see what I was doing. Personally I think he came in to make sure I wasn't sobbing, and maybe to see if I'd fix him dinner." She pressed the last plant into the dirt. "I didn't. And the tuna sandwiches were pretty good."

Peeling off her gardening gloves, she seated herself; leaned against the headstone, warmed by the sunshine; and looked out over the valley. From here she could see cattle peppering the pastures far away near the bend in the valley, and closer at hand a cowboy riding along the road. She could see the house and Dan's figure as he made his way to the barn. She could see Samson in his pasture. But she couldn't hear anything except the breeze through the budding leaves, and with the silence came a peace she hadn't experienced since . . . since she didn't know when. For sure not since she'd dropped those books in the parking garage.

Pulling the letter from her pocket, she looked at the ragged envelope. Mrs. Dreiss had said to read this one last, but it appeared to be the oldest in the stack. When Pepper opened it, she saw why.

A multitude of different-colored inks striped the pages, and the handwriting grew progressively shakier. Mrs. Dreiss had written the letter at different times during the last nine years.

Dear Pepper, I'm going to start this letter and put the really important stuff in it, and add things as I think of them. It'll contain all my wisdom. Don't worry, this won't take long.

Pepper grinned.

First, I hope you didn't run away because you feared you disappointed me. In the end, a day of skipping school, a stolen case of beer—how had Mrs. Dreiss found out about that?—*and a romp with Dan Graham aren't such*

big deals. I disappointed a lot of people in my life, includ-
ing my dear mother when I married Mr. Dreiss, but I made
my choices. You made yours. Let's be happy with them.
Remember, raising flowers and making the best cookies in
the county are no small accomplishments.

Aloud, Pepper answered, "How about if I help open
an Internet site that sells Rita's quilts and our plants? We
can make it a success, and during the bad years in ranching, I'll need the extra income."

The light blue ink changed to black:

If you haven't already done it, go and find your family.
You've spent your life feeling hurt because you need them
and they didn't come and find you. Have you never
thought that they might need you?

"I'll write the letters tonight," Pepper muttered. She
had already composed the one to Hope. But why was
everyone nagging her about her family? Saying things
like *They need you* and *What if they're ill?* And reminding
Pepper that she could die before she took the time to discover where they were and what had happened to them.
According to Mrs. Dreiss and Dan, her grudges weren't
worth much when she faced the great unknown. Worse,
Pepper knew they were right.

The last entry was written in red:

The doctor down in Boise told me that if I don't have
surgery, I'm going to have a heart attack and die. If I do
have surgery, I have to have it at St. Luke's Hospital, then
go to a rest home, then have a nurse come to the ranch
with me—if I get to come home. I don't trust doctors worth
a damn, and I sure don't trust people to think it's important
for an old lady to die in her own bed. So I'm not doing it,

and I'm not telling anybody what he said. I'm not afraid, and dying fast of a heart attack beats going slow.

Pepper wiped a tear off her cheek. She knew Mrs. Dreiss meant what she said. But what a hard, cold choice to make, to live longer and maybe unhappily, or to die soon and suddenly in the place she loved.

Stop feeling guilty!

Pepper jumped to see that Mrs. Dreiss had realized what she would feel.

We'll see each other again, I know we will, and I've enjoyed the letters and the seeds you sent.

Mrs. Dreiss would have appreciated the irony that it was a gift for her, a book taken by Pepper to be auto-graphed by General Napier and dropped with the signed books in the parking garage, that had sent Pepper fleeing to the ranch. Fleeing home.

Long ago I wondered who would inherit this land when I died. When you came into my life, I knew I would give it to you, because you love it as I do. I know people in Diamond (specifically that old fart Russell Graham) think it'll go up for sale. You'll do me a big favor if you stay and be a thorn in his side.

And maybe a thorn in Dan's side too? That boy came home from the military, and he's angry. He's wounded, and more in his soul than in his body. Help him. You're the one he needs. You're the one he's always needed.

Pepper dropped her hands into her lap. The letter made a crumpling sound that echoed some of Pepper's despair. "But, Mrs. Dreiss, I'm in such trouble. I've got this general after me, and she wants to kill me." Pepper swallowed. "It's been ten days since I sent an e-mail to

Senator Vargas. Someone has to have read it by now, and nothing has happened. I'm afraid it's sitting in a pile of e-mails marked *Crackpots*. Or that General Napier was called in, she disdained it, and they believed her. She twisted the facts on television so she would sound blameless. She showed a police sketch of some fake person who didn't bear any resemblance to me. She's leading the police astray, and she hasn't been arrested yet, that's for sure. I want to go to the FBI office and tell them the truth, but I'm afraid they'll tell General Napier and she'll have me assassinated." Pepper swallowed, and in a softer voice she said, "Dan wants me to confide in him, but Rita says he's ruthless with criminals and when I think of having him look at me and not believe me, I just can't. I don't dare . . . Oh, what should I do?"

She heard the answer, clear as a bell, in her head.

Warn Dan.

She looked around, expecting to see Mrs. Dreiss standing there.

Instead she heard the words again.

Warn him.

She looked at the letter she held in her trembling hand. Mrs. Dreiss had sent an appeal across time, and Pepper wanted to consent. Pepper had asked a question across space and received an answer.

Warn him.

Mrs. Dreiss was right. Pepper had to put aside her distrust and tell Dan about General Napier. He would know what to do, whom to contact. Yes, he might think she was guilty, but by confiding in him she would save not only her own life but perhaps his too.

Irresistibly, the hay barn drew Pepper's gaze. Dan was in there, doing something—welding or hammering, something manly—and he was angry and wounded in his soul. Mrs. Dreiss said so, and Pepper believed her. She had spent so much of her life doing the wrong thing, yet she couldn't kid herself; she and Dan shared a connection that time and separation had not destroyed. She wanted to help him. She wanted to be with him.

Last night they had gone to their separate beds, as primly as if the previous night of debauchery had never occurred. But she had slept in minutes and quarter hours, haunted by the memory of all they had done and tortured by the knowledge that she could go to him, have him whenever she pleased—and she would always please.

He had been so close. In the next room. If she had got up and found her way in there, his hands would have risen to meet her. He would have pulled her atop him and . . . Pepper caught herself before she could imagine more. She put her hand over her pounding heart. Tried to catch her breath. It seemed as if they'd pulled the cork out of the bottle and found the wine within sweet and addictive . . . and endless.

Maybe he wouldn't want her forever. Maybe tomorrow he would shoo her away like a stray cat. But Mrs. Dreiss had liked him, had wanted Pepper to like him too. Surely that counted for something.

Surely that softly whispered message—*Warn him*—meant more than mere words.

Pepper would go to him, talk to him about General Napier. Then she would tell him she was going to stay.

She would say they needed to slow down, to build trust in each other before they again wrecked on the rocks of suspicion. Then . . . then they would see what developed.

Standing, she brushed the grass stains off her seat. "You're right," she told Mrs. Dreiss. "I have to warn him, let him help me. Then I will help him." She smiled. "Whether he wants me to or not." Gathering her gardening tools, she walked back to the house.

In her bedroom, she went to the closet and brought forth the light-blue camisole, the one she'd worn all those years ago to tease Dan. Carrying it into the bathroom, she hung it on the doorknob. She discarded the floppy gardening hat and ran a comb through her hair, washed her face and hands, and removed her shirt and her bra. Slipping the camisole over her head, she smoothed the slick material over her skin . . . and smiled.

She only wanted to talk with Dan, of course, but sometimes a girl liked to know she looked good, just in case there's another chance to, say, tease a guy.

She donned her shirt again. Picking up her buff-colored cowboy hat, she perched it just so on her head. As she smoothed the edge, the texture felt like velvet, and she remembered how awkward and eager Dan had looked when he gave it to her all those years ago. And like it had all those years ago, the hat fit perfectly . . . *like Cinderella's slipper.*

But she had to remember, she wanted to talk. She only wanted to talk. Intent on reaching Dan, she repeated that like a mantra, walked out of the house—and almost tripped over Hunter Wainwright, the cowhand she'd met her first day here, squatting by the window, a screwdriver in his hand.

Her heart leaped into her throat, yet she managed a high shriek.

"Ma'am!" He straightened up. "Sorry, I didn't mean to scare you. I thought no one was here."

"It's all right." Pepper put a hand on her chest. "I'm jumpy." In the briefest of moments, between seeing the cowboy and screaming, the possible irony struck her. She was going to tell Dan the truth about the general, to trust him as she hadn't trusted anyone for far too long. How dreadful if she were murdered before she could reach him.

She needed to go to him. She needed to go *now*. She glanced around. Mrs. Dreiss had warned her. Time was running out.

But Hunter took off his hat, displaying a wealth of silver hair and a startling tan line that cut straight across his forehead. "Miss Watson, isn't it?"

Pepper remembered her pseudonym and her story. "Yes, that's me. I left, but I had a chance to come back, so I did."

Hunter didn't seem interested. He almost spoke over the top of her as he explained, "I'm supposed to keep an eye on this old house, make sure everything's in repair. I had a moment, so I was looking it over."

"Oh. Okay. Good. I appreciate it."

His brow crinkled. "Ma'am?"

"I mean"—she couldn't tell him she had inherited the house—"it's nice of you to help out in that way."

"That's what they pay me for." He was really a charming man, with his winsome smile and his self-deprecating manner.

She liked him, so she smiled back, then stiffened when that obnoxious cowboy, Sonny Midler, strode up on the porch as if he owned the place.

He paid her no heed, but with a direct stare at Hunter, he said, "Hey, Wainwright, I thought you were going to go down to the south pasture and help move the herd."

Hunter chuckled, an indulgent older man humoring a young, cocky cowboy. "I was looking for work, and I found some repairs here."

"I didn't know you ever went looking for work," Sonny said sharply.

"I've got a few surprises up my sleeve, but if you want me to move the herd, I sure will." Hunter ambled down the stairs and disappeared around the corner toward the garage.

Sonny stared after him. "I wonder what he was really doing here."

Irritated, she asked, "What are *you* doing here? Don't *you* have work to do?"

Recalled to her presence, Sonny slipped into his I'm-such-a-hunk persona. "I came to check up on you, ma'am. To see if you needed anything."

"If I did, I could get it myself," she snapped.

"Yes, ma'am." He tipped his hat. "I know you could, ma'am."

She closed her eyes in disgust, and when she opened them, he had disappeared. She jumped as hard as when she'd seen Hunter Wainwright. Where had Sonny learned to move like that, so silently? Was he imitating Dan?

With a snort she started toward the barn and muttered, "I know he is." Dan was the kind of man lesser men mimicked in the hope of being like him. *Good luck to Sonny.*

The big barn doors on either end stood open, catching the breeze that sang through the valley, and when she stepped inside, she smelled hay, fresh paint, and leather. It was dim inside and warm, and she walked along searching for Dan.

She found him in the open part of the barn, right below the hayloft, sitting with his back against the wall. A half-painted chair lay across the workbench. The other chair stood nearby. And Dan held something cupped in his hands.

As she walked up, he looked up and smiled. The unexpected tenderness of the smile caught at her heart and stopped her in her tracks.

"You didn't do a very good job of searching for eggs," he said.

Realizing what he held, she knelt beside him. "That old hen hid her nest."

In his palm he cradled a fragile white oval. "She's got another three eggs behind the welder, and they're hatching. She's a sly old bird."

The chick within had cracked the shell with its beak. Pepper could see a glimpse of one wide, black eye. The white down was damp and glued to its little body, but the chick pecked frantically, working to be born.

Pepper laughed rather breathlessly. "It wasn't my fault. She hid them before I got here, or they wouldn't be hatching now."

The chick chopped out a big section of the shell and fell out into Dan's palm. It squatted there, stunned by its freedom and the immense world of the barn stretching high above it and far around it.

"Look at that," Dan marveled. "It's a whole new life." Cupping his hands around the bird, he blew on it to warm it.

Pepper watched with a catch in her throat. This brief moment of creation involved him as nothing else she'd seen . . . nothing else except the act of mating with her.

The wave of love that struck her almost knocked her off her feet.

When Dan opened his hand, the chick flexed its knees and staggered to its feet. It wobbled and looked around.

"Oops." He closed his hands around the bird again. "I don't want it to think I'm its mother. That old biddy would peck my eyes out." Going to the welder, he leaned down. The old hen screeched furiously, and Dan protested, "I didn't hurt it. I'm putting it back."

He stood and watched until the squawking died away. He beamed like the proud papa. "My guy's the first one out."

"Your guy is probably a girl, because girls are always ahead of guys, and you look"— Pepper laughed briefly— "positively mushy."

"That's me. I'm a mushy guy." Going to the sink, he washed his hands and dried them on a paper towel.

When he turned, he looked her over. His gaze lingered on the cowboy hat perched jauntily on her head, and his expression became something different. Something intense, sexual, passionate. He said, "Pepper, you came to me."

With a jolt, Pepper realized what Dan thought. He thought she'd come to him for sex.

He started toward her as if it were the most natural thing on earth for her to seek him out.

She backed away. "That's not why I'm here."

He strolled forward, his walk smooth and predatory. "Why *did* you come, sweetheart?" He didn't believe her. Or didn't care to believe her.

"I wanted to tell you something." She stumbled backward over a bench.

He caught her before she fell backward into the pile of clean hay below the loft. He slid an arm around her waist. Taking her hat off her head, he tossed it on the clean pile of straw.

As he gazed at her face, her throat, her bosom, his lids grew heavy and developed that sexy, bedroom-eyes look. Without saying a word, he conveyed his need. The atmosphere between them grew heated, scented with impatience and thick with desire.

And she knew it was true. She could heal him.

Because she loved him.

But first she had to give him all her trust.

Putting her hands over his heart, she said, "Listen to me, Dan. I have to tell you the truth."

She told him about General Napier, about the murder, about her flight. She told him all about the events that had driven her here. She told him everything except why she came to him now. She didn't think this stolid, stern, pragmatic man would believe that Mrs. Dreiss had given her advice.

When Pepper was done speaking, Dan said, "Stay right there."

Going out of the barn, he fitted the receiver into his ear, waited until the colonel picked it up, and said, "Sir, I know what—or rather, who—the terrorists are waiting for." At Colonel Jaffe's squawk, Dan lifted the receiver away from his ear.

Before he finished explaining, Colonel Jaffe was swearing at Army Intelligence for keeping secrets from Special Forces because they wanted to make the nab themselves. Dan could hear buttons being punched and speakers blaring, then Colonel Jaffe said, "There she is, giving an interview in Salt Lake City—which, incidentally, is not far from where Schuster is currently hiding out. The goddamned missing link right before our eyes." He yelled at his aide, "Get someone to keep an eye on General Napier!" Then back at Dan, "This better not screw this whole operation, or I'll by God make someone sorry. Lieutenant, I'll get back to you." Colonel Jaffe slammed down the phone.

So for the moment, Pepper was safe. Dan smiled. Safe, and his. He strode back into the barn, making sure that his security measures were in place, checking and rechecking for signs of ambush. There was none. Thank God, for Pepper rose from the chair by the workbench. Slender, strong, she watched him as if he could be the answer to her prayers, yet she stood ready to take action if needed.

This woman, this fragile, secretive woman, had managed to evade a general in the United States Army and the web of terrorist informants around the country. This woman, this beautiful, graceful woman, had gifted him with her trust in a way he would never forget. His mind, bent on revenge to the exclusion of all else, reeled in wonder. His heart, frozen by the sights and sounds of horror and cruelty, war and terror, melted in amazement.

She watched him, head cocked, eyes wide.

She was not the most beautiful woman in the world. Somewhere in his mind, he knew that was the truth. Yet to him, the combination of dark, curly hair and bold candor, of hazel eyes and tentative trust, was the most exquisite sight in the world.

She loved him. She hadn't said so, but for her to tell him the truth, all the truth, without hesitation, not knowing all of what he'd done in the military, yet sure in her mind that he would somehow save her . . . Yes, she loved him.

Reaching for her hands, he cradled them in his own. "I wish you had come to me sooner."

"I didn't . . . I couldn't . . . I had to . . ." She smiled at him, that marvelous smile that made him rejoice. Made him want her beyond sense. "First I had to find out a few things on my own."

"Does everything make sense now?"

"I think it does." Her smile brightened until he was almost blinded by its light, then softened to a blush. "I know it does."

He kissed each knuckle. Her hands were gardener's hands. Her thumb showed a callus caused by using a trowel. Her nails were short, her cuticles ragged.

Calluses lined her palms right beneath her fingers, and her grip was strong on his fingers. "What'll we do?" she asked.

Dan was a soldier. He knew the facts, he weighed the odds. He would have at least two hours of warning before the terrorists arrived. He was as prepared as possible, had been for weeks. He also knew the odds of surviving the coming battle and the necessity of making each moment count. "What'll we do?" He grinned. "We can do two things. We can wait, and we can make love."

Twenty-three

"What? Now? Are you crazy?"

Pepper wanted to demand answers, but Dan slid his arms around her waist, bent his head, and kissed her, one of those deep, satisfying kisses that drank in her breath, sapped her determination, and made her want what he wanted.

Desperate and confused, she broke his grip and backed out of his embrace. "Right now, General Napier could be coming after us."

His eyes smoldered a deep, dark brown. "Not yet."

"How do you *know* that?"

"I made a call."

He looked . . . happy. She had told him they were in danger, and a half smile curved his lips. She looked at the phone, then back at him. "What are you talking about?"

"You don't know the truth. No one in Diamond knows. But I haven't been discharged from the army. I'm still in the military. In Special Forces." He seemed cheerfully unconcerned as he dropped his bombshell.

General Napier's threat hung over every movement, every thought, but Pepper could handle that. It was a peril she'd lived with for almost two weeks. It was Dan's statement that terrified her. "Wait! You're *in* the military? No." He was wrong. "You were wounded. You're retired."

"There's more to it than that."

She dug her nails into his shoulders. "What do you mean, 'There's more to it than that'?"

Still he rubbed her in long, slow strokes as if that would make her forget that he . . . that he was still in the army. In the most dangerous branch of the service! "Right now I can only promise you that you're safe here with me—at least for the moment."

She glanced around the barn and saw things she'd never noticed before. The shotgun over the door looked normal, but the butt of a pistol protruded from one of the open nooks on the workbench. While she'd been waiting for Dan to return, she had noticed that the workbench itself looked heavy. Now, she realized, it was heavy enough to stop a bullet, and that dark green insulated vest hanging there—it was body armor.

Dan wasn't kidding. He was . . . he was in the *military*.

In a daze she heard him say, "In an hour, everything could change. Will change. I'm going to have to send you away to safety, so let's seize the moment. We'll celebrate life. Let me show you how." He was forceful, bent on seduction, again. Always.

Nothing was right. Everything she knew had changed. Pepper's mind whirled in the confusion of love and worry and pain and peril. "Where are you going to go? What's going to keep you safe? You're not on active duty, are you?"

With his hands around her waist, Dan backed her up against a wooden stall, leading her as elegantly as a dancer, and he didn't answer her.

She had thought that telling him the truth would save them both. She had thought they would go to the police, to the FBI, to somewhere safe. Instead, he confessed he was still in the military, where he'd almost been killed twice! He could die today, tomorrow, in a year. She pressed her hand against his chest. Her own thumped in a mixture of fear and exhilaration, anguish and desperation. "We can't make love now."

The trouble was, he paid no attention to her words; he listened to her body instead. "Do you trust me?"

"Yes, I do, but—"

"Then trust me with your whole heart." He was odd, jubilant, reckless, touching her as if time no longer stretched before them in limitless abundance. As if they could postpone death by a simple act of passion. His dark eyes glittered with excitement. "I'll keep you safe. Let's make love as if tomorrow will never come."

"That's not what I want. I want you to be safe too."

"Don't worry about that." He dismissed her concern as if it were of no importance. Pressing her head to his chest, he put his cheek on her hair. He seemed to think she was the most precious woman in the world, and he handled her as if he valued her above all else. "We'll get married."

"What?" If he hadn't been holding her, she would have fallen at his feet. *"What?"*

"I said that wrong." He didn't let her go. He didn't sink to one knee. His voice still commanded. But he did ask, "Will you marry me?"

As if that made it better! "Why?"

"Because you love me. You love me." He kissed the top of her head. "Don't you?"

She hid her head in his chest. A few moments ago she had realized she loved him. She hadn't come to terms with what that meant. And he knew? How had he divined such a thing? Had it been obvious to everyone except her?

He ran his hands up and down her spine. "We're mated. We should be married."

"I never said that!" *Marry him?* When she had lived in Diamond before, he had been the wild boy, and she had never wanted to tame him.

Since she had come back, she had concentrated on the danger posed by General Napier and the more immediate danger from Dan and his exhilarating blend of passion and promise. She looked into his face and her words were no more than a breath. "Marriage has never occurred to me."

"How flattering." But he sounded amused and looked confident. He unbuttoned her shirt. As the blue camisole came to light, he gave a deep groan of delight. "You come to me like this and think to deny me? Think about it. We'll sleep together every night and wake in each other's arms every morning."

"Forever." She didn't understand the concept.

But he seemed to. "Absolutely. Forever."

Marriage. Permanence. She had never dared think of

him as hers forever. Everyone in her life had managed not to love Pepper Prescott. Was he saying he did?

No, he didn't love her. He said they were *mated*.

The sex was good. He could imagine *wanting* her forever. What was that worth? Not enough.

She loved him. How silly of her to think that made everything okay. Love had never done anything but hurt her. "You think that because I want you, that makes everything all right."

"Darling, it doesn't hurt." He ran his fingertips over the pale lace that trimmed the front of the camisole.

Meticulously she picked the words that would test him. "If I hadn't consented to have sex—"

"Make love," he corrected, and caressed her through the silky material.

"Make love with you the other night, would you still want to marry me?" *Lie*, she urged him silently. *Please, please lie.*

He chuckled, and the sound rumbled in his chest. "It probably wouldn't have occurred to me to ask you now," he admitted.

Stupid man. He had told the truth.

Well, she could tell the truth too. Stiffly she said, "Thank you for the offer, but no."

The laughter faded from his face. His scar shone white against his skin. "I think you will."

Bit by bit she withdrew from his embrace. "Why?"

"Because you're a minister's daughter. You know right from wrong. And because we can't do this"—he tugged her shirt free of her jeans—"without wanting this"—he slid the camisole down. His eyes grew heavy-lidded as he gazed at her breasts, and he smoothed one nipple with his thumb. "So pretty," he murmured. "Like the downy skin on a fresh peach."

"Stop looking at my fruit-like breasts and listen. Don't . . ." But when he put his mouth to her nipple, she pressed her head against the boards and suppressed a whimper.

When he looked into her eyes again, he said, "I *am* paying attention to you. I can't *not* pay attention to you. Marry me, because we need to be together."

She was afraid he was right. They did need to be together. She had only to look at him, to think of him, and her body prepared itself. Her breasts ached from need; she wanted him to suckle her. Inside her belly, muscles tightened in anticipation, while at the same time, a dampness grew between her legs. When he unzipped her jeans, she didn't stop him. But the words she spoke came from her heart. "With you, sex is so intense, so important, so earthshaking . . ."

"God, yes." He removed her shoes, slid her jeans and the camisole down to her ankles. "Take them off, honey."

She stepped out of everything. "Yet I've got to stop before my sins come crashing down on my head." When he stood, she took his face in her hands. "And, I'm afraid, on yours." She spoke the deepest fear of her heart. "What if you die?"

He smiled so sweetly, her heart, her knees, her whole being melted. "I can't die now. Now . . . Let's make love one more time. Today. Now."

General Napier. The military. Marriage. The combination of disasters swirled in Pepper's head, yet lust and a fear of death that lurked too close urged her acquiescence. The glow in his eyes warmed her whether she wished it or not.

He murmured, "This is the last time we'll make love before we send out the wedding announcements—"

"No." She shook her head.

He continued as if she hadn't spoken. "So enjoy it. Now wrap your fingers around the rope."

She glanced off to the left, up to the coil of rope hanging on a twenty-penny spike. What was he planning?

He didn't explain. Instead he caught her hand and lifted it to the rope, then waited until she grasped the coil.

"Now there." Another coil hung on the other side of her, up high. She gripped it too.

She was spread across the wall, her shirt hanging open, the blue camisole slipping across her breasts. Her jeans were kicked away, and she looked, she suspected, like a ravished maiden in an old, bad movie. But ravished maidens didn't enjoy the look on their ravisher's face quite as much as she enjoyed the look on Dan's.

Color burned on his cheekbones, and his eyes glowed hot with passion. He knelt between her legs.

Alarmed, she tried to draw them together, but he slid his hands up the insides of her thighs and tenderly opened her to his gaze. His finger barely stroked her, a hint of touch that sent riots of sensation along her nerves, and promised more. "Do you believe I'll save you? Do you believe in me?"

She could scarcely speak for the anticipation. "Yes. Yes."

He looked up at her from his kneeling position, and

she saw a dangerous gleam in his dark eyes. "Then know this—I always get my way."

Her hands tightened convulsively on the ropes. How could he say that? What did he mean? Was he *threatening* her with marriage?

Then he bent his head and tasted her, driving all thought from her mind.

She whimpered as his tongue teased her with the promise of ecstasy. His breath warmed her even more, preparing her for the moment . . . for the moment . . .

"Oh, Dan. Please, Dan." Her head sagged. She fought to stand, and clutched the ropes so hard the stiff strands of the jute poked into her palms.

He took her in his mouth and sucked on her, enfolding the sensitive flesh and tasting her with a delicacy that drove her to sweet insanity.

She quivered. She gasped.

As if he found pleasure in her small moans, in the way her hips moved, he moved deeper, sliding his tongue inside her. Then out, then in. He imitated intercourse, and it wasn't as good. It wasn't as deep. It wasn't as big. But with each thrust, his momentum increased and she wanted more.

More of him. All of him.

If she didn't have him soon, she would lose her mind. "Please, Dan, please, I need you. I want you to make love to me."

In one smooth, long motion, he rose to his feet. He leaned against her, provoking her with his strength. He seemed taller than he'd ever seemed before, more powerful. His shirt was buttoned, but his hard, corded chest pressed against hers. She thought she felt a strap that crossed it—a holster?

My God, did he carry a gun?

Then his callused hands stroked her arms, his hips moved against her in blatant demand, and she forgot danger and distress, for at some point he had managed to get rid of his boots and his pants. His bare cock pressed against her belly, and she wanted the heat of it inside her.

She knew he wanted to *be* inside her. More faintly, she said, "Please, Dan."

Sliding his hands between her legs, he clasped the globes of her bottom and lifted her. He pressed her against the wooden boards, opened her knees wide with his elbows. She was spread-eagled, as exposed as possible.

"There." His eyes gleamed with satisfaction when he looked down at her. At them. "That's the way I want you."

She stared at him, stricken by an unexpected panic at her vulnerability.

He saw it. Of course he did. She suspected he had even set her up so he could say, "Trust me. I won't hurt you."

But the alarm lingered as he moved closer. She felt the probe of his penis as he searched for entrance. Finding it, he pressed up, into her passage. The motion stretched her, and he felt so huge, so invasive. She whimpered, writhed on him, but she was slick from his mouth, wet from her desire, and he moved into her steadily, taking her, making her his.

At last he was all the way inside her, his whole body

leaning against her, holding her in place. As he breathed, the hair on his chest rubbed her nipples beneath the camisole. The coarse boards against her back caught the material of her shirt. His hands on her bottom held her steady. Her hands clenched the ropes, her arms flexing in anticipation.

And he stared down at her, his blond hair falling over his forehead, his eyes rich with the sexuality that drove him to possess her again and again, in every way, in every place, until nothing she did and nowhere she went would be without the scent of him, the memory of him.

As he held her gaze, he flexed his hips, a small motion that pulled him back only a few inches. Then he came back. Back . . . and forth. Back . . . and forth. Short, slow thrusts that touched all the way inside her to the base of her womb. With each thrust, he pressed against her pelvis, inciting a riot of nerves made possible only because she was so open to him. He incited her inside and out with his lingering assault. At the same time he possessed her with his gaze, demanding more from her than she could give. Sounds broke from her, short cries of thwarted ecstasy.

"Am I hurting you?" he asked in that low, deep voice that had visited her dreams for far too many years.

She couldn't fight off the languorous rapture enough to speak.

But he stopped and repeated the question. "Am I hurting you?"

She knew he wouldn't start again until she had reassured him. She wet her lips. "No." God, no. He wasn't hurting her. He was . . . she didn't know what he was doing, but it was deep and dark and so intimate she struggled with the knowledge that she had no control. That he dominated her. That whatever pleasure he chose to inflict, she would allow him.

Because . . . because . . . She closed her eyes against his knowing gaze. She allowed him to do these things because they gave her joy.

Not because he had proposed to her. Not because they were soul mates who had been separated for too long. Not because she understood, better than anyone, that life was short and the time should be celebrated with the one she loved. She didn't want him for those reasons. She didn't love him for those reasons.

Yet right now love filled her to the exclusion of all else. Love drove out the fear. Love possessed her whole being.

His motion started again, deep inside her, and went on and on. She experienced Dan in every cell of her body. He provoked her to a fever of impatience. She wanted to move too, but there wasn't room between him and the wall. She tried to lift herself, but he held her too tightly.

She was drowning in inexorable desire. Her nipples puckered, hard and almost painful. Her heart pounded. A violent delight swamped her. She went under with a small scream, straining against him, her hips bucking against his, trying to absorb every remnant of bliss from his possession.

Inside her, her muscles clamped on him, each spasm growing greater and greater as the need he had so assid-uously cultivated found culmination in a blazing climax. Glorious release seized her body.

And he . . . At last, as her body demanded and his gave,

his eyes closed. He groaned, a heartfelt sound of anguish and euphoria. He stabbed into her, impaling her on his orgasm. He flooded her with his semen, and even knowing she could become pregnant, she reveled in it.

In the final throes of orgasm, he wore an expression of savage satisfaction. His forehead dropped to hers. He rubbed it back and forth, and his opening eyes caught her gaze before she could look away. He stared at her, unsmiling, his fierce expression proclaiming he was a conqueror, triumphant in his victory over overwhelming odds. He was a lover, made mad with passion.

And for the first time she was thoroughly pleased with her vulnerability. She had accepted every inch of him, given him the license to enjoy her body. And he had. My God, he had.

Every time they made love it was better, stronger; every time bound them more closely.

As she caught her breath, it hitched and hiccuped. The breeze from the doors touched her face. Up in the loft, the birds sang as they sailed out the open window. The world hadn't stopped, yet for Pepper, for one moment in time, it had narrowed to one woman and one man.

To Pepper and to Dan.

"Let go of the ropes, sweetheart." He spoke into her hair. "Sweetheart, let go and hold on to me."

Easier said than done. In her climax she'd been clutching the ropes so tightly her fingers were stiff.

Gradually she loosened them. She lowered her arms, slid them around his shoulders, and laid her head on his chest.

She heard the rumble of his low laughter. Pressing her hard against the wall, he slid his hands around her waist. "Wrap your legs tightly around me." When she didn't move, he added, "Unless you want to walk."

With an exhausted groan, she did as he instructed.

Lifting her away from the wall, he moved to the pile of hay strewn beneath the loft. He lowered himself onto his knees, then lowered her until the hay crackled around her.

As she sank down, the scent enveloped her. As Dan descended on her, his male scent overlaid the barn smells, bringing with him the sharp memory of good sex and inexplicable tenderness. She relished the weight of him on top of her and the length of him inside her.

But the hay poked at her bare skin. She squirmed. "The hay itches."

He lifted his head, looked down at her, and said, "Well, I love you too."

The words shot through her like a volt of electricity. Was he being sarcastic?

No matter. He had no right to say that to her. No right at all.

It wasn't funny.

He rolled so that she was on top of him, protecting her from the hay, and he brushed off her back as if nothing important had happened.

But something had. He had reminded her why she'd come in here, and what he'd said.

He had asked her to marry him, to be with him forever.

Reality, held briefly at bay, returned with a vengeance. It was one thing to love him today. To be with him for a while. But marriage . . . that meant forever, and she didn't dare love a man so much that his death would kill her, that the absence of his love would be a void in her soul.

Was it already too late for her?

She had to get away from him. She struggled up on her elbows. She buttoned her shirt with shaking fingers, then separated herself from him. As he slipped from her body, he generated another shiver of ecstasy—a small cataclysm, one that told her how easily he could again beguile her.

At least for a time.

But if she left him, would he die?

Frantically she searched for her underpants, finding them at last tucked inside one leg of her jeans.

Was this the last time they would make love?

Everything in her urged her to run. Everything except that small voice inside that insisted she wanted him no matter what the terms.

She donned jeans and panties in a rush, started to zip up, then turned to find him stretched out in the hay, naked from the waist down.

His legs were long, dark, and deliciously hairy. His penis rested against one thigh, appearing flaccid and harmless, much like Superman looked while he was masquerading as a mild-mannered reporter. Dan's arms were tucked behind his head. He watched her, that enigmatic expression on his face, and he was waiting. "Pepper, I don't like the way you're acting. Tell me, are you going to marry me? Or are you going to run away again?"

Twenty-four

In Zack's study Gabriel paced across the Oriental carpet.

Zack helped Hope sit down in his most comfortable chair. He pushed the ottoman under her heels and handed her a bottle of water. She looked at it with loathing. "Of all the times I could use a cocktail, and I can't have one." Ferociously she twisted off the cap. She took a drink and turned to Zack. That fierce, protective glow lit her eyes. "Now, what is it?"

Zack grinned with savage satisfaction. "Jason Urbano came through. He was interviewing Pepper's clients, trying to discover where she might have fled. He met Senator Vargas from Arizona, who after some questioning, admitted he had received an e-mail from Jackie Porter, his landscaper, sent from an Internet café in Denver, accusing General Napier of the murder of her aide and of collaborating with terrorists."

Hope sat straight up. "Has he told the government?"

The two men exchanged glances, and Gabriel said, "He assured Jason he had, but he was considerably less forthcoming about what the government was going to do."

Color burned in Hope's cheeks. "Why?"

Zack took Hope's hand and held it between both of his. "Think, honey. This is a matter of national security."

"Zack, you've got connections. You find out what they're doing!"

"I did contact them," he said patiently. "I explained who Pepper truly was. They don't say much—people like that don't ever say much—and while they wouldn't commit about the issue of terrorists, they admitted they want Pepper almost as badly as we do."

The color faded from Hope's face. "And General Napier wants Pepper dead so she can't tell law enforcement what really happened. Why didn't we find her sooner? Why didn't I—"

Gabriel interrupted before Hope could blame herself. "Because Pepper didn't want us to find her."

That distracted Hope. "What? Why?"

"She hated being a preacher's kid. She hated that people expected her to be a model child, and she did everything to be a bad example."

"I know." Hope was eight years older than Pepper. "Mama always said she was our wild child."

Gabriel continued, "When Dad and Mama were killed, remember how the church folk said she was unattractive and no one would ever adopt her?"

Zack had never heard that. "Bastards! They said that about an eight-year-old child?"

Gabriel nodded darkly. "The members of the church board were convinced Dad and Mama had stolen the church funds. They never looked for another culprit. They divided us kids up like garbage."

"Pepper was so upset when they took Caitlin, and she screamed bloody murder when they came for her." Hope clutched her hand in a fist on her belly. "I helped them with her. Told her it was only temporary."

"I told her that too. The two people in the world she loved, and we lied to her."

As Hope realized the truth, tears spilled down her face. "She doesn't want us to find her. She believes we abandoned her."

"That helped," Zack muttered sarcastically to Gabriel. Sitting on the arm of Hope's chair, Zack rubbed her neck and said aloud, "But we are finding her. We'll make her listen."

Gabriel offered his sister a box of Kleenex. "The worst that can happen is that we'll save her life."

"The *worst* that can happen is that we *won't*." Hope scrubbed the tears off her cheeks. "So what are we doing *now*?"

Picking up the house phone, Zack called Griswald. "How's it going? Can you come down?" Griswald's squawk of excitement made him hold the phone away from his ear. Putting it back, he said, "Good. I'm glad it worked."

Slowly Gabriel came to his feet.

"What?" Hope asked. "What worked?"

"It's good news," Zack assured her. "Let's wait for Griswald and he—"

"What worked?" Hope fiercely demanded.

Before Zack could appease her, they heard the thump of footsteps across the hardwood floor in the foyer.

Griswald shot through the door, his coat half on, his vest unbuttoned. In all the years he'd been working for Zack, Zack had never seen his butler in such a state.

Hope pointed at the floor in front of her. "Tell me."

Griswald smoothed the flyaway hair that fringed his skull. "Earlier in the day Mr. Givens called me from Washington and said he had an idea."

Hope trained her stern eye on Zack.

Zack explained, "It occurred to me that you were sent to Boston, as far away from Hobart as they could send you. So because the guilty party was trying to separate the family, perhaps Pepper was sent in the opposite direction."

Griswald took up the tale. "I went looking for Miss Pepper in the public school records in Seattle, Washington, and the vicinity."

Hope clutched Zack's hand so hard his knuckles ground together.

"Did you find her?" she asked.

In triumph Griswald produced a piece of paper from his inner coat pocket. "Pepper Prescott, eight years old, a ward of the state, first appears seventeen years ago in Seattle with no records whatsoever. She was placed in a foster home. It didn't work out due to excessive belligerence on her part. She was placed in another foster home. She threw tantrums. She was sent to another home in Bellingham, Washington. It didn't work out because—"

Hope half rose in her chair.

"Cut to the chase," Zack instructed.

"Yes, sir." Griswald read, "At the age of sixteen, she was sent to the small town of Diamond, Idaho. She lived with a Mrs. Patricia Dreiss for almost a year, the longest time she lived anywhere. From there she ran away and disappeared from sight." He handed Hope the sheaf of papers. "Sir, if you send people to her foster homes, surely there will be a clue as to her current whereabouts, and perhaps we shall find Miss Pepper herself."

Hope handed Zack one of the papers. "You two go to Diamond."

Zack handed it to Gabriel. "Gabriel will go to Diamond. Take the corporate jet, Gabriel."

"Zack, I want you to go," Hope said.

Gabriel glanced at the sheet. "Idaho. Where's Idaho?"

"In the West, sir," Griswald answered.

"Zack." With little success, Hope tried to heft herself out of the comfortably padded chair. "You go!"

Gabriel and Griswald walked out the door, ignoring her and leaving Zack to face Hope's wrath. He shook his head at her. "I'm willing to go away for a day, knowing I can get right back to you. But my darling, I don't care what you say or how you cry or how you rage. I'm not going. I'm staying here with my wife, who is going to have a baby."

Twenty-five

*H*e *had offered marriage to Pepper.*
Dan's spontaneous proposal had surprised even him.

But if he had been surprised, Pepper had been shocked. Was still shocked, if her stark, agonized expression meant anything at all. Her hands stilled on the button of her jeans, and she stared at him with a mingling of hope and despair in her eyes that told him she loved him—and hated loving him.

"Marriage makes sense," he pointed out. It did. He lusted after her; he needed to claim her in every way he could, and that included marriage. When they were teenagers, he had loved the whirlwind of freedom and excitement they created when they were together. He'd dreamed of how they would be free . . . together.

He'd been an idealistic fool.

Now he was practical, an adult who knew what he wanted and how to get it. Best of all, he'd seen evidence that Pepper was practical too. Standing, he picked up his jeans and slowly donned them. "Before when you lived here, you weren't ready for a permanent relationship. Neither of us was. But time has changed both of us. You've owned a business. I've commanded a platoon. We're not kids anymore."

She fussed with the buttons on her shirt. "No. We've both grown and changed."

"You own a ranch." He pulled on his boots. "You need help running it. I can help you."

She shot him one sharp glance, then turned away. "So now you're marrying me for my ranch?"

"That's not what I said. I've made money in the service. I've invested it. It'll go a long way toward helping you upgrade this place, and I'll contribute something to the marriage." He tried to joke. "You bring the land, and I'll bring the cash. It's a marriage made in heaven."

"I don't want you to pay to marry me. If you save my life, don't you think that's enough?" she asked truculently.

His blood heated at the suggestion that he fought for profit, for admiration, for a bride. "So if I save your life, you'll consider that some kind of dowry and you'll marry me?"

She had the grace to look ashamed. "No. No! I didn't mean that."

"Just for the record, I'm going to protect you no matter what you decide. It's something I have to do."

"That's got nothing to do with our suitability."

"Really?" Sarcasm dripped from his tone.

"You don't want to marry someone your family doesn't approve of, someone who's not from the area." Leaning against the wall, she tugged on her socks and tied her shoes. "Someone who's always getting in trouble."

At her stubborn refusal to look at him, he became more savage. "You're not making sense. An hour ago you came to me and told me about General Napier and trusted me to set everything straight. Now you're worried about whether you're from the area? Whether my dad approves? The dad you compared to"—he pointed toward Samson's empty stall—"a horse's ass?"

"I told you about General Napier because I didn't want you to get killed. *You* were the one who proposed."

He had tried to appeal to Pepper's common sense, but there was more to the situation than that, and while he preferred to keep this sensible, he was willing to do whatever was necessary to keep her by his side. If that was what it took, he would talk about emotions. "You love me."

She didn't deny that.

"You need me."

She didn't deny that either.

"We'll make a good life together."

She jumped on that. "We wouldn't be together. You admitted it. You're still in the military. You wouldn't be here. You'd be in Iraq or the Philippines or South Africa." Her cool, direct gaze considered him, and it was as if she had never moaned and tossed in his arms. "You'd be off doing whatever it is you do, and I'd be here—I guess—wondering when I'd hear about your death."

Of course. He should have known. She didn't want him to be in the army. And with the number of loved ones she had lost, he supposed he understood. Yet even if he could, he wouldn't change the course of the coming events. Not now, with the whole weight of an international terrorist organization posed to crash down on him. He had a vengeance to exact.

Taking the microphone from his wallet, he looked at it, although he knew that even in the frenzy of passion, he would have heard the alarm. But Colonel Jaffe hadn't called. Dan and Pepper had a little more time to straighten this out. Only a little. "You're not my only responsibility."

"Of course not. You're still in the military. You're in Special Forces. I can't believe it." She staggered as if she would fall. "Nine years ago, when I was with you, I felt such an intensity of . . ."

When she didn't finish right away, he finished the sentence. "Love."

"Passion." She glared at him, and her voice grew stronger, bolder, like the young, defiant Pepper's voice. "An intensity of *passion,* and I knew from experience that no one I cared for stood by me. Not my foster families. Not my real family. No one."

He absorbed the information, realized what she meant, rejected it. "Do you mean that you left me because somebody *else* left *you?* That you're going to do it again? What is that, some kind of twisted revenge?"

"I knew you wouldn't understand."

He had no patience with such nonsense. "I've heard that before." His temper simmered, waiting to boil. "Make me understand."

She was loud, belligerent. "I ran to save myself the pain of your leaving me."

"You ruined my life—our lives—because you thought I might betray you?"

"Everyone else—"

"To hell with everyone else! I'm not everyone else!"

"You would have—"

"When? When did I ever betray you?"

"Even my parents—"

"But not Mrs. Dreiss. And not me. I never betrayed you."

Pepper thought Dan was going to grab her, drag her off to bed, and prove how puny were her past fears. He wouldn't have to work at arousing her; she wanted him. Her body yearned for him.

Instead he pivoted on his heel, grabbed the unfinished chair and straddled it. Seating himself, he gripped the rungs on the back. "Listen to me. I am not any of those people who hurt you. I *swear* I will never hurt you."

"Maybe not, but when I try to let myself go"—her arms opened wide—"I find myself hanging on to control like a cat clinging to the top branch of a tree. It's terrifying up there, and lonely, but it's scarier to jump down." She closed her arms around herself. "I might not make it, because sleeping with you is all torture and bliss and gut-wrenching desire that leaves me helpless and hurting because I can't be with you forever."

His dark gaze absorbed her distress and her awkwardness. He nodded as if he'd heard something she hadn't meant to reveal. "Say it."

She played dumb. "What?"

"Tell me."

"You already know."

Silently he insisted.

Softly she surrendered. "I love you."

He stood. He threw the chair aside. He swept toward her with the speed of a tornado, caught her to him, looked down at her wide, trusting eyes. She pressed her fists to his chest, trying to slow his advance, but he was a master strategist. The heat of him enveloped her. He smiled at her, a tender smile that disarmed her because he used it so rarely. "I swear to you, you won't regret marrying me."

"I don't want—"

He interrupted her with kisses, small, sweet kisses on her lips. Slowly, he introduced his tongue, playing with her, enticing her with gentle ease.

Her eyelids fluttered closed. Then open. Then closed.

His hands roamed. One skated down her spine, spreading warmth in its wake, to cup her bottom and lift her hips toward his. The other slid around to the back of her head and cradled it. His fingers massaged her, easing the tension in her neck, in her back.

As she returned to the state of ready arousal, she realized, of course. She didn't have to surrender. He would simply ignore her struggles, ride over them as if they didn't exist.

Her head tilted, her mouth opened. She tasted him, sipped at his tongue, loved the texture of each deepening kiss.

He crafted sensuous seduction at its best. Each motion of his fingers lifted the tiny hairs on her skin. Each sweep of his lips wrested another soft moan from her. Perhaps her body had been warmed by his earlier possession. Perhaps she yielded more eagerly as the promise of passion swept her. But how could she resist a man who made promises without words, who craved nothing more than to leisurely give her pleasure?

As gradually as blossoms unfurled to the sun, her fists opened and splayed across his chest. Her hands inched upward toward his shoulders, toward his neck. She cradled his head, loving the jagged sensation of his newly cut hair against her fingertips. He warmed her whole body with his, lulling her into the belief—false, she knew it was false!—that his closeness vanquished all her misgivings, all her troubles.

She breathed with him. Her heart beat with his. He tuned her to match his rhythms.

Then, little by little, he drew back, lessening the impact of each individual kiss. At last he drew back completely.

She knew he was staring down at her, waiting for her to open her eyes.

Dan wanted to marry her, but he hadn't said he loved her. Not like he meant it.

What was it he *had* said? Oh, yes, she remembered.

Marriage made sense. No passionate avowals from him, just an indulgent affection, a constant lust, and a maddening, patronizing protectiveness.

Her eyes snapped open. She pushed on his shoulders. "That's not enough."

He let her go. "Damn it, Pepper! You are the most stubborn woman in the world. What do you want from me? Blood?"

Her hand flew to her throat. She stared at him. She saw the scar on his face, the scar that ripped across his belly, and she remembered why she couldn't have him.

"No. No blood. I don't want you to bleed for me." She started toward the door.

He caught her arm. "Are you going to throw away everything we are together because you're afraid?"

"Yes. Yes, I am. So what? You don't know what I feel! You don't know what's happened to me all my life."

He stood over her like a judge. "You won't even ask me to quit the military?"

She didn't know what to say. Ask him? To quit?

"What if I said I would?" he demanded.

If he said he would leave the army and stay with her, would she marry him then?

She didn't know. She just didn't know. Yanking herself free, she said, "You said you were going to send me to safety. Why don't I go now?"

He didn't follow her as she stormed toward the house, and she was glad, because she was so angry. So angry that the tears spilled from her eyes and dripped off her cheeks. Impatient, she wiped at them, but they kept coming.

She stormed into the house and slammed the door. The small violence made her feel better. He was going into battle, was he? He had to have sex before he died, did he? He wanted to marry her . . . A sob caught her unprepared. She rushed into the bathroom and grabbed a handful of tissues.

She had to stop crying. She had done the right thing. She had trusted him with her secret. He had known the right authorities to contact, and she was being sent to safety. And he might never return to her—this time, or the next time, or the next.

She couldn't live like that, knowing, wondering . . .

Why hadn't he told her before she fell in love with him again? Then she could have protected herself from this anguish. It was his fault. All his fault.

She didn't want to love him.

As she walked past his bedroom, something inside caught her gaze. The room looked exactly as it had when Mrs. Dreiss was alive: neat and old-fashioned, with a brass double bed, lace curtains, a chest of drawers, and a wooden chair, except that something brown and shapeless had made itself a nest on Dan's bed. A squirrel? Pepper paced across the floor, intent on not alarming the brown creature, and felt stupid when she realized the thing was a doll. A homemade, stuffed, filthy doll. It would have been barely recognizable except for the two black button eyes sewn into its canvas head, and one hand stuck out from under its long, shapeless dress.

Bewildered and cautious, she picked the poor thing up. The legs flopped so perilously, she was afraid they would fall off. Instinctively, she cradled the doll like a baby, supporting its head and its back, smoothing her fingers across its parched face. She could see where someone had sketched a red mouth in ink, and black wisps of hair across the forehead, but the color had almost disappeared. A faded blue cloth wrapped the doll's head and was stitched at the base of its skull to hold it in place.

The doll had been hand sewn with exquisite care, and the poor thing looked as if she had been well loved at one time. But what had caused the scorch marks on the side of her face and her dress? What had torn off one arm?

Dan spoke from the doorway. "She's a mess, isn't she?"

Pepper wasn't surprised that he had followed her. "What happened to her?" Still caressing the doll, Pepper imagined a house fire. Something disastrous, but not earthshaking.

The answer *was* earthshaking. "She was blown up— along with the four-year-old girl who was her mommy. The doll survived."

Her shocked gaze swung to him. "Someone deliberately killed a child?"

He now wore his pistol strapped across the outside of his shirt under his arm where he could easily get to it, and an insulated vest to conceal it from plain sight. "They deliberately killed the child's mother and father. Killing the child was a bonus, a chance to intimidate anyone else who dared to help the U.S. Army." He spoke calmly of a horrific event, even a cataclysmic one. And he had the doll.

Stupefied with shock, she asked, "Did you . . . were you there?"

"I was the one the parents informed to. I told you I was in Special Forces. It's more than that. I led a counterterrorist unit." He touched his scarred cheek. "In the right light with the right hair color, I can look South Asian or Middle Eastern or Mongolian."

Her gaze searched his features, seeing how it could be done. "Do you speak those languages?"

"Some of them badly. Some of them pretty well. I've played a lot of roles, thwarted a lot of plots, saved a lot of people. But not all of them." He indicated the doll. "I assured these folks no harm would come to them. I didn't think anyone had recognized me. I thought I had been *so* vigilant." He touched the wisps of drawn-on hair on the doll's forehead. For a second, his mask dropped. "I held the little girl on my lap while I talked to her father. She was the sweetest kid, with big brown eyes and a beautiful smile. She was why her dad would talk to us. He wanted a better life for her."

Pepper wanted to be angry at him, to tell him that *she* was the one with the haunting memories. But she saw a man in pain, and she faced an ugly fact. She was selfish, bone selfish. She had been whining about her problems. Now Dan was telling her what he had done, and why, and his reasons were larger and more excruciating than anything she had ever faced.

"The next day, I heard there was trouble. I grabbed some of my guys and we ran." As Dan stared, his pupils widened until his eyes were holes into the darkness of his soul. "We got there in time to see the house blow up in our faces. No screams. Just that blast that knocked us off our feet. I couldn't hear anything for hours, but I could see. And I could smell. Smoke and fire. The stench of burning flesh. All that was left of their home was rubble."

She had watched the scene often enough in the movies. A loud boom. Plaster and stones flying from the force of the blast. Blood and bones scattered everywhere.

But this was real. It had happened. In her mind's eye she saw Dan, shocked and battered, running toward the devastated house, trying to find the child he'd met the day before. "And the doll?"

He looked at Pepper as if startled to see she was there. "Yeah. The doll. Thrown almost at my feet."

With horror Pepper recognized the brown stains on the doll's skirts. "This is the little girl's blood."

"No. It's mine." He touched his belly. "I wouldn't let

the doll go, not even in the hospital." Sharp as a blade, his dark gaze flicked to her. "All of us who work against the terrorists end up the same way—scarred, quitting in agony, dead . . . or wanting revenge."

She flinched at the finality of his words.

"All I could think of was that poor little girl and who she could have grown up to be. What a waste. What a goddamn waste of beauty and talent and intelligence, all for some toxic ideals and a whole lot of money."

Pepper placed the doll on the nightstand. She turned to Dan, wrapped her arms around his waist, and held him as tightly as she could, trying to absorb the pain that walked with him every day.

He didn't hug her back. "I did my job. I did the right thing. When I got out of the hospital, I went looking for the one who betrayed them and us."

She stiffened in fear for him. Didn't Dan understand he could have been one of the good guys who ended up dead?

Of course he did. Dan would have known the facts better than anyone. "Did you find him?" she asked.

"Of course. I killed him." Dan's body shook, a jarring motion as if he'd been struck by an earthquake. "He almost killed me too. But I *did* kill him."

She pressed her head to his chest and listened to the beat of his heart. "I'm proud of you."

He stood immobile in her arms, as if he didn't want to respond to her fierce embrace. Finally, his arms enclosed her, and he held her as she held him.

His heart beat against her cheek, the sound rumbling through her head. The hard muscles of his body absorbed her life essence and gave it back tenfold. She loved him so much, and for the first time, she loved him without bitterness or envy. How could she envy a man who walked with these kinds of memories?

She looked up into his immobile face. She recognized it for what it was now—a mask he donned, not to confound her, but to hide his pain from his dad, from the people in town who didn't know what he had done to protect them, from her.

Now she saw everything, and she ached for him. "You didn't save that little girl."

He flinched, and once again she saw the raw anguish he lived with every day. "No."

"You can't save the world."

"You think you're the first one to tell me that?" His eyes . . . his eyes were so sorrowful, her own filled with tears.

"But you don't believe it." Taking his hand between hers, she kissed his palm. Holding it between both of hers, she told him, "I'm so proud of you."

"You don't have to feel sorry for me."

"I don't feel sorry for you. I would never feel sorry for you. I'm not glad you had a difficult time either, but knowing all this"—she touched the doll on the nightstand— "changes things."

"What things?"

She coughed, trying to clear the embarrassment. "Like that there are worse things than being a foster child without a family. You and I—we're two wounded souls, and somehow we make each other better."

His eyebrows rose in surprise. "Yes. Yes, I suppose we do. That's no small thing, is it?"

"It's a very huge thing."

"I promise I'll never hurt you. But I have one more thing I have to do." His generous lips flattened into a grim line. "Payback. Revenge. Whatever you want to call it."

She knew she wasn't going to like the answer, but she had to ask. "What . . . what do you have to do?"

"The guy I killed—his father has eluded us for years. He's one of the men who makes the plans for the international terrorists, and he's the wiliest son of a bitch ever born. But he has a weakness. He wants me dead."

"So you let him know that you're here." All was clear now. "That's why there's so much security here. That's why you're always wearing a pistol. You're not just recovering from a wound. You're a decoy!"

"Yeah. We haven't got a lot of time left, but I want you to know when this is over, I can get an honorable discharge from the army, and I will."

"I didn't ask that of you."

"I know you didn't. It's my gift to you."

Did he love her? Maybe so. Maybe this was the way a man uncomfortable with emotion showed his love. Pepper could barely speak. "I've brought General Napier down on you too."

"I can handle it."

In memory of a four-year-old girl, Dan put himself in harm's way. Now she understood why. He was brave, doing the right thing no matter how difficult and deadly.

Pepper could do no less.

Twenty-six

As softly as a summer breeze, Pepper touched Dan's lips with hers. "You've got things you need to do. Preparations to make so your men don't get hurt. And I need to pack a bag to take with me when I go to safety."

It was true. He did have preparations to make, and she should pack a bag, but he could hardly stand to let her go. And that was a dereliction of duty. He kissed her again, just once, and let her go. "A small bag," he instructed. "Toothbrush, change of underwear, the essentials. You'll be back before the week is out."

"Great." She smiled, but her lips looked as if they were stiff, and her eyes were wide and anxious.

"Don't worry." He used a soothing tone. "We'll get you out in time."

"I know you will." She kissed him again. "And you'll be fine, right?"

"I've got two men in town. I've got a man on the ranch. The unit is in place, waiting to move as soon as the terrorists close in, and we wouldn't be worth much if we weren't used to fighting against the odds."

His words didn't seem to noticeably appease her. If anything, she looked more frightened. But her chin rose. "Me too. And everything always comes out okay in the end. Doesn't it?" Like a soldier going off to war, she walked toward the door of his bedroom. She paused before she stepped out, and looked back at him for a long moment. In a voice that sounded painfully sincere, she said, "I love you. And as soon as this is over, we'll get married."

As she disappeared toward her bedroom, he stared after her. Funny. She'd expressed the fear he would die, yet at the same time, she acted as if she couldn't wait to get out of here. An ugly thought wormed its way into his mind.

Was she only interested in her own safety?

He found himself moving quietly so the old floorboards didn't creak. Into the kitchen. Into the dining room. To the door of her bedroom . . .

A swift glance proved she wasn't there. As he paced toward the bathroom, he tried to tell himself that panic was a normal reaction among civilians. Yet when she wasn't there either, he headed out the door, and he was angry. When faced with the idea of battle, most people ran for their lives.

But Pepper . . . Pepper always ran, especially when it came to him. He found himself gritting his teeth as he stepped out onto the porch and looked out and saw her hurrying toward his truck, wearing her old coat, a backpack slung over her shoulder, his keys dangling from her fingers.

She had said she loved him. She had said she'd marry him. And she'd used the words to cover up the truth. She was running away again. After all those vows of devotion, she was leaving him. He raced toward her with the softest tread, across the lawn, over the gravel drive.

Right before he grabbed her, she sensed something behind her. She whirled. He saw her frightened glance, saw her instinctive leap toward the truck. Catching her around the waist, he tackled her. As they flew through the air, he twisted so she landed on top of him. The backpack skidded away.

As they rolled in the grass beside the drive, they were both talking.

She said, "You've got to let me go. I've brought disaster on you again."

"You're mine. You never took another lover." He was astounded at the words, at the sentiment. He hadn't even known that he thought such a thing.

"Listen." Pepper rested on top of him and cupped his face in her hands. "General Napier is after me. *Me.* If I get out of here, she'll give chase. She'll divide the terrorists and you'll have a chance against them."

"You liar. You're running because you're afraid."

Her gaze fell under his slashing contempt. "I'm leaving to help you."

He was furious. "Don't give me that crap. All these years you never indulged in another relationship because a relationship is permanent." She stilled, and he knew that at last he was on the right track. "Yes, that's it. If you loved someone, anyone, you'd have to stay in one place and work at keeping your love alive. It's easier to run away."

She twisted, trying to get away from him. "That's ridiculous."

He understood her now. He understood everything now. "That's why you were so angry when I wanted you to find your family. You don't want to know them. You're afraid you're not good enough for them."

She struggled in earnest. "My family's not the problem here."

"No, the problem is you said you loved me. You promised to marry me when this is over, and you're making a break for it. Do you realize that if you drive down that road away from me, you'll ruin the whole operation that took months and a million dollars to set up?"

"No. *No,* you never said that."

"I didn't think I needed to. I thought you'd wait for the right moment to be transported out of here. And *hm,* why did I think that? Because you said you were only going to pack a bag!" He roared his anguish at being abandoned by the woman he loved—again. *The woman he loved.* The woman who had brought him back to life with her compassion and her admiration. The one person to whom he had confessed his torment at failing to save that child. *The woman he loved.* The woman who, as soon as she realized she was in danger of being killed— or worse, of being part of his life forever—scurried like a cockroach for the exit.

She flinched. "It's not what you think. I'm going to come back, be with you forever—"

Disgusted by her show of earnestness, he shoved her off him, let her land on her rear. He sat up. "Don't worry, if I live through this, I won't hold you to your promise to marry me. I wouldn't have you. You're a coward in every way possible."

She curled up, drawing her knees to her chest, staring at him as if he had broken her dreams. Her eyes . . . He recognized the expression in Pepper's eyes. He'd seen eyes like hers one other time, when he had held that child in his arms and seen the shock of painful death and the blankness of bitter eternity.

The shock of seeing that expression in her face acted like a slap to his senses. This was the girl he had loved as a boy and now loved as a man. She was a complicated woman who didn't give her trust easily, if at all. He, the man who believed in listening to his instincts, had never sensed any taint of treachery about her.

But he heard his instincts in regard to himself, heard them loud and clear, and they shrieked that he had been expecting trouble. He'd been ready for betrayal. He had accused Pepper of letting the past influence her to the detriment of all her relationships, when he had done exactly the same. He'd admitted to himself that he loved her, panicked, run off at the mouth, ruined everything. Worse, he'd hurt the one person he loved above all things. He muttered, "I'm a fool."

Her shoulders slumped. Her lower lip trembled. Her eyes filled with tears.

"Listen, Pepper . . ." How was he going to explain himself?

Like a woman on the verge of an emotional break-down, she awkwardly scrambled to her feet. She gave a heart-wrenching sob, one so loud it almost sounded fake.

"I'm sorry. Don't do that." He stood and tried to fold her in his arms.

She leaned against him—hard. The weight of her caught him off guard. And he never saw it coming.

She grabbed his wrist, hooked her heel behind his knee, and knocked his feet out from under him.

He landed flat on his back. His training took over. He rolled and came up in one smooth movement.

All signs of the betrayed and wounded lover had been vanquished. Pepper Prescott stood straight and tall. Her eyes considered him as if he were vermin, and as rapidly as she could, she backed up, out of his reach. She held a smooth, straight pistol in her hand. A Beretta 9mm, like the one in his holster at his side.

Like the pistol in the holster at his side.

He groped for his Beretta. It was gone.

She had done what no man had ever succeeded in doing. She had picked him clean of his firearm.

Pepper should have been chilled by the way he stared at her and the pistol, but she was so damned angry. No, not angry. Furious, enraged, ready to kill him for hurting her in every way possible. For betraying her as every single person in her life had betrayed her. She hated him . . . because she loved him, and he had tried to destroy her.

In a voice that sounded as calm and cold as General Napier's, Pepper said, "Thank you for reminding me of an eternal truth, Dan. For a second I forgot. Everybody's out for themselves, and nobody trusts a nobody like me."

His glance flicked between her and the pistol, her and the truck, as if weighing his chances of bringing her down. "Put that thing away. You're not going to shoot me."

Softly, keenly, she said, "Please. Test your theory."

He looked at the cold, black eye of the pistol, held steady in her hand. He looked into her eyes.

She allowed him to see the rage that drove her.

He didn't move.

She smiled, a slight lift of the lips, a motion almost painful in its anguish. "Good decision. And remember. I'm either a coward and a liar, or I'm the woman you just insulted. I would truly enjoy a reason to shoot you."

"I got that."

"Now tell me the plan. If I can't leave on my own, I need to know where I'm going when I'm sent away, and how I'm going to get there."

"I've got a guy watching your back—" Dan glanced around as if anticipating his arrival.

"Watching me," she said cynically.

He took a step toward her. "No. He's making sure you're safe."

She backed up. She was willing to shoot him, and he looked mad enough to take his chances. She had allowed rage to take her; she hadn't thought this out. She didn't know where she was going to go. On the other hand, with Dan's pistol in her hand, she didn't have to listen to his insincere apologies. "Can you get me out of here early?"

"No, but we've got two hours from the moment the terrorists start to move—" Dan stopped. A buzzing came from his pocket. With a courtesy that seemed out of place after their enmity, he asked, "Do you mind if I answer that?"

"Please." She gestured with her free hand. "Be my guest. But make sure you don't accidentally retrieve a weapon when you get the microphone."

"Understood." As if she weren't standing there pointing his own pistol at him, Dan placed his receiver in his ear and listened, his face chill and calm. "Colonel, I did suggest it was a trick. How many men?"

The pistol was growing heavy. Pepper picked up her backpack and slung it over her shoulder.

Dan's tone grew crisp. "I'll send her to the cabin. There's no help for it." He listened again, then added, "I'll do what I can." He signed off, and he followed her, at a safe distance, to the truck. His hands were empty, and his eyes were narrow and calculating.

"What's happened?"

"The terrorists—Napier, Schuster, and their men—hired performers to take their places so they could move on the ranch undetected. One of the substitutes got suspicious and contacted authorities. We've got a situation on our hands."

Pepper laughed, a thin sound that lacked amusement. She opened the door to the truck. "Follow me if you want, but please remember, I shoot very well and I *really* want to kill you. Right now I want to kill you even more than I want to kill General Napier, and that's saying something."

"With my assistance, you can survive."

The rage she thought she had under control lashed out in words as sharp as razor blades. "I've had your assistance. I don't think I can stand any more of your assistance!"

He held up his hands. "Go to the old cabin. It's reinforced, stocked with ammo. I took you there on purpose, so you'd know where to run if things went bad." He nodded toward the truck. "But you're going to have to walk. I'll open the cabin door from here."

She mocked, "And open it again when you want in?"

"Once you get inside, you'll see. It's impregnable."

"What about you?" She heard a shrill alarm go off in the house.

He looked down at his pager, and before her eyes, he became a man possessed by the need for revenge, a soldier who would win by any means—a warrior. "That's Yarnell. A troop of armed men just passed through Diamond. You've got no way out and about a half hour before they get here. Get going." He didn't appear to move quickly, yet in a moment he had disappeared into the house. Just disappeared as if he'd never been there at all.

She hesitated, then reality hit her. Her heart jumped. She didn't dare take the chance.

General Napier had found her at last.

The sun was setting as Pepper tucked the pistol into her coat pocket and started up the path behind the house toward the old cabin. At a brisk pace it would take her ten minutes to get there. It would take her eight if she ran, but the path wound uphill, the backpack was heavy, and she didn't dare arrive out of breath. She needed her breath, and she needed her wits.

This was the showdown she had feared for so long, and as she had feared, she would be alone. She would probably die . . . alone. Amazing how that scene in the driveway had both ruined her life and stiffened her spine. She might die, but she would go down fighting, for she desperately wanted to live. To live so she could hear Dan Graham apologize for his misconceptions about her, and she really and truly wanted to see him grovel as he again begged her to marry him. . . .

But here her imagination failed her. She couldn't bring up that picture. Dan Graham? Grovel? She laughed briefly, but the laugh turned into a sob and she swallowed it down.

She couldn't think of Dan now. She had to concentrate on survival.

The forest got thicker as she climbed. The pine needles slipped under her feet. She could smell fear on herself. Fear, and sex, and Dan. Not exactly the perfume she had hoped to breathe with her last breath.

Breaking into the small clearing, she saw the cabin and for the first time, realized why Dan had had the area cleared. No one could sneak up on this cabin.

Swiftly she made her way to the porch. The door opened smoothly at her touch, with a weight that made it feel like the door to a bank vault. Bulletproof? Undoubtedly. Would it resist the blast of a rocket? She didn't dare wonder about that. Her skin crawled as she stared into the dark interior.

And it *was* dark. The cabin sat on the shadowed side of the mountain. The sun was going down. The windows were tinted so that no light came in, and probably no light went out. The single room was partially a cave, and the odor of damp earth and impregnable rock made her realize—this would probably be her grave.

Pulling her flashlight from the backpack, she shined it around the walls and in the corners. As it had before, the place looked deserted. The table, stools, bench, and trunk still squatted in the center of the room, and the huge fireplace rose against one wall. She took a cautious step inside and heard the scuttle of rodent feet. She gritted her teeth, but she knew the mice would be eating her carcass if she didn't set up *now*.

She almost jumped out of her skin when, out of the shadows behind her, she heard, "How's it going, little lady?"

"Sonny!" Turning swiftly, she saw him swaggering up the steps, young, overconfident . . . a terrorist?

He touched his hat with one finger. "Is there something I can help you with?"

She put her back against the wall. "I . . . just . . ." She groped in her coat pocket for the pistol. "What are you doing here?"

He smiled, but the open charm he had displayed before seemed shadowed now. "Didn't Dan tell you? I came up to help."

From the other side of the porch came a man's voice. "Help what?" Hunter Wainwright stepped into view. "Help her? She's a smart woman. She isn't going to believe that."

"What the hell are you doing here, Wainwright?" Sonny shifted his weight to the balls of his feet. "As if I had to ask."

Before he could spring, Pepper pointed the pistol at him. "Don't do that."

Sonny teetered on the brink of movement. He stared

at her through incredulous eyes. "What are you doing? I'm your man."

Dan had said he had a cowboy on the ranch to protect her. But Sonny? Swaggering, obnoxious Sonny?

Hunter laughed scornfully. "She's not going to believe you." He walked toward her.

She pointed the pistol toward him. "I didn't say I believed you either." But he was older, sensible, where Sonny seemed nothing but a rash boy given to impulsive decisions, like the decision to take a bribe and kill her.

Yet she couldn't cover them both with a single pistol. General Napier was coming. Pepper had to get inside the cabin. She had to make a choice.

Then Sonny made the choice for her. He rushed Wainwright, bowling the old cowboy over. Wainwright landed with a thump, but he showed a remarkable ability to brawl. He kicked the feet out from under Sonny and landed atop him with a vicious punch. The two of them rolled toward Pepper, pummeling each other with a very real hate.

Pepper found herself making a decision she didn't want to make. A decision on the spur of the moment.

With the butt of the pistol, she knocked Sonny flat. The young man groaned as he hit the porch facedown.

Pepper shuddered and broke into a sweat. His skull had made a hollow sound. She didn't hate him that much, but she didn't dare take him inside either.

Grabbing Wainwright by the collar, she dragged him inside the cabin as he scrambled to his feet. She examined the locks and realized again that Dan was right. No one could come through this door unless she let them.

She shut the door. It latched as silently as it opened, with a finality that made her want to fling herself back outside and take her chances.

But that was stupid. If Dan could defend himself from here, so could she, especially with the help of his man. She glanced worriedly at Wainwright. He didn't look any too helpful. In fact he seemed more concerned with blotting his bloody nose with his pristine white handkerchief than with helping her set up for the fight. "Do you suppose Sonny will be all right when the terrorists show up?" she asked. "I'd hate to think they'd kill him for failing."

"I hope they gut-shoot him. He always acts like he's so smart, you know?"

"I do know." As Wainwright reminded her of Sonny's faults, she felt a little more cheerful about her choice.

Still she kept an eye on Wainwright as she pressed her hand on the surface of the table. It didn't jiggle. The furniture was like everything else in here—unexpectedly strong. Placing her backpack and the Beretta down, she opened the lid of the trunk, shined the flashlight inside, and gasped when a mouse scurried out.

As she jumped back, Wainwright picked up her pistol. "Ma'am, I appreciate you dropping this gun, because I got to tell you, I don't like hitting a lady, but I would have done it if I had to."

She stared at the pistol Wainwright pointed at her, and realized she *had* believed Dan sent someone to help her. She'd simply made the wrong choice.

Twenty-seven

ainwright pulled another, smaller pistol out of his jacket, handling both guns with daunting familiarity. He slouched back out of reach of her lashing feet, and with a smirk, he commanded, "Move toward the door and open it like a good girl."

Pepper was sick of being patronized. She was sick of being afraid and of pretending to be someone other than herself. She was sick of men with their war games, their plots, and their stupid assumptions. She wanted her land, she wanted her freedom, and she, by God, was going to live through this battle so she could do whatever she wanted for the rest of her life without interference from anyone, and that included Daniel Graham. Planting her hands on her hips, she asked, "What are you going to do, Wainwright? Kill me?"

At the annoyance in her tone, Wainwright's smirk disappeared. "No way, lady. I'm going to turn you over to that fellow who's been paying me good money to watch you and Dan, and he's going to hand over a wad big enough to get me a long, long ways away from here."

She couldn't help it. She grinned. "How far do you think you'll have to go to escape a madder-than-hell Dan Graham? A Tibetan monastery doesn't seem your sort of place."

Wainwright's lower lip protruded. "I can get away from Dan."

"Sure you can." She stepped toward Wainwright.

He stepped back. "Stay away. Mr. Graham told me about your judo or karate or whatever it is you know."

Couldn't Russell keep his mouth shut about anything? She kept talking. "That's assuming this guy who's paying you isn't going to put a bullet between your eyes because he's done using you."

"Hey! There's no call for that kind of talk." Wainwright's indignation seemed unfeigned. "It isn't seemly, coming from a pretty girl like you."

"Hey!" she mocked. "These people are international terrorists. Do you think they really give a damn about you or me or anybody else?"

The pistols wavered. "Terrorists? Don't be silly. There's just those guys who want to get even with Dan for being such a smart young cuss . . ." Seeing her lip curl, Wainwright gestured with the pistols. "You don't know what you're talking about. Open the door."

"You don't like anybody that's younger than you or smarter than you, do you? So I guess you're mad at the whole world."

His little pistol steadied on her chest. "Open the door."

She should have handled him better, let him know the kind of scum he'd made a deal with, coaxed him into letting her go. One by one, she unlatched the locks. She pulled the door open to a world blessed by the last rays of the sun. With a glance behind her, she realized he still maintained a substantial distance from her. She dashed out and to the side, where the wall would protect her.

She didn't see him. Didn't hear a sound. As she rounded the corner, there wasn't a whisper of warning, yet a man's hand wrapped around her wrist.

Dan said, "It's me."

Pepper had never screamed in fear in her life. She did now. Her blood pressure hit its limit.

Through the thumping of her heart, she heard him repeat, "Pepper, it's me."

Dan. *It was Dan.*

That bastard. He wore the same clothes he had been wearing, with the addition of a bulletproof vest that strained across his broad chest.

She saw a horse trotting back down the path toward the ranch.

Samson.

Wainwright thundered after Pepper.

Dan flung her to the floor beside the still-unconscious Sonny. Stepping up, Dan punched Wainwright in the face, using Wainwright's momentum to knock him ass over teakettle. Wainwright skidded across the porch on his face. The Beretta 9mm went flying. Pepper scrambled after it.

Dan started toward Wainwright.

With his own small pistol, Wainwright shot at Dan.

"Goddamn you, Wainwright." Dan flinched and kicked the gun out of Wainwright's hand hard enough to send it soaring far off into the grass. "You're the dumbest son of a bitch to ever work this ranch. If you live through this, you're going to prison." Hoisting Sonny over his shoulder, Dan headed for the cabin. "Come on, Pepper, they're almost here."

Fine. The terrorists were almost here. Dan *was* here. She knew who she hated most, but it was a close contest.

Pocketing the Beretta, she followed him. "What about Samson?" He deserved better than to die out there.

"He's a smart old horse," Dan assured her. "He'll take a detour and find his way home eventually."

Pepper shut the door. "Wainwright?"

Dan nodded toward the window. "Take a look."

She looked out and saw Wainwright running after Samson, catching his mane, scrambling onto his back. Samson never slowed as he went under a low-hanging branch and scraped Wainwright off.

Wainwright hit the ground on his back. Getting up, he chased after Samson again, but Samson would have no more of the old cowboy. His steady trot became a gallop, and he veered off the path and into the woods.

Dan laughed and placed the limp Sonny on the floor at the back of the cabin.

Pepper ignored them both. More important things needed attention than two macho men who thought they were the hottest stuff on the block. Going to the open trunk, she surveyed the contents with lethal satisfaction. She had found the only thing that could make her smile—Dan's stash of weapons. She unloaded it onto the table. A heavy rifle, with a good long scope. Goggles . . . night goggles? She slipped them over her eyes, and viewed everything with a yellow tint. In the back, dark corner, she saw Sonny reach up and touch his head. Yes, these were definitely night goggles.

Sonny groaned.

"Waking up?" Dan asked.

"Oh, God," Sonny said. "I'm dizzy. I'm sick."

"I'll bet you are." Dan sounded a little odd himself.

She swung her head toward him.

He was ripping away his torn shirt sleeve. It took a minute to realize—blood stained the material.

Pulling off the goggles, she asked, "What happened?"

"That idiot shot me with his stupid popgun." Dan sounded disgusted. "Give me a hand, will you, Pepper? This stupid hole won't stop bleeding." He had retrieved a first aid kit, and he handed her a roll of gauze.

She hesitated.

"It's not bad. The bullet went right through. Just wrap it up," he instructed in a kind tone, as if she were squeamish.

It wasn't that. He was hot and perspiring, and he smelled. Not badly, of course not. Only Dan could get ready for battle, catch his horse, ride up a steep hill, and still make her want to lick his sweaty skin. There was no help for it. She had to touch him. Pressing one end of the bandage on his arm, she wrapped the gauze around and around. With as much venom as she could manage, and right now she was a striking rattlesnake, she said, "I should have killed you while I had the chance."

"If it makes you feel any better, no one, man or

woman, has ever brought me down and taken my weapon from me. Only you."

"I would feel *better* if I had *shot* you." She had never meant anything so much in her life.

"You've never shot anyone. I'm telling you, it isn't usually this pretty." The warning sounded clear in his voice. He nodded toward Sonny. "Did Wainwright knock him cold?"

She said nothing.

"Pepper?"

"I did." She tied off the bandage and went back to the table. "You failed to mention who your backup was."

"My mistake." Dan chortled. "Wait until the other guys hear the great terrorist-fighter was defeated by a female civilian."

Sonny groaned.

Dan was suddenly as serious as a heart attack. "Sonny, you going to be any good to us?"

Sonny didn't answer.

Remembering the sound of the gun butt against his skull, Pepper confessed, "I hit him pretty hard."

In a voice so calm and confident Dan might have faced this situation every day—and, she reminded herself, he had—he said, "He's had worse. When we get him out of here, the medics will take him."

He didn't show an ounce of concern. What an obnoxious prick.

"The guys in town will be leading the rescue, but because of the terrorists' trick, they won't be here right away. It's up to us to stay alive until they get here. We've got to be smart, and we've got to be fast." Going to the table, Dan picked up the heavy vest. "Bulletproof." He held it for her.

She slipped it on. It was big, built for Dan's broad shoulders.

"Buckle it."

Even when she fastened the buckles, it slipped back and forth across her chest.

Dan took up the rifle. "Sniper rifle," he informed her. "A Parker-Hale M-85, and enough ammo to bring down a small army." He pointed at what looked like a large calculator. "Electronic detonator for the claymore mines." He showed her the handguns. "Two Mark XIX Desert Eagle .44 Magnums with detachable scopes." He indicated a padded computer sleeve. "Turn that on."

She unwrapped it and found herself staring at an electronic panel. She ran her fingers over the edges and along the back and found the switch. She flipped it on and saw the land as it sloped away from the cabin. Each tree, each branch was as clearly outlined as if it were daylight. Somewhere out there, Dan had affixed cameras to help him fight off his attackers, and they showed the terrain as clearly as she could see it with her own eyes.

Dan glanced over. "Pepper, look at the screen. What do you see?"

Something glowed red as it slipped from tree to tree toward the cabin.

Not something. *Someone.*

With a shock, she realized the lighted shape was human.

Her focus swung from Dan to the danger. Her heart thumped, then beat like a runner's at the end of a race.

But she had only begun. "General Napier," she whispered.

"No, she won't be here yet. Not her, and not my man, Schuster. The first rule of being a general: Send in the expendable soldiers first. The fight will be almost over before either one of them makes an appearance." He pulled a small scope from his pocket and handed it to Pepper. "Put this on the Beretta. We'll need it before it's all over."

Pepper picked up the pistol. Looked at it, looked at him, thought about the things he'd said to her. Decided she needed Dan too badly to put him out of his misery now. She picked up the scope and affixed it to the pistol. "You're mighty trusting considering an hour ago you called me a coward and said all I was good for was running away."

"An hour ago I was an ass. Now I'm not."

In as snotty a tone as she could manage, she said, "You should get a second opinion. In fact, I'm glad to give it to you. You still are. An ass. The biggest ass I've ever had the misfortune to meet."

He slanted a glance at her. His tone never changed as he indicated the glowing soldier on the screen. "Do you want to know why he glows like that?"

Yes, she wanted to know why he glowed like that. But she snapped, "If it makes you feel smarter to tell me, go ahead."

"The cameras see the combatants in color." From the corner of the trunk he pulled a small, dark box that fit in the palm of his hand.

Behind the first attacker, she saw another. For some

reason he seemed brighter, more vibrantly red. Another attacker followed behind him. He glowed with a spark of green.

She hated to ask, but her life might depend on her knowing. "Why are they different colors?"

"I adjusted the sensors so different weapons glow distinctly." Dan glanced at the screen. "Green. He has a grenade launcher. These walls won't hold up to that. We'll take him out right away."

"How are we going to do that?"

Dan showed her the box. "Claymore mines."

She could shoot, but she knew nothing about stuff like this. About military weaponry. But she nodded as if she did.

She didn't fool Dan, for he explained, "When I got this place ready, I placed mines on the trees. They're set to explode with this. It's an electronic charge."

She nodded again. She got it now. "Right."

More men appeared on the monitor. Six, moving with speed and stealth toward the cabin.

"There they are." Dan sounded almost pleased. When he saw her staring incredulously at him, he explained. "It's the waiting I hate."

She couldn't keep back her corrosive response. "It's the lack of faith I hate."

"Forgive me." He sounded sincere, and what she could see of him looked sincere.

"When I die." She glanced at the screen. "You might not have to wait too long."

He had the nerve to tuck his finger under her chin and lift her face to his. "I pledged safety to a child, and I lost her. I'm not losing you too."

"You also promised not to hurt me." Pepper shoved his hand aside. "I've seen how you keep your promises."

"Do your part, and you'll come out all right."

She wanted to retort that he was wrong, but that was stupid and childish. She wanted him to keep this promise.

He pointed to the ammunition. "Keep the rifles loaded. When I tell you, press the buttons for the land-mines. The walls are reinforced, the glass is bullet proof. Stay low, and stay away from the rifle holes."

Pepper had never before heard that tone in Dan's voice: calm, instructional, and deadly. It had an odd effect on her. It made the moment seem both less frightening and more real. She wiped her sweaty palms on the sides of her jeans. "Rifle holes?"

"There are three holes on either side of the door at irregular intervals low on the front walls, and one on each side wall."

She knelt on the floor and ran her fingers along the wall.

Dan knelt beside her, so close she could feel his warmth. "Keep an eye on your monitor."

She glanced over. Another four shapes had joined the first ones. Most of them glowed red, but she could see occasional sparks of yellow and blue.

She didn't ask what that meant. What difference did it make? She and Dan had to kill everyone or die. It was as simple as that. "Dan, these aren't our troops, are they? Did General Napier dupe American troops into coming and fighting for her?"

"It's not that easy. No one, not even a general, can

move American troops into battle without clearance." Dan picked up the sniper rifle. He pointed at the monitor. "See that guy right there?"

She saw a glowing red form running from tree to tree, coming toward the cabin. "Yes."

"If he were one of our guys, my equipment would recognize his weapons as ours. It's possible for mercenaries and terrorists to carry American equipment, but not for American troops to carry anybody else's equipment. Okay?"

"Much better."

"I'm going to take him out as soon as he gets to here." He pointed again. "We're trying to make the grenade launcher swerve toward this mine."

She saw a clear, flat light against a tree. The mine. "Good."

Dan caught her chin again, and this time he cared nothing for her struggles. He pressed a hard kiss on her. "For luck," he said, and he lay down on the floor. He thrust the rifle through the wall, shot and withdrew in one smooth motion.

The red glow dropped.

A fusillade of bullets raked the walls. She could hear them striking the wood outside, hear the ping as they hit the reinforcement, and she couldn't stop herself. She shrank back, sure she was going to die.

Instead, in that calm tone, Dan said, "Good. Our grenade launcher is swerving. See."

She opened her eyes, the eyes she hadn't realized she had closed. She looked at the screen. The green blip was running sideways.

"All right?" Dan asked.

"Yes." She was. The primitive instincts that had carried her so far in life kicked in.

"Good." Dan handed her the little box. "When the grenade launcher gets here, push this button."

Her hands shook, but she nodded. She could do that. She could do anything she had to do. Her emotions sharpened to a razor's point. Survival. That was all that mattered now. Survival.

With a grace and speed that amazed her, Dan moved from hole to hole, shooting, taking men out, moving the grenade launcher closer to the mine. Dan was good. He was probably the best. With the preparations he had made and his skill, they had a chance.

"Four men down," he said.

The grenade launcher was in position. She pushed the button.

The floor shook from the blast.

The green blip went down and didn't move.

Eight more blips appeared on the screen.

It looked like a video game, one of those with a warning about violence.

"They brought a lot of men for a double prize, you and me. All right. We've got six mines left." He showed Pepper which buttons to push, and his hand didn't shake at all. "Take out as many as you can. We're going to go out fighting."

"We're going to win."

After that the battle blurred for Pepper into a series of buttons, rifles, and explosions. The terrorist troops kept coming, more and more of them, overwhelming the cabin in a tide.

"It's almost over," Dan announced, "because there they come. There's your general and my man."

Not even the prospect of death could dim Pepper's irritation. "She's not *my* general." She saw two purple blips on the monitor. "Why are they that color?"

"Body armor. Got any mines left?"

"One."

"Make it count."

"I made them all count."

He grinned at her. "I know. You can guard my back any day."

It was, she realized, his farewell tribute.

Damn it. She was going to die. Dan was going to die.

She sent a prayer winging to God. A prayer to save Dan.

She snatched a moment from the study of her monitor to glance at him. He shot with precision and efficiency. He moved with an economy of motion. His hair was tousled. His face was dirty. She hated him for betraying her, and she prayed that he lived.

She didn't want to contemplate what that meant.

A whole group of assailants ran for the grenade launcher.

"Dan—"

"I see it." Dan started firing, one shot after another. Men went down.

Someone picked up the grenade launcher and aimed it at the cabin.

Dan used his command voice. "Pepper, go to the back and get down."

She didn't give a damn about his command voice.

He was still shooting.

She had one more mine. Three combatants moved into place. She fixed her eyes on the screen. A little closer. A little—

Dan's voice rose and snapped. "Pepper."

"No." It was the last word she would say. How appropriate to go down defiant. And, more quietly, "I forgive you."

The grenade launcher pointed at the house.

She pushed the button.

And a double explosion rocked the cabin.

She found herself on the floor, her hands over her head, Dan on top of her.

Dust rose. The whole cabin creaked. But nothing crumpled around them. No timbers fell.

"What the hell?" Dan's voice rumbled through her. "They missed."

She pushed at him. "Get off me."

He held her for one more moment, she supposed to prove he could.

Then he reached for the monitor, which was lit up like a Christmas tree. "Well, about time. The cavalry has arrived."

Twenty-eight

Dan watched Pepper as she placed her folded coat under Sonny's head. "I'm sorry," she apologized for the fifth time. "I thought Wainwright was the good guy."

"It's okay," Sonny mumbled. He maintained consciousness, but he was obviously suffering from a splitting headache. He needed the medics, and as soon as all the terrorists had been rounded up, Dan would open the door.

His caution made Pepper furious. She was also dirty, bleeding from a cut on her chin—and alive.

It was a miracle. She was alive.

He hadn't let her near the windows, although the American troops had illuminated the whole mountain with floodlights. He said he didn't intend to lose her now from a stray bullet.

To Sonny she said, "Dan didn't tell me he had the whole U.S. Army on call by satellite."

"Didn't matter," Sonny said. "They would either arrive on time or they wouldn't."

She cast Dan a furious glance. That was what he'd been saying to her.

Dan added, "Because the terrorists tricked us, the unit wasn't in position when the attack started."

"All right. I got it!" She pointed at the monitor and leaped to her feet. "Okay, you can let me out now. They've got them all."

Dan rose too. "They'll give us a hail when they're ready for us."

She hopped with impatience. "How will they do that?"

"Here they come now." He watched one man separate from the others and head toward the cabin.

A knock sounded.

Casting her a significant look, Dan said, "They'll knock." He opened the door.

"Sir, the area is secure." The sergeant snapped out a salute.

Dan saluted back. "About goddamn time you got here, Yarnell."

Then, as Pepper watched in amazement, the two of them slapped their hands together in a hearty handshake.

"Good to see you alive, Lieutenant." Yarnell smacked Dan on the shoulder. He was tall and lanky, with black boots each the size of Texas, and apparently camouflage was his favorite color.

"Good to be alive. Got medics nearby? Sonny's in the cabin. He managed to get knocked out, got a concussion." In the interest of giving Sonny a bad time later while he was fully conscious, Dan kept the how of it to himself.

Yarnell whistled for the medics, and two soldiers hustled into the cabin.

"Don't worry," Dan said to Pepper. "They'll handle him."

Dan glanced over the scene. Bodies were covered with tarps. Prisoners gathered in a sullen clump. Rifles and ammunition had been stacked in piles. "Did you get the two principals?"

"Napier is nice and secure. She says she doesn't know anything about this, of course."

Dan's mouth flattened. "She wouldn't. It was a coincidence she was in the area."

"Don't be ridiculous. It was no coincidence." Yarnell smirked. "She was trying to stop it."

"God save me from her kindness," Dan said.

"She . . . wasn't . . . trying . . . to stop it," Pepper ground out.

The two men looked at her, smiles twitching. "He was joking," Dan said.

"Oh." Pepper's indignation deflated.

Dan turned back to Yarnell. "Schuster?"

Yarnell gave a single shake of his head.

With quiet intensity Dan said, "Damn."

"What happened to him?" Pepper asked. "Was he killed?"

"Suicide," Yarnell said. "Terrorist commanders don't let themselves be captured. But we've got some of his men."

"Almost as good." Dan was pleased. "What are the plans for the general?"

Yarnell twitched a shoulder. "The brass asked that we

keep her here tonight. The winds are tricky for a helicopter landing, or so they say."

Dan considered him for a long moment. "Do they think she can highjack an army helicopter?"

"They seem to think she can do just about anything, and they're not taking any chances."

Dan whistled.

Pepper said nothing, but she agreed. General Napier had sayings for situations like this. *If defeat is inevitable, go out fighting. Death is the only acceptable surrender.* Of course Pepper had imagined her taking a heroic last stand against the terrorists, not aiding them.

"They want to make sure she gets to Washington for questioning. They'll fly her out in the morning."

"Hey, Lieutenant, hey, sir, why did you take us away from the bar?" Soldiers crowded the porch, at least a dozen of them, and all of them knew Dan. Each of them was armed to the teeth, wore camouflage streaked on their faces, and grinned at their old leader. They slapped his shoulder and shook his hand, and he slapped and shook back. They spoke a language Pepper didn't understand, about M-16s and HEs, and they laughed about death and dying.

She stood back and shivered in the cool air, feeling ridiculously alone and excluded.

She had always been alone. Why did it matter now? Now after she'd faced her own death? She didn't need to be the center of a group of friends. She could slip away, go back to the house, make a life for herself. Maybe send letters to Hope and Gabriel . . .

She didn't notice as Dan began to introduce her to his

compatriots, because a single man walked toward the porch. He wore a camouflage green shirt and pants and black army boots, like the rest of the soldiers, but he wore no insignia on his sleeve. His hair was black, his eyes were green, his face resembled a Mayan statue. He was looking at her. Staring at her. Staring so hard she shifted from one foot to the other in discomfort.

So much for slipping away. The FBI agent had arrived to take her for questioning.

But when he stopped a few feet away, he smiled at her, a whimsical, *glad* smile, as if he were happy to see her. As if he knew her. As if she should know him.

And there was something about him . . .

The hair. The eyes. The face.

Her eighth birthday party. Blue and gold streamers draped across the room. She looked around the table at her friends and her family. She looked up at the boy leaning in the corner. He smiled at her.

"Gabriel," she whispered.

Her brother. He was her brother.

It couldn't be true.

But he nodded. He held out his hands.

"Gabriel," she said a little louder.

The love she had felt for Gabriel rose from the basement of her soul where she had banished it. The love overwhelmed the memories, the resentments, and the loneliness of so many years in exile. She caught her breath on a sob. Putting her hands in his, she said, "Oh, Gabriel, I've missed you so much!"

As if he feared she might break, he pulled her into a delicate embrace, then as she hugged him back, his grip grew fiercer and stronger. "We thought we'd lost you. Darling sister, we thought we had lost you forever."

Dan watched Pepper descend the hill with her brother's arm draped across her shoulder.

He was a fool to be jealous, but envy clawed at his gut. He had cherished the dream that she would find her family. He had hoped she would welcome them back into her life. But he'd also imagined he would be the one who found them for her. He had been sure she would be his when it happened.

He was a selfish bastard. He couldn't even be glad she had found her brother.

Because . . . because she wasn't his. She was withholding her glances, her words, herself. He had wrecked everything with his distrust and his cruel words. He winced when he remembered what he had said and how he had rejected her. He didn't know how to get back to where they'd been before.

Dan shook his head and started down the hill after them. "I can't let her go. She's mine."

Pepper stumbled along the well-lit path beside Gabriel. All her doubts about finding her family had been swept away. She knew Gabriel had looked for her and for all of the family. She trusted him. She had always trusted him.

Now a different loneliness clawed at her soul. Dan had made clear what he thought of her, and so she banished him from her hopes. If only she could banish him from her heart. She walked away from him without looking back, and wondered whether he even noticed she had left, and wished she didn't care enough to wonder.

They were almost all the way down the steep path when Gabriel said mournfully, "I should have known."

She glanced at him. "What?"

"You've got man troubles."

With a jolt she realized she hadn't asked him a single question about his life, what had happened, what he knew. She laughed shamefacedly. "I am so selfish. Forgive me. You've come all this way to find me. You helped rescue me, and I'm so bound up in my own problems, I haven't even thanked you."

"Remember your manners, they're the grease of life," he said, teasing her, using the phrase their mother had used.

Pepper stopped to let some soldiers go by and found herself smiling at Gabriel. "So tell me, are you married?"

"Not ever. I haven't had the good fortune to find the right woman."

"Maybe the right woman hasn't found you." Pepper started walking again, sliding down the last steep stretch to Mrs. Dreiss's yard. She could see the house, lit by floodlights, and soldiers on guard at every corner. "Do you live in Texas?"

"Boston."

She blinked. "That's a long way from Texas. How did you . . . ohh. *They* sent you there, didn't they?"

"The kindly church board who separated us all?" he asked grimly. "No. I went there to find Hope."

Hope. Her sister. The one person Pepper truly blamed for her own loneliness and exile. But in the last few days

Pepper had grown up, and a great longing to see Hope clutched at her. "Did you—" Pepper could hardly speak around the lump of excitement and dread. "Did you find her?"

They walked across the yard toward the back porch, where a tall, well-dressed woman waited. A dark-haired man stood behind and off to the side, a protective presence. The woman was heavily pregnant. Her hand rested on her belly, and she watched Pepper come toward her with a hungry intensity that both beckoned and broke Pepper's heart.

It was her sister. It was Hope. Pepper walked faster, then ran, calling, "Hope. You're here; you came at last!"

Hope clutched the handrail to descend the stairs. The man helped her with his hand under her arm. The two women met in the middle of the yard, their arms outstretched.

Hope's belly got in the way of their first embrace.

Pepper's tears blinded her. Burning with joy and love, she rested her head on Hope's shoulder and sobbed.

Hope's voice broke and wavered as she repeated over and over, "At last I've found you. At last I've found you."

It sounded as if she'd been practicing the phrase for a long, long time.

Lifting her head, Pepper stared into Hope's face. The last time she'd seen her sister, Hope had been sixteen—a mature, responsible sixteen, but sixteen in appearance.

Now she was a matron, thirty-three years old, strong, glowing . . . pregnant.

"How?" Pepper pressed her hand to Hope's belly. "When?"

Hope hiccuped and dug two tissues out of her pocket. She offered Pepper one. "The usual way, and really soon."

Accepting it, Pepper blew her nose. She looked toward the dark-haired man standing not far away with Gabriel. "Your husband?"

"Zack. Zack Givens." Hope sounded proud. "Isn't he beautiful?"

Pepper laughed, a burst of hiccuping laughter. "He is, yes."

"What about *him*?" Hope pointed back toward the path. "Is he yours?"

Pepper didn't have to look to know of whom Hope spoke. Dan stood on the other side of the yard, watching them. She could feel his gaze, and she resented that he intruded on this private moment. A little too sharply, she said, "No. I thought he might be, but it didn't work out."

"Oh." Hope's gaze lingered on Dan, then shrewdly observed the ravages on Pepper's face. "I see." Licking her thumb, she rubbed it on Pepper's chin. "I'd recognize you anywhere. Your face is always dirty." Her smile wavered and broke. "I thought General Napier was going to kill you. I thought we were too late."

"Just in time." Hope sobbed, and Pepper embraced her and said, "Don't, dear. We're together now."

"This time I won't let you go," Hope answered forcefully. "I'm so sorry. Pepper, I'm so sorry. I've said it before and I'll never stop saying it. I should never have let them take you. Take any of you. I should have run away with you, kept us together any way I could."

"It's not your fault." Seeing Hope's furious regret,

Pepper believed it for the first time. For the first time, she put aside the feelings of an eight-year-old child and saw the truth. "They would have found us. They would have brought us back and nothing would have been any different."

In a whisper, Hope said, "They murdered Mama and Daddy. I know they did."

Pepper squeezed her harder. "What?"

Hope winced.

And Pepper realized—not only was her sister pregnant, but her stomach muscles were drawn up tight into a cramp. "Is it supposed to do that?"

Hope shushed her, but Pepper's voice had carried.

A few large strides brought Zack to Hope's side. "Hi, Pepper, good to meet you at last."

His voice was nice, she noticed, deep, with that oddly crisp Massachusetts accent, but he wasn't looking at her.

"Hope, is there something you want to tell me?" He didn't wait for her reply but pressed his hand on Hope's belly. He fixed her with a stern gaze. "How long has this been going on?"

"A few hours."

Gabriel drew closer.

So did Dan.

Hope was in labor, Pepper realized. "Oh, my God! Oh, my God!" An hour ago Pepper had thought she was going to die. Now a new life was coming into the world. She wanted to clap her hands, to dance, to shout. Instead she said, "Hope, you're going to have a baby!"

Hope smiled through a pain. "Yes, dear."

"How many hours?" Zack demanded.

Hope tried to smile and failed miserably. "Six."

"Damn it to hell, Hope." Gabriel threw his hat on the ground. "I told you to stay home!"

In a bright tone Hope said, "We brought the midwife."

Wrapping his arm around her waist, Zack helped her toward the house. "You promised we wouldn't have to use her."

Pepper stayed on her other side and listened in a mixture of dismay and envy. They were a family—Zack, Gabriel, and Hope. They sounded like a family; they loved each other like a family; they knew all each other's secrets like a family. And she had been doing everything in her power to avoid them.

Dan was right.

She had been a fool—about so many things.

As the three of them made their way toward the house, Dan walked up to Gabriel. He held out his hand, and when Gabriel shook it, he said, "I'm Dan Graham. I live here with Pepper." Dan was proud of his less-than-subtle claim on her. "Come with me. I think we're supposed to boil water."

Lana Pepper Givens was delivered in Mrs. Dreiss's bed at four o'clock in the morning. The infant shrieked loud enough to wake every soldier camped out in the yard. Her screams brought the three men and the woman playing cards at the kitchen table to their feet.

"I get to go smoke a cigar!" Russell said triumphantly, and rushed out onto the porch.

The crying came clearly through the walls of the tent pitched in the middle of the army camp. General

Jennifer Napier lay in her sleeping bag and stared at the tent top, at the lights that shone through the nylon, and cursed the tracking device Sergeant Yarnell had fastened around her ankle with a steel rope. That baby guaranteed attention would be focused elsewhere. General Napier could probably escape now, but she would be prey, entertainment for the troops as they dogged her through the mountains. Even in these unimaginable circumstances, even in the depths of what looked like disaster, General Jennifer Napier did not lose her dignity in such a manner.

In Mrs. Dreiss's bedroom the midwife cleaned the infant, ignoring its high-pitched crying and its ineffectual kicks, and reflected with satisfaction that mother and baby were doing well. Wrapping Lana in a blanket, the midwife placed a pink cap on her bald head and handed her to the mother.

From a safe distance Pepper watched the proceedings and marveled at how natural and yet how extraordinary this was. She had a sister. She had witnessed her sister give birth. Now she had a niece.

With delight Hope accepted her squalling infant. "She's beautiful."

Zack leaned over them both. "She's gorgeous." His deep voice rose an octave, and to the baby he murmured, "Yes, her is. Her is the most beautiful girl in the world."

Pepper grinned to hear the tough, taciturn man reduced to a babbling idiot by a red-faced, screaming baby.

"Pepper, come and see your niece," Hope commanded.

Pepper didn't really want to. She didn't know what to do with babies, especially babies this small. She had just spent hours locked in this room with a midwife and her brother-in-law, seeing parts of her newly found sister she had never dreamed of seeing, and now she had to coo over that ugly little . . . She leaned over the bed.

The baby stopped squalling, looked at Pepper, and like a monkey, she thrust out her lower lip.

"Oh, Pepper." Hope laughed and cried at the same time. "She looks like you."

"Poor kid." Pepper smoothed the little fist.

She didn't see the look Zack and Hope exchanged, but suddenly she found herself holding her niece. *"Oh."*

The skinny arms flailed, Lana's eyes opened and closed, sometimes separately, sometimes together, and the little mouth stretched and yawned.

Pepper's eyes swam with tears. "Oh. Her is beautiful."

Hope said, "Pepper, you'd better take her to see Gabriel before he breaks down that door."

But Dan was out there somewhere, waiting to see Pepper, wanting to talk to her. She stammered, "D . . . doesn't Zack want to do the honors?"

"I'd like one moment alone with my wife." Zack picked up Hope's hand and held it close to his heart, and the way he looked at Hope made Pepper hug the baby a little tighter. Any question she might have had about their relationship was answered right then. He adored his wife.

As Pepper tiptoed out of the room, she whispered to the baby, "They need privacy. Don't worry, it doesn't mean they love you less. It means that you're secure because you know they love each other and they'll always be together." She remembered what Hope said about Daddy and Mama, and wondered, Was it true? Had they been murdered? Were the wonderful parents she remembered real?

Had they been victims of the most horrific crime imaginable?

Pepper walked through the dining room and into the kitchen, staring down at the small human being in her arms, desperate not to drop her, determined to be the best aunt ever.

Three chairs scraped back as she stepped inside the room. She knew Gabriel and Dan. In fact, Dan she knew only too well. And although she had met the lady only once in her sojourn here nine years ago, Pepper recognized her: Dan's mother, Barbara Graham. She stood almost as tall as her son. Like him, she was dark-skinned, but she had dark hair and high cheekbones that made her the spitting image of Dan's Indian great-grandmother.

Like a good mother, Barbara had come because her son had almost been killed. She said, "Good to see you again, Pepper," and she sounded as if she meant it. She had always seemed to be nice, and Pepper could hardly blame her for raising a jackass for a son.

Lana blinked at the overhead light, and her little monkey face screwed up in an exaggerated frown.

Gabriel rushed forward. "Is everything all right? Hope? The baby? Let me see." He looked stunned when he looked down at that scrunched little infant face. "Is she supposed to look like that?"

Barbara pushed her way in. "Let me see. Oh!" She crooned, "Yes, her is supposed to look like that. Her is beautiful."

"If you say so," Gabriel replied doubtfully.

Pepper wanted to concentrate on the baby in her arms. She didn't want to glance up. But she couldn't help it. Dan was looking at her, she could feel it, and irresistibly he drew her gaze.

He watched them all impassively, not indicating by his face or form that he cared about the baby or about Pepper or about joining the celebration of Lana's birth. Yet a warmth slid down her spine.

He wasn't indifferent.

But, Pepper told herself, she didn't care. Yes, he had saved her from death. He had also stripped her of the pride and independence she had worked so hard to develop. She had promised to marry him, and he had believed the worst of her. His contempt had burned away the love she'd felt for nine long years. She was free of him at last. Looking down at little Lana, Pepper smiled. She had other things to occupy her mind.

The back door slammed. Leaving an obnoxious cloud of cigar smoke on the porch, Russell hurried to Dan's side. "Is it a girl?" he asked.

Dan observed the way Pepper cradled the baby, saw how Gabriel hovered over them both, and torn between gladness and sorrow, he said, "It's a family."

Twenty-nine

An hour later, when Pepper came into the kitchen, Dan, Barbara, and Russell were still awake, drinking coffee around the kitchen table.

She nodded at everyone, even made casual eye contact with Dan, and joked with what she thought was admirable aplomb, "These all-night parties are killers, aren't they?"

"You said it." Barbara propped up her eyelids with her fingers. "I'm too old for this."

Russell stopped scratching his stubbled chin long enough to ask, "How's the kid?"

"Asleep. So are Hope and Zack. The midwife's in my bed." Stretching the kinks out of her back, Pepper headed for the coffeepot. "Thank God someone made this."

"Danny did." Barbara patted his arm. "He said you'd need it."

"Danny was right." Pepper grabbed a mug and lifted the pot. "Thanks, Danny."

In that deep, low, warm voice that sounded like sex on the prowl, he answered, "You're welcome, Pepper."

She slopped the coffee onto the counter.

Trouble. Right away he made trouble. She looked at him without a twinge of affection.

An awkward silence filled the kitchen as Pepper wiped up the spill and loaded her coffee with sugar. "Did someone find Wainwright?"

Russell said, "He's in the county jail with buckshot in his rear."

Turning, Pepper raised her eyebrows at him.

"He tried to take refuge in the bunkhouse, and one of the cowboys took exception." Russell grinned. "I'm giving him a bonus tomorrow."

Barbara laughed a deep and hearty laugh. "Russell, you're a scoundrel."

"Yeah." Russell held her hand in that way that clearly proclaimed that she was his.

Pepper said, "I hadn't realized you two were together again."

Dan looked startled. "Neither had I."

"People can change," Barbara said. "Even your father."

"Even your mother." Russell nudged her.

Barbara shot an enigmatic glance at Dan and Pepper and finished smoothly, "Sometimes it's necessary to first find out how miserable you are apart."

Pepper stiffened. Had that been aimed at her? Or did it just feel that way?

Russell cleared his throat. "Dan, you and I might as well go down and get those chores done. Then you can move back home, since there aren't enough beds here."

Russell was right. There weren't enough beds, the danger was over, and Russell would send someone over to help work the ranch. Dan could go home.

As Pepper considered the good news, the silence in the kitchen stretched out forever.

Finally Barbara said, "Russell, you're an old pain in the ass."

"Yeah, Dad, you really are." Dan stood. "Pepper, can I talk to you out on the porch?"

"She doesn't want to talk to you," Russell said.

At the same time Barbara said, "That would be a good idea."

Dan's parents glared at each other.

Pepper said, "Sure." Whatever Dan had to say to her, it didn't matter. She didn't care.

Grabbing her coat off the rack, Dan put it around her shoulders. He placed her buff-colored cowboy hat on her head.

But she would have none of that. Cinderella was dead, and he had killed her. Removing the hat, she tossed it onto one of the chairs. In clear, precise tones she said, "I don't want that anymore."

Barbara said, "Ouch."

Dan looked for a moment as if he wanted to jam it back on her head.

Pepper stared back at him, challenging him, daring him.

"All right. I'll keep it here until you want it back." He sounded sincere and looked confident.

What a jerk.

A nice, clean jerk who had at some point in the night

taken a shower and now smelled like shampoo and warm skin. She didn't need this kind of enticement. As she stepped out onto the chilly porch, she huddled into her coat. "Don't hold your breath."

Her lawn had been transformed into a temporary army camp. Dozens of tents were pitched all over, with a spotlight on the tent in the middle of the yard, and armed guards around it. General Napier's tent.

A few soldiers were stirring. The cooks were awake. But for the most part it was silent, cool, fresh with the approaching dawn of a new day.

Pepper said softly, "Guess we'd better keep it quiet, huh?"

As if she hadn't spoken, Dan asked, "Are you going?"

She knew him. He was trying to shake her with his directness, but she could fend him off. In an upbeat, civil tone she said, "To Boston? Yes, you were right. I want to get to know my family. I can help with the baby and—"

"When are you coming back?"

She sucked in an annoyed breath. Couldn't he play the game?

Of course not. Not Dan Graham. Only when the game served him. "I don't know if I am."

The shadows and the light slashed his face into angles, and his eyes shone with dark power. "You own this land."

All right. She could speak plainly too. "I don't know if I'm going to keep the land. I can't ask you to care for it for an indefinite time. I know your dad will buy it."

"Mrs. Dreiss left it to you."

Oh, no. He wasn't going to play the guilt card. "She

didn't want me bound to it. She wanted to help me. And she did."

"What about me?" He stepped closer. "You promised to marry me."

A little too loudly she said, "You changed your mind."

He lowered his voice so the words barely reached her ears, so she had to strain to hear the wisps of temptation. "It would be very good between us. You love me, and I love you—"

"Oh, please. Don't. Don't even try to tell me you love me." She hated this. She hated him. She hated that the scent of him wrapped her in passionate memories when he was standing there lying to her without an ounce of shame. "Is that supposed to make my little girlish heart flutter? Because I don't need your kind of love. Love isn't believing the worst of me because of the evidence. Love is believing in me *despite* the evidence."

He took a breath, let it out, then took another breath. "Love is being vulnerable after too many years alone, and being scared so shitless I seized the evidence like a gun to fend you off." He spoke too rapidly, as if his every word embarrassed him.

She had no patience for this. She had no patience for herself and that part of her that wanted to pay heed and maybe admit he might be, not justified, but telling her the truth. "What a pile of crap."

"I know. I lost my head."

Well. Now that was an admission.

"I've done the wrong thing. I've *believed* the wrong thing. I should never have lost my faith in you." Taking her resisting hand, he held it against his heart. "But you said you forgave me. In the cabin, when we thought we were going to die. I heard you."

She didn't want to be close to him. She didn't want to suffer his excuses, and she didn't want to touch his chest. But struggling would be undignified, and she would lose, so she allowed her hand to rest limply in his. "I did say I forgave you, but it was the kind of forgiveness bestowed on people I will never see again."

Quizzically he said, "I didn't know there were different kinds of forgiveness."

"You learn something new every day. Anyway, I never said I still loved you. Sometimes love dies, and sometimes it's beaten to death. You took my trust and my love—the things I had never given anyone in all the years since I lost my family—and you spit on them."

"I'm sorry. I'm so sorry. Please believe me." Which was a lovely apology, but he didn't pause long enough to let her savor it. He went right on to the truth as he saw it. "But your love hasn't died."

The nerve. "And you would be the expert on my feelings?"

With compelling power he said, "Pepper, what we have between us isn't easy. It's not some lightweight emotion that can be crushed by disillusionment or broken by absence. You love me, and I love you."

She rolled her eyes.

"Don't be like that!" With his hair hanging over his forehead and indignation growing on his face, he looked less like the self-assured soldier who always had everything his own way and more like the young Dan Graham.

Good. Because at least the young Dan Graham had

had honest feelings. Crossing her arms over her chest, she leaned against the railing.

He was struggling now. The words weren't quite as glib. He let her hand go. "More than anything, you and the love I feel for you have defined my life." He grimaced as if he didn't want to talk anymore.

She couldn't resist prodding him. "Please. Go on."

"Yeah. Yeah." He leaned his hands against the railing and looked out over the makeshift army camp. In a voice so low she had to strain to hear him, he asked, "Do you remember when I told you about my belly wound and that I had peritonitis?"

"I remember." Carelessly she asked, "You almost died, right?"

"I did die, a couple of times."

She didn't like that. "Really?"

"I always came back."

"I guess you did." He was standing beside her, she reminded herself, quite alive.

"Each time I drifted back to consciousness, I returned to this body wracked with fever and ripe with agony, and always because the thought of you called me back. As long as you were in the world, I couldn't leave."

He hated admitting his need, and that, more than anything else, forced her to realize that he was telling the truth.

Yet . . . did he think he could use a speech to put a bandage on a wound he had inflicted?

He continued, "Not without knowing where you were, whether you needed me . . . Not without searching for you, finding you, and making you mine one more time."

"Well, you made me yours, and more than once." In a tone as insulting as she could make it, she asked, "Why aren't you satisfied?"

"Because it's not making love to you that's important." He held up his hands in a stop gesture. "I don't mean that the way it sounded." His eyes shone with frustration. "Having you proved that there's so much more between us. You're part of my being. You're my light at the end of the tunnel. You make my existence worthwhile, and I have to do everything in my power to keep you at my side."

"Except be the man I want to spend my life with."

"I *am* that man. Give me a chance. I beg you. Don't let one moment of panic—my panic—ruin our lives." Dan sounded, and looked, like the epitome of candor.

But she didn't care. "I can't take another chance on you. I would always wonder when you were going to hurt me again."

"I can't promise that between us we won't have words, but I can promise I will always face the world at your side." He kissed her cheek, a warm and gentle caress. In her ear he whispered, "Please, Pepper, marry me."

"No." She was still bleeding inside from the things he'd said, and she was scared. "I learned my lesson. I'm not going to be that stupid again."

"You're the one who said it best. We're two wounded souls, and somehow we complete each other. Let's complete each other forever."

Damn him. His sincerity caught at her throat. If she weren't careful, she would yield, and she couldn't. Not yet. Probably not ever.

She heard the stirring of many bodies, and grateful for the distraction, she looked out over the camp. The sun was lightening the eastern sky, and out of the center tent stepped General Jennifer Napier, fully dressed in combat fatigues, every hair in place, her face set in stern lines. She spoke sharply to the guards, who sprang to their feet around her, and they saluted as if she had done nothing wrong. Sergeant Yarnell joined them, a grim expression on his face.

Pepper fixed her gaze on the general; General Napier was not to be trusted. Ever. "What will they do with her?"

"She's going to Washington for questioning." Dan reminded her, "So are you."

"Yeah." Pepper watched the general as she strode toward the cook tent, her guards following on her heels. "Dan, you do realize she's dangerous?"

"Everyone realizes that."

A deep uneasiness stirred in Pepper's veins. "More dangerous now that she's cornered?"

Reaching inside his jacket, Dan pulled his Beretta out of its holster and handed it to her. "Does that make you feel better?"

Was he patronizing her? She didn't think so. It seemed more of a chivalrous gesture, one that showed his trust in her and her abilities. Another courtship gesture in his futile courtship. "Thank you." Holding the weight of the gun, feeling the warmth the metal had absorbed from his body, did make her feel better.

At that moment General Napier caught sight of Pepper. Her eyes narrowed. Her slight lips smiled. She came toward the porch, a strong, wily old mountain lion who faced the last fight of her life and planned to rend her share of flesh.

Yarnell stopped her at the foot of the stairs. "Ma'am, you can't go up there."

General Napier flashed him a look of scorn but stopped as instructed. She lifted her face toward Pepper's, and too clearly Pepper saw the age lines that marked her cosmetic-free face. She must have lied about her age, as she had lied about everything else.

"If it isn't little Jackie Porter. Or is it Pepper Prescott?" General Napier's glance flicked at Dan, and her eyes widened. "And Lieutenant Dan Graham."

Dan looked unimpressed by her venom. "Good to see you, ma'am."

"So," General Napier purred, indicating Pepper with a flick of her hand. "That's why *she* managed to escape me. She found you."

The sun peeked over the hill, lighting Dan's blond hair to gold. "You underestimate her, General Napier. She would have saved herself."

Yarnell watched General Napier with dislike. The soldiers surrounding her listened with interest.

Pepper's uneasiness deepened. No one except her seemed to realize how potentially precarious this situation was. The soldiers, the *men*, seemed to think that because General Napier was a woman and defeated, she no longer posed a threat.

"Don't be ridiculous." General Napier brushed his conviction aside. "She's pathetic. She told me about herself at that book signing. She's an orphan from, of all places, Texas. Her parents were cheap criminals who dumped her as soon as they could. She didn't have any resources. She must have been thrilled to latch on to you."

With a lack of intonation that was insulting in its disinterest, Dan said, "I'm sorry I had to see this, General Napier. I had hoped you would be a better loser."

Yarnell stepped close and took her arm. "Ma'am, I'm afraid you're going to have to come along with me."

As if everything happened in slow motion, Pepper saw General Napier pull the sidearm from the sergeant's holster. Smoothly the general aimed it at Dan's chest.

Pepper couldn't hear the shouts of warning. Didn't notice the soldiers' frantic attempts to stop General Napier. With deadly intent Pepper brought up Dan's pistol, held her breath, aimed. And fired. The percussion jerked her hand. The heat of the Beretta warmed her fingers. The shot screamed in her ears.

And Dan still stood, unhurt.

As General Napier fell, her pistol went flying. She grabbed her shattered arm and screamed in agony—and in fury.

The soldiers pointed their firearms at the general.

Picking up his pistol off the ground, Yarnell stared at it in dismay. "How did she do that?" he asked the air.

Gently Dan removed his pistol from Pepper's shaking hand. "Don't feel bad, Yarnell. Napier must have been an expert on disarming a man. I bet she gave instructions in her book. Right, Pepper?"

Grimly Pepper met his gaze. He was alive, and she had saved him. They were even. "Right."

"Ms. Prescott, that was the finest marksmanship I've

ever seen." Yarnell stared at General Napier as she writhed on the ground. "You shot that pistol right out of her hand. I am grateful, ma'am. Damned grateful."

"You're welcome, Sergeant." When the general had stopped her high-pitched screaming, Pepper walked down the steps to her. Leaning over, Pepper met General Napier's furious gaze, and in a voice that reached only the general's ears said, "I was aiming at your heart. But then, your heart is a very tiny target."

Thirty

*P*epper held the four-week-old Lana and argued with her brother-in-law. "It wasn't a gas pain. I tell you, she smiled at me."

Zack retorted, "Dr. Banks says babies can't smile until they're five weeks old."

"Lana is smarter than most babies," Pepper said loftily. As far as Pepper was concerned, Lana was the smartest baby in the world. Pepper looked around affectionately. It was good to be here in the Givens's conservatory in the bosom of her family.

She'd spent the first week of her exile—or rather, her return to civilization—in Washington, D.C., talking to the FBI and other law enforcement agencies about what she'd seen and heard in that parking garage.

Even Colonel Jaffe came down to introduce himself to her. Although he said very little, she found herself disarmed by his genial eyes and ready smile, and amazed and alarmed at his impression that she was Dan's woman.

She set him straight right away, but he still smiled.

She found it interesting that while the law enforcement agencies made clear their disapproval about her flight, they were extremely polite to Zack Givens's sister-in-law. Perhaps part of their courtesy was due to the presence of Zack's lawyer friend, Jason Urbano, who attended the hearings with her.

When she wasn't being questioned, she was shaking the hand of Senator Vargas and thanking him for believing her e-mail and taking action. She was packing up her apartment, putting her furniture into storage, collecting her plants, and gently passing her customers on to other landscapers. She hadn't decided what she was going to do with her plants or her furniture.

She hadn't decided what she was going to do with her life.

Nothing was the same. She had different options. She had different obligations. She had a niece, an older sister, a brother, a brother-in-law . . . and somewhere in the world, a younger sister to find.

"I heard Lana say her first word the other day." Gabriel smirked. "She looked in the mirror and said, 'Monkeyface.' "

"She did not!" Hope and Pepper said together.

"You only say that because she looks like me," Pepper added.

"That's right." Gabriel tugged on one of her curls. "Monkeyface."

"Actually," Hope said, "she looks like Caitlin."

The room got very quiet. Hope, Gabriel, and Pepper all remembered their sister as a baby. They had held her, kissed her, loved her, and they hadn't seen her since she was nine months old. Griswald had found no trace of her, but they knew that a baby who had been adopted had a different last name and maybe a different first name. The search would continue for Caitlin, but she was a teenager now. Would they ever get to see her again?

For that reason as well as for herself, Pepper cherished Lana. Zack's family welcomed Pepper with enthusiasm. At least one of Hope's friends came by every day, and they talked to Pepper as if they had known her for years. Even the servants beamed when they saw her. It was as if all the dreams she didn't know she'd dreamed had come true.

Except for one.

But she didn't think about *him*. She was busy with the holding, rocking, and burping. And if for the last week she had been aware of a certain restlessness, she attributed it to the need for employment. After all, she had worked hard for years. Spending time in the lap of luxury was bound to be unnerving. And if her restlessness took the form of erotic dreams involving a certain Idaho rancher, well, that didn't mean a thing.

Griswald stepped in the door. "Miss Pepper, you have a phone call."

"A phone call?" Gabriel lifted his eyebrows in surprise. "From who? She doesn't have any friends."

Everyone laughed, because at Lana's christening Pepper had been the most popular person there, but Pepper found herself annoyed. So what if no one in Boston was her personal friend? Gabriel had no reason to call attention to her isolation.

She had forgotten that in addition to being her favorite brother—her only brother—Gabriel could be a pain in the rear. In fact sometimes he reminded her a little bit of Russell Graham, who was probably now gloating at his success in disconnecting his son from the unsuitable Pepper Prescott.

"It is a young lady, and she is a great deal more polite than you, Mr. Gabriel," Griswald said with freezing politeness. "A Mrs. Rita Domokos, of Diamond, Idaho."

Pepper froze, unable to imagine why Rita would call her here.

Dan. One of the terrorists had returned. Dan was injured, he was dying . . .

Still in that same pompous butler tone, Griswald said, "She said to tell you everything is fine and she wants to talk."

Pepper blew out her held-in breath. She transferred Lana into Gabriel's arms.

"She's on line two. You can take it in Mr. Givens's study." Griswald transferred his disapproving gaze to Zack. "Since Miss Lana has been born, *he* never uses it."

While Zack lodged a laughing protest, Pepper hurried into his study and shut the door behind her. She punched line two and said eagerly, "Rita? How are you?"

Rita's voice came clearly across the wires. "I'm great. I've started the Web site. Barbara's helping me, and I need to know, do you want to sell seeds?"

"Oh! Oh, yes, I want to . . ." But Pepper had forgotten about that plan, and she wasn't there. She didn't know how the plants in Mrs. Dreiss's garden were doing, or even if they were still alive. She slithered into Zack's big leather chair. "I don't know. I've got a bunch of plants here that need to be transplanted soon, but I've been . . . How is everyone up there?"

"Good. Barbara and Russell are going to get married again on the Fourth of July." Rita sounded amused. "Russell keeps saying it's Independence Day for everyone but him. It's going to be a big party. You ought to come up."

Pepper soaked up the news, but she said, "I don't think Russell would invite me to a pig slop."

"I don't know. Let me ask him." Pepper heard Rita holler, "Hey, Russell, Pepper says you wouldn't invite her to a pig slop!"

Pepper wanted to smack her friend. "No! Rita, don't tell him that."

But it wasn't Rita's voice that spoke next. It was Russell Graham, and he sounded as irate as ever. "Damned right I wouldn't invite you to a pig slop. You go off and leave Dan again. I haven't seen the boy so bad since he got home from the service sliced to bits."

Pepper loved hearing that. She *loved* it. Of course she didn't want to think what her glee might mean or whether being happy at Dan's depression was an indication of a vengeful soul. "He should be able to forget about a miserable coward like me pretty quickly."

Russell snorted. "He gave me a bachelor party, ordered up some strippers from Boise, then spent the evening staring at their boobs and telling me they weren't as good as yours. Now I don't know the truth of that, but those girls had some pretty nice hooters, if you know what I mean, and for him to even *think* of yours when he could have been—"

Barbara's voice intruded. "Hello, Pepper. No, Russell, you can't have the phone back. So, Pepper, how's Boston? When are you coming home? Can you make it to my wedding? We'd love to see you there."

Russell's voice shouted in the background. "We need new towels and sheets! Our colors are blue and white!"

"Russell, shut up," Barbara snapped. "Pepper, honey, you don't have to bring a thing."

"We like red wines," Russell shouted. "And I drink Canadian Club!"

"Russell!"

The phone there hit the floor hard enough to make Pepper hold the receiver away from her ear. She heard a scuffle.

Rita got the phone again. "He's been dipping into the Canadian Club early," she advised Pepper. "But see? They'd like to have you at their wedding. It's going to be at the Congregational church at two, followed by a reception at their house, which should last all night."

"Rita, is it true Dan's moping after me?" Pepper couldn't believe she had asked. "Not that I care, you know, but Russell said—"

"Moping after you? No. I've talked to Dan a lot."

A lot? Pepper straightened in Zack's chair. What did Rita mean by *a lot?*

Rita continued, "He feels like he treated you badly, said a lot of stuff he shouldn't have, but you know Russell. He overreacts about everything."

"Yes, he does." But he said Dan thought she had better boobs than a stripper. The man had good taste. "Where's Dan living?"

"At Mrs. Dreiss's place. Someone has to stay there until you return. He got that honorable discharge already, and a bunch of medals, which his commander said he had coming to him. But don't worry about being selfish." Rita sounded breezy and unconcerned. "We all understand you want to get to know your family. You get here when you get here. Pepper, I'm on the Grahams' phone and I'm running up their bill. Let us know what you want to do about those plants. And do try and come up for the Fourth. Everyone's going to be there. Gotta go. Bye!"

Slowly Pepper hung up the phone and wondered if she'd been invited—or challenged. Was Rita dating Dan? And why would Pepper care if she was? Pepper had made it clear to Dan she didn't want him. He should find another woman and marry her and have children with her and see the winter snows fall and the spring tulips bloom . . .

Pepper stepped out of Zack's study. She looked around vaguely. She had nowhere to go. Then she realized, Lana was in the conservatory with Hope. Lana needed her. Hope loved her. Pepper had a place in the world.

When she got there, Hope sat alone, nursing a sleepy Lana. Hope looked up at Pepper, smiled, and indicated the seat next to her.

And Pepper felt a tingle of warning. She recognized Hope's expression. Recognized it from all those years ago.

Hope was going to fix Pepper's problems, whether Pepper liked it or not. In a low, gentle tone Hope said, "Lana's going to miss you when you leave."

Pepper sputtered, "L . . . leave?"

"We're all going to miss you. But you've got that land in Idaho to care for. I imagine you're ready to get back."

Pepper hadn't decided anything about her land, and she sure hadn't thought about leaving her family and going back up where chickens hatched in a man's hand and he made coffee every morning at five o'clock, then woke her up and dragged her out to do chores.

"It's been almost a month since you left," Hope said. "Have you heard from Dan?"

Pepper spoke too quickly. "No. Why should I?" Then, feeling foolish, she relaxed. "Oh, but you mean about the ranch."

"No, I meant about you and him." Hope pinned Pepper with her gaze. "You did shoot a general of the U.S. Army for him."

Pepper straightened. "I did not shoot her for him. I shot her for myself. That woman destroyed my life and my ideals. I hope they fry her."

Hope mulled for a moment, then said, "I don't know if I'm supposed to tell you this, but Zack says she reported all her knowledge of the terrorist network for a plea bargain."

Pepper hissed her exasperation. "Then I hope they set her free so her terrorist friends can take appropriate action."

"No, she's going to rot in prison for the rest of her life." Hope cupped Pepper's cheek. "But whatever you decide, you have to go back to Idaho."

Only half joking, Pepper asked, "Are you throwing me out of the nest?"

"Not throwing you out, simply giving you a little nudge." Hope looked in her eyes. "Pepper, we love to have you here, but you've been hiding. Hiding from that nice man."

"*Dan?*" Pepper snorted loudly enough to make Lana start. Pepper lowered her voice. "You don't know him at all."

"I think the same thing could be said about you."

At that moment, Pepper realized she liked having a family, yes, but she had liked living alone too. She liked spending time with her plants, talking to green leafy things that couldn't talk back. She missed them. She missed her greenhouse. She missed the long valley and the wide blue sky and the hens who hid their eggs in snake-ridden cubbyholes. She had missed it the whole nine years she had been gone, and she missed it still.

And Dan. She missed him. Damn it to hell, she missed Dan. When she realized he had achieved his revenge, she was thrilled for him. When she realized he had lived through that fight and that he was alive somewhere in this world, her heart blossomed with joy.

Hope continued, "You two have got some issues to work out."

Pepper knew she was fighting a losing battle to keep her resentment alive, but she had to try. "Like the fact that he thought the worst of me?"

"I know you, Pepper, and you have a tendency to encourage people to think the worst of you. Or at least you don't discourage them."

Resentfully Pepper said, "Maybe."

"Is there any reason why he thought the worst of you?" Hope asked.

"He's stupid."

"Besides that?"

"He caught me leaving him."

Hope quizzically tilted her head. "Some men might take that badly."

"He should have believed in me."

"Just as you should have believed in him all those years ago rather than assuming he would hurt you?"

Furious at what she saw as a spilling of her confidences, Pepper demanded, "Who told you that?"

"You did."

"Oh. Yeah." When Pepper had told Hope about her years alone, she hadn't thought that Hope would see beyond the stated facts, or use the knowledge against her.

Hope lifted the baby away from her breast, put Lana on her shoulder, and patted her back. The baby gave a huge belch, and Hope smiled fondly. "Listen to that. She's just like her Aunt Pepper. I hope she's like her Aunt Pepper in other ways too."

"What ways?" Pepper asked suspiciously.

"When you were a child, you never ran from a fight. You never ran from anything."

A fight? Pepper recognized she had lost this one. Standing, she walked toward the door. Looking back, she said, "I wanted him to be Prince Charming."

Hope laughed. "The trouble with wanting Prince Charming is you've got to be Snow White, and Pepper, you've drifted."

The Fourth of July in Diamond, Idaho, was always a huge celebration. The fireworks display was the grandest in the county. There was a parade with the fire truck and the 4-H horses.

But at two o'clock in the afternoon on that particular Independence Day, the streets were empty. Every single person in town sat in the Congregational church watching Russell and Barbara Graham be reunited in holy matrimony.

Dan stood beside his father at the altar and reflected that it was a rare son who was lucky enough to serve as his dad's best man while his parents got married. It was truly rare for a son to observe his parents as they smiled into each other's eyes and feel envy.

He wanted this to be his wedding. He wanted to be the groom. He wanted Pepper to be the bride. He wanted the figures on the cake to be them.

Instead he was standing up here with Mrs. Hardwick, his mother's matron of honor, and contemplating the hours he would spend hosting his parents' reception. It wouldn't be so bad, except he knew his dad had a dozen girls set up to ambush him. Sharon Kenyon, Teresa Cannon, Beth Kauffman . . . the list went on and on. He could feel their eyes on him now, admiring him, assessing his worth, planning their assault.

Dan listened to the minister drone on in a monotone. Dan sighed, then took a long breath redolent with the scent of flowers, and felt a puff of fresh air against his neck.

He turned quickly.

No one stood there. He saw the filled pews, the smiling faces, Teresa Cannon's bouncy blond hair and chipper smile.

Yet the breeze touched his face, and the door of the church swung shut as if *she* had been there, watching him.

Dan stood beside his parents in the reception line in the basement of the church, shook hands, and in an undertone, said, "Dad, I'm going back to the Dreiss place to do the chores and change before I come to the party."

Russell whipped his head around. "You can change at the house."

"But I can't do the chores at the house."

"I can send a cowboy to do that."

Cynically Dan reflected Russell must really have promised a lot of women a shot at him. "Dad, it's not a big deal. It'll take me an hour, and I've got to go get my jeans anyway."

"You are coming to the party, aren't you?" Russell played the guilt card. "Your mother would be hurt if you don't celebrate our marriage."

"I wouldn't miss it, Dad." With even less conscience than his father, Dan played the wounded soldier card. "I need a little time alone before I face another barrage of people."

"Oh." Russell struggled between compassion and disbelief. Compassion won, but only by a hair. "Sure, son, you go and take an hour to get refreshed. Then come home and have a good time! We've got the Beefy Barbarians playing until two A.M.!"

"I'll be there. Wouldn't miss it." Dan inched away, smiling and shaking hands until he was out of the crowd, then out of the church, then into his truck. Putting it in gear, he laid rubber all along the pavement.

What difference did it make? There wasn't any traffic. Even the sheriff was at the wedding.

Dan raced through Diamond and down the highway until he hit the gravel cutoff going onto the Dreiss ranch. Then he slowed down. Steers were unforgiving when you hit them, and not smart enough to move out of the way of a desperate man. He reached the house in record time, and as he leaped out of the truck, he looked around.

No cars were parked in the garage. No one sat in the porch swing, rocking and smiling at him. He saw no evidence that any person had been here.

Yet he *had* felt that breeze on his neck.

Hurriedly he strode into the house. He took in the living room with one quick glance, and he saw no one.

He looked in Mrs. Dreiss's bedroom. No one. He stepped into the dining room, looked in Pepper's bedroom. Nothing. No one. He opened the cabinet and checked the computer, but nothing had broken the laser beam that guarded the ranch. Not a car, not a bear, not a rabbit. Dan would have sworn . . . All his instincts said *she* had come back.

He walked into the kitchen. Empty.

He sat at the table. He stared out the window at the garden. Pepper wasn't out there. Pepper wasn't in here. He had wanted her so badly, and she hadn't come back.

He had been so sure she would. Maybe not for him— probably not for him—but because she loved it up here. Her plants, her land, the home she had always wanted— from the time she'd been a teenager, this had been her dream. She'd chased herself away the first time. He'd chased her away the second time. But he had resolved, when she came back a third time, he would woo her, he would grovel to her. Hell, he would crawl for her if that's what it took to get her back into his arms.

Because what he'd told her was true. It wasn't only the sex that drew him to her. She completed him. She made him come alive, and he couldn't live without her.

He hoped she couldn't live without him.

He couldn't stand it anymore. He couldn't stand the loneliness or the waiting. If she wasn't going to come to him, he would go to her. To hell with his folks' reception. He might as well start packing.

He stood. He strode into his bedroom.

And there, in the middle of his comforter, rested a woman's buff-colored cowboy hat.

Without comprehending, he stared at it.

Pepper's hat. The hat he had given her. How had it. . . ?

Then a great, glorious relief filled him.

With a thud, the door shut behind him.

He turned, and there stood Pepper, her back pressed against the wall, that wonderful, irrepressible smile lighting her face.

Joy rode like fire through his veins. She was all he needed to be happy.

Taking the hat, he came to her. He placed it on her head. He kissed her lips. He looked into her eyes, and he said, "Welcome home."

Enjoy the following preview of Christina Dodd's
SOME ENCHANTED EVENING
Coming soon in hardcover from William Morrow

One

Never call attention to yourself. A princess's reason for existence is to fulfill her duty as a representative of the royal family. Nothing more.

—THE DOWAGER QUEEN OF BEAUMONTAGNE

Scotland, 1808

The valley was his, the village was his, and the woman rode into the town square of Freya Crags as if she owned it.

Robert MacKenzie, earl of Hepburn, frowned at the stranger who cantered over the stone bridge and into the bustling crowd. It was market day, and booths of brown canvas were set up along the perimeter of the town square. The place rang with the sound of a hundred voices calling out their wares, but the stranger dominated the crowd, towering above them on a fractious two-year-old colt. The chestnut stepped high, as if proud to carry her, and the quality of the horse alone would have turned heads.

The lady in the saddle attracted even more attention—first fleeting looks, then open stares.

Robert glanced around at the small circle of old men gathered in the sunshine in front of the alehouse. Their wrinkled mouths sagged open as they gawked. Around them the sounds of shoppers and merchants haggling turned into a buzz of speculation as every eye turned to view the stranger.

Her riding costume swathed her from neck to toe with black wool, preserving the illusion of propriety, yet outlining every curve of her trim figure. Her black hat was tall, with a broad brim, and black veiling floated behind. The red trim on her sleeves matched the red scarf at her neck, and those small bits of vivid color shocked and pleasured the eye. Her bosom was generous, her waist narrow, her black boots shiny, and her face . . .

Good God, her face.

Robert couldn't look away. If she'd been born in the Renaissance, painters would have flocked to her door, begging that she pose for them. They would have painted her as an angel, for her wavy golden hair glowed with a light of its own. Copper glints in the curls seemed to possess a power to warm the hands, and Robert's fingers itched to sink into the waves and discover the heat and the texture. Her softly rounded cheeks and large amber eyes under darkened brows made a man think of heaven, yet the stubborn set of her chin saved her face from a cloying sweetness. Her nose was slight, but her lips were wide, lush, and red. Too red. She rouged them, he was sure of it. She looked like an Englishwoman of good quality, except, of course, that no young lady of good quality ever rouged her lips, and certainly none ever traveled alone.

She smiled, giving him a glimpse of straight, white teeth. He planned to explore that mouth.

Robert straightened away from the wall of the alehouse.

Where in blazes had that thought come from?

Hamish MacQueen was boisterous. "Who do ye suppose she is?"

A good question, and Robert intended to get an answer.

"I dunna know, but I'd like t' part her beard," declared Gilbert Wilson, his sly wit taking a wicked turn.

"I'd like t' give her a live sausage fer supper." Tomas MacTavish slapped his skinny knee and chortled.

Henry MacCulloch said, "I'd like t' play dog in the doublet wi' her."

All the old men cackled, remembering the days when they would have wooed a beautiful visitor. Now they were content to sit in front of the alehouse and play checkers—or they had been until *she* rode into town.

Robert's gaze narrowed on the female. He was smart enough, and in his travels had seen enough, to recognize trouble when he saw it.

"Ye damned auld fools." The alewife, Hughina Gray, stood with her apron wrapped around her hands. "Canna ye see she's na guid?"

"I'd wager she's verra guid," said Tomas's brother Benneit, and the old men laughed until they wheezed.

"Ye shouldn't talk so in front o' the laird," Hughina reproved. She was a striking widow, and she'd made it clear she had room in her bed for Robert.

He hadn't accepted the invitation. When the laird

slept with the women of his lands, trouble was sure to follow, so when the urge was on him, he traveled over the hills into Trevor and visited with Lady Emundson. She enjoyed his body and his driving sexuality without caring a crumb whether he loved her, and that made a very satisfactory arrangement for them both.

Lately he hadn't suffered from the urge.

His hand crinkled the much-read letter in his pocket. He'd been too busy making plans, vengeful plans, and now those schemes had been set to naught because one woman failed to fulfil her promise. Damn her.

But for the moment he was distracted as the exotic stranger circled the booths, giving everyone a chance to watch her; the villagers' expressions were suspicious or inquisitive, but she beamed a friendly smile.

Her gaze found and considered the new seamstress.

The seamstress stared back with all the hostility of a plain woman before a beauty.

So for all her timid homeliness, Miss Rosabel had sense. He glanced back at the still-guffawing old men. More sense than the men who'd lived here all their lives.

The stranger rode right to the middle of the square, where a statue honored Robert's ancestor Uilleam Hepburn. A raised platform surrounded the statue, and there she slid off her horse.

Of course. Already Robert knew she liked to be seen.

She tied her horse to the iron ring and lifted her saddlebags onto the platform, which raised her above the multitude. The curious throng gathered. For one moment the female sobered, touched the silver cross around her neck, then took a breath and flung her arms wide. "Good people of Freya Crags, allow me to introduce myself. I am a princess in exile!"

Hamish tucked the end of his shirt over the stump of his arm. The old soldier had his weaknesses, and a pretty woman was the main one. "Eh, a princess! We've got guid taste."

All the old men cackled, wild with the joy of having such a colorful distraction in their sedate lives.

Robert glanced at them, distracted from the pageant in the center of the square by their surging excitement.

The larcenous wench of a princess made another outrageous claim. "I've come to bring youth, beauty, and joy to your lives!"

Robert's head snapped back toward the royal minx. The words of his aide, Waldemar, came back to him so clearly, Waldemar might almost have been standing beside him. *Lor love ye, Cap'n, there's ne'er a person what falls into yer life without a purpose. Ye just 'ave t' discover what that is, and use 'em like the instruments they are, and always ye'll get yer way, see if ye don't.*

With the lightning-quick calculation he had developed in the army, Robert realized why this female had arrived in his town and what purpose she would serve. Yes, he would use her like the instrument she was. She would do as he instructed because she had no choice, and yes, he would get his way.

Fortified with resolve, Robert made his way through the crowd toward the statue and the princess.

At long last justice would be served.

*   *   *

Clarice Lilly took a breath and awaited as the curious throng surged forward.

They stared at her, silent and dreary. The place was clearly prosperous, yet she saw not one smile, not one colorful gown or frivolous hair ribbon. It was as if somehow they'd lost their spirit, as if they couldn't see God's good sunshine or smell the flowers sold in bunches in the stalls.

It was true what they'd said in England. The Scots were dour and drab. These people needed her, needed what she had to offer.

Again she rubbed the silver cross that hung around her neck. The cross was supposed to bring her luck—a luck that had signally failed in the last few months. That was why she had crossed the border into Scotland; her welcome in England had worn thin, and she had to make a living.

She couldn't fail. Too much depended on her.

Everything depended on her.

With the skill of a born mimic, she allowed the slightest Scottish accent to slide into her voice. "Good people of Freya Crags, I can make a plain girl beautiful. I can cure her spots. I can bring a blush to her pale cheeks and make her the object of every man's attentions. Of course I can do the same for any gentleman who needs help. But ladies"—she winked broadly—"don't you find that a little soap makes even the ugliest man irresistible?"

A few of the older women grinned and nudged their men. The men grumbled and looked sullen.

She smiled at them. She always smiled at them, no matter what, and the men eventually smiled back.

Clarice settled into her pitch. "Who am I, you ask, to claim I can solve all your amorous woes? I'm Princess Clarice, one of the Lost Princesses."

A gentleman of about thirty years was making his way toward the front, a disbelieving smile on his lips. At the sight she forgot what she was doing. She straightened. She stood staring. Up there, on the stage she had created, she was aware of only one thing: A man watched her with all his attention.

Clarice was used to attention; indeed everything she did and said and wore encouraged it.

But this man was different from the usual spectators. He wore clothes of a finer cut than most of the townsfolk. Clarice pegged him as a gentleman farmer or perhaps a businessman from Edinburgh. He stood taller than the other men by a good three inches and was completely, blazingly masculine in a way that challenged all that was feminine in her. His hair was black. Not dark brown, black, like black silk that absorbed nothing but the brightest sunlight and transformed it into glints of silver. His face was tanned from the sun, a harsh face that had seen too much of the world and liked little of it. He had a hooked nose and a strong jaw, and his eyes . . . ah, his eyes.

She tried to look away, but she couldn't break the contact.

A woman could write poetry about his eyes. Clear, blazing blue like royal sapphires set in gold, they watched Clarice with the kind of confidence that said he understood what pleasured a woman and would use his knowledge ruthlessly, again and again, until he was exhausted, or she was, or they both combusted with mutual joy.

She didn't want his attention. She didn't need to fight that kind of temptation. She never indulged in flirtations or frivolities; she dared not. So she would make sure she stayed far away from him.

Dragging her gaze away from his, she repeated, "I'm one of the Lost Princesses. My country's gone, my family scattered, but I can't avoid my destiny. And, good people of Freya Crags, do you know what that destiny is?"

She'd been doing this for almost five years, and well, for she saw heads shake in response. She told them, "A princess is bred for one purpose and one purpose only—to catch a prince."

Amusement rippled through the crowd. She saw smiles. Ugly, cynical smiles on the older, experienced faces. Bewilderment and a shy interest on the younger faces, and from a few, forlorn curiosity.

"Can I help you catch a prince?" She stepped to the edge of the platform and made a play of lowering her voice. "Well, to tell you the truth, princes are a little thin on the ground these days."

The amusement grew louder and more open.

"But from the time I was a wee child, I had a directive drummed into my head: Find a prince and marry him. No other man will do. Since I can't do that, I must turn to my other talent—helping you catch *your* prince. Ladies, these bags"—she pointed at the saddlebags her horse carried—"contain royal secrets from around the world! Of course"—she allowed her mouth to droop—"I have to charge you for them. Exiled princesses have to eat too." Her voice strengthened. "But I'm not making a fortune, and I guarantee my work." She'd convinced all of the villagers.

Well, almost all. A few stood with their arms crossed over their chests. A handsome woman back by the alehouse. A short, middle-aged, mean-eyed man with a chip on his shoulder the size of an iceberg. Those were the ones Clarice depended on to make trouble—and to help her clinch the sales.

The fascinating gentleman watched her, apparently entertained. He was an unknown entity. Yet he felt far too familiar, as if she knew him from somewhere—a dream she'd had, or a wish unfulfilled. She did *not* like him.

The alewife shouted, "Ye've got a glib tongue."

The short man yelled, "She can't do anything she claims."

"Can I not?" Clarice's gaze landed on the homely seamstress, engrossed and standing close. "What's your name, miss?"

The seamstress glanced around as if hoping Clarice was speaking to someone else "I'm . . . um . . . I'm Miss Amy Rosabel."

"Come up here, Miss Rosabel. Don't be shy."

Reluctantly, she climbed up to stand beside Clarice. She was at least two inches taller than Clarice, but she hunched her shoulders so much, she looked shorter. Her brownish blond hair was pulled tightly back from her face, accentuating the thrust of her narrow nose and her pointed chin. She had dark rings under her eyes, and her complexion was pasty white. Her brown wool gown was appalling.

Clearly, to every eye, she needed help. "Miss Rosabel, I'm going to make you beautiful," Clarice said.

Miss Rosabel pulled her tattered shawl closer around her shoulders. "Nay, miss, but thank ye."

Her heart leaped to her throat, and for a moment she thought she had gone too far. He would beat her right here in front of everyone.

The fascinating gentleman put a restraining hand on his arm.

In a rage Billie swung around, ready to kill the one who halted him. But when he saw who accosted him, he dropped his fist and glared.

The gentleman shook his head, chiding Billie without a word.

Billie backed away.

So. The gentleman must be good with a roundhouse. Handsome, tough, and dynamic. He commanded respect—and perhaps some fear.

Clarice shivered. Certainly he commanded fear from her.

Her fingers were shaking as she opened her saddlebag and brought forth a clay jar. "This is a powerful extract of herbs and roots in a gentle cream that refreshes the complexion and brings the first tingle of beauty. Watch as I apply it." Miss Rosabel tilted her chin up as Clarice smoothed on the cream and rubbed it in. "It has the lovely scent of rosemary and mint, and a special secret ingredient known only to the women of my royal family."

"Gold, frankincense, and myrrh," the alewife mocked.

"You're partly right," Clarice responded, and was gratified to see that the woman looked taken aback. "Of course my kingdom is far from Bethlehem, but the trade routes were established long ago, back in the mists of time, and my country is known for its mountains, its treasures, and its beautiful women." She laughed at the old men who stood under the eaves of the alehouse, craning their necks to watch her.

Five identical, almost toothless smiles shot back at her, and one ancient fellow collapsed against the wall, his hand on his chest in faked spasms.

Clarice loved old men. They said what they thought, they laughed when they wanted, and they always like her, no matter what. Always.

With the cloth Clarice gently wiped the cream off Miss Rosabel's face. She urged Miss Rosabel to stand straight with her shoulders back, gentled the severe line of hair around her face, and pushed her toward the front of the platform.

The crowd gave a gratifying gasp.

"Yes, imagine that—an improvement in only five minutes!" Clarice pointed as she spoke. "Her dark circles are gone, and her skin is pink and healthy-looking." More important, Clarice thought with satisfaction, Miss Rosabel's nose and chin were no longer pointed, and the softened hairstyle gave her a girlish loveliness. "Give me an hour and think what I can do!"

Cautiously, Miss Rosabel touched her face. "Am I pretty?"

"Very pretty," Clarice assured her.

"My skin feels so clean and fresh!" For the first time, a smile broke across Miss Rosabel's face, and the men rumbled in admiration. They hadn't noticed her before. Now they did. She wasn't yet beautiful, but she was young and healthy, and she would be swamped with offers to walk in the evenings.

Extracting a swath of soft blue material from her saddlebag, Clarice draped it across Miss Rosabel's bosom. The color made an already attractive face more attractive, and she said, "So, ladies and gentlemen, is this improvement worth ten pounds from Billie MacBain?"

"Yes!" the crowd roared, and everyone looked around for Billie.

Clarice laughed. Laughed with the pleasure of a win and a dozen guaranteed sales. "He sneaked away. But you can buy the face cream from me, and if you'd like to know more royal secrets, I'll be staying at the inn—"

The handsome gentleman reached up and caught her hand. He spoke at last. "It would be best if you stayed at the manor . . . Princess."

She'd seen MacKenzie Manor as she rode into Freya Crags. Set well off the road on a rise, four stories high and twenty glass windows across, with gargoyles poised on the roof and bronze double doors so big they should have been at home on a cathedral. The gray, forbidding stones weighed down the ground and chilled Clarice's heart.

Perhaps she disliked the place because of her knowledge of its owner. Her spy in the town had written her about Lord Hepburn, a man who ordered his lands like a despot. Clarice didn't want to stay in the house, and she didn't want to be anywhere near this fellow, who was probably the steward or the butler or . . . or a man too gorgeous for his own good. Or hers.

With a superior smile that frightened off most men, she tugged to free her hand. "You're very free with your master's invitations."

He didn't release her, and he didn't look frightened.

A rustle of laughter spread through the onlookers.

"No!" Miss Rosabel pinched her elbow hard.

Clarice flinched. She'd made a mistake, although she couldn't imagine what it was.

In a soft voice with a hint of brogue, he said, "I'm free with the invitations to MacKenzie Manor for good reason."

A suspicion flicked at her mind. *No. It couldn't be.*

But it was. "I'm Robert MacKenzie, the Earl of Hepburn. I'm the laird of Freya Crags and the master of the manor." He kissed her fingers. His breath warmed her flesh, and for one moment she thought his tongue touched her skin. "I'm not a prince, but still I insist. Stay at the manor with me."